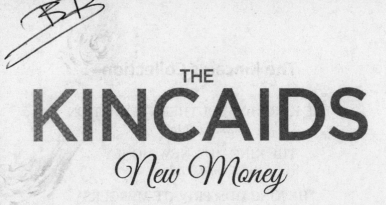

THE
KINCAIDS
New Money

New money. New passions. Old secrets.

Two passionate reads from fantastic authors
Jennifer Lewis and Heidi Betts

The Kincaids Collection

THE
KINCAIDS
New Money

JENNIFER
LEWIS

HEIDI
BETTS

MILLS & BOON

First published in Great Britain 2013
by Mills & Boon, an imprint of Harlequin (UK) Limited, Eton House, 18-24 Paradise Road, Richmond, Surrey TW9 1SR

THE KINCAIDS: NEW MONEY
© Harlequin Enterprises II B.V./S.à.r.l. 2012

Behind Boardroom Doors © Harlequin Books S.A. 2012
On the Verge of I Do © Harlequin Books S.A. 2012

Special thanks and acknowledgement to Jennifer Lewis and Heidi Betts for their contributions to the Dynasties: The Kincaids series.

ISBN: 978 0 263 90603 5

009-0413

Harlequin (UK) policy is to use papers that are natural, renewable and recyclable products and made from wood grown in sustainable forests. The logging and manufacturing processes conform to the legal environmental regulations of the country of origin.

Printed and bound by
CPI Group (UK) Ltd, Croydon, CR0 4YY

BEHIND BOARDROOM DOORS

JENNIFER LEWIS

Jennifer Lewis has been dreaming up stories for as long as she can remember and is thrilled to be able to share them with readers. She has lived on both sides of the Atlantic and worked in media and the arts before she grew bold enough to put pen to paper. She would love to hear from readers at jen@jenlewis.com. Visit her website at www.jenlewis.com.

Dear Reader,

I still remember the first time I discovered romance novels. I was working in mid-town Manhattan, around the corner from the Donnell Library. On my lunch breaks I often headed to the library looking for something to read and before long I noticed the big rack of series romance novels. I don't remember which book I picked up first, but it didn't take me long to get hooked.

I loved the strong, savvy characters in every book and the interesting mix of settings. I looked forward to plunging into each new romance and following the ups and downs of the couple's road to their happy ending. I also enjoyed the short length of the stories, which allowed me to ride the whole rollercoaster in a day.

Eventually I grew daring enough to try my hand at writing, though it took many years before I honed my craft enough to bear the precious logo. This book is my fourteenth and I hope you enjoy Brooke and RJ's romance!

Happy reading,

Jennifer Lewis

For Pippa, international pony of mystery and cherished member of our family

One

"There is one good thing about this situation." RJ Kincaid slammed his phone down on the conference table, his voice cracking with fury.

"What's that?" Brooke Nichols stared at her boss. She failed to see a bright side.

"Now we know things cannot possibly get any worse." His eyes flashed and he leaned forward in his chair. The other staff in the meeting sat like statues. "My calls to the prosecutor's office, the police, the courts, the state senator—have all been ignored."

He stood and marched around the table. "The Kincaid family is under siege and they're firing on us from all angles." Tall and imposing at the best of times, with bold features, dark hair and smoky slate-blue eyes, RJ now looked like a general striding into battle. "And my mother, Elizabeth Winthrop Kincaid, the finest woman in Charleston, will be spending tonight behind bars like a common criminal."

He let out a string of curses that made Brooke shrink into her chair. She'd worked for RJ for five years and she'd never seen him like this. Normally he was the most easygoing man you could meet, never rattled by even the most intense negotiations, with time for everyone and a nonchalant approach to life.

Of course that was before his father's murder and the revelation that his privileged and entitled existence was founded on lies.

RJ walked over to his brother Matthew. "You're the director of new business—is there any new business?"

Matthew inhaled. They both knew the answer. Even some of their most stalwart clients had fled the company in the aftermath of the scandal. "There is the Larrimore account."

"Yes, I suppose we do have one new account to hang our hopes on. Greg, how are the books looking?" RJ strode around to the CFO and for a moment she thought he was going to collar him.

Mild-mannered Greg shrank into his chair. "As you know, we're experiencing challenges—"

"Challenges!" RJ cut him off, raising his hands in the air in a dramatic gesture. "That's one way of looking at it. A challenge is an opportunity for growth, a time to rise up and seize opportunity, to embrace change."

He turned and walked back across the room. Everyone sat rigid in their chairs, probably praying he wouldn't accost them.

"But what I see here is a company on the brink of going under." RJ shoved a hand through his thick, dark hair. His handsome features were hard with anger. "And all of you are just sitting in your chairs taking notes as if we're at some garden party. Get up and get out there and do something, for Chrissakes!"

No one moved an inch. Brooke rose from her chair, unable to stop herself. "Um…" She had to get him out of here. He was acting like a jerk and if he continued like this he'd do himself permanent harm in the company.

"Yes, Brooke?" He turned to face her, and lifted an eyebrow. His eyes met hers and a jolt of energy surged in her blood.

"I need to speak to you outside." She picked up her laptop and headed for the door, heart pounding. He could probably fire her on the spot in his current mood, but she wasn't doing her job if she let him insult and harangue employees who were already under a lot of pressure and stress through no fault of their own.

"I'm sure it can wait." He frowned and gestured to the gathered meeting.

"Just for a moment. Please." She continued toward the door, hoping he'd follow.

"Apparently my assistant's need to consult with me in private is more urgent than the imminent collapse of The Kincaid Group, and the imprisonment of my mother. Since it's the end of the day I'm sure you also have better places to be. Meeting dismissed."

RJ moved to the door in time to hold it open for her. A wave of heat and adrenaline rose inside her as she passed him, her arm almost brushing against his. He closed the door and followed her out. In the hush of the carpeted hallway Brooke almost lost her nerve. "In your office, please."

"I don't have time to loll about in my office. My mother's in the county jail in case you hadn't noticed."

Brooke reminded herself his rudeness was the result of extreme stress. "Trust me. It's important." Her own firm tone surprised her. She walked ahead into the spacious corner office with views of the Charleston waterfront. The sunset cast a warm amber glow over the water reflected on the walls in moving patterns. "Come on in."

RJ sauntered into the room, then crossed his arms. "Happy now?"

"Sit down." She closed the door and locked it.

"What?"

Her resolve faltered as her boss glared at her.

"On the couch." She pointed to it, in case he'd forgotten where it was. She almost blushed at the way it sounded as she said it. What a lovelorn secretary's fantasy! But this situation was serious. "I'm going to pour you a whiskey and you're going to drink it."

He didn't move. "Have you lost your mind?"

"No, but you're beginning to lose yours and you need to step back and take a deep breath before you damage your reputation. You can't talk to employees like that, no matter what the circumstances. Now sit." She pointed at the sofa again.

A stunned RJ lowered himself onto it.

Brooke poured three fingers of whisky into a crystal tumbler with shaking hands. Everything really did seem to be going to hell in a handbasket for RJ. Until now he'd faced each disaster with composure, but apparently he'd reached his breaking point.

Their fingers touched as she handed him the glass, and she cursed the subtle buzz of awareness that always haunted her around RJ. "Here, this will settle your nerves."

"My nerves are just fine." He took a sip. "It's everything else that's screwed up. The police can't really believe my mother killed my father!"

He took a long swig, which made Brooke wince. She bit her lip. The pained expression on his handsome face tugged at her heart. "We both know it's impossible, and they'll figure that out."

"Will they?" RJ raised a dark brow and peered up at her. "What if they don't? What if this is the first of many long nights in jail for her?" He shuddered visibly and took another swig. "It kills me that I can't protect her from this."

"I know. And you're still grieving the death of your father."

"Not just his literal death." RJ stared at the floor. "The death of everything I thought I knew about him."

She and RJ had never discussed the scandalous revelations about the Kincaid family, but they were both aware she knew all the details—along with everyone else in Charleston. They'd been splashed all over the local media every day since his father's murder on December 30th. It was now March.

"Another family." He growled the words like a curse. "Another son, born before me." He shook his head. "All my life I was Reginald Kincaid, Jr. Proud son and heir and all I wanted to do was follow in my father's footsteps. Little did I know they'd been wandering off into some other woman's house, to sleep with her and raise her children, too."

He glanced up, and his pain-filled gaze stole her

breath. It killed her to see him suffering like this. If only she could soothe his hurt and anger.

"I'm so sorry." It was all she could manage. What could she say? "I'm sure he loved you. You could see it in his face when he looked at you." She swallowed. "I bet he wished things were different, and that he could have at least told you before he died."

"He had plenty of time to tell me. I'm thirty-six years old, for Chrissakes. Was he waiting until I hit fifty?" RJ rose to his feet and crossed the room, whiskey splashing in the glass. "That's what hurts the most. That he didn't confide in me. All the time we spent together, all those long hours fishing or hunting, walking through the woods with guns. We talked about everything under the sun—except that he was living a lie."

RJ tugged at his tie with a finger and loosened his collar. Recent events had given him an air of gravitas that he'd never had before. The strain hardened his noble features and gave his broad shoulders the appearance of carrying the weight of the world.

Brooke longed to take him in her arms and give him a reassuring hug. But that would *not* be a good idea. "You're doing a great job of keeping the family together and the company afloat."

"Afloat!" RJ let out a harsh laugh. "It would be a real problem for a shipping company if it couldn't stay afloat." His eyes twinkled with humor for a split second. "But at the rate we're losing clients we'll be belly up in the bay before the year is out if I don't turn things around. For every new client Matthew brings in, we're losing two old ones. And I don't even have a free hand to guide the company. My father—in his infinite wisdom—saw fit to give his illegitimate son forty-five percent of the company and only leave me a measly nine percent."

Brooke grimaced. That did seem the cruelest act of all. RJ had devoted his entire working life to The Kincaid Group. He'd been executive vice president almost since he left college, and everyone—including him—assumed he'd one day be president and CEO. Until his father had all but left the company to a son no one knew about. "I suppose he did that because he felt guilty about keeping Jack secret all these years."

"As well he might." RJ marched back across the room and took another swig of whiskey. "Except he didn't seem to think about how much it would hurt the rest of us. Even all five of us Kincaids together don't have a majority vote. Ten percent of the stock is owned by some mystery person we can't seem to find. If Jack Sinclair gains control over the missing ten percent he'll get to decide how to run The Kincaid Group and the rest of us have to go along with it or ship out. I'm seriously considering doing the latter."

"Leaving the company?" She couldn't believe it. Selfish thoughts about her own job disappearing almost toppled her concern for RJ.

"Why not? It's not mine to run. I'm just another cog in the machine. That's not what my dad groomed me for or what I want for myself." He slammed the empty glass down on a table. "Maybe I'll leave Charleston for good."

"Calm down, RJ." Brooke poured another three fingers of pungent whiskey into the glass. Right now it seemed a good idea to get him too drunk to go anywhere at all. "It's early days yet. Nothing will be decided about the company until the shareholders' meeting and, until then, everyone's counting on you to steer the ship through these rough waters."

"I love all your nautical lingo." He flashed a wry grin as he took the glass. "I knew there was a good reason I hired you."

"That and my excellent typing skills."

"Typing—pah. You could run this company if you put your mind to it. You're not just organized and efficient, you're good with people. You've managed to talk me back off the ledge today, and I thank you for it." He took another sip. The whiskey was certainly doing its job. Already the hard edge of despair and anger had softened.

Now was not the time to mention that she had applied for a management job, and been turned down. She didn't know if RJ was behind that, or if he even knew.

"I didn't want you to upset people any more than they already are." She pushed a hand through her hair. "Everyone's temper is running high and we need to work together. The last thing you want is for key employees to quit and make things worse in the run-up to the shareholders' meeting."

"You're right, as usual, my lovely Brooke."

Her eyes widened. Obviously the whiskey was going straight to his head. Still, she couldn't help the funny warm feeling his words generated inside her, almost like a shot of whiskey to her core.

"The most important thing right now is to find your dad's murderer." She tried to distract herself from RJ's melting gaze. "Then your mom won't be under suspicion."

"I've hired a private investigator." RJ peered into

his glass. "I told him I'll pay for twenty-four hours in the day and he shouldn't stop until he finds the truth." He looked up at her. "Of course I told him to start with the Sinclair brothers."

Brooke nodded. Jack Sinclair sounded like a man with an ax to grind, though her vision could be skewed by the fact that he'd inherited her boss's birthright. She hadn't met Jack or his half brother Alan. "They must be angry your dad kept them secret all these years."

"Yup. Resentment." RJ sat down on the sofa again. "I'm beginning to know what that feels like."

"Very understandable." Her chest ached with emotion. She wished she could bear some of the burden for him. "This whole situation came out of nowhere for you."

"Not to mention my mom." He shook his head. "Though sometimes I wonder if she knew. She didn't seem as surprised as the rest of us."

Brooke swallowed. Elizabeth Kincaid would have had at least some motivation for the murder if she'd known about her husband's adultery. And she had seen her in the office on the night of the murder. She shook the thought from her brain. There was no way such a quiet and gentle person could fire a bullet at another human, even her cheating husband. "Let me pour you some more."

She brought the bottle over to the sofa and leaned down to fill RJ's glass. The whiskey sloshed in the bottle as he stuck out a strong arm and pulled her roughly onto the sofa with him. She let out a tiny shriek as her hips settled into the soft leather next to his.

"I appreciate the company, Brooke. I guess I needed someone to talk to." His arm had now settled across her shoulders, his big hand wrapped around her upper arm. She could hardly breathe. And when she did his warm, masculine scent assaulted her senses and raised her blood pressure.

RJ settled into the sofa a little, caressing her shoulder with his hand. Heat bloomed under his fingers, through her thin blouse. She still held the whiskey bottle and wondered if she should pour from it, or if he'd had enough. He answered the question by taking it from her with his free hand, and putting it on the floor along with his glass. His hand then settled on her thigh, where she could feel the warmth of his palm through her smart gray skirt. Her heart quickened when he turned to look at her.

RJ's expression was one of intense concentration. He seemed to be examining her face like she was a table of container ship sailings. "I never noticed how green your eyes are."

Brooke had a sudden urge to roll those eyes. How many women had he used that line on? RJ was famous throughout the Southeast as a Most Eligible Bachelor and had enjoyed his single status as long as she'd known him. "Some people would call them gray." Was she really sitting almost in RJ's lap talking about her eyes, or was this some kind of manic dream?

"They'd be wrong." Again his expression was deadly serious. "But lately I'm learning that people are wrong a lot of the time." His gaze fell to her mouth. Her lips parted slightly and she pressed them back together. "I'm having to question a lot of my assumptions about the world."

"Sometimes that's good." She spoke softly, wondering if she'd said the wrong thing. Sitting this close to

RJ was dangerous. Arousal already crept through her limbs and strange parts of her were starting to tingle.

"I suppose so." RJ frowned. "Though it doesn't make life any easier."

Poor RJ. He was used to being the golden child, his entire life mapped out at birth and his every need taken care of before he could even voice it.

"Sometimes challenges can make us stronger." It was hard to form sensible thoughts with his arm around her shoulder and his other hand on her knee. She could feel the power of his sturdy body right through her clothes. Part of her wanted to stand up and go organize the papers on his desk. The other part wanted to wrap her arms around his neck and...

RJ's lips crushed over hers in a hot, whiskey-scented kiss that banished all thought. Her body melted against his and she felt her fingers do what they'd wanted all along—roam into his stiff white shirt and the hard, hot muscle beneath.

His hands caressed her, making her skin hum with arousal. Her nipples thickened and a powerful wave of heat rose in her belly. RJ's raw hunger for affection—for help—gave urgency to his touch. She could feel how badly he needed her, right now, here in his arms.

She kissed him back with equal force, affection for him overpowering any more sensible urges. She wanted to heal his hurt, to make him feel better, and right now she almost felt that was within her power. Emotions surged within her. She'd adored RJ almost since the day she met him and his strength under adversity only made her admire him more. She'd never dared imagine for a single second that he'd return her feelings.

Their kiss deepened and heated and for a moment she thought they'd fuse and become one, then RJ pulled back gently. "Brooke, you're an amazing woman."

His soft sigh contained a thick aroma of all those fingers of whiskey she'd poured him. Would he regret this in the morning? Still, hearing him call her an amazing woman stirred something powerful inside her. Was this the beginning of a totally new phase in their relationship? Maybe they'd start dating and she'd be able to help him negotiate the minefield of his life and come happily out the other side with him—arm in arm. His arms felt fabulous around her right now.

Or would she remember this as the moment she destroyed her hard-earned career at The Kincaid Group and permanently alienated her boss by getting him drunk and compromising their professional relationship? A ball of fear burst open like a mold spore inside her.

What was she doing? She'd gotten him drunk, then let him kiss her. It was all her fault, even she could see that.

RJ stroked her cheek and she fought a sudden urge to nuzzle against him like a cat. Was it so wrong to give him the affection and comfort he craved? Again, violins and visions of a rose-scented courtship hummed in her mind. She was strong enough to help him through this. Her own background had made her a resilient person.

RJ caressed her, taking in the curve of her breast with his fingers then trailing over her thigh. The musky scent of him filled her senses for a second as his lips met hers again and kissed her softly.

Cigar smoke clung to his suit from the long business lunch he'd hosted at a local restaurant, and mingled rather intoxicatingly with the whiskey. Everything about RJ seemed delicious to her right now. She wanted to wrap herself up in him and stay there forever.

But he withdrew again, leaving her lips stinging. Then he frowned and pushed a hand through his hair as if wondering what he was doing.

An icy finger of doubt slid down Brooke's back. Perhaps that smoky smell came from the smoldering ruin of her career and reputation. Instinct pushed her to her feet, which wasn't easy with her knees reduced to wobbly jelly. "Maybe it's time to get out of here. It's after seven."

RJ leaned his head back against the sofa, eyes closed. "I'm beat. I don't think I can take another step today."

"I'll call you a cab." She certainly didn't want him driving with all that whiskey in him. He didn't live far away, but driving or walking him home didn't seem like such a great idea, either. If he invited her in, she wasn't sure she could say no, and she knew she'd regret being that easy.

"Don't worry about me, Brooke. I'll sleep here on the sofa. I've done it many times before. If I wake up in the middle of the night I'll go through some of the paperwork I need to read."

"You'll wake up sore."

"I'll be fine." Already he was sinking into the sofa, eyes sleepy. "Go home and rest and I'll see you in the morning."

Brooke bit her lip. Somehow it hurt to be dismissed like this after their steamy kisses. What did she expect? That he'd want her by his side every moment from now on? Maybe after so much whiskey he'd already forgotten he even kissed her.

"What about dinner?"

"Not hungry," he murmured.

"There's half a plate of sandwiches in the fridge left over from a luncheon meeting today. I could get them for you."

"Stop trying to mother me, and go home." His tone was almost curt. Brooke swallowed and turned for the door. Then she noticed RJ had sat up again, head in his hands. "I can't believe my mom is in jail. It's just so wrong. I've never felt so powerless in my life."

Brooke walked back toward him. "She's a strong woman and she'll survive. You've done all you can for now and it won't help her if you worry yourself sick over it. Get some sleep so you'll be ready to make the most of tomorrow. You've got a company to save."

He blew out a hard breath. "You're right, Brooke, as usual. Thanks for everything."

Already he'd lain down, eyes closed. A fierce pang of tenderness for him ached in her chest. So tall and strong and proud and so anxious to go immediately into battle to save his mom. RJ was the kind of man any woman would adore. And she was only one among the many who did.

She slipped out of his office and closed the door, then picked up her jacket and bag from her own desk outside it. *Thanks for everything.* Was that his way of wrapping up the evening's events—memos typed, letters filed, kisses received. All in a day's work.

"Bye, Brooke."

She startled at the sound of her name. She'd totally forgotten there might still be other employees on the floor. Usually everyone was long gone by now, but PR assistant Lucinda was donning her jacket two cubicles away. Brooke wondered if her cheeks were flushed or her lips red. Surely there must be some telltale signs that she'd locked lips with her boss.

"Bye, Luce." She hurried for the elevator, hoping no one else would see her.

When the doors opened Joe from Marketing was inside. "What a day," he exhaled, as she stepped in. "This place is coming apart at the seams."

"No, it isn't." She bristled with indignation. "We're going through tough times but a year from now this will all be forgotten and the company will be back on top again."

Joe raised a sandy brow. "Really? If old Mrs. Kincaid did it I don't think the family reputation will recover. And it's sure looking like she did. I bet she's enjoying life as the merry widow now."

"She didn't do it." Still, a sliver of doubt wedged itself into her mind. Anyone could be pushed past their breaking point, and Elizabeth Kincaid had been pushed pretty far from the sound of it. "And don't go spreading rumors that she did. You'll make things worse."

"Are you going to report me to your boss?" He shifted his bag higher on his shoulder.

"No. He's got enough problems right now. He needs all of our support."

"You're like a wife to him, so supportive and attentive to his needs." His grin was less than reassuring. "If only we could all be as lucky as RJ."

She froze. Could he know something had happened between her and RJ? The doors opened and she stepped out with relief. "I'm not his wife."

Though maybe one day I could be. Fantasies already played at the edge of her mind. Dangerous fantasies. Dreams that could explode in her face and destroy her career and reputation.

Still it was hard not to let her imagination wander just a little....

Two

Brooke had a sleepless night. In the morning her hair was a mess and she had to whip out the curling iron to bring some life back to the limp brown locks brushing her shoulders. She applied her makeup carefully, wanting to look as beautiful as RJ had made her feel last night. Did she look different now that she'd kissed him?

Not really. At least her eyes weren't red from crying—yet. RJ would be able to blame his sudden enchantment with her on the whiskey she gave him. She, on the other hand, could blame only her years-long fascination with him. She'd fallen into his arms without a protest, and kissed him with passion that came from the heart.

She wore her smartest black suit. She'd bought it on sale at a fancy boutique, and with its well-cut designer lines it was something a rich girl would wear. She stood back and surveyed herself in the full-length mirror. Did she look like a potential girlfriend of RJ Kincaid?

She knew what her mom would say. *You have a nice figure, you should show it off more.* But that wasn't her style. Besides, the last thing she wanted was a man who only cared about her breasts and not her brain.

She donned her Burberry raincoat, a cherished consignment store find. She preferred a demure, somewhat conservative style that said, *I mean business.* She wanted people to take her seriously. She'd never flirted with RJ for a single instant, as her job meant far more to her than the prospect of a quick kiss and cuddle.

Fear licked around the edges of her brain. Would RJ be embarrassed by last night's indiscretions and find a way to shunt her aside? Her heart pounded as she walked into the Kincaid building.

Her throat dried as she stepped out of the elevator on their floor. How would she greet him? Would he be furious she'd made him drunk and landed them in a compromising position?

Maybe he wouldn't remember that he'd kissed her at all.

His office door was closed. Was RJ still in there sleeping on the sofa? She hung her coat with shaking hands and wiped sweaty palms on her skirt before approaching. She lifted her hand to knock, then hesitated.

Maybe she should wait for him to come out. He might have a major hangover he needed to sleep off. She turned and went to sit at her desk. She was always the first person in each morning. She liked to get her in-box dealt with before the phones started ringing.

Brooke checked her email, then pulled the mail from her tray and started to sort through it. But her eyes kept straying to the closed door. Was he still upset about his mom being jailed? Who wouldn't be? He could probably use a coffee and some breakfast.

She rose from her chair and approached the door again. She inhaled deeply and raised her hand—and the door opened.

The polite greeting she'd rehearsed fled her lips at the sight of RJ. She'd expected him to look rumpled and tired, but he didn't. Well groomed and wearing a perfectly pressed suit, he looked every inch the business titan his rivals feared.

"Morning, Brooke." His eyes twinkled with amusement.

"Morning." The word burst out fast and loud. Somehow he seemed even more gorgeous than usual. Maybe because she knew just how his mouth tasted in a kiss. She struggled to drag her mind back to practical matters. "Did you sleep okay?"

"I slept very well under the circumstances." He leaned against the door frame, eyes resting on her face. "It wasn't easy sleeping alone after that kiss." His deep blue eyes smoldered and his hushed tones carried more than a hint of suggestion.

Brooke bit her lip to stop a huge smile creeping across it. "For me either." Her admission was a relief. He wasn't trying to forget the kiss ever happened. "I'm glad you're feeling better this morning."

"I took your advice to heart. No sense weakening under pressure when I need all my energy to fight. Onwards and upwards, Brooke."

"That's the spirit." She let the big goofy smile widen her mouth. This was the RJ she'd grown to know and love. "What's first on the agenda this morning?"

He tilted his head slightly and lowered his voice. "The first thing on my agenda is to secure a date for tonight."

Brooke's heart almost stopped. Did he mean with her, or did he intend for her to call some strange woman and...

"Are you free after work this evening?"

"Yes," she stammered. "Yes, I am." How cool. Oh well, not like she had an image as a seductress to uphold.

"I'll make reservations and will pick you up at your place at seven-thirty."

"Great." Already her mind spun with worries about what to wear. Her cherished collection of business suits would be too stuffy for dinner and she didn't have that many—

"I'm off to a meeting and I've left a pile of items in your inbox."

"Great." Apparently that was the only word left in her vocabulary. "See you later," she called, as he swept into the elevator.

A date with RJ. Tonight. And she didn't even have to make the reservation! But she did still have to go through his correspondence and coordinate his sched-ule, just like any other day.

She felt as if she was stepping onto a board of chutes and ladders. Three steps forward and dinner with RJ leads up the tall ladder! What next? Would she roll a five and plunge to estrangement and unemployment at the bottom of a chute?

With no idea what kind of restaurant RJ would choose, Brooke decided to go smart-casual. She donned a floral patterned dress she'd never worn to work and a cute cashmere shrug she'd found in a boutique walking home from work one day. Her hair was shiny, her complexion clear for once and except for the heightened redness in her cheeks she looked pretty darn good!

Still, she jumped when the doorbell rang. She'd never given RJ her address, but no doubt he could just look in her personnel file. She drew in a breath as she walked across the living room to open the door.

"Hi." She felt yet another huge goofy grin spread across her face at the sight of RJ, several inches larger than life, as always, standing right there on her doorstep. "Won't you come in?" She'd spent at least an hour cleaning the place to within an inch of its life.

"Sure." He smiled, and stepped inside.

"Would you like a martini?" She knew he loved them.

"Why not?" RJ managed to look both classic and hip in a jacket that hung elegantly from his broad shoulders, and loose khakis. He often had the air of an old-time matinee idol, which perfectly matched his bold, aristocratic features and easy confidence. Right now she felt like his leading lady, since her dress had a vintage flair to it.

She mixed the martinis and poured them into long-stemmed glasses while RJ complimented her place.

"Thanks, I like it here." She'd lived in the two-bedroom condo near Colonial Lake for five years now and was proud of how she'd decorated it. A mix of timeless pieces and funky touches that reflected her personality. "I'm renting right now but I hope the owner will sell to me when the lease is up." *As long as I still have a job by then.* She smiled and handed him the drink. "Bottoms up."

RJ raised his glass. "I never know which end will be up lately." He took a sip, and nodded his head in approval. "You look gorgeous." His gaze lingered on her face, then drifted to her neck, and she became agonizingly conscious of the hint of cleavage her dress revealed.

"Thanks." She tried not to blush. "You don't look too bad, either." He'd obviously taken the time to go home and change after work, which touched her. She knew how often he headed out to dinner straight from the office.

"I clean up okay." He shot her a sultry look. "I'm glad to do something fun for a change. Lately I feel like I'm running from crisis to crisis, either in the company or in the family."

"Crisis-free here." She offered him a plate of tiny puff pastries she'd picked up on her way home. "Want something to nibble?"

"Why, sure." His eyes rested on her face for a second longer than was entirely polite. All the parts of her body that never knew how much they wanted to be nibbled by RJ started to hum and tingle. Then he took a pastry, put it in his mouth and chewed.

Brooke quickly swallowed one herself. She could see his gleaming black Porsche parked outside. She'd never ridden in it before as he used a more practical Audi sedan for work. She could imagine the neighbors whispering and peering through their miniblinds. "Where are we going for dinner?"

"A new place just off King Street. It's a grill, of

sorts, with a Low Country twist to it. A friend told me it's the best food he's eaten in ages."

"Sounds great, but isn't that kind of central? What if people see us together?" It probably wasn't the best idea for them to hang out right in the historic district. She'd assumed he'd pick somewhere discreet and out of the way.

"People see us together every day. Let them assume what they like."

Was he implying that this evening meant nothing so there was no need to worry if anyone saw?

The steady heat in his gaze suggested otherwise. If she didn't know better she'd suspect he could see right through her dress.

"I'd prefer to go somewhere more private." Her nerves jangled as she said it. He was her boss, after all, and not used to hearing her opinion on such things. "I'd hate for people to start talking."

"Let them talk. Everyone in Charleston is talking about the Kincaids right now and it hasn't killed us yet." His face darkened.

He must be thinking about his father's murder. Why was she bickering over restaurants when RJ was under so much pressure already? "All right, I'll stop worrying. We can always tell them we were testing it out as a place to hold a client party."

"Always thinking." He smiled and took another sip of his martini. "That's a damn good martini but I think we should get going. I made a reservation for eight and it's the hottest table in town right now."

Uh-oh. That meant there might be people he knew there. What if people started to gossip about them and things didn't work out? Her hands shook slightly as she put on her shrug and grabbed her purse. She was hoping for a promotion. What if people thought she was trying to sleep her way to the top? She was hardly from RJ's usual social circles. She swallowed hard. Still, it was too late to back out now. "I'm ready." She was heading out to dinner with her boss, for better or worse.

The reclined seats in his black Porsche felt every bit as decadent and inviting as she'd imagined. Excitement raced through her as RJ started the engine. She wouldn't be able to resist telling her mom about this. She'd be impressed for sure. Then again, maybe she was starting to think too much like her mom. She did not like RJ because he had a Porsche, or a large bank account—she liked him because of his intelligence and kindness.

And his washboard abs and fine backside.

"Why are you smiling?" His eyes twinkled when he glanced at her.

"I think the martini made me giddy."

"Excellent. I like you giddy."

He pulled into a parking space in the historic district, then opened her car door before she even had time to unbuckle her seat belt. He took her hand and helped her out, and she felt like royalty stepping onto King Street with RJ Kincaid. Which was funny because she'd been to restaurants here with him before—as part of a business party, of course. Now everything was different.

Her hand stayed inside RJ's, hot and aware, as they walked down a picturesque side street to a restaurant with a crisp green awning. The maître d' took them to their table on a veranda overlooking a tiny but perfect garden behind the building, where flowers climbed an old brick wall and water trickled in a lion's-head fountain. The table was set with a thick, starched tablecloth and heavy silverware, and a bright bouquet of daisies in a cut glass vase.

RJ pulled back her chair, again making her feel like a princess.

"A bottle of Moët, please," he said to the waiter.

Brooke's eyes widened. "What are we celebrating?"

"That life goes on." RJ leaned back in his chair. "And dammit, we're going to enjoy it no matter what happens."

"That's an admirable philosophy." Along with everyone else in Charleston, he must be wondering what could possibly happen next. His dad was dead and his mom was being held at the county jail under suspicion of murder. Bail had been denied as, with money and connections, she was considered a flight risk.

And there was something he didn't know.

Brooke had told the police she'd seen Mrs. Kincaid at the office that night. She hadn't mentioned this fact to RJ. In light of the arrest she wasn't sure he'd be happy she told the truth. Of course she knew Elizabeth Kincaid was innocent, but still… Guilt trickled uneasily up her spine. She really should tell him she'd seen his mom there. Just to clear the air.

"My dad would have wanted me to hold my head up and keep fighting." He watched as the waiter poured two tall glasses of sparkling champagne. "And that's what I intend to do. I spent all afternoon trying to get the D.A.'s office to agree to set bail for Mom, but they've refused. And I talked Apex International down from the ledge in between phone calls to the D.A."

"The toy importer?"

"Yup. Getting ready to jump ship to one of our competitors. I convinced them to stick with us. Told them the Kincaid Group is the most efficient, well-run, cost-effective shipper on the east coast and we intend to stay that way." He raised his glass and clinked it gently against hers. "Thanks for brightening a dark day."

His honest expression, weary but still brave and strong, touched something deep inside her. "I'm happy to help in any way I can." That sounded odd. A bit too businesslike, maybe. But it was hard to step out of her familiar role and embrace this new one, especially when she had no idea what role she'd be in tomorrow. *You know I'd do anything for you.* She managed not to say it, though she suspected he knew.

"You're helping already." That little flame of desire hovered in his pupils and sent a shiver through her. "Your loyalty means a lot to me. You've proved I can count on you in a crisis. I don't know what I would have done without you in the last few weeks."

His deep voice echoed inside her. Did she really mean that much to him? Her heart fluttered alarmingly. "I'm glad."

Further words failed her and she distracted herself by looking down at the menu, which had an array of elegant yet folksy-sounding local dishes. After some hemming and hawing, RJ chose roast pork shoulder with mustard barbeque sauce and sautéed greens. She chose a shrimp dish with a side of grits and an arugula salad.

"It occurs to me that I don't know too much about you, Brooke Nichols." RJ raised a brow. "I know you live in Charleston, but other than that you're a bit of an enigma. You don't talk about yourself much."

She inhaled slightly. "There isn't much to know." Did he really want to learn that her college quarterback father had resisted all her teenage mother's attempts to trap him into marriage, and how she'd grown up with a succession of stepfathers? "I was born in Greenville, and I went to high school in Columbia. Mom and I moved here after I graduated and we both adore it."

"Does your mom live with you?"

"No, she lives in the 'burbs." With her latest boy-friend. "I enjoy having my own place."

"Do you? I find I'm getting tired of living alone. I miss Mom's cooking." He smiled, then a shadow of pain passed over his features.

A jolt of guilt tightened her stomach. Was her police interview the reason Elizabeth Kincaid had been ar-rested? She really should tell RJ about that right now. *Did you know I told the police I saw your mom at the scene of the crime?* How did you say something like that without sounding accusatory? "I'm sure they'll let her out soon. They have to know she's innocent. She's the sweetest lady I've ever met." She wasn't exagger-ating. And now she knew what Elizabeth Kincaid had put up with over the years. She must have suspected her husband was cheating, at least, even if she hadn't known about his second family. "I wish we could help them find the real killer."

"Me, too. Mom's always been the linchpin of the family. I'm trying to hold it together for everyone but we're all tense and anxious."

Her heart swelled. "I envy your large family. It must

be reassuring to have siblings you can turn to as well as your parents."

"Or fight with." He grinned. "I think we probably argue as much as we get along. Maybe not so much these days, but when we were kids…" He shook his head.

"I never had anybody to fight with, and I'm not sure that's a good thing. Sibling spats must teach you how to negotiate with people."

He laughed. "Are you saying I honed my business bargaining skills over the Hot Wheels set I shared with Matt?"

"Quite possibly." She sipped her champagne, a smile spreading across her lips. RJ was visibly relaxing, his features softening and the lines of worry leaving his face. "Whatever you did as children has made you close as adults. I don't think I've ever seen a family spend so much time together."

RJ sighed. "I really thought we were the perfect family, but now the entire world knows that was just an illusion."

"No family is perfect. Yours is still close-knit and loving, even after everything that's happened."

The waiter brought their appetizers, fried calamari with a green tomato salsa.

"We'll get through this. I need to focus on what makes us stronger, not what's threatening to tear us apart. And somehow you've managed to deflect the conversation off yourself again." He raised a brow. "You're a mysterious character, Brooke. What do you do when you're peacefully alone in your private palace?"

She shrugged. It would have been nice to be able

to chatter gaily about flamenco dancing sessions and cocktail parties, but she wasn't one to embroider the truth. She had friends over once or twice a month, but mostly she valued the peace and quiet of her sanctuary after a long day at work. "I read a lot." She paused to nibble a crispy piece of calamari. "Not very exciting, is it?"

"I guess that depends on how good a book you're reading." His blue gaze rested on her face, and she warmed under it. "Sometimes I think I should make more time for quiet pastimes like reading. Might improve my mind."

She laughed. "I can't see you sitting still long enough to read a book."

"Maybe that's something I need to work on." He hadn't touched his food. If anything he seemed transfixed by her, unable to take his eyes off her face. Brooke felt her breathing grow shallow under his intense stare. "I used to go out to our hunting cabin at least once a month with my dad. We'd mellow out and recharge our batteries together. I haven't been there since he died."

"Can you still go visit it?"

"It's mine now. He left it to me in his will." A shadow passed over his face. The same will that left almost half the company to Jack Sinclair. "It's been sitting empty since he died."

"Why don't you go there?"

He shrugged. "I never went there without Dad. I can't imagine going alone and I can't think of anyone I'd want to go with." His expression changed and his eyes widened slightly. "You. You could come with me."

"Oh, I don't think so." She shifted in her chair. Their

first date wasn't even over yet and he was inviting her on an overnight trip? She knew his family never went there just for the day. It was probably a long drive. She'd likely be expected to share a bed with him and so far they'd only kissed once. Already her heart pounded with a mix of excitement and sheer terror.

RJ's face brightened. "We'll go this weekend. Just you and me. We'll get Frankie Deleon's to pack us some gourmet meals and we'll spend a weekend in peace."

"I don't know anything about hunting." The idea of killing things made her cringe.

"Don't worry, we don't have to really hunt. Dad and I mostly just walked around in the mountains carrying the guns as an excuse. It's so peaceful up there it seems a crime to pierce the air with a shot."

She smiled. "That's a funny image. So there aren't racks of antlers on the living room wall?"

"There's one set but we bought it at an antiques auction." His eyes twinkled. "We call him Uncle Dave. We did sometimes go fishing and eat the fish, though. Fishing was the only time I ever saw Dad sit still for more than a few minutes."

"I used to fish with my friend June's family years ago. They'd take a camper to a lake and stay there for a week every summer. I caught a huge rainbow trout once."

"Excellent. Now we know what we're doing this weekend." He rubbed his hands together with enthusiasm. "Nice to have something to look forward to as this promises to be a long week."

Brooke didn't know what to say. He'd already planned her weekend without even waiting for a response. Yes, he was her boss, but going fishing on the weekends was not part of her job description. She should be mad at his arrogance.

On the other hand, a weekend in the mountains with RJ... What girl would say no to that?

Her. "I don't think I should come. I'm sure you have other friends you could invite." Her gut was telling her to slow this whole train ride before it went off the tracks. "I have...things to do here at home."

"Are you afraid I'll take advantage of you, out there in the lonesome woods?" He tilted his head and lifted a brow.

"Yes." Her blood sizzled at the prospect.

"You're absolutely right, of course."

"I think it's a bit premature."

"Of course, we've only known each other five years." A dimple appeared in his left cheek, emphasizing his high cheekbones.

"You know what I mean."

"Sure. One amazing kiss is not enough to plan an entire weekend around."

She shrugged. "Something like that."

"How many kisses? Two, three?" He looked impatiently at the expanse of tablecloth between them. Humor twinkled in his eyes.

"Probably somewhere around five." She fought to keep a smile from her mouth.

"Five years and five kisses." He looked thoughtful. "Let's see what we can do before the night is out."

The handsome waiter whisked their appetizer plates away and settled their mains in front of them while the sommelier poured two glasses of white wine. She'd barely made a dent in her champagne. Maybe that was her problem. She needed to drink a bit more to take the edge off her inhibitions. The whiskey had certainly done wonders for RJ yesterday. On the other hand, the prospect of four more kisses before the evening ended made her light-headed.

She could see the glow of impending victory in RJ's eyes. She'd become familiar with that look in meetings right when he knew he'd clinched a big deal. RJ hated to lose, and sometimes went after quite small clients just for the satisfaction of beating the competition.

Apparently she was to be his next conquest. Her blood pressure ratcheted up a notch. RJ in motion was hard to stop. "Can you really get away for the weekend with everything that's going on right now?"

RJ raised a dark brow. "That's exactly why I need to get away." He reached out and touched her fingers gently where they sat at the base of her glass. A tiny shiver of arousal ran through her. "And you're just the distraction I need."

His voice was husky, thick with the arousal that weighted the air between them. Did he expect her to go home with him tonight? Just what had she gotten herself into here? Him calling her a "distraction" did not entirely bode well for a lifelong commitment.

Then again, she was getting way ahead of herself. And already her lips tingled in anticipation of the second kiss he'd promised. She tried to distract them with a piece of shrimp, but the sauce proved surpris- ingly spicy and only made things worse. "I suppose some fresh air won't do either of us any harm." That sounded lame. She should probably be making sug- gestive and witty comments. Soon enough RJ would realize he'd made a terrible mistake thinking she was an attractive and desirable woman.

If he even did think that. Maybe it was more of an "any port in the storm" thing. Even your assistant started to look good when your entire world was falling apart.

"What *are* you thinking about?" RJ peered into her eyes, mischief sparkling in his own blue depths.

"Just wondering where this evening is heading." The truth seemed as good a response as any other.

RJ's mouth broadened into a sensual smile. "Somewhere beautiful."

It was dark when they parked near Waterfront Park and strolled along the promenade looking out at the lights reflected on the dark water. They were dangerously close to RJ's apartment, or at least she suspected so, but he'd shown no signs of trying to take her home. He hadn't even tried to kiss her.

Her skin craved his touch and each time she hoped for it and didn't get it, the longing only grew more bone-deep. Five years of suppressed yearning were unleashed by one kiss, and if she didn't get another kiss soon she might just burst into flame.

Moonlight mingled with the streetlights to illuminate RJ's dramatic features. "So your mom is your only real family?"

"Since my Gran died five years ago, yes." RJ had been plumbing her for information all evening. Not in an unkind way. He seemed genuinely curious.

"Did you ever want siblings?"

"All the time," she admitted. "When I was little I wished for a sister to share my dolls with. Then when I was a teenager I wished I had a brother to bring home handsome friends."

He chuckled. "My sisters weren't shy about asking me to do just that. But I bet you managed fine, anyway."

He caressed her with another one of those lingering glances that made her feel like a supermodel. No need for him to know her last date had been nearly a year ago. Since her best friend got married she hadn't been out much at night and she knew better than to have an affair with someone at the office.

Until now...

He stepped toward her and slid his arms around her hips. Her breasts stirred inside her dress as he pulled her close. Her lips parted and her hands rose to the soft wool of his jacket. She ached for his kiss, a long, deep ache that rose inside her and pulled her closer into his embrace. When his lips finally met hers sensation sparkled through her. All day she'd dreamed of this moment, craved and hoped for it, despite all her misgivings. RJ's arms around her made her feel safe, protected and adored. He kissed with exquisite gentleness, touching her lips gently then pulling back, letting the very tip of his tongue touch hers, teasing and tasting her until she was in a frenzy of arousal. It took all her strength not to writhe against him in full view of the other people enjoying the breezy moonlit night.

"Yes, it's a good idea." RJ's words surprised her. "Us kissing." They'd barely pulled apart and she hadn't even had time for doubts to creep back into her consciousness. No doubt he was trying to preempt them.

"Certainly feels like one." A silly smile plastered itself across her face. A sense of euphoria suffused her entire body, and she'd only had two glasses of wine so she couldn't even blame the alcohol.

She was high on RJ.

His lips touched hers again, and again her synapses lit up like a Christmas tree. She'd never experienced such a sharp physical reaction to a simple kiss. It was a full-body experience. By the time he pulled gently back she was sure she'd broken out in a sweat.

Already her lips itched to meet his again. But if she gave him all five kisses, was she agreeing to the weekend away? "I really should get home now."

"No way." His hands held her steady. "Five years, five kisses."

"There's nothing about kisses in my employment contract." She attempted to look fierce.

"There wouldn't be, since we don't use an employment contract." That naughty dimple appeared again as he lowered his lips to hers. Brooke's lips parted instinctively, and a tantalizing tip of his tongue probed her mouth, sending a shiver of suggestion down her spine. Her knees wobbled and she was forced to hold him tighter. With her pressed against his hard chest, kiss number three was broken only by a quiet whisper. "Brooke, why did we wait so long?"

She didn't answer. Boring explanations about her long-term career prospects had no place in this electric moment. Kiss number four crept up on them and her eyes shut tight as sensation swept through her. RJ's hard chest felt like a safe foundation to lean on, so she let the world drift away and lost herself in his kiss. An hour could have passed before their lips finally pulled apart, she had no idea.

The streetlights, even the reflected glow from the

water, seemed painfully bright when she opened her eyes.

"I expect you're wondering if I'm going to ask you back to my apartment." RJ looked down at her, arms still wrapped around her, holding her close.

The thought did cross my mind. She kept her mouth closed, though. She still had no idea what she'd reply if he did ask.

"I'm not."

A tiny frisson of disappointment cascaded through her. Had this evening led him to decide he was no longer interested in her? Maybe he just liked talking to her and didn't want to take it further. Perhaps those kisses that lit her whole body on fire had simply been a series of tests that she'd failed.

"I have the utmost respect for you, Brooke." His expression was serious.

Her heart sank further. Was this the "you're too valuable an employee for me to fool around with" speech?

"I know you're a lady and would be offended if I asked you in on our first date." He moved his hands until they were over hers. "And I'm still enough of a gentleman to resist the temptation."

His fingers wove into hers and the full force of that temptation rushed through her. He was taking it slow because he respected her. Somehow that truly touched her.

He leaned in until she could inhale his enticing male scent. "But I'm not letting you go without one last kiss."

Relief swept through her as their lips pressed together. He wasn't rejecting her. She held him tight and kissed him back with passion.

"And I'm already anticipating the pleasure of an entire weekend with you, so asking for tonight as well would be greedy."

Misgivings still crept in her veins. An entire weekend was a long time. If things got out of hand there would be no turning back. Though likely it was already too late to return to their normal workaday existence. "What should I bring?" Would she need waders, or an evening gown? Or both?

"Just yourself. The house is fully stocked for entertaining guests so there's loads of extra gear there."

"Will anyone else be there?" What if other Kincaid siblings were around to witness her liaison with RJ? She cringed at the thought of them laughing behind her back, or exchanging shocked whispers.

"I certainly hope not." RJ pressed a quick kiss to her lips. "Since the house is mine now and I haven't invited anyone but you we should have the whole two hundred acres to ourselves."

Two hundred acres. It must be in the middle of nowhere. Of course that was probably the point with hunting cabins. Less chance of shooting one of the neighbors. She and RJ would have more than enough privacy to do anything they liked.

Which reminded her she was arm in arm with him in a popular spot in downtown Charleston. Did she really want coworkers or his family to see them kissing? They might think she was trying to sleep her way to a promotion. Or even take advantage of him when he was under stress. "I think it's time for me to go home. I have to work tomorrow—and so do you in case you've forgotten." It was nearly eleven last time she'd checked.

"I don't have to worry. My capable assistant handles everything for me while I take long lunches."

Brooke made a mock gasp. "I'll have to schedule some of those investor conferences you so look forward to. Perhaps some early breakfast meetings."

"Now you're scaring me. I'll do my best to roll in after a late breakfast."

His cocky attitude didn't annoy her. In fact she was proud he could count on her to keep his work life on track. He looked so relaxed and happy right now you'd never guess his family was in turmoil. Maybe she could take some credit for that, as well.

A warm sense of satisfaction bloomed inside her, along with the delicious arousal RJ had stirred. If things went well this weekend, who knew what the future might hold?

Three

"**Y**ou're going to spend the weekend in the woods with *your boss?*" Her friend Evie had been speechless for a few seconds. Now apparently she'd recovered.

Brooke moved the phone back closer to her ear again. "He's quite different than I thought. Much more sensitive."

"I don't care how sensitive he is. What will happen when he gets bored with you?"

"Ouch." Brooke walked across her apartment. "Am I that dull? You've been friends with me for nearly eight years."

"You know what I mean. Most men, especially in his position, just want to fool around and have fun, and after a few dates they're ready for someone new. Didn't you tell me yourself that he's a bit of a Casanova?"

"Sure, he used to date a lot, but this big family scandal has made him more serious." He hadn't been going out much lately. At least not that she knew of.

"So he's turned into the white picket fence type and is looking for a nice, quiet girl to settle down with."

"Maybe he is."

"You could be right, but what if he isn't? You've put five years into the company. Didn't you say something about a management position?"

"I applied to be the events coordinator but I didn't get it." Yes, it smarted a little, especially since the woman they'd hired from outside was more than a bit flaky. "I just have to keep trying."

"And you think an affair with your boss will help?"

"It's not an affair yet. All we've done is kiss."

"After a weekend in the woods it will be an affair. Do you genuinely believe he'll decide you're the girl of his dreams and ask you to marry him?"

Brooke took in a breath. "Is it a crime to dream? You're married."

"To the guy in the next cubicle, not the one at the head of the boardroom table. I care about you, Brooke, and I know how much your job at Kincaid means to you. It really is a place where you could take your career to the next level and I don't want to see you throw that away for a quick sympathy fling."

"I can always find a job somewhere else."

"In this economy? I'm being very careful with the job I have as there's not a lot out there."

"You're so supportive." Her joy had deflated. One minute she'd been swanning around the air castles of her mind as Mrs. RJ Kincaid. Then the castle went poof and she was now single again and jobless, too. "Maybe I want to have some fun."

Evie sighed. "I miss our nights out together. I know being married is no reason to stay in every night, but we have our hands full with this renovation project right now and—"

Brooke laughed. "I wasn't trying to guilt trip you into a night on the town with me. I know it sounds crazy but the roller coaster has already left the station. I can't go back to before the kiss, so I might as well enjoy the ride and hope for the best."

"My knuckles are turning white just thinking about it. And I want to hear *all* the details on Monday."

RJ left his keys and wallet on the tray and walked through the security machines at the detention center. His entire body reacted to the oppressive atmosphere of the building. A place where hardened criminals were locked up awaiting trial, and where his kind and gentle mother was forced to suffer their company.

A silent guard led him to a private interview room. His lawyer had apparently gone to great trouble to arrange a face-to-face meeting with his mom, otherwise he could only speak to her from the lobby over a video link. The guard opened the door to a small room with a metal desk and two chairs.

She looked tiny, sitting alone at the desk, dressed in the regulation jumpsuit. He walked toward her, unable to govern his features into any kind of polite greeting. "Mom." He took her in his arms and held her tight. She seemed so frail and helpless, not at all the steel magnolia he'd always proudly bragged about.

"No contact." He'd forgotten the no touching rule, and the gruff voice behind him reminded him. With great reluctance he pulled back his arms.

"I won't do it again." He turned to the guard. "Can we be alone for a few minutes?"

"I'll be standing right here, watching." The tall, older man gestured to a square of window in the door, then slipped outside.

His mom's face was pale and drawn, with tiny blue shadows under her expressive eyes. Her trademark auburn hair was slicked back in a way that only made her look more gaunt and slender.

"I'm trying everything to get you out of here."

"I know." The barest hint of a smile lit her eyes. "My lawyer says you won't even let him sleep."

"He can sleep later, once you're free. I'm going to see the D.A. again this afternoon, before I go away for the weekend."

"Are you going to the lodge?" Her eyes brightened. He nodded. "I wondered how long it would take before you went there again. I know how much you love it up in the mountains. Who's going with you?"

"Brooke." Why not tell the truth? Anticipation rose in his veins like sap in the spring. He couldn't wait to be alone with Brooke on that peaceful mountainside. He could already picture sunbeams picking out gold in her hair, and those soft green eyes gazing at the majestic views. She'd love it there. He knew she would.

"Your assistant?" His mom's shocked response drew him from his reverie. Her pale eyebrows lacked their usual flourish of pencil, but he still saw them rise.

"Yes. She and I... She's been a great help to me lately." His brain filled almost to bursting with a desire to tell his mom all about his newfound relationship with Brooke. Brooke was sweet and kind as well as beautiful and he was sure his mom would love her.

Still, he could tell his mom was shocked by the idea of him dating his own assistant and somehow it seemed premature, so he held his tongue.

She nodded. "She seems a bright girl, and very pretty. I hope you have a lovely time. You certainly deserve a break and some fresh air. I know how hard you've been working."

"Thanks, Mom." His chest tightened. How sweet she was to wish him a good weekend when she'd be stuck in here. Anger and frustration raged inside him again. "Why are they holding you? No one will explain. I can't understand why they won't let you out on bail. I had a hell of a time even coming to see you in person."

His mom glanced around the room. "Sit down, will you." She gestured politely as if inviting him to take up residence in one of her beautifully upholstered Liberty print chairs at home, not a scarred metal folding chair.

RJ sat.

She leaned toward him. "They know I was in the office on the night…the night your dad was shot." Her voice faded on the last word and he saw pain flash in her eyes.

"You were there?" He kept his voice as hushed as possible.

"I was." Her lips closed tightly for a second, draining of blood. "I brought him a plate of food as he'd said he'd be home late."

RJ frowned. "They didn't say any food had been found."

She shook her head. "He didn't want it so I took it home with me." She let out a sigh, which rippled through her body as a visible shiver. "I know it seems odd, me bringing him dinner. I only did it that night as I was worried your dad had been so distant, like he was troubled by something. I'd been short with him the night before and I wanted to show him I cared."

"Dad knew you cared about him." RJ's heart filled with red-hot rage that his dad had caused her so much pain by carrying on with another woman. "If anything, he didn't deserve you."

Her eyes filled with tears, but she managed to blink them back. "I do miss your father, even after all that's happened."

"Of course you do." He took her hands in his. They were cold and bony, and he chafed them lightly, trying to warm them. "But you bringing dinner doesn't make you a murderer."

"It makes me a murder suspect."

RJ frowned. Something was seriously off here. "But how did the police know you were there?" The front desk didn't bother logging family members or employees, who were allowed to come and go as they pleased.

"Someone saw me."

"Who?" What kind of person would finger his mom at the crime scene?

She hesitated. Looked away. "Does it really matter? I don't even remember if anyone saw me. As I said, I was there."

"The accusations still don't make sense. You have no motivation to kill Dad. For one thing, you were as much in the dark as the rest of us about Angela and her sons." The words soured in his mouth. "I wish to God none of us had ever found out."

She pulled her hands back and placed them in her lap. "I have a confession to make, RJ."

RJ's eyes widened. "What?" Was she going to admit to killing his dad? His stomach roiled.

"I did know about Angela." Her eyes were dry, her expression composed. "I'd known for some years. Ever since I found an earlier version of Reginald's will in his desk while looking for a calculator."

RJ swallowed. So his suspicion was correct. "Why didn't you say anything?"

"Your father and I had words, but he convinced me to stay with him for the sake of the family. The reputation, the company, you know how important all that was to him." She smoothed back her hair. "And to me."

He blinked, unable to process this. "So you were sitting there with us at family dinners, week after week, and you never breathed a word to anyone?"

Her head hung slightly, and lines of pain formed around her eyes. "Your father and I were married for a very long time. There was a lot of history there. Maybe too much to throw away for an affair that began so long ago."

"But that was still continuing, unless I understand wrong."

He watched his mom's throat move as she swallowed. "You're not wrong. Reginald loved Angela." It took visible effort for her gaze to meet his, and he fought the urge to take her in his arms again. Her rigid posture told him to keep his distance. "He loved me, too." A wry smile tugged at her lips. "He was a man with a lot of love to give."

"That's one way of looking at it, though I'd like the opportunity to give him a piece of my mind." He realized his hands were clenched into fists, and he released them. "I know you didn't kill him." He had to say it, because he had thought it for that split second after she announced a confession, and he needed to clear the air.

"Of course I didn't, but the police and the courts don't know that, and I don't have an alibi for the time of the murder."

"We need to find out who really did it. Do you have any suspicions?"

She shook her head. "Trust me, if I had even the slightest inkling, I'd tell everyone I know."

RJ glanced around the grim room. "This place is a nightmare." He remembered the bag he'd brought with him. "I brought you some books. Flannery O'Connor, William Faulkner. Lily said you'd want something more cheery, but I wasn't so sure. They put them through the metal detector downstairs. Apparently razor-sharp wit doesn't show up on the screen."

She smiled, and peered into the offered paper bag. "RJ, you're so thoughtful. And you're right, I feel like reading about experiences darker than my own." She sighed. "Hopefully I won't have time to read them all."

"Not if I can help it."

"I've never flown in a small plane." Brooke's hands trembled as she buckled the seat belt in the Kincaid jet. "Couldn't we drive there?" Her wide green eyes implored him.

A protective instinct surged inside RJ and he took hold of her hand. "It's almost 150 miles away, near Gatlinburg, Tennessee. We'll be fine." Strange to see ever-capable Brooke looking worried. He squeezed her trembling fingers gently to reassure her. "At least we have a professional pilot today. My dad used to fly it himself sometimes and while he claimed military flying experience, I never saw any kind of license."

"Scary!"

"Tell me about it. I even toyed with getting a license myself so I'd be able to take over in an emergency. One time we got caught in a wind shear coming out of the mountains, but Dad handled it like a pro." His chest tightened as a wave of sadness swept through him. He still couldn't believe that he'd never see his dad again. Never hear his chesty laugh or another tall tale about his days in Special Ops.

"You're not making me feel better."

"We'll be fine." He lifted his arm and placed it around her shoulder. Her soft floral scent filled his nostrils. Soon they'd be alone together in the mountains. The fresh air would lift the cares off both of their shoulders. He couldn't wait to hear her infectious laugh echo off the wooded hillsides, or see the morning sun sparkle in her lovely eyes. And then there would be the nights… He'd instructed the caretaker to put the best fresh linen on the beds—he planned to offer her one for herself, then tempt her out of it. The prospect of Brooke's lush body writhing under those sheets made his pulse quicken.

Yes, she was his assistant. Doubts did force their way to the forefront of his consciousness from time to time. Mixing business and pleasure was always risky, and in a family business it could be downright explosive. His father had warned all of them to keep their personal affairs out of the office and RJ had never had an affair with an employee before, despite considerable temptation over the years. Funnily enough he'd never seen Brooke in that way until their whiskey-flavored kiss in his office. She'd been his right-hand woman, his trusted friend, his rock—but their kiss had opened up a new world of possibilities.

Now he knew his assistant was a sensual woman, with passion flickering behind the jade of her eyes and excited breaths quickening in her lovely chest when he looked at her, the temptation was irresistible. He'd never have dreamed anything could take his mind off the hailstorm of disaster raining down on the Kincaid family over the last few months, but when he was with Brooke, all his burdens seemed lighter. It was such a relief to be with someone whom he could totally trust.

He heard Brooke's breath catch as the plane lifted off the runway, but she soon relaxed as they rose high over the Charleston suburbs, heading toward the sunset and the distant shadow of the mountains. If only they could fly away from all his troubles and worries. Those were hitchhiking along, but with Brooke by his side they'd stay in check.

"How's your mom doing?" Brooke's soft question revealed her natural empathy.

"She's hanging in there. She's a brave woman and she doesn't want us to worry. I visited her this afternoon and took her some books she wanted. I told her we're doing everything we can to get her out. The police have been pretty closemouthed so I hired a private investigator to work full-time on the case, and he's going to work with Nikki Thomas, our own corporate investigator. The lawyers are still trying to negotiate bail. They keep promising she'll be released but it gets shot down at the last moment. Apparently someone saw her in the office that night. Hey, are you okay?"

Brooke's face had turned so pale, even her lips lost color. "Sure, just a little queasy. I'll be okay."

He squeezed her hand. It was easy to dismiss your own problems, but you couldn't always help the ones you cared about. Lately that made him feel powerless, an unfamiliar experience he hated. At least he could show Brooke a glorious and relaxing weekend in the country. She deserved the best of everything and he intended to give it to her.

Brooke gripped his hand tightly during their descent into the airport at Gatlinburg, then exhaled with relief as the plane taxied to a halt.

"See? You survived."

"Only just. And my nails have probably left permanent scars on your hand."

"I'll wear them with pride."

RJ was pleased to see the caretaker had dropped the familiar black Suburban off at the airport then discreetly disappeared. The first sign that his plans were going smoothly. He'd told the caretaker he didn't need any staff on hand, as he suspected Brooke might be spooked by the presence of other people. Much better that they enjoy peace and privacy.

A now-familiar pang of grief hit him as he climbed behind the wheel. His dad usually drove, maintaining the familiar patterns of father-and-son even though RJ had been driving for nearly twenty years. "Dad loved it up here. He always said the whole world fell away if you got high enough up into the mountains."

"It's beautiful. The light is different here." That light illuminated Brooke's hair and her delicate profile as she looked out the window. For a split second he longed to press his lips to hers and lose himself in a kiss. Instead he started the engine.

"Dad wrote me a letter when he made his will." He frowned. He'd never spoken to anyone else about it. "Said he wasn't sure how much longer he'd live and he wanted to make sure the lodge would be mine."

"Oh." Brooke turned sharply, shock written on her face. "Sounds like he almost knew he was going to die."

"He never said a word to anyone." He shook his head. "His lawyers told me he redrew his will every few years, so they didn't think much of it. He included letters each time. But when he died there was one for everyone in the family…except my mom."

"Did he leave any hints of who he suspected?"

"That is odd. Nothing I could figure out. He does mention his other family that none of us knew about. Well, except Mom."

"Your mom knew about his other woman and her children?"

RJ swallowed. "Apparently so. She didn't say anything to us. She learned about them while he was writing his will. She found a copy in his desk." It was good to get that awkward truth off his chest. He knew he could trust Brooke not to tell anyone. "She didn't want any of us to know."

"Is that why police think she has motive?"

"I suppose they think she wanted revenge." He heard Brooke's intake of breath. Did she think it was possible that his mom could wield a gun against her husband of nearly four decades? "You do know she's innocent."

"Yes, of course." The color had fled her cheeks again. "It's just a shame she had to find out that way."

Brooke seemed distracted, staring hard out the window, not even noticing the bait and tackle shop and the quaint country inn he'd intended to show her.

"I brought Dad's letter with me because he mentions something in the lodge." He paused while a big truck crossed at the intersection ahead. "Something else he wanted me to have."

"An object?"

"I don't know. It's rather mysterious. He said to look in the third drawer down, but he didn't say what piece of furniture."

"Hmm. I guess you'll just have to open every third drawer down in the house, and hope for the best."

He didn't mention the other things his dad had said in the letter. For now those were between Reginald Kincaid, Sr., and his namesake, and maybe it was better that no one else knew about them.

Brooke was lost for words when they pulled up at the lodge. Then again, what had she expected, a shack with an outside toilet? This was a Kincaid residence. The vast log home rose up out of the surrounding woodlands, high gables braced with chiseled beams and walls of windows reflecting the sunset. RJ strode up the steps and unlocked the impressive double doors, then ushered her inside.

Golden sunlight illuminated the foyer from all directions. RJ put down their bags then walked through a door in the far wall. "Dad named it Great Oak Lodge. Come see why we built the house here."

Brooke followed him into another grand room, decorated in an updated, minimalist interpretation of hunting-lodge chic: pale sofas with muted plaid accents, a painting of a stag and an impressive stone fireplace. The last rays of sunlight blazing in through a wall of windows largely obscured the view, until RJ opened a pair of patio doors and she saw an endless vista of tree-cloaked hills.

She walked out and stood beside him. There were no signs of civilization at all, just peaks and valleys filled with more trees. "It feels like we're on top of the world."

"Maybe we are." He stepped behind her and slid his arms around her waist. Her belly shimmered with arousal. They hadn't kissed since their date two nights ago, and on the plane she'd been too nervous to think much about kissing. Or any of the things that might follow.

RJ bent his head and pressed his lips to her neck. "You smell sensational." Excitement trickled through her, peppered with anxiety about where this was all going. Now his hot breath warmed her ear, making her shiver with anticipation.

"Shouldn't we put our bags away?" She could hardly believe that was her voice interrupting the sensual moment.

RJ chuckled. "Trying to delay the inevitable?"

"Just being practical. That's why you hired me." Ouch. Why did she have to remind him—and herself— that she was his employee?

"Let's leave the office at the office." RJ still held her tight in his embrace, and his mouth had moved barely an inch from her skin. "Do you think any of those trees care about memos and meetings and deadlines? It's a whole different world up here. Breathe in some fresh mountain air."

"I think I am." Surely if she wasn't she'd have passed out by now. Which was a distinct possibility the way RJ was tantalizing her earlobe with his tongue and teeth.

"Mountain air is restorative. Draw it all the way to the bottom of your lungs."

She drew a breath deep down into her belly the way she'd learned in yoga class. Evening cool, scented with pine and fresh soil, the rich air filled her lungs, and she exhaled with gusto. "That does feel good."

"Standing up here restores perspective. Out here it seems like time doesn't exist—the sun rises and sets and everything stays the same except the slow change of the seasons."

"RJ, you're turning out to have more dimensions than I expected."

"And you've known me five years already. Just shows how important it is to step out of context. Now kiss me."

Before she could protest he spun her around and pressed his lips firmly to hers. Her eyes slid shut and her hands rose to his shoulders. The kiss was delicious, golden and heady as the sunset warming their skin. The slight stubble on RJ's chin tickled her and she felt his eyelashes flutter against her cheeks as he deepened the kiss.

She hugged him, enjoying the closeness she'd craved, letting go of her worries and losing herself in the powerful sensation of his strong arms around her waist, holding her tight.

When they finally pulled apart, by only a feather's depth, his eyes sparkled and she knew hers did, too.

Happiness swelled in her chest and the moment felt so perfect.

"You're a very beautiful woman, Brooke. The sunset suits you."

"Maybe I should wear it every day."

"Most definitely. And I have a feeling that sunrise will become you, as well."

"I guess we'll have to get up early and find out." A tiny blade of anxiety poked her stomach. By morning they would have slept together.

Or would they?

After they disentangled themselves from each other's arms, RJ took her to a bedroom with panoramic views and invited her to unpack. Then he disappeared. Maybe they weren't going to sleep together at all. The closet was empty, except for a few hangers and a plain white terry bathrobe. The room had an adjoining bath, with freshly unwrapped soap and tiny bottles of expensive Kiehl's shampoo and conditioner. The rustic yet elegant bentwood bed was covered with a thick, soft duvet and the whole room was decorated in neutral colors that complemented the jaw-dropping view out the window. It was like being in a very high-end hotel.

Brooke hung her few items in the cavernous closet, then changed out of her work suit into her favorite jeans and a green shirt that highlighted her eyes. The carpets were soft pure wool, so she left her feet bare to better enjoy them and show off her rather daring jade-green toenails.

She peered out into the hallway. She followed the sound of whistling and found RJ in a similarly spacious bedroom, with a large bed made of rustic planks, checking his phone. "Settled in?"

"Perfectly." There was his bag, half-unpacked, on top of a pine chest of drawers. So they were sleeping in separate bedrooms. She should be relieved, but instead she felt disappointed. Maybe she was hoping for a whirlwind romance and he just planned to cast some flies and kick back in the sunshine.

"I've never seen you in jeans before." His eyes roamed down her legs, heating her skin through the denim. "Clearly, I've been missing out."

"I've never seen you in jeans before, either." She smiled, glancing at the pair peeking out of his duffel bag.

"Mine don't hug me quite the way yours do." A dimple played in his cheek.

"Shame." A sudden vision of RJ's body flashed in her mind. Even in his suit—the jacket hung over a corner of the wardrobe door and his sleeves were rolled up—you could see he was built and muscular. He played a lot of tennis and squash and sailed competitively. No doubt his muscles were bronzed by all that time in the sun. Hopefully soon she'd get to compare her imagination to reality.

If that was really a good idea.

"Are you hungry?" RJ's expression suggested he wanted for something entirely different than food.

"I am. All that shaking with terror on the flight built up an appetite."

"Good, because I'm making dinner."

Her eyes widened. RJ Kincaid in front of a stove?

"Don't look so shocked. You should know by now that I'm a man of many talents."

"I'm impressed."

"One of my talents is delegating to skilled professionals." He strode out of the room, leaving his phone on the bed. "Frankie Deleon owns the best restaurant in town and this afternoon I had the fridge stocked with provisions." She followed him into a bright kitchen with gleaming professional quality appliances. He pulled open one door on the fridge. The inside revealed a collection of smart earthenware dishes, each labeled with a Post-it note. "Let's see, jambalaya, baby back ribs, black-eyed peas and greens—hey, those need actual cooking. Poached salmon, sesame noodles." He moved a dish aside to reach behind it. "Macaroni and cheese, rice salad, green salad, beet and goat cheese salad... Where do you want to start?"

Brooke's mouth was already watering. She could get used to this Kincaid lifestyle. "It all sounds sensational. What are you in the mood for?"

His blue gaze settled on her face and she read her answer loud and clear. A smile crept across her mouth as her nipples tightened under her green shirt.

"You decide."

A challenge. She knew RJ liked people who could think on their feet and make executive decisions. "Ribs with sesame noodles and green salad."

"I like." RJ pulled the containers from the shelves and placed them on a butcher-block island large enough to have its own sink. Brooke turned on one of the stainless steel ovens, and RJ pulled some fine china dishes from one of the cabinets. They picked a chilled white wine to sip while waiting for the ribs to bake.

"Did you check the drawers yet?"

RJ looked up from the bottle opener. "What drawers?"

"The one mentioned in your dad's letter." Maybe

that was too personal. He probably wanted to search for the item alone.

He looked back down at the bottle. "I'm not sure I'm ready yet. I still hardly believe he's gone."

"I can't imagine what a shock it must have been."

"I keep expecting him to walk around the corner and say it was all an elaborate hoax." He gestured toward a wing-backed red chair in the great room adjoining the kitchen. "That was his favorite chair. I feel like he's going to get up out of it and rib me for not catching any fish yet this year."

The cork popped out with force, almost making Brooke jump. "I know he's proud of you for how you're handling things."

RJ nodded. "He's got to be watching from somewhere."

She fought an urge to glance over her shoulder. She wasn't sure she wanted RJ's dad watching the things she hoped to get up to with him tonight. Then again, maybe she should think more about how this would look to all the other people around them. What would RJ's siblings think of her spending the weekend with him? She worked closely with his brother Matthew in the office—would she be able to look him in the eye on Monday? And what about his mom? Would she see sleeping with his assistant as somehow beneath a Kincaid?

Of course Elizabeth Kincaid had much bigger problems to worry about right now. Partly due to information that she, Brooke Nichols, had provided to the police. She really needed to get that off her chest. Maybe now was a good time. She could casually say she'd seen his mom in the building and then... No.

Better to say the police had interviewed her and she just happened to mention—

"I'm glad you're here with me." RJ's soft voice jolted her from her fevered ruminations. He handed her a cool glass of clear white wine and she took a hasty sip. The moment for telling him had passed. Now he was getting romantic and she'd ruin it all if she said anything. "I've been wanting to come up here for a while, but didn't know how I'd feel."

"How do you feel?" She squeezed her guilt back down. He wanted a relaxing weekend, not more to worry about. It was probably better if she didn't mention it until they were back in the everyday world of Charleston.

"Okay. It's as beautiful as ever, peaceful and a perfect escape from reality."

"Can you ever really escape from reality?" Somehow it kept sneaking back into her consciousness.

"Sure." He smiled. "You file it away in a drawer."

"The third drawer down, perhaps?"

"Maybe that one, maybe another. Maybe more than one." He raised a brow. "Then you lock it and lose the key until some later date."

"That does not sound like the RJ I know."

He laughed. "It doesn't, does it? Maybe I'm trying to change."

"I don't think you should change." She said it in earnest, then wondered if she'd revealed too much about herself. "You're up-front and honest. You tackle things head-on and don't beat around the bush or try to people-please."

"And you've been the victim, more often than not."

"I'd much rather have you tell me what you think than have to guess it."

"I suppose that's one thing I got from my dad." His expression darkened. "Or I thought I did. He was blunt and truthful, and I never doubted a word he said." He swirled his glass of wine and peered into its depths. "Now I can see I should have been wary of all the things he left unsaid. Maybe you can never really know anyone."

"I don't suppose you can, but most people don't have secret families, so I don't think you could have seen it coming." It was hard to know what to say without overstepping the mark.

"No? My mom knew about them, and she kept quiet, too."

"She was probably trying to protect you from pain."

"Instead, she accidentally set herself up as a possible murderer." He shook his head and took a swig from his wine. "There's no justice in this world."

Brooke's stomach clenched. She hated to see RJ sounding so bitter. He was usually the most upbeat and positive person she knew. "There will be justice, but it might take some time."

"I wish I believed you. How can there be justice in a world where the Kincaid Group, the company I've devoted my working life to, is now forty-five percent owned by a half brother—" he said the word with a growl "—that I never knew existed." He looked up at her, eyes cold. "And who despises my entire family and the company he's just been handed."

Brooke put her wineglass down on the island. "It's all very strange and hard to understand right now." How could his father have been so cruel as to take away the company RJ saw as his birthright and hand it to an unknown rival?

"You know what?" RJ's voice was low with anger. "I do want to see what's in that third drawer. I want to see exactly what Dad wrote that would help me to understand why he stopped seeing me as his eldest son and heir." He slammed open the third drawer down on one side of the kitchen island. "Napkins and napkin rings. Can you see the significance?"

Brooke swallowed. She wanted to laugh, just to ease the tension, but it wasn't funny. "Did he have a desk?"

"Yes, there's a study." He strode from the room. Brooke glanced at the oven and saw the ribs still needed a few minutes. Always the trusty assistant, she followed him.

RJ marched into a bright study with cathedral ceilings and a leather-topped desk. "Ha. Two rows of three drawers." He pulled open one bottom drawer and rifled through the interior. "Bullet casings, ballpoint pens, paper clips, a broken golf tee." He slammed it and pulled open the other. "Reginald Kincaid letterhead and matching envelopes." He lifted the papers. "What's this?" He pulled out a manila envelope. "It has his name on the front. Or my name—since according to my birth certificate I'm Reginald Kincaid, as well." The envelope was sealed. Thick too, like it had a wad of papers, or even an object. "It's heavy."

"Are you going to open it?"

RJ hesitated, weighing it in his hand. The oven timer beeped in the kitchen.

Four

"I'll go check the ribs." Brooke seemed relieved at the excuse to leave him alone. Once she'd gone, RJ glanced down at the envelope in his hands. The writing was his father's familiar script, neat and commanding. He slid a finger under the sealed flap and ripped the paper carefully, aware he was frowning.

Then he lowered the open envelope to the desktop and eased the contents out onto the desk. Papers, mostly, a pair of cuff links, a ring he'd never seen his dad wear and some old photographs.

"They're done. I'll just toss the salad," called Brooke from the kitchen.

"Great." What was this envelope of things supposed to mean? He picked up the ring and looked at the design. Gold with a flat top, it was shaped almost like a class ring. As he stared at the shield he realized it was probably from his dad's time in special forces.

He recognized the bird holding a lightning bolt. The ring was worn, the gold scratched by use, but he didn't remember ever seeing it on his dad's finger. A relic from another lifetime, the lifetime in which Angela had been the woman he loved—and unbeknownst to him, the mother of his firstborn son.

"It's ready." Brooke's voice tugged him back to the present.

There was a lovely woman waiting for him in the other room, and painful memories could wait. He pushed the items back into the envelope and slid them into the same drawer. "Coming."

Brooke looked so beautiful standing silhouetted against the last rays of light. Her lush body beckoned to him, promising an evening filled with pleasure. Much better to tuck all that other stuff away in a drawer for now.

"Looks delicious." He stared directly at her as he said it.

A pretty smile played around her pink mouth. "It sure does. Where do you want to eat?"

"There's a table on the deck." He served the ribs onto two plates, and Brooke spooned out the salad and noodles. He grabbed cutlery from a drawer, picked up the wine and glasses with one hand, and Brooke brought the plates. The last rays of sun lit the polished wood table and chairs in a fiery reddish gold. He lit the decorative hurricane lamps with the BBQ lighter, and topped up their wine.

"Okay, this really is paradise." Brooke couldn't stop staring at the view. "This must be the only house for miles around."

"There are cabins and people out there, they're just hidden by the trees."

"The trees are kind to cloak everyone in peace and privacy." Her sweet smile made his chest fill with emotion.

"They're in charge around here. Dad always said that coming up to the mountains put everything into perspective. Problems shrink away and so does the human ego."

Brooke laughed. "I can't picture your father saying that."

"He could be quite introspective when the mood caught him." He could tell Brooke was rather intrigued by the new side of him she'd seen lately. Usually he didn't think too much about the impression he made on people, but right now it pleased him to show Brooke he wasn't just a hard-partying playboy. "It's easy to see why, now we know his life was a lot more complicated than any of us imagined." He took a bite of his food.

Being out here in the mountains brought a sense of equanimity that dulled the pain of recent events. He could think and talk about his dad calmly. Brooke's peaceful presence helped. He couldn't imagine her getting upset about anything. She was always the voice of reason in the office, ready to pour oil on troubled waters. "Did I ever thank you for taking me by the scruff of the neck and getting me out of trouble the other day?"

"When I marched you to your office and plied you with liquor?" Her pretty green eyes sparkled.

"Yes, that. A wise executive move."

"More an act of desperation. Still, I'd like to be an executive one day."

"You'd be good. You have an instinct for how to deal with people—getting them to deliver weekly updates so we know where everyone stands, for example."

"I got the idea from a management video I watched."

"I had no idea such bold ambition burned in your chest." RJ took a swig of wine. Brooke probably was wasted as his assistant, much as it pained him to admit it. HR had recently informed him that she'd submitted her application for a management role in the Events department and he'd told them he couldn't spare her right now. He needed an assistant he could trust with all that was going on in the wake of his father's death. Still, holding her back for his own reasons was selfish. He'd have to look around the company for the right role for her.

Brooke's sparkle had dimmed slightly. "I hope I didn't overstep the mark. I do really enjoy working with you."

"Of course you're looking to the future. I'm glad to hear you have big plans. You have a lot to offer the business world." He was relieved to see her lips curve into a smile again. "We'll have to talk about your future when things settle down."

She nodded. He felt a twinge of guilt that he didn't want to talk about her future right now, but frankly that was too big, complicated and potentially disturbing a subject for what was supposed to be a relaxing weekend in the mountains.

They chatted more innocuously about Charleston and their favorite music while the sun set and plunged them into the familiar velvety darkness. They swept the plates and glasses back inside. "Should we wash the dishes?" Brooke glanced at them where they lay on the counter. RJ had already disappeared into the next room.

"Don't worry about them. Come relax."

Brooke shrugged and followed him into the living room. It was hard to remember she was his guest, not his assistant right now. She hated leaving loose ends but maybe that was part of becoming the kind of person who managed others, rather than one who did everything themselves. RJ had changed the conversation rather deftly after her mention that she'd like to go into management, but maybe he just didn't want to be reminded of the office when he was trying to relax.

RJ leaned over a sleek device, and suddenly the room filled with music. Ella Fitzgerald, mellow and sultry. He looked up and smiled. "I thought we should dance."

Excitement stirred in her chest, along with a flutter of nerves. "Sure."

Dancing would get them close. Closeness would get them… RJ wound his arms around her waist. She could feel the heat of his body through his thin shirt. His back muscles moved under her hands as they swayed to the music. He pulled her against him and soon the rise and fall of her breath matched his. Or was it the other way around?

The song ended and another started, while they moved slowly around the big room. Dancing this way with RJ felt oddly natural, unhurried and relaxing. Arousal crept through her like wine, making her giddy but happy. They didn't even kiss until the third song started. RJ's lips brushed hers. Their mouths melded together slowly, tongues meeting and mingling.

Her chest pressed against his, her nipples tightening

against his hard muscle. Their hips swayed in rhythm and his hands roamed over her back. By the fifth song the kiss deepened to the point where their feet stopped moving. She felt RJ's fingers tugging at the hem of her shirt, then sliding over her skin. She shivered with pleasure and let her fingers roam into his waistband.

Soon they were plucking at each other's shirt buttons and pressing bare skin to bare skin. The music wrapped around them as RJ guided her onto the sofa and together they eased off her jeans. Her body throbbed with desire that gave urgency to her movements. The zipper of his pants got stuck as she tried to undo it and she found herself struggling with desperation that would be funny if she wasn't so…desperate!

RJ took over and together they shed his pants then wrapped themselves into each other on the wide surface of the sofa. RJ's big body fit perfectly around hers. His muscled arms held her close and his strong legs and hard abs made her pulse quicken.

Was she really lying semi-naked on a sofa with RJ Kincaid? Perhaps this was one of her more elaborate fantasies getting out of hand?

But his hot breath on her neck felt so real. So did the broad fingers slipping inside her delicate panties, and the lips closing over her nipples through the lace of her bra. Brooke gasped when he sucked on her nipple and sensation shot through her. She pushed her fingers into his thick hair and gave herself over to the sensation, arching her back and pressing her pelvis against him.

They both still wore their underwear, but she could feel RJ's intense arousal through his cotton boxers, and soon found her hands pushing down the elastic waistband and reaching for his erection. She shivered when she discovered how hard he was, how ready.

"Let's go into the bedroom." RJ's voice was thick with need. Without waiting for her response he picked her up in his strong arms and carried her across the room. Supported by his strong body, Brooke felt weightless and desirable. RJ swept her into his bedroom, and laid her gently on the soft duvet.

"You're so beautiful." His gaze roamed over her body, making her skin tingle with excitement. He caressed her skin, starting at her shoulder and trailing his fingertips over her lacy bra and along her waist. When he reached her skimpy panties he hooked a finger into each side and slid them slowly over her legs, devouring her with his gaze as he pulled them down to her toes.

Excitement built in her chest as she waited for him to finish. Then he rose back over her and she leaned forward while he unhooked her bra and released her breasts. He kissed each freshly bared nipple and cooled it with a flash of his tongue. Breath coming faster, she pushed his boxers down over his thighs.

At last they were both naked. RJ climbed over her, kissing her face and murmuring how pretty her eyes were, and how soft her hair. The simple compliments made her feel like a goddess. She let her fingers roam over the thick, roping muscles of his arms and back and wished she could find words to admire them, but words deserted her as sensation overtook her body.

He entered her very gently, kissing her as he sank deep. Brooke arched against him, relishing the feel of him inside her, his powerful arms wrapped around her. The weight of his body settled over her, pushing her into the mattress as she clung to him.

"Oh, RJ." The words slipped from her mouth as she brushed his rough cheek with her lips. She'd waited years for this moment. She could feel him inside her, hard, yet so gentle as he moved with her.

A shiver of pleasure crept over her as he slid deeper, and she felt herself opening up to him. She snuck a peek at his face, and their eyes met in a single, electric moment. The expression on his face was almost pained, so intense, his blue eyes stormy with emotion.

Brooke felt her heart swell with feeling for this man. So strong and capable, he led the company with such energy and pride, and at this moment his entire being focused on her. His arms wrapped around her, enveloping her in their protective warmth, while he moved with precision and passion.

"You're an amazing woman, Brooke." His whispered words stirred something deep inside her. He shifted slightly, sending arrows of pleasure darting through her. Was she amazing? She certainly felt special right now.

Or were they both just caught up in the moment? Or in the madness that had brought her into his arms that night in his office.

A ripple of fear made her hold him tighter. "I'm not amazing." She couldn't bear for him to be making love to some imaginary woman who had nothing to do with the real Brooke Nichols. "I'm just…me."

RJ paused for a moment and their eyes met. Again that fierce gaze almost stole her breath. "You're amazing because you are just exactly you. The most beautiful, capable, sweet, organized, sexy and irresistible woman I've ever met."

A giggle rose in her chest. "That's quite a mix of adjectives."

"You're a unique person." He brushed soft kisses over her cheek and the bridge of her nose, making her smile. "And it's my very great pleasure to be sharing this bed with you." His penis stirred inside her, sparking a ripple of laughter along with a rush of erotic pleasure.

Her eyes slid closed as she kissed him on the mouth, drinking in the rich taste of him. She'd imagined moments like this, but not that she'd feel so totally swept away on a tide of intense pleasure.

RJ's strong arms eased them into a new position where she was sitting in his lap. As they moved together, the powerful penetration took her deeper into the mysterious otherworld they shared. RJ's hands on her skin, his thighs wrapped around her, his hair brushing her forehead...

Feelings raced through her. She wanted to shout, or cry. *I love him.* The thought flashed in her brain and she held him tighter. *Is it just my body talking?* Her brain grappled with powerful emotion while her body clung to his, moving with him in a thick sea of pleasure.

I love you, RJ.

She let her mind release the thought, though she didn't allow her lips to voice it. It was enough for her to know. She didn't want to throw pressure at him and ruin this beautiful moment. She'd never felt closer to anyone, and maybe she never would again.

For now, it was precious.

Her climax crept over her gradually, starting with

little waves that lapped at her fingers and toes, and ending in a big breaker that crashed over her.

RJ joined her, exploding with a gruff cry, crushing her against his chest and pressing his face to hers as they collapsed back on the bed. Overwhelmed by sensation and emotion, she lay limp in his arms.

"I don't remember the last time I felt this good." RJ cradled her, stroking her softly. "You're a miracle."

Brooke's chest, already bursting with happiness, almost exploded. Being here with RJ felt so absolutely right. It seemed odd that they hadn't come together earlier, when they were so perfect for each other. He stroked her cheek and she sighed. She'd made RJ feel good, too. Maybe that was the best part of all.

Lying here in his embrace she could imagine them living happily as a couple. They'd worked together successfully for five years, which was quite an accomplishment already. They'd always got on and never argued, and he obviously respected her opinion. "I'm glad I dragged you out of that meeting and plied you with liquor."

"Me, too. Not many people would have dared." He kissed her cheek softly and nuzzled against her. Again her chest swelled with joy. "You're a brave woman, Brooke Nichols."

She was, wasn't she? Not many women would chance a weekend away with their boss. For a moment the familiar doubts started to creep back in. How would they behave at the office? Would he be affectionate or would they go back to professional cordiality? What would she do if he kissed her in front of the other employees?

She blushed just thinking about it. She'd love it, of

course. She'd be so proud and happy to be RJ Kincaid's girlfriend. A dream come true. And here she was, living it.

They kissed, then dressed and went to enjoy more music and dancing, then undressed and made love again. This time they fell asleep together, with seductive music still throbbing away in the living room. Brooke slept deeply, totally relaxed and at ease in RJ's arms.

In the morning she awoke with an odd mix of anticipation and anxiety. They had two whole days to spend together with no interruptions.

Then again, what if they had nothing to talk about? What if he grew bored with her?

"Morning, gorgeous." RJ pressed a kiss to the back of her neck.

"Hi." A wave of pleasure lapped over her at the touch of his lips and her doubts scattered. "Did you sleep okay?"

"Never slept better in my life. You're the best medicine in the world."

She smiled. "I'm glad. Last night was fun."

He kissed her cheek. "More than fun. You're full of surprises, Brooke."

"I am?"

"I had no idea you had such a sensual side."

"I try to keep it under wraps when I'm at the office." She winked. "Might not be appropriate."

"There's a whole different Brooke that I never knew about."

"Actually I think the Brooke you know is about ninety percent of the real Brooke." She didn't want him to start thinking she was really a temptress superspy or something, and then be disappointed. "There are just a few facets of me best not viewed under fluorescent lighting."

RJ glanced down at her body and lifted the covers to reveal a peaked pink nipple. "I think you'd look amazing under any lighting."

The way he stared at her made her feel beautiful. She worked hard to keep her body in reasonably good shape, but she'd never felt ultra gorgeous—until RJ's appreciative blue gaze touched her skin.

She trailed a finger over his muscled chest. "I'm not sure what I expected under all that crisp suiting, but let's just say I can tell you work out."

"I play a lot of tennis and squash. They're a full-body workout."

"I used to play tennis in high school." She said it shyly. She'd been their team's star player, but never pursued it in college since she didn't want to take too much time away from her studies and she needed to work almost full-time.

"No kidding? We'll have to hit some balls together. We can go to the club when we get back."

The club? The ultra-exclusive country club that cost over fifty thousand dollars a year just for the privilege of membership? She swallowed. "I haven't played in years. I probably wouldn't even be able to hit the ball over the net."

"We'll have to find out, won't we? Tennis is like riding a bicycle, at least I think so. After ten minutes or so you'll feel like you never put down your racquet."

"Maybe, if you promise to take it easy on me." She slid her finger down over his hard belly, which contracted under her touch.

"I don't know. That's not really the Kincaid way."

"You're more into crushing your opponents then dancing over their shattered remains?" That was their business reputation to a certain extent. RJ looked surprised. Had she stepped over an unspoken boundary by talking about the family? "I don't mean that literally, of course. Just that I—"

RJ laughed. "Don't back down now. That's exactly what I meant. We're not able to lose gracefully. It's not in our DNA. If we were, maybe we'd be able to fit in better with crusty old Charleston society, where you need to suck up to someone whose great-great-granny came over on the *Mayflower* just so you'll get invited to their garden parties. We're constitutionally unable to do that."

"But the Kincaids are part of Charleston society."

He laughed again. "As if there was only one Charleston society. Believe me, there are plenty of people in this town who look down on the Kincaids as nouveau riche upstarts who won't be around for long." He looked thoughtful. "It's never bothered me before, but with everything that's going on lately I'm more determined than ever to prove them wrong."

"The Kincaid Group will weather this storm. So far it doesn't seem so much worse than the time we lost the Martin account."

"The Martins went out of business. This time people are leaving just because they can, and they're going to the competition."

"So, you'll have to show them what they're missing. And now's a good time to build up the company's real-estate portfolio."

"It is. We've been moving assets in that direction.

When the real estate market comes back we'll be sitting on a gold mine, especially along the Charleston waterfront. Hey, why are we lying here naked talking business?"

"Because we're that kind of people." She smiled at him.

He lifted a dark brow. "We're a lot alike."

Brooke shrugged. She wasn't sure how alike they really were. Not being accepted into the highest echelons of Charleston society had never been one of her most pressing problems. And a relationship with her would hardly boost his social standing, which apparently was a big concern for him.

"We are alike." He obviously sensed her doubts. "We're both teetering on the brink of being workaholics, we like good restaurants, we play a mean game of tennis and we're both lying in this bed."

Brooke chuckled. "When you put it like that... But you're making a lot of assumptions about my game of tennis."

"I know you well enough to know you wouldn't have mentioned it unless you were practically on the tour."

"I'll have to be careful what I tell you. You have dangerously high expectations."

"Only because you never disappoint." He said it plainly, no hint of teasing.

"Never? Surely I've made a few typos along the way."

"I sincerely doubt it, but I'm talking about you as a person, not an office appliance. Don't think I haven't noticed how brilliant you are."

Brooke beamed inside. "I enjoy a challenge."

"And I enjoy you." He nibbled her earlobe gently,

sending a rush of sensation through her. Suddenly they were kissing again, then twisted up in the duvet making mad, early morning love.

Love? No. Not that. Having crazy, wild, before-breakfast sex. She'd never had so much sex in a twenty-four-hour period, and they were barely twelve hours in. Energetic and passionate, RJ soon brought her to new heights of arousal and excitement. They climaxed together, with a lot of noise, followed by laughter as they tried to disentangle themselves from the duvet.

"I'd suggest we shower together," said RJ, once they stopped panting long enough to form a sentence. "But I'm worried we may never make it to breakfast."

"What are we doing for breakfast? I don't recall too much breakfast food in the fridge."

"That's because there's an excellent diner up the road, and I always go there. You'll love it. It's a real slice of life in the mountains. I'll shower first, then leave you with some privacy."

Brooke couldn't resist sneaking a few long, lascivious peeks as RJ rose from the bed and strode naked across the room. His body was magnificent. Broad shoulders tapered to a slim waist, and his backside… ooh la la. She would probably never be able to keep a straight face in the office again.

She fanned herself as she heard the rush of water in the shower. She'd expected RJ to be a romantic charmer, but not that he'd drive her so completely over the edge. Maybe all the years of fantasizing about him in secret made their actual coming together so intense.

She loved that he was so affectionate. He seemed to really enjoy holding and hugging her, as well as kissing and licking and all that other good stuff. And, boy, was he deft at sliding a condom on at just the right moment. He didn't even need to interrupt the flow of events. He must have had the packet ripped open before they even started.

She frowned. This should remind her that he was no innocent boy next door on his first date. RJ Kincaid had bedded a lot of women, and she wasn't likely to be the last.

Her chest tightened, then she realized how foolish it was to be thinking about the future when they still had the whole weekend ahead of them. She had no idea what the future would bring. Who could have predicted that Reginald Kincaid, one of the most vibrant men she'd ever met, would be shot dead by a mystery assailant, let alone that his wife would be accused of his murder?

Brooke let out a long sigh. If only she could figure out who else might be responsible. She was in the office on the night of the murder and left less than half an hour before it happened. The police had even interviewed her as if she was a suspect at first. Whoever killed him might have been in the building the entire time. But who?

"Why the serious face?" RJ appeared in the doorway, toweling off his spectacular bronzed body.

Already she felt a smile creep across her lips. Who could stay serious when confronted with such a vision? "What serious face?"

"Much better."

They ate an enormous breakfast in the 1950s-style diner, served by the owner who had probably been doling out grits since the 1950s. He made a big fuss of both RJ and Brooke, treating them like visiting royalty. His great-granddaughter, aged about seven, brought them flowers she'd picked in the garden and handed the bouquet to Brooke. "You're very pretty."

Brooke smiled. "You're very pretty, too. And I'm impressed with the standard of service here. You don't get flowers and compliments every day with break-fast." When the little girl had skipped back outside she whispered, "I wonder if they pay her to flatter the guests."

"It's a good strategy. Maybe The Kincaid Group should try it out on our customers." Humor twinkled in his eyes. "On the other hand, most of our clients aren't nearly as easy on the eyes so it might come across as phony."

"Oh, please." She wanted to protest that she wasn't pretty, but she didn't want to appear to be fishing for more compliments. She'd certainly never felt prettier in her life. "I hope you don't have anything too strenuous planned for this morning. I'm not sure I'll be able to move after that fantastic meal." Perfectly crisp bacon, golden scrambled eggs, freshly baked rolls and spicy fried potato. And the ubiquitous bowl of grits.

"We'll save the hike to the summit for this afternoon then. How about we stroll to the lake and pretend we're fishing?"

"Sounds good."

She had no idea how good. While they'd been re-laxing in the diner, a member of staff had packed the trunk of the Suburban with an icebox of chilled beer and a packed lunch.

"I feel like elves are following close behind us wait-ing on us hand and foot."

"Just takes a little organizing."

Again, Brooke wondered if he did this sort of thing often. Bringing girls up to the cabin and scheming with all the locals to pamper and spoil them. Maybe right now the people in the diner were shaking their heads and clucking their tongues and discussing how long "this one" would last.

How long would it last?

RJ opened her car door, always the perfect gentleman. Right now she didn't feel like his admin at all. It was almost impossible to imagine showing up at the office on Monday and going through his in-box. On the other hand she could imagine any number of intriguing things that could happen between now and Monday.

RJ seemed like a different person than when they left. For the first time since his father's death he appeared truly relaxed, his face crinkling into smile lines rather than the frown he'd worn so much lately. His broad shoulders looked at ease, not tight with tension.

She felt different, too. Their night of passion had awakened something inside her. She was no virgin but she'd certainly never experienced pleasure like that before. This morning she'd grown into a more deeply sensual person than she was yesterday. Colors were brighter and smells sweeter and even the air tasted bright and crisp as champagne.

By Monday they'd both be different people, one way or another. Her fantasy of a relationship with RJ was coming true and happiness seemed right within her grasp.

Though if it didn't work out, if this weekend was all they had, she'd have the agony of knowing just what she was missing—for the rest of her life.

Five

A lazy morning of casting flies from a grassy river-bank, followed by their luxurious picnic, led to a re-laxed walk in the woods. RJ was easy to talk to. Which was hardly a surprise given that she'd known him for years. It was odd, and wonderful, how quickly and to-tally their relationship had altered from being purely professional to…utterly unprofessional.

They carried a thick foam camping pad out onto the broad balcony of the cottage, and now lay on it, naked, covered only by a thin sheet swiped from the linen closet. Warm spring air caressed their skin, still damp from the exertions of a heated afternoon love-making session. RJ traced patterns on her belly with a lazy finger, stirring little rivers of sensation that made her want to giggle.

His hair, tousled at some point by her fingers, hung

down to his eyes, which shone, dark with arousal. "Maybe we shouldn't ever go back."

Brooke's stomach contracted slightly under his fingers. "Tempting as that sounds…"

"Come on. Would they really miss us?" Humor deepened his dimples. "That unpleasant Jack Sinclair can take over running the company and you and I can just live in the woods on trout."

"We didn't catch any trout." The idea held marvelous appeal. No more early morning commutes. No more taking minutes in meetings. But at heart she was a practical girl. "We didn't even see any trout."

RJ's grin was infectious. "Berries, then."

"Okay, berries. Supplemented with orders from your favorite restaurant." She played with the lock of dark hair on his forehead.

RJ planted a kiss on her stomach. "I've never contemplated any other life than the one I was born to. Lately, though, with all this madness surrounding the family and the company, I can't help thinking that there are other possibilities out there." His expression darkened somewhat. "And that in making his will my dad was giving me permission to explore them."

Was he serious? She couldn't imagine The Kincaid Group without RJ, or RJ without the company that seemed to be his lifeblood.

But she wanted to be supportive. "What would you like to do, if you could do anything?"

RJ traced the line of her thigh with his broad thumb. "I think I'm doing it." His mischievous expression teased her. "And maybe I could branch out into this." He lowered his head and licked her nipple, tightening it to a hard peak. "And this." He raised his mouth to hers and kissed her with exquisite tenderness.

Brooke's heart swelled inside a chest already very full with the wonder and excitement of their new relationship. RJ spoke as if he'd just discovered the love of his life—her.

Don't get carried away! Up here in the clouds it was easy to forget all about the real world, but sooner or later they'd have to go back to it.

After another delicious dinner from the bounty in the fridge they watched a classic Hitchcock movie together. RJ held her tight during the scary bits and Brooke loved enjoying such a normal, everyday couple activity with the man who'd once seemed wholly unobtainable. After the movie they shared a dish of caramel ice cream, then kissed with cold tongues and warm hearts.

Sunday was a lazy day. They didn't even rise from bed until nearly noon, and only then because RJ decided it was time to confront the manila envelope of memories his father had left him.

RJ brought a new sense of calm back into the study with him. He'd closed the door on Friday night determined to enjoy his weekend with Brooke. By Sunday, however, a sliver of guilt was intruding on their shared paradise. Sunday dinner was a Kincaid tradition. They all gathered in the big family home and shared a traditional roast or some other delicacy their mom had conjured up. Now she was in jail, the family tradition was temporarily suspended. How could they face each other across the table with neither the matriarch nor the patriarch of the family present?

Their dad would never sit there again. They'd stubbornly kept the tradition going at their mom's insistence in the weeks and months since his death. It was no doubt his responsibility as the eldest to gather the clan in their mom's absence, but he didn't have the heart.

He'd spent two enjoyable days here on the outskirts of his life, with the lovely Brooke for company. But he had decisions to make and avoiding them didn't sit well with him.

Brooke had cooked pancakes from a packet mix while he made coffee, and after they'd eaten she tactfully excused herself, saying she needed time to make a couple of phone calls. She went out on the terrace, where the reception was strongest, and he headed back into his father's inner sanctum with a heavy heart.

The envelope lay there in the drawer where he'd left it. He wondered if his dad had prepared it all at once in a typical flourish of brusque efficiency, or if its contents were the product of hours of thought, packing and unpacking.

Probably the former. With a swift inhale he pulled the packet from the drawer and emptied its contents on the desk in a rude clatter and rustle. Amongst the yellowed papers was a crisp, new sheet, folded in two. RJ snatched it off the desk and pulled it open. His scalp pricked with discomfort as he saw the handwritten lines. Another letter. The letter he'd opened and read so hastily after the funeral had cut a dark scar in his heart and he suspected this would only reopen and deepen the wound.

While you bear my name, you are in truth not my firstborn son.

He'd seen Angela and her sons at his father's funeral, but refused to believe the gossip about who they were. When he opened the letter, that one brief line had knocked away the foundation of his life. So swift and brutal was the blow that he'd been hard-pressed to act like himself for the rest of the day. He no longer was himself. Since birth he'd been Reginald Kincaid, Jr., chip off the old block. All he'd wanted was to be just like his dad, a proud family man, successful in business and in everything else he turned his hand to, from fighting foreign wars to scoring birdies on the club golf course.

In that letter his father had revealed he was not the man they'd all assumed him to be. Fathering a child before his marriage was one thing—and as he'd posthumously explained, he didn't know about his son Jack until years after his birth—but resuming his relationship with his son's mother and maintaining them as a second family went beyond the common accusation of adultery and into the realm of almost criminal deception.

Steeling himself, he focused on the handwritten script that covered most of two pages.

Dear Reginald,
We all make choices in life and, as you are by now well aware, I made choices that many would disapprove of. You may well be angry with me, and knowing your proud and honest spirit, I bet you are. You've had some time to think about how all this affects you, and above all I want to make you aware that you have choices, too.

RJ growled. Did his father think he was some beardless sixteen-year-old looking for a pep talk? He'd been a man himself now for a decade and a half.

My parents took away my choices when they forbid me to marry Angela, the woman I loved.

RJ suppressed a curse. How he wished he'd never heard the name of Angela Sinclair, or her accursed son.

Being an obedient son, I didn't marry her. Instead I ran away from them all, from all of their plans and hopes and dreams for me. As you know, my time in the service was a defining period in my life that shaped me like a blade in the furnace, and I look back on it with pride as well as regret. I'm enclosing the ring I wore for many years as a symbol of my commitment to my unit. It was a wedding ring of sorts, when I wore it, as I had thrown away all other allegiances. I sought to escape my former life and forge a new one all my own. I also enclose the pilot's license I earned all those years ago and that you used to tease me about. As you can see, it really does exist, along with the other, less savory, realities of my life.

Escape is an illusion. No matter how far you run, or how fast, the truths of your life—of who you are and what you've done—dog your heels over all terrain, and sooner or later you have to turn and face them. When I returned home I had to face the parents who'd waited and worried every day I was gone. This time, obeying their wishes that I take a suitable bride and start a family seemed a far more livable kind of escape, and I soon met and married your wonderful mother. My happiness was complete and

I barely thought of the lives I'd left behind, until I learned by chance that the woman I once loved had borne my child and raised him in my absence.

By this time I had children of my own with your mother and knew the force, and felt the commitment, of the paternal bond. I hope you'll one day understand that there was no way I could turn my back on my own flesh and blood. When I met Angela again, I felt the full power of our grand passion that I'd tried so hard to leave behind in my attempts to be a good son.

Don't be a good son, RJ.

RJ blinked and thrust the letter down, growling with a mix of fury and disbelief. All his life he'd been proud to fulfill his parents' goals and dreams, to now be told it was all some kind of colossal mistake? He snatched the pages up again, anxious to get to the end.

All your life you've been told where to go and what to do. Your mother and I carefully chose the best schools and groomed you for your future role in The Kincaid Group. We never asked you what you wanted. RJ, my son, I want you to take this opportunity to look inside yourself and decide what you truly want from your life.

RJ threw the letter down with another curse. How arrogant of his father to assume that he'd blindly followed along with their plans for him. He'd been successful in school and in business and everything in between because of his own hard work and dedication and because he'd wanted to. He knew plenty of men with all his advantages who'd thrown them away and run off to pursue alternate dreams. His old pal Jake ran a beach bar in Jamaica, for Chrissakes. He could have dropped out of the Caine Academy, or flunked out of Duke and opened a surf shop. He hadn't done those things because he'd chosen the life he was living. He'd fully intended to spend his entire career building The Kincaid Group until his father decided to pull the rug out from under him.

He was nearly at the end of the letter anyway. Blood boiling with a mix of anger and frustration, he focused his eyes on the neat handwriting again.

The defining fact of my life, son, is that I loved two women.

RJ shook his head. Surely love was an act of choice. In his opinion his dad should have told his parents to shove it and married Angela. Of course he would never have been born, but right now that didn't seem like such a bad deal.

I never claimed Angela and our son during my life as my role in society was important to me. I wanted those invitations to the black tie affairs, the yacht club memberships and the satisfaction of being a leading member of Charleston society.

RJ snorted. *Thanks for setting fire to all that and leaving us in the ashes.*

His father had always put a lot of stock in what other people thought. More than a man of his standing should have to. It likely went back to the Kincaids never being on quite the upper tier of Charleston society. His mom's family was one of the old guard. In retrospect he could see that was probably the chief reason his dad married her. And now look where marriage to Reginald Kincaid had put her.

I'm not proud of the choices I made. I've long carried the burden of keeping Angela and her sons secret. In making my will I tried to redress some of the wrongs I committed against Jack. He grew up on the sidelines of society, as the child of a single mother, and without many of the advantages you enjoyed. In giving him a majority share in The Kincaid Group I aimed to give him the opportunities he was denied as a boy. I realize this may seem unfair to you, but I also know you're wise enough to understand my reasoning and strong enough to forge ahead and make a success of your life, either in the company or outside it. If you're reading this letter it's because I'm dead, of natural causes or otherwise. I wrote it to explain myself to you after you'd had some time to reflect on the terms of the will, since knowing you as I do I suspect you tore up my first letter and threw it on the fire.
I love you, RJ, and I'm proud of you.
Dad.

RJ sank into the chair. His anger had evaporated, replaced by a wounding sorrow. Apparently his dad hadn't known him as well as he'd thought. Far from tearing up his first letter, he'd carried it with him since the day he received it. Maybe his dad really hadn't known how much he'd loved him? They'd never been much for words or hugs.

Angry as he was at the choices—no, the stupid mistakes—his father had made, he'd give almost anything to see him just one more time.

But life—and death—didn't work like that.

He folded the letter and thrust the ring, the license, the photos and other stray bits of paper that commemorated milestones in his dad's life, back into the envelope.

His dad had given him permission, perhaps encouragement, to leave The Kincaid Group if he wanted to. He could move away, start a new life in a different city.

A cold shiver ran through him at the limitless possibilities, the many routes his life could take. Right now the only thing he wanted was to see Brooke's lovely smile again.

"Brooke! You promised you'd tell me everything!" Evie's voice rose with exasperation.

Brooke moved the phone further from her ear. "I'm trying. The weekend's not even over yet. I'm sitting on a balcony with a ridiculous view over what must be the entire range of the Great Smoky Mountains." The morning "smoke" or fog had evaporated, leaving a crystal-clear vista of wooded slopes and sapphire blue sky. How could she even describe what she'd experienced over the last two days? "It's just a romantic weekend. You know what that's like." She wanted to downplay the whole thing. It was their first weekend together. Yes, it was fantastic. More than fantastic. But it didn't mean RJ would be shopping for a ring later.

"You had sex with him?"

"No, we meditated together."

"Oh, stop! Okay, that was a bit crude. You slept together."

"We did that, too. He's a very heavy sleeper, who makes this adorable purring noise right before he's about to wake up." A vision of his powerful chest rising and falling filled her brain. She'd watched him for over an hour, afraid that if she moved she'd wake him and spoil the pleasure of watching him sleep in her arms. He'd looked both powerful and vulnerable at the same time. Irresistible.

"Aw, like a big kitty. So when are you seeing him again?"

"I imagine I'll see him first thing tomorrow when I give him his mail." She swallowed. Would she be able to maintain her usual professional demeanor now that she knew exactly what he looked like beneath those elegant pin-striped suits? Now that he knew exactly what she looked like beneath her tailored skirts and blouses.

Her nipples pricked to attention as she remembered his blue gaze raking over her skin, drinking her in like a long, tall glass of water in the desert.

"Hmm, mad passionate love on the office desk, papers sliding forgotten to the floor while the phone rings."

"Definitely not." Brooke blushed at the vivid image her friend had conjured.

"Never say never. Would you have thought a week ago that you'd be locking lips in his office?"

"Not in a million years. I won't say I didn't fantasize about it, but I never thought it would happen."

"See? Anything could happen. Before the year is out you could be Mrs. Brooke Kincaid."

"I very much doubt it. The Kincaids are apparently obsessed with their social standing in Charleston. In addition to being illegitimate, I don't have a drop of blue blood in my veins. RJ's father didn't marry his mistress because she wasn't from the right social class, and from the sound of it not much has changed since then."

"Don't be silly. RJ's crazy about you, and he's far too self-assured to worry about other people's opinions of his lovely bride."

"Stop! I thought you were the one warning me to go slow in case it all ends in tears."

"The way I see it, you're in over your head already. Might as well enjoy it and worry about the tears later. Did you ever figure out what to get your mom for her birthday?"

Brooke gasped. "I can't believe it. I totally forgot! And it's tomorrow. No, it's today, Sunday! I haven't even called her. I'm supposed to be at her place for dinner."

Becoming involved with RJ had totally derailed her brain. She hung up and called her mom to confirm they were still on. As she was speaking, she heard the sliding door to the balcony whisper open, and RJ stepped out. She waved hi and finished the conversation, telling her mom to book a table wherever she wanted.

"I missed you." RJ's deep voice wrapped around her at the same time his arms did.

"We weren't apart more than twenty minutes."

"Felt like an eternity." He nuzzled her neck, then rested his head on her shoulder for a moment.

"Are you okay? Did you read the letter?"

She felt his chest rise as he sucked in a breath. "I read the letter. My dad apparently gives me permission to abandon all my responsibilities and seize a new life by the…" He looked up and his gaze met hers with blistering force. "All I can say is thank heaven for you being here in my arms right now."

"Don't let it get to you. Maybe we should go for a walk in the woods to blow off steam."

A sparkle of mischief crept into his eyes. "I can think of another way to blow off steam."

Brooke wasn't at all nervous on the flight back. Hand in hand with RJ, she felt they could stride across the world together and nothing could harm them.

Back in her condo, she shrugged out of the chic "country attire" she'd bought for her weekend in the woods, showered and dressed in something her mom would approve of. "You have such a nice body. You should let people see it." By people, she meant men. Barbara Nichols's life revolved around men and the chance of being admired by them.

She stopped by a mall and picked up the most expensive tennis bracelet she could find. Expensive was always good as her mom would know exactly how much it cost. When she arrived at 14 Pine Grove, as usual her mom was dressed for a night on the town. "Oh sweetheart, you shouldn't have!" The sparkly bracelet hit its mark, and was immediately added to the collection of bling on her thin wrist.

"Where's Timmy?" Her mom's boyfriend had been a regular fixture around the house for nearly two years.

"Moved to Charlotte."

"Why?"

"His job transferred him to their plant there." She shrugged as if she couldn't care less. Brooke could see the lines in her face had deepened.

"Oh, Mom, I know you two got along well. Did you talk at all about going to join him?"

Her mom's pale blue eyes had a hollow look. "He said he thought it was better if we made a clean break. He started talking about kids and you know how that goes." She swatted the air dismissively with her mani-cured hand. Timmy was at least fifteen years younger than her. This had happened before.

"I'm sorry to hear that, because I thought he was nice." Not interesting, or funny, or charming or gor-geous, like RJ, but he treated her mom well.

"Yeah, well. Sooner or later it's time to move on. Maybe we'll meet Mr. Right tonight. I booked us a table at Dashers, it's a new place just up the road."

Brooke's heart sank. The prospect of sitting at a bar booth, eyeing potentially eligible males with her mother, was enough to suck every last breath of wind from her sails. Again, this had happened before. Still, it was her birthday.

Twenty minutes later they sat in the shiny black booth, which looked just as Brooke had imagined it. Her mom's sculpted legs were artfully draped outside the booth where they could catch the eye of any pass-ing males. "How about you, sweetheart? Are you still spending the weekends holed up in your apartment practicing yoga or do you ever go out into the world?"

All of Brooke's better judgment told her to keep quiet about RJ. "Actually I'm seeing someone." Apparently her better judgment had disappeared with her first sip of Frascati.

Her mom's mouth and eyes widened. "Who? Someone from work?"

Brooke gulped. "Um, yes, actually."

"Did you finally catch that gorgeous boss of yours?" She leaned in conspiratorially. "I'm always telling you you're beautiful enough for even the richest man in Charleston, if you'd just shine a light on your assets." She glanced approvingly at the cleavage revealed by her blouse. "You do have a glow about you, now I'm looking closer." Her penciled brow lifted. "Well, don't sit there in silence. Tell me more!"

Brooke took another sip of her wine. "It is my boss." She said it quietly. "RJ. He's been through a lot lately and I think I've been a shoulder to cry on for him."

"Oh God, not a crier! I can't stand them and they usually drink like fish, too."

Brooke laughed. Her mom had a way of disarming anyone's inhibitions. "Not literally. He's just been going through a lot. I'm sure you've seen the stories in the papers."

"About his mom killing his dad." She grimaced. "Nasty stuff."

"Mrs. Kincaid didn't do it, I'm sure of that."

"Papers said they have evidence that she was at the scene of the crime around the time that it happened. That sounds pretty guilty to me."

Brooke's back stiffened. Was her admission to the police that she'd seen Elizabeth Kincaid in the building shortly before the murder the entire reason RJ's mother had been arrested? She'd yet to hear of anything more concrete.

"She came to bring him his dinner or something. Probably, I mean. I don't know for sure." She didn't want anyone to know she was involved in the investigation. At least not until she'd found a chance to tell RJ. If only she could take back her words and tell the police she hadn't seen or heard anything. "She's a really nice lady. Very quiet and sweet."

Her mom clucked her tongue. "Those quiet ones. There's always more to them than meets the eye. You don't work in my business for more than thirty years without learning a thing or two about people." As a waitress, she claimed to have gained astonishing insight into the human psyche. "She probably smiled her way through decades of marriage, being the good little wife, then when the revelations about his second family came out, she snapped." She clapped her hands together and Brooke jumped in her seat.

"I'm sure it must have been someone else. But the problem is no one else has a real motive."

"What about that newly discovered son who inherited a whole lot of money?"

Brooke nodded. "He seems to have gained the most by Reginald's death. And I hear he's not very nice, either." She drew in a breath. "Don't tell anyone I said that, okay?" Her mom loved to gossip with the customers. "He is part of the family, after all. Or at least sort of."

"Bitter." Her mom puckered up her lips and took a sip of her Manhattan without leaving any lipstick on the glass. A skill she was proud of. "I bet you anything it was him that did it. But we seem to have gotten off track here." Her lips widened back into a smile. "Are you getting serious with Reginald Kincaid, Jr.?"

Brooke laughed. "It's RJ. No one calls him Reginald."

"Well, don't you let him get away. You won't get many opportunities like that in a lifetime."

"I don't know where it will lead, but I really like him."

"Don't let him treat you badly because he's a rich boy. Not that you would. My Brooke has a good head on her shoulders." Their plate of nachos arrived and her mom took one and crunched it. "I never got my big break. Not yet, anyway." She winked. "But it sounds like you'll soon be living in fine style."

"Mom!" Suddenly Brooke could picture her bragging to her customers about how her little Brooke was dating one of those big-shot Kincaids that were all over the papers. "Will you do me a huge favor and keep it to yourself, at least for a while?"

"And spoil all the fun of bragging about you? Aww." She pouted. "I'll do my best. You'd better get engaged quick, though, as I'm not sure I'll be able to hold my tongue for long."

"I have no idea if we'll ever get engaged. We only started dating this week."

"You could always try telling him you're pregnant." Her mom lifted a brow.

Brooke stiffened. "If that had worked for you we'd still be living with my father. As it is, I've never even met him."

Her mom drew in a breath. "You're right. I forgot. Now why did I ever tell you about that?"

"Because I kept asking until you broke down." Brooke smiled. "And you knew it was better for me to finally hear the truth rather than all those crazy stories about a traveling salesman who'd be back from the Far East any day now."

"Well, it sounded more exciting than a balding ex-quarterback who owns a shoe store in Fayetteville. I looked him up on Facebook and let me tell you he's not aging well. He sure was handsome in his day, though."

"And maybe he did us both a favor by letting you go." Her mom had tearfully admitted that he'd left town—for good—the day after she'd happily told him about her surprise pregnancy.

"We'd been dating for six months. I thought it was a sure thing." She shrugged her slim shoulders inside her silky dress. "But you never know what people are made of until their feet are to the fire."

"Well, RJ's feet are in several different fires right now, and I'm doing my best to be the water that cools them."

"Just make sure you don't get left to run down the drain when the fire's been put out. And you don't want to lose your job over him, either. One thing I've always prided myself on is keeping my job. Men come and go, but work will put food on the table if they're there or not, and don't you forget it."

"Don't worry." Brooke picked up a nacho and nibbled it thoughtfully. "I won't."

Six

"You took Brooke to the cabin?" RJ's brother Matt stared at him. They were alone in RJ's office with the door closed. "Things aren't so desperate that you need to work on weekends. I did score the new Larrimore Industries account after all, and that should start bringing in revenue as early as—"

"Matt! I didn't bring her there to type my memos."

He watched while understanding dawned in his brother's green eyes. "You and Brooke... Oh, RJ, are you sure that was a good idea? She's such a key member of the company and you know how you are with women."

RJ bristled. "Exactly how am I with women?"

"Enthusiastic."

"So now I'm enthusiastic about Brooke. She's beautiful, intelligent, kind and she gives great hugs." He couldn't stop a smile creeping across his mouth. Even thinking about Brooke gave him a warm glow. "There's quite a different side to her than the one we see at the office."

"I bet she's saying the same thing about you." Matt raised an eyebrow. "Are you going to be kissing in meetings and sneaking off for afternoon trysts?"

RJ fought a grin. "Appealing as that sounds, I think we'll both have enough self-control to maintain a semblance of professional decorum."

"And what happens when you get tired of her?"

"Unimaginable."

"Maybe I have a more vivid imagination than you. I know what it's like when a relationship starts to sour. You do realize she could sue you for sexual harassment and win?"

RJ frowned. "Brooke would never do that."

"Let's hope not. We can't afford another scandal right now. I guess you'll just have to marry her." There was not the slightest glimmer of humor in his brother's steady gaze.

RJ's stomach tightened. "Let's not get too carried away. We haven't even been dating for a full week, yet."

"See? That's the RJ I know. You're crazy about them for a while, then something better comes along."

"These days I never know what's going to happen next, so I'm going to seize the moment. Did you guys visit Mom over the weekend?"

"Both days, just like we promised. She says she's doing fine but she's looking rather thin and drawn. We've got to get her out of there."

"I've been on the phone to the D.A.'s office every day. Three times today already. If they have evidence they need to produce it. You can't keep someone behind bars without a trial in this country. It's not like she's accused of an act of terrorism." He felt his hackles rising again. "The assistant D.A. said something about a witness at the scene, but then she clammed up. I know there wasn't an eyewitness to the murder or we'd have heard about it. If there was, we'd know what the hell happened and Mom would be home where she belongs. The private detective I hired is trying to break down the blue wall of silence that is our local police department right now, but no luck so far."

"Lily's going to visit her again this afternoon."

"I'm going, too, after the meeting. I bought some of her favorite chocolates." He shook his head. "Though I'm sure even Ghirardelli doesn't taste all that great when you're locked up in a tiny cell sleeping next to a toilet. It makes me sick."

"I know, RJ. Honestly, I understand about the Brooke thing. This nightmare is hard on all of us and I can see the temptation to fall into the nearest pair of soft arms." He clapped RJ on the shoulder. "Let me know if you hear anything new from the police or the D.A.'s office, okay?"

"Will do."

Brooke darted away from RJ's office door and back to her desk, heart pounding, before Matthew emerged.

He looked right at her and smiled, and she managed to stammer a greeting, sure her face was red as fire. She'd been unable to resist listening in on RJ's conversation with Matt—horribly unprofessional, not to mention totally uncool, but she couldn't help herself. She'd pretended to rearrange some files in the tall cabinet next to his door, but every nerve in her brain and body was fine-tuned to pick up all sound from inside.

Her heart had soared as RJ said such sweet things about her, then crashed when Matt muttered about lawsuits and accused him of falling into the nearest pair of soft arms. That rang painfully true. None of them knew where this was going, and it could be heading to a lot of very dark places.

The door was now wide open, and she glanced inside to see RJ, head bent over some papers on his desk. He looked up. "Are you going to sue me for sexual harassment?"

"Never." She said it too fast and too loud. Did he know she'd been listening?

"Never say never." RJ raised a brow. "You could, you know."

She walked into his office and closed the door gently behind her. "What happened between us was entirely mutual." She kept her voice composed and professional, though her heart was hammering. How typical of RJ to come right out and say what anyone else would want to brush under the carpet. Right now she adored him more than ever. "I don't regret it."

Though maybe I will one day.

RJ rose and came around the desk. In his dark suit he looked imposing and elegant. Different from the rugged charm of the RJ she'd enjoyed all weekend, but every bit as irresistible. He wrapped his arms gently around her waist and pulled her close for a kiss. Her insides bubbled with pleasure and she let her hands slide under his suit jacket and caress his back through his cotton shirt.

"This is fun." RJ's breath heated her neck.

"It feels naughty."

"It is naughty." He squeezed her backside gently. "And I could think of even naughtier things we could do."

She giggled. "Don't you have a ten o'clock?"

"I'm the executive vice president. I can cancel it." His deadly serious expression only made her want to laugh harder.

"It's with a potential new client." She ran a finger along his shirt buttons. "A large manufacturing company with factories in China."

"Hmm. You're making this all very confusing and difficult for me."

"Then as your personal assistant I'll have to insist that you go to the meeting."

"Can you do that?"

"Apparently I just did." She kissed his dimple. "Though only time will tell if you listen." She could hardly believe she was being so bold. The chemistry between them must be affecting her brain.

"I'll only go if you'll come, too." Humor sparkled in his eyes. She would have been at this meeting anyway.

"If you put it that way, how can I refuse?" Her lips tingled as he feathered one last kiss over them. She pulled herself away, slightly breathless, opened the door and went to get her laptop.

Everyone on the floor must know something by now. Or they'd figure it out from her burning cheeks. Or the loopy expression on her face.

And RJ had come right out and told Matthew! Did he plan to tell the entire family they were seeing each other? Surely the others would also worry about lawsuits. It hadn't occurred to her that she'd have a case against him, but her friend Evie had told her about a woman at her company who sued her boss when he dumped her. She'd won, even though it was consensual, because he was her direct boss and should not have embarked on a relationship with her.

It was easy to forget about all the pitfalls when she was in RJ's arms, or even gazing at his handsome face. The moment she moved away she felt exposed again to the chill winds of reality.

Brooke sat next to RJ during the meeting, which was normal since she sometimes needed to show him correspondence or data on her laptop. Opposite her, a tall blonde with a very large mouth was representing the Xingha Corporation, a manufacturer of children's toys that did a lot of business with U.S. supermarkets. Three non-English-speaking Chinese men in gray suits sat further along the table, and occasionally she turned to repeat something to them in Chinese.

"Oh, RJ, you must come to Beijing again soon. You'll love what they've done with your favorite hotel. Hot tubs in every room." Her dark eyes clashed with her blond hair, and gave her face a sense of drama that really annoyed Brooke. Already she found herself anxiously casting her mind back to RJ's trips to Beijing—had he even been to Beijing?—and wondering and worrying how intimate he'd been with Ms. Claudia Daring.

"I'm sure I'll be in Beijing sometime soon, but right now we have a lot happening here."

"I've heard." She leaned forward, and reached out to clasp his hands. "It's terrible. If there's anything I can do…anything at all."

Brooke barely managed not to roll her eyes, but

inside her stomach was churning. RJ and this woman had obviously had an affair.

She tried to glance sideways at RJ without moving her head. Were his eyes lighting up at the sight of Claudia's smile? He leaned back in his chair so she couldn't get a good look at him.

Matt sat farther down the table. What was he thinking about right now? Was he laughing at RJ being confronted with his own woman-loving ways at the first meeting of the day? She wished she could slide under the table and hide.

She was just the latest in a long line of Kincaid conquests. She knew that. You didn't work for RJ for five years and not realize that he enjoyed the company of women every bit as much as James Bond.

"You'll recall that we moved our account to Danmar Shipping in 2009 over pricing issues." Claudia lifted her rather pointy chin. "We understand you might be in a position to offer a more competitive price." One slender brow lifted slightly.

"Yes." Matthew chimed in from far down the table, although Claudia had addressed RJ. "We'd like to bring the Xingha Corporation back to The Kincaid Group, and we can provide some strong incentives. We understand that some of your new products are temperature sensitive and we can provide climate controlled…"

He continued speaking but Brooke no longer heard a word he said. She was staring directly at Claudia, who never took her eyes off RJ. Her breath caught as Claudia's tongue sneaked out and flicked over her upper lip. Probably supposed to look sensual, but it made Brooke think of a lizard.

Her eyes flew to RJ's face, and horror crept over her as she saw his familiar dimples deepen.

"Excuse me." She rose from her chair and hurried for the door, unable to contain herself for a single second longer. Once outside the meeting she walked quickly to the ladies' room. RJ was flirting with that woman, in front of everyone, when he'd slept with Brooke only yesterday!

And despite the fact that his brother knew about their affair and had taunted RJ for his womanizing ways not half an hour earlier.

Her breathing was rushed and unsteady and she wasn't surprised to see her face looking pale, except for a nasty flush spreading across her neck. That only happened when she was really embarrassed. How could she survive this meeting? If RJ had coolly rebuffed Ms. Daring, and perhaps said, "I'd love to come to Beijing, with my fiancée, Brooke Nichols," and gestured proudly toward her, she'd feel quite different.

"Ugh!" She said it aloud. This is what happened when you let your imagination run away with you. Even after RJ's conversation with Matt, she'd focused on the moment when he said it was unimaginable that he should tire of her, not the part where he had a new woman every week. Within an hour his dimples were deepening over some scrawny executive with an account to dangle.

Still, she had to go back. A bathroom break was one thing, ditching the meeting was another. And her laptop was still in there. She drew in an unsteady breath, patted cold water on her hot cheeks and dried it with a paper towel. *You're a professional and you can do this. You actually want The Kincaid Group to get*

*this account because you care more about the future
of the company than your future as RJ's latest female
conquest.*

It wasn't working. Nevertheless, she gritted her teeth
and strode out the door.

She plastered a smile on her face as she entered the
meeting and sat down.

RJ turned to her. "Brooke, we came to an arrange-
ment with Xingha, and we're going out for a celebration lunch. Can you book us a table at Montepeliano?"

"Sure." She maintained her stiff smile and picked
up her phone. "How many people?" Was she invited
or was she merely making reservations for RJ and his
new bilingual playmate? She cursed the angry flames
of jealousy that licked inside her. How had a few days
of intimacy with RJ turned her into an irrational, emotional wreck?

"All of us." He glanced around the table. "Nine." A
quick count revealed that did include her.

"Will do." She made the reservation in hushed tones.
Great, now she had to sit through lunch watching Ms.
Daring make eyes at RJ. And vice-versa. The restaurant was a short walk from the offices, and a favorite
for business lunches.

"Do excuse us." RJ spoke to Claudia. "My assistant
and I need a moment." He glanced at Brooke, and her
heart jumped. Was he going to scold her for running
out of the meeting? She was there to take minutes and
she'd obviously missed the most important part—the
deal. Of course Matt or RJ could fill her in on the details, but it was unprofessional of her to just vanish.

She followed him out of the room, and he gestured
for her to come around the corner toward an empty

conference room. Once inside, he closed the door. He looked at her and a tiny line appeared between his eyebrows.

"I'm sorry I left like that, I…" The rest of her words were lost when his mouth crushed over hers. His broad hands settled on her hips, and she shuddered, once, as his tongue slipped into her mouth.

Brooke heard a tiny moan leave her as the kiss deepened. Relief and the shock of excitement stirred her blood. Her nails scratched at RJ's strong back through his shirt, and she got a sudden urge to pull off his stiff suit jacket and feel his warm skin.

"Whoa, there." RJ pulled back, dimples deeper than ever. "Let's not get too carried away. The door's not even closed."

Brooke flushed. "Whoops."

"We'll use up all that energy later, and that's a promise." His blue eyes shone with dark fire. "Though it'll be hard to keep my hands off you for the rest of the afternoon. I guess this is why they say office romance is a bad idea."

"Just one of the reasons why it's a bad idea." A naughty smile crept across her mouth. "Makes it hard to stay focused in meetings, too."

"Or does the desire to get out of the meeting sharpen one's focus enough to make a deal in record time?"

"Yes, how did everything happen while I was in the washroom?"

RJ raised a brow. "I guess you'll never know." He gestured for her to leave the room before him, and she felt his fingers trail across her rear end as she turned to go. That sparked a little ripple of laughter. What did she care how they made the deal so fast? RJ had let her know he wanted her, not their glamorous client.

She walked to the restaurant on a cloud of joy. She didn't even mind RJ chatting with Claudia Daring. Now she had the perspective to see him using his charm to build the business, not to lure another woman into his bed. Her earlier flash of jealousy seemed petty and foolish.

She noticed Matthew casting wary glances at his brother. Was Matt worried she or RJ would somehow reveal their clandestine relationship? She knew the company couldn't afford even a wisp of scandal, so she made sure to sit at the far end of the table and did her best to make conversation with the Chinese men who had about twelve words of English among them.

That night she and RJ stayed at his place. His large, modern apartment had stunning views of the Charleston waterfront. They ordered in Thai curries and played a game of strip Go Fish then made lazy, intoxicating love on his oversize bed. After midnight they called a cab so she could go home, sleep and get ready for work.

By Thursday, at RJ's suggestion, she'd left a robe and a spare dress there, to avoid having to rush home. She took to carrying extra makeup and hair implements in her purse, because she now spent more time at his house than her own.

Her clothes looked strange hanging in the spare closet next to his off-season clothes. Of course if they lived together here, this would be her closet.

"I've decided to reinstitute a family tradition this week. Sunday gatherings at the old homestead."

"Your mom's house?"

She turned to see RJ frowning at the phone. "Yes. It may seem strange for us to go there when she's not in it, but she insists she wants us to get together and she'll be there in spirit. We've met for dinner nearly every Sunday since we were kids, and it doesn't feel right to drop the ball because everything's a mess right now. Besides, it'll be nice for you to meet the whole gang."

Her eyes widened. "Me? I don't know. Your family has a lot to talk about. And I don't want to scandalize them. They're sure to think it's odd that you're dating your assistant." Her stomach clenched as she immediately regretted the use of the word dating. That sounded so…serious, and RJ had plainly told Matt he had no idea where things were headed.

"Matt knows already."

She didn't plan to admit she'd heard Matt's reaction. "I don't want to be in the way."

"You won't be. My sister Lily will bring her new fiancé, Daniel, and Laurel—who you know—will bring her fiancé, Eli. Kara is planning both of their weddings. Then you already know Matt and you've probably met his fiancée, Susannah."

"Yes, I met her when she brought Flynn in to meet him for lunch." Flynn was Matt's toddler son, who'd recently scared everyone by getting some rare disease that had the family hovering over his bedside around the clock.

"Did you know Susannah is Flynn's mom?"

"But I thought Matt was married when… I mean, I know his wife passed away, but…" She felt her face heat. Matt's wife, Grace, had died in a small plane crash a year or so ago. Flynn must be just three, or thereabouts.

RJ laughed. "Matt didn't cheat on his wife. They'd hired her as a surrogate since Grace couldn't carry a child. What Grace and Matt never told us is that they used Susannah's egg, so Flynn was actually Susannah's biological child. She came back to Charleston in case he needed a compatible bone marrow donor when he was ill, and she and Matt fell in love. Pretty crazy, huh?"

"It's wonderful. For both of them and for Flynn."

"Romance is in the air amongst the Kincaids lately. It only seems fair that they get to know you, too."

"It would be nice to get to know your sisters. Sure, I'd love to come." Already caterpillars crawled in her stomach at the idea of them all looking at her. No doubt they would wonder why their brother was interested in someone ordinary like her.

"They'll love you." RJ crossed the bedroom and rested his hands on her hips. Her belly swirled with arousal. "And I know you'll love them, too."

I sure hope so. She sank into his embrace and enjoyed the warm, protected feeling of his arms around her. She was getting far too attached to RJ. Now she knew he was thoughtful, passionate and sexy as well as smart and gorgeous....

Brooke let out a small sigh. Everything was going so well. Somehow she'd climbed the tallest ladder on the chutes and ladders board and was sunning herself on a lofty square near the top. Why did she feel like a long chute was just around the corner?

Seven

Brooke agonized over what to bring to the meal, especially since she wasn't sure who the host was in Elizabeth Kincaid's absence. She didn't want to bring flowers and have them die alone in an empty house. She settled on a bottle of champagne and a hand-painted ceramic bowl filled with gourmet fudge.

She'd agreed to meet RJ there, and she felt a growing sense of trepidation as she walked past the other large, elegant mansions on tree-lined Montagu Street. As she approached the imposing Kincaid residence, she heard muffled voices through an open, lace-curtained window.

"You're kidding me!" A woman's voice. "Who invited him?"

"I did." Another female. "He's making a big effort to be a member of the family."

Brooke paused on the brick walkway to the front

door. Both voices were raised. She didn't want to enter into a scene.

"He's not even related to us. Alan is from Angela's second marriage."

"I invited Jack, too, but he didn't reply. Maybe he'll come anyway."

"Jesus, Kara. Why did you invite either of them? I just wanted a quiet family dinner, like we used to have." RJ's voice. His sister must have invited the sons of Reginald Kincaid's second family.

"I think we should give Alan a chance. He's been perfectly pleasant. He even seems interested in working for The Kincaid Group. Why not get to know him?" Brooke couldn't tell his sisters apart by their voices. She still hovered outside on the path, pretending to look for something in her purse.

"You always were too nice for your own good." RJ again. "At least Alan didn't inherit part of the company. He isn't even a relative. He's just an innocent bystander as far as this whole situation is concerned."

"Exactly. So let's welcome him into our midst. Anyone bring champagne?"

Brooke decided this was her cue, and she marched up the front steps and rang the bell. RJ greeted her with a warm kiss on the cheek and summoned her into a large, airy room with high ceilings and comfortable sofas. Everyone exclaimed over the champagne and fudge and she heaved a sigh of relief that she'd gotten off to a good start.

"This is my sister Lily." He gestured to a pretty woman with red-gold hair cascading over her shoulders. Her blue eyes were bright as she shook Brooke's hand.

"We've run into each other a few times at the office. Sometimes I hang around just to annoy RJ and Matt."

Matt, seated on a sofa with his toddler son on his lap, waved a cheery hello. She tried not to blush at the recollection of him discussing her with RJ.

"Daniel is Lily's fiancé," continued RJ. Brooke shook hands with a tall blond man with a warm smile. "And this is Kara. She's the event planner in the family."

"And right now I'm being blamed for overplanning this event." Her green eyes sparkled. "Trust me, people, I know what I'm doing."

RJ continued, "Of course you know Laurel." A striking beauty with long, auburn hair, Laurel Kincaid worked for the company as public relations director. She stepped forward and gave Brooke a kiss on the cheek, and introduced her fiancé, Eli, a tall, handsome man who Brooke knew owned a respected resort chain.

"We're glad you could come. It's nice to see RJ more relaxed lately." Laurel gave her brother a quick nudge.

"Brooke is definitely helping me keep things in perspective."

The doorbell rang again. The siblings looked at each other. "That must be Alan," whispered Laurel.

"I'll get it." Kara smiled and marched for the door. Brooke hadn't met either of the Sinclair men. She couldn't help a spark of curiosity at what the sons of Reginald Kincaid's former mistress would be like. All eyes swiveled to the door as Kara returned with a blondish man of medium height, smartly dressed in a wool jacket and pants.

RJ introduced her, and Alan Sinclair smiled and shook hands—firmly, Brooke noted—with everyone.

"Delighted to be here. So kind of you to invite me. What a stunning room!" He marveled over the crisp, Federal-era plasterwork.

Brooke had a feeling she'd seen him somewhere before. Maybe he'd come to the office for one reason or another. His hair curled just over his collar and gave him a raffish air, like a professor who slept with his students.

Now, now. You're as bad as the rest of them. Give him a chance. She didn't even know this man. She just knew RJ didn't want him here.

"Actually a lot of the details have been restored," Lily chimed in. "The house was a wreck when the family bought it. Dad's mother insisted on buying it and she spent years bringing back all the original features and furnishing it in period style."

"Which is why it looks more like a museum than a real house," murmured RJ.

"It is a museum, of sorts," Laurel spoke up. "A monument to an era that Grandma loved. She always wished she'd lived back in the 1800s, so she could swan around in long dresses and spend entire afternoons playing whist."

"She pretty much did that anyway," teased RJ. "Mom likes to have card parties, too. Mint juleps and cutthroat bridge."

There was a moment of silence, while they no doubt all thought of poor Elizabeth Kincaid sitting in the county jail.

Alan cleared his throat. "The house is obviously a labor of love. I don't suppose one of you would give me a tour?"

Laurel said, "Of course, I'd be happy to. Lily, is the meal under control?"

"Almost. Pamela should go away for the weekend more often. I love having the kitchen house to myself."

"Let me come help in the kitchen." Brooke was eager to make herself useful. In truth she was much happier working at an event rather than trying to make small talk, especially when they all must be wondering exactly why she was there.

She followed Lily outside into the manicured garden, and along a small brick walkway to the large, bright kitchen house. The building was a relic from the days when servants and their steamy labors could be kept separate from elegant family life, but had been renovated into a chef's kitchen with marble work tops and tall painted cabinets. Something delicious simmered in three pots on the stove and salad fixings sat, still bagged, on a long wooden table in the middle of the room. "Shall I make the salad?"

"That would be great. I'll just toast the garlic bread." Lily ripped off a hunk of French bread from one of three loaves and popped it in her mouth. "I'm in the second trimester of my pregnancy right now, and I'm absolutely ravenous."

"How exciting. Do you know if it's a boy or a girl?"

She pulled romaine lettuce from its bag and started to peel leaves off into a colander. "Not yet. We can't decide whether to find out. I know it's easier to know the gender because you can decorate the room, but I've also heard people can get really stressed about picking family names and creating expectations before the kid is even born. We went through a lot of drama just getting to this point, and I just want to enjoy our pregnancy without stirring up any more excitement."

Brooke rinsed the lettuce under a high, arched tap. "Having a baby must be one of the biggest adventures there is. You're bringing a brand-new person into your family, who you'll be spending the rest of your life with. It's magical, really."

Lily turned to her, eyes bright. "That's exactly how I feel. I admit I didn't intend to get pregnant, but it's brought Daniel and me closer than we would have dared become otherwise." She lowered her voice. "So are you and RJ...an item?"

"I guess we are." Brooke felt a little thrill of nerves. "Just since two weeks ago. I never intended for anything to happen, but..." She shrugged.

Lily's face turned more serious and her blue eyes looked steadily at Brooke. "Do be careful."

"What do you mean?" Brooke swallowed hard.

"Emotions are running high right now and the media's watching us all very closely."

Brooke's hands grew cold. "I'm not sure what you're saying."

Lily leaned in close. The lettuce dripped water onto the marble sideboard. "In case things don't work out between you, you know, it's important not to stir up any bad press."

"You think he'll break up with me and I'll go to the media?" First Matthew, now Lily. No doubt all the Kincaids suspected she'd betray the family. What would they say if they knew she'd told the police about their mom? Suddenly she felt like an intruder at their family gathering. If only she'd told RJ about it right away. Now there was so much water under the bridge she could hardly come out and admit her involvement. The deception by omission ate at her insides.

"No! None of us expects you to cause trouble." Lily put a hand on her arm. Her fingers felt soft, not accusatory. "I just want you to be prepared for anything and to handle it calmly. RJ's a smart, fun guy and a stand-up brother, but he's always sworn he'd never marry or have children." She gave a wry expression.

Brooke's stomach clenched. He'd actually said that? His own sister would know. And she was warning her to be careful not to get her heart broken. Brooke took the lettuce back to the wood table, and started to tear the leaves with shaking hands.

"I'd never deliberately stir up any trouble for the family," she said quietly. "I care very much about RJ, and about The Kincaid Group."

"I'm sure you do." Lily came close again. "I can see RJ looks different lately. More like his old self before Dad died. I'm sure that's attributable to you. I hope everything works out well."

Brooke heard the doubt in her voice. Brooke knew herself that RJ changed girlfriends like most men changed ringtones. She should be grateful for the wake-up call.

She and Lily chatted innocuously about a recent music festival, and Brooke prepared the rest of the salad, then they heard Alan's house tour coming toward the kitchen house.

"Stunning plasterwork in the archways." Alan's confident voice boomed outside the doorway. "She must have hired craftsmen from Italy."

"She did." Kara accompanied him into the room.

"Only the best for Grandma Kincaid. Do you ladies need some help with the food?"

"It's all ready." Lily smiled. "Perhaps you could both help us carry it into the dining room?"

The long mahogany table gleamed under its load of antique porcelain and sterling silver flatware. Obviously someone was polishing and dusting in Elizabeth Kincaid's absence. Not that she would clean things herself even if she was here.

Alan picked up one of the crystal glasses and peered underneath. "I knew it. Penrose Waterford. The original Waterford crystal." He beamed at the gathered group, taking their chairs. "It's a privilege to be surrounded by such treasures."

"It's fun to meet someone who appreciates them so much," said Laurel. "We tend to take everything for granted since we've seen all these things since we were babies." Little Flynn had picked up a scrolled silver spoon and raised it, ready to bang it down on the burnished wood surface before his father caught his hand with a laugh. "See! No appreciation for the finer things."

Alan laughed, showing even white teeth. "Born with a silver spoon in his mouth, lucky little devil. And surrounded by such a warm and loving family, too." He beamed at the gathered crowd.

Brooke shrank into her chair. He seemed perfectly comfortable here. She felt they were all watching her, wondering what would happen when RJ dumped her. RJ made such a handsome head of the family, carving the big roast and passing plates around. She helped herself to minted potatoes and steamed asparagus and raised her glass in a toast to the family and the fervent hope that Elizabeth Kincaid would be at next Sunday's gathering.

"What I want to know," said Matthew, "is who gave the police the information that led to Mom's arrest. They won't even say what the information is. The investigator RJ hired says someone saw Mom in the building, but the police aren't confirming."

Brooke's fingers tightened around her glass of white wine. She put it down carefully.

"Damn, but I wish I was there that night." RJ looked up. "I went out to a dinner across town and left around six, so I didn't see a thing."

Brooke swallowed, and stared at her asparagus. She'd been there until shortly after seven, finishing a report and PowerPoint presentation for one of RJ's upcoming meetings. That's when she'd joined Elizabeth Kincaid on the elevator and exited the building with her. Had RJ's mother been so upset because she'd found Reginald dead…or worse…killed him? No, no she couldn't believe it of her. Maybe she should just say something right now. She hadn't done anything wrong in speaking to the police, but sitting here in silence felt terrible. Perhaps she could just—

"If an employee told the police they saw Mom, they should be fired," RJ spoke loudly.

Brooke's knife rattled against her plate, and she cleared her throat and busied herself cutting some meat. Speaking up right now was not a good idea. She'd definitely have to tell RJ alone, not surprise him in front of his family. If only she could pluck up the courage.

"Be fair, RJ," Laurel said. "If they were just speaking the truth they've committed no crime. Mom did say she was there that night, bringing Dad's dinner."

"No way. It's a police investigation and they should have pled the fifth. It's a simple matter of company loyalty."

"Maybe they had no idea what was going on?" Lily peered at RJ over her glass of sparkling water.

"Hardly. The police were crawling all over the office for weeks investigating the murder. No one could have thought they were simply making casual conversation. Someone out there is responsible for our mother being behind bars right now, with a bunch of real hard cases and nut jobs, and that's not something I can forgive."

Brooke's breathing had become so shallow she started to feel faint. RJ would surely find out it was her who spoke to the police. Part of her wanted to confess right now and get it over with. Have them all shout at her and blame her and throw her out of the house. She silently twisted her napkin in her lap.

No, apparently she was too weak to speak up and face the music. And worst of all, she couldn't bear to hurt RJ.

And there was her job. And the rent to pay. And her dream of buying her little condo. She should probably start looking for another job, since they'd fire her for sure once they found out and it was bound to happen sooner or later.

"Brooke, are you okay? You look pale?" Kara turned to her.

"Sure, fine!" Her voice came out loud and forced. "Delicious dinner." Her lame comment echoed down the table.

"Marvelous." Alan smiled and lifted his knife.

"Quite the most succulent roast I've had this year. My congratulations to the chef."

Lily smiled. "Mom taught me everything I know. She's an amazing entertainer. Speaking of which, Laurel, she wanted to know how your wedding plans are coming along. Did you choose the dress yet?"

Laurel looked slightly startled. "Choose a dress? I can't possibly get married until Mom is out of…that place."

"She wants us to forge ahead with all our plans so she can leap right back into life once this ordeal is over. She and I spent ages poring over menu ideas for my wedding. And she thinks I should go for the Vera Wang dress I showed you."

Laurel bit her lip. "I don't know. It just seems wrong to think about dresses and cakes and reception venues at a time like this." She turned to Eli. "Don't you think?"

"Absolutely." He patted her hand. "No need to rush. We have the rest of our lives together."

"I agree with Mom and think you're being silly. Come on, Eli. Don't you think Mom would be cheered up by pictures of your lovely bride in sixty or seventy different fabulous gowns?" Eli shrugged in response to Kara's question. "I tell you, I'm more excited about this wedding than the bride or groom. If they didn't have a party planner in the family, there probably wouldn't ever be a wedding.

"I think everyone needs a party planner in the family. Come on, I'm up to three weddings right now, Lily and Daniel, Matt and Susannah, Laurel and Eli— who's next?"

Brooke felt a sudden raw flush of irrational hope in her chest. Why not her and RJ?

Well, there were any number of reasons why not. RJ didn't say anything and she forced herself not to look at him. Lily's warning reverberated in her mind.

"Alan, how about you? Have you got a blushing bride hidden somewhere?"

"Not yet, I'm afraid." He smiled around the table. "I'm still waiting for that perfect lady to enter my life." Brooke noticed his eyes skip right past her as he shone his klieg-light charm on the gathered group. He probably wasn't interested in her since she wasn't a member of the mighty Kincaid family. She was just a nobody who happened to be there. "And who knows, it could happen any day now." He let his blue eyes fall to rest on Kara, and Brooke watched the slight suggestive lift of his eyebrow.

"That's the spirit." Kara smiled. Then she clapped her hand over Eli's. "I still think you should be pushing your bride to make some decisions. One couple I helped recently had been engaged for sixteen years. They hadn't planned it that way, they just never got around to setting the date."

"Maybe they just weren't all that crazy about each other." RJ topped up the glasses of those seated on either side of him. "When people realize that they really like each other, things happen fast." His bright gaze settled on Brooke, who couldn't stop a smile rushing to her lips.

"Maybe you'll be next then, RJ?" Kara looked at him with an arch smile.

RJ laughed. "Or maybe you will, Kara?"

Brooke deflated as suddenly as she'd filled with

hope. Which was absolutely ridiculous after two measly weeks of dating. You'd think she'd never been in a relationship before.

"Since I'm not even seeing anyone right now, I'm not entirely sure how that could happen." Kara took the bottle from him and refilled the next two glasses down the table. "But I suppose you never know what life is going to bring."

"Truer words were never said." Alan beamed around the room. "I never imagined I'd find myself in the midst of such a charming family. I'm honored to be here and delighted to find that I truly feel at home among you."

Brooke wished she could say the same. But, kind as they were, she still felt like an outsider. The kind of outsider who was responsible for putting their beloved mother behind bars. And when they found out, she'd be on the outside for good.

Eight

"I guess Alan's not so bad after all." RJ piloted his Porsche back to his apartment. Brooke sat beside him, looking gorgeous in a green dress that gracefully hugged her curves.

"He's certainly making an effort." Brooke seemed a little tense, her pretty mouth tight and her lovely green eyes darting around a lot. He'd be sure to release all that tension with a nice, soothing massage when they got home. His fingers tingled with anticipation at the prospect.

"Was it overwhelming being surrounded by Kincaids?"

"Everyone in your family is lovely. They couldn't have been nicer."

"Still, there are a lot of us. And more all the time, it seems. The clan keeps growing." He beamed. He loved the way she'd pitched in with Sunday dinner and he could tell she'd made a positive impression on his sisters. "You fit right in." There weren't many women as intelligent and fun as his sisters, but he'd managed to find one. That she was gorgeous, too? Icing on the cake.

"Thanks. I've had practice, being in the company so long, I knew half of you already."

"But socializing is different. For one thing you look a lot hotter in that dress than in your power suits." How could he not have noticed how breathtakingly beautiful she was until recently? He must have been blind. He took the briefest of red-light opportunities to admire the way her dress draped over her slender thighs, and saw her smile out of the corner of his eye.

"Thanks."

"I can't wait to peel it off you."

"You won't have to wait long."

He pulled into the parking garage under his building and they hurried upstairs, laughing at their own eagerness. Every glance, every touch that passed between them only ratcheted the tension higher. RJ's muscles ached to wrap themselves around Brooke again. He'd made an effort not to paw her in front of the family, as he didn't want to embarrass her. He could tell she still felt a little shy and awkward, probably because she was used to having a much more formal relationship with all of them.

In the elevator, RJ seized the opportunity to steal a greedy kiss. Brooke's mouth tasted like honey and flowers, and her skin was smooth silk under his fingers. How could he have worked with her for five years and never realized such a delicious and inviting woman was right under his nose?

So much for being sensible and keeping work and play separate for five years. If it hadn't been for that one crazy whisky-fueled night he could have missed out on becoming intimate with the most appealing woman he'd ever met.

They tore into the apartment, flushed and breathless. Brooke fumbled with the buttons on his shirt while he unwrapped the complicated sash around her waist. Her nipples poked eagerly through the delicate fabric of her bra when he unzipped her dress and let it fall to the floor.

He circled her waist and held her against his chest. Brooke let out a shuddering sigh. He could tell she'd been anxious today, maybe nervous about making the right impression on his large family. Now they were alone again her reserve melted away, leaving her warm and eager in his arms.

Their kisses had a dimension he'd never experienced before. Something more than taste and touch, a thrilling quality that never failed to surprise him. Her mouth fit his so well, he could kiss her for hours and not notice the time passing.

Brooke's hand covered his erection through the pants they'd not yet managed to shed, and he released a little groan of his own.

"I feel like a teenager when you're around." He breathed in her ear and nibbled the nape of her neck. "I had a hard time keeping my hands off you today."

"Lucky thing you don't have to anymore." She stroked the hard length of him, then unzipped his pants and took him firmly in her hand. RJ arched his back at the sensation.

"I think we'd better get horizontal."

Brooke squeezed again, making him breathe harder. "Horizontal is so…predictable." She spoke quietly. He cracked open his eyes to see her mischievous grin.

"Brooke, you never fail to surprise me." They shrugged off his pants and he lifted her onto the back of the broad leather sofa, which was just wide enough to hold her gorgeous ass while he held her steady.

It drove him crazy to see how wet and ready she was. He entered her slowly, and enjoyed her sweet moan of pleasure. Her breasts bounced gently against his chest as he rocked back and forth. He loved the feel of her hands on his back, clinging for balance as he moved with her. When she wrapped her legs around his hips and pulled him deeper, he thought he'd explode right there and then, but he pulled himself back from the brink and teased her lips with licks and kisses.

"Oh, RJ." His name on her sigh heightened his arousal. He sensed her climax growing close. Her nails dug into his skin and she moved with increasing speed and passion, legs still wrapped firmly around him. When she finally let go, he felt the force of serious relief ripping through him, and they almost toppled backwards onto the sofa together until he managed to right them.

Still in the same position, he picked her up and carried her into the bedroom, where they settled on the bed. Brooke's eyes were closed, her lashes long and thick against her rosy cheeks. Her hair splayed over the pillow and her lips were red and slightly parted.

"What a vision," he murmured.

Her eyes opened a little, a sliver of jade green glory, and he saw the spark of a smile in them. Brooke's smile did something really odd to his chest. In fact he was currently experiencing a host of unfamiliar sensations. Is this what love felt like?

He settled next to her onto the pillow. Brooke had already drifted off into a sweet sleep, and he was almost ready to do the same until he realized he'd better go remove the condom.

Which was when he realized he hadn't used one.

Brooke woke up to the first rays of lazy sunshine peeking around the heavy curtains. She'd slept like a corpse. The anxiety of the family dinner knocked her right out. Or maybe her brain was hiding from the ugly reality of the truths she had to reveal. She turned to find RJ, but his side of the bed was empty.

When she glanced at the clock it was only 6:30. Early for him to be up already.

"RJ?" How odd. He didn't seem to be in the bathroom, and the bedroom door was closed. She tried to settle her head back on the pillow, but found she couldn't relax. She climbed out of bed and pulled her robe from the wardrobe, then stepped out into the living room.

Still no RJ.

The kitchen was empty, and so was the spare bedroom. The door to his office was closed. Not exactly an early riser, RJ usually rolled out of bed at the last minute when it was time to head to work. She'd never known him to work in his study in the morning. Maybe something was going on with his mother's case?

That now-familiar knot of fear reappeared in her stomach. Had he realized it was her who spoke to the police?

"RJ, are you in there?"

She heard a rustle, and the sound of a chair being pulled back, then the door flung open. RJ's face was dark, his eyebrows lowered.

Immediately Brooke felt the blood creeping from her body. He knew. "I'm sorry, I never meant to—"

"Don't blame yourself. I screwed up, Brooke."

"What?" She was confused.

RJ shoved a hand through already disordered hair. "I've been taking responsibility for birth control, so it's my fault I forgot to use a condom."

Brooke's mouth fell open. She'd been so excited and aroused it never crossed her mind. "I didn't even think of it."

"You could be pregnant."

The words hung in the air for a moment. Her hand flew to her belly as if life was already taking shape in there. Which it might be.

"I can't believe I was so stupid." RJ's tone made it clear there was nothing positive about the possibility.

Brooke shrank back into the living room slightly. For an odd, irrational second, she'd welcomed the idea of RJ's baby. Now she could plainly see he was horrified by the possibility of having a child with her. "It was my fault, too. I should have said something."

"It's not your fault. I've taken care of it every time, so you could reasonably expect me to continue." He hesitated. "I don't suppose you're on the pill or anything, are you?"

She swallowed. "No. I should have gone to the doctor for something, but everything happened so fast…." Their whirlwind romance had seemed above prosaic matters like birth control. And the sad fact was she hadn't had a relationship in so long that she hadn't thought about contraception in ages. She had an old diaphragm buried somewhere in her bathroom cupboards, but it probably didn't even fit anymore.

RJ shook his head. "With everything that's going on, the last thing we need is more worry. And considering that our current situation was precipitated by my dad's illegitimate son, you'd think I'd be more careful." He wasn't looking at her, but right past her, into the living room.

Our child wouldn't be illegitimate if you married me. The thought penetrated her brain before she had a chance to stop it. The man right in front of her looked like he had no intention of marrying anyone, ever. Just as his sister had warned her.

"How soon will we know?" He turned his gaze back to her, where it hit her like a blow.

"Uh, I think it's at least a month." Didn't you have to miss a period, or something? She'd never been in a position to worry about it before. Her periods were as regular as tax bills. She hugged her robe about her. The mood had morphed from fevered excitement to worry and regret. "I guess I should get ready for work." Where she'd be sitting outside his office all day, knowing he was in there wishing he'd never met her and hoping and praying that she wasn't pregnant with his child.

The reality of the situation settled like a stone in her stomach.

"I'm sorry, Brooke." The pain in his blue eyes scratched a tiny hole in her soul. She wanted to say, "Don't worry about it," or something equally banal, but RJ's grim countenance made her keep her platitudes to herself. She turned and walked back to the bedroom, each footstep feeling like a mile. She managed to shower and climb into the clean suit she'd left there. Her eyes looked hollow as she brushed her teeth at RJ's sink. She'd been tiptoeing along, enjoying her romance with RJ and skirting all conflict for as long as she could. She'd finally hit that game board chute she'd worried about, and now she'd landed in a heap back at the bottom of the board, sitting on a pile of shattered dreams with an aching heart.

"Oh, Brooke, I won't say I told you so." Evie sat opposite Brooke on the sofa in her living room, sympathy in her big brown eyes and her freshly made martini sitting un-sipped in her hand. "But I had a feeling something like this would happen. I've never heard of anyone having an affair with the boss and going on to enjoy decades of happy marriage afterwards."

Brooke put her own martini down on the coffee table. Making it had been a welcome distraction, but she didn't have the heart to drink it. Besides, alcohol might make her more emotional, which was definitely not a good thing right now. And there was the possibility that she might be pregnant, which meant she shouldn't be drinking at all. "Trust me, I know! I never intended to have an affair with him. It just happened. I knew it wasn't a good idea from the moment we first kissed, but it was so…" She groped around her brain for words.

Perfect…magical…dreamy…wonderful…sensual… amazing…

She didn't feel like voicing any of those out loud right now.

"I've told you before that I see a pattern in your relationships." Evie drew her brows together slightly, the way she did when she was about to get serious.

"What relationships? I haven't had a date in over a year."

"Is it that long? Well, you did say you wanted to take a break. And I don't blame you, after the blond guy."

"Sam." Brooke grimaced slightly. "He seemed sweet at first."

"He seemed needy." Evie sipped her drink. "He was needy. I think that's why you were drawn to him. He wanted someone to tell all his problems to, a shoulder to cry on and someone to have lots of warm sympathy sex with."

Brooke chuckled. "Not lots of sex. Trust me."

"And that guy you dated in college, Ricky. He was seriously high maintenance. I'm not sure how you managed to attend your classes and hold a job while tending to his many needs."

"RJ's not needy. He's extremely capable, independent, brilliant...."

"And going through the biggest personal crisis of his life. At any other time he'd probably be a different person, but in the last few weeks he's been a strapping, muscular bag of needs, and you've been doing your best to meet them all."

"You are right about the strapping and muscular part." A tiny smile tugged at her lips. Then she wiped it away. "I was crazy about RJ for years. Long before all this latest drama. I can't believe I forgot all about contraception and gave him yet another thing to worry about. If only I could turn back the clock and—"

"Stop trying to save everybody."

"My desire to save everybody may be what makes me such a good executive assistant."

"Then stop doing it at work, too. I thought you wanted to move into management."

Brooke stared at her untouched martini. "I hope I still have a job to go to. If RJ gets tired of dating me he's not going to want to see my face every day."

"So, apply for another job before it happens. Didn't you say the HR lady thought you had potential for promotion?"

"I think she was just trying to let me down easy when I got passed over for the Events job. She did tell me to come back and try again, though. She almost hinted that RJ wasn't willing to give me up just yet."

"What?" Evie sat up. "Did you ask him about it?"

"No." Brooke sighed. "I never even told him I'd applied. I thought it would be awkward if I got rejected."

"You'd better believe he knew about it. His family owns the company." Evie raised a brow. "They'd better not try any funny business, especially if you're pregnant. Then you'll really need the job."

"I know." Brooke hugged herself. "I've heard pregnant women can't even get health insurance these days unless it's through an employer."

"Don't panic yet. You don't even know if you are pregnant." Evie leaned forwards and rested her chin on tented hands. "Would you marry him?"

Brooke shrank under her inquiring stare. "You mean if I was pregnant?"

"Yes, and he decided to be a gentleman and face up to his responsibilities."

Brooke pulled further back into her chair. "Not if it was an obligation for him." What a horrible thought.

That RJ might feel compelled to marry her out of duty. "I'd hate that."

Not that he'd seemed at all inclined to propose this morning. His grim expression still haunted her mind, and he'd managed to be out of the office most of the day in "meetings" that weren't on the calendar. They'd made no more after-work plans.

Maybe this was the end?

Perhaps he'd simply grow more distant and there'd be no more mention of kisses or weekends in the mountains. They'd go back to sharing memos and emails, rather than hugs and sly glances.

Her hands grew cold just thinking about it.

Or worse, maybe he'd want her out of sight. She might get transferred to a "crucial position" at the dockyard, or maybe even one of the overseas offices. She'd lose her job—and her health insurance—just when she needed them most.

"Don't look so grim." Evie tapped her hand, drawing her back into the present. "No one's died yet!"

"Except RJ's father."

Evie grimaced. "I forgot. Poor RJ, he really does have it coming at him from all angles. Do they still think his mom did it?"

"Apparently so. She's still being held without bail."

"I bet if you could spring her you'd make him the happiest man alive."

"I'd love to, but that would mean knowing who murdered his dad." She didn't want to admit, even to Evie, that she was the person responsible for his mom being arrested. "Apparently there's a paper log kept at the security desk of everyone who enters and leaves the building, but the page for that day is missing."

"The killer must have taken it."

"I'd imagine so." The killer had been in the building with her that night. She suppressed a shiver. "It's scary knowing there's someone out there who could kill Reginald Kincaid in cold blood."

"And no one knows why."

"That's the weirdest part. I know RJ has suspicions about Reginald's oldest son, Jack, who he left a huge stake in the company to. He keeps his distance from the rest of the family, almost as if he has something to hide."

"Sounds very guilty."

"But apparently Reginald knew, or at least suspected, that someone was out to get him. He wrote letters to all the family members, to be read in the event of his death. If he suspected his son Jack, why would he leave him almost half his company?"

"Maybe it was RJ?" Evie lifted a brow. Humor glittered in her eyes, which was enough to prevent Brooke getting upset.

"Yes, and maybe he'll kill me next so I won't sue him for sexual harassment. His brother Matthew actually warned him I might do that."

"Would you?" Evie's eyes widened.

"Never. It was utterly consensual so I'd be a real loser if I sued."

"Might be easier than winning the lottery, though."

"I'd rather take my chances with the Powerball."

"I notice how you deftly dodged my question about RJ being the murderer. Just for the sake of argument, he does have motive. Maybe he found out about his dad's second family and was so mad he wanted revenge?"

Brooke shook her head. "That's not his style. He's too smart to risk spending his life in prison, for one thing. And he really loved his dad. It's easy to see. He told me about all the time they spent together at their cabin in the woods, and how much he misses him every day." Her heart filled with emotion just thinking about the look in his eyes when he spoke of his father.

"Shame, because discovering he's a killer would really help you go off him if things turn sour."

"Maybe this crisis will help us grow together."

"See, there you go again, looking for troubled waters to pour oil on. You need to find a nice, uncomplicated guy without a care in the world," Evie said.

"Except that I'm in love with RJ." She said it aloud, needing to admit it to her best friend as well as herself. The word *love* gave her a rush as it sounded in the air of her condo. "I truly am."

"I can tell." Evie tilted her head and gave Brooke a sympathetic look. "Go on. Call him. You know you want to." She looked at Brooke's phone where it sat on the coffee table next to her keys.

A rush of adrenaline prickled Brooke's fingers and toes. Did she dare? Maybe he'd be thrilled to hear from her and tell her to come on over. Then they could spend the night making love in his big bed and share a sleepy breakfast in their robes before walking to work together.

She picked up the phone and dialed his number.

"Who?" RJ stood up violently from his chair and shoved his hand through his hair. Matt was in his office, along with Laurel and corporate investigator Nikki Thomas. Tall, with shoulder-length black hair and blunt bangs that framed intense blue eyes, Nikki had found the private investigator RJ had hired to look into the murder. Tony Ramos, a tall man with a shaved head and a way of making you feel he could read every thought in your head. "We all know someone saw Mom here on the night of the murder. She told me so herself, but who the hell was it and why won't anyone tell me?"

"Yeah, who was it?" Matt paced in front of the door. They were all on edge, as the D.A.'s office had just turned down their umpteenth request for bail.

"Brooke Nichols."

The name fell like a stone in the crowded office. All eyes swiveled to RJ.

"You're kidding me." He looked from Matt to Laurel. Everyone in the room seemed frozen to the spot. He felt his head begin to pound. "It couldn't be Brooke. She would have said something."

Laurel swallowed, and Matt looked down at the carpet.

"You got this information from the police?" Anger and confusion rose and snarled in his chest. His phone started vibrating in his pocket, and he reached in to turn it off.

Ramos nodded. "Yes. They interviewed all the employees the next day, and there were only five people in the building after seven that evening. Unfortunately security only had people sign in on a paper log, and—as we all know—it went missing. These are the people who admitted to being there, and Jimmy, the security guard who was on duty that night, said these are also the only people he remembers seeing. Alex Woods, the night shipping clerk, Reginald himself, his wife, Elizabeth, and Brooke Nichols."

RJ blew out a hard breath. Brooke, the person he trusted more than anyone else in the world, had kept this from him. "Why didn't she tell me?"

"Maybe because she was afraid you'd react like this?" Laurel raised a brow. "All she did was tell the truth, RJ. Would you have wanted her to lie?"

"None of the others saw Mom?"

"Jimmy says she waved hello. Nothing out of the ordinary. Apparently Brooke later told the investigating officer Mrs. Kincaid seemed anxious, or stressed."

"Dammit." RJ banged his fist on the desk. "Poor Mom stuck in that place with all those criminals because of a thoughtless comment. Brooke couldn't possibly suspect Mom."

"I'm sure she doesn't, RJ." Matt rubbed his eyes. "This situation is a giant quicksand swamp that everyone is getting sucked into. What we need is to find the real killer. Any news on that, Tony?"

"The police have eliminated all the other people who were here from their inquiries, and I admit I've done the same. The only possibility is an intruder no one saw."

"We have security on the desk 24/7," said RJ. "We're in a competitive business, and shipping containers can hold a lifetime's worth of trouble so we're ultra conscious of who comes and goes from this building and all our other facilities. Everyone has to come through the lobby. There's no other way into the building."

The investigator narrowed his sharp eyes. "I've checked all the windows and the former cargo doors that were sealed shut. The building is as tight as one of your container ships. The assailant could only have come through the lobby. He also must have removed the log page at some point. Jimmy says the only time the desk is left unattended is when he goes to the bathroom. He said he always bolts the lobby doors before leaving the desk, and he's sure he did so that night." Tony looked from Laurel to RJ. "But when he came back from the can and went to unlock the door, the bolt was pulled."

"So someone left the building while he was in the bathroom." Laurel's hand flew to her mouth. "And it wasn't Mom because Jimmy said she left much earlier."

"Exactly," Nikki chimed in. "The big snag is, other than Jimmy's word, there's no concrete proof of when she left the building, and even if there was proof, she came and left right around the time of the murder."

"When did Brooke leave?" RJ's gut churned. He hated that she was now involved in this mess. His fury at her deception was tempered by worry that she'd be somehow implicated.

"She left at the same time as your mother. They came down in the elevator together. Apparently Brooke got on the elevator as Mrs. Kincaid came down from visiting your dad's office."

"But Brooke isn't a suspect."

"Nope. Never was."

RJ felt a small wave of relief. Then his head started to ache again when he wondered why she'd never told him any of this. They'd been intimate in every way. He'd shared stories about his dad that he'd never told anyone, and she never mentioned that she'd said anything to the police. Her behavior was bizarre and troubling, especially since the subject had been discussed openly with her in the room, including at the family dinner. Why had she kept such crucial information from him?

And what if she was pregnant, right now, with his baby? Choosing to have a baby was a huge, lifetime responsibility that should grow from careful thought and planning, not spring from a steamy night of sex. The situation was further complicated by him being her boss. At this point, that was a nightmare. He couldn't keep a straight face while she walked in and out of his office with letters and files, acting like everything was completely normal and they'd never done more than hold hands.

"RJ, are you still with us?"

"What?" He realized Matt had been talking to him.

"Tony wants to know if he should talk to Brooke, hear exactly what she told the police."

"No. I'll talk to her myself." He'd avoided her all day, wary of the effect her big green eyes had on him, but there was no avoiding the conversation they needed to have right now.

He tried hard to tug his attention back to the reason for this meeting. "We need to find out more about the suspected intruder. Has the building been combed for fingerprints?"

Tony shrugged. "This office building is fifty years old. There are tens of thousands of fingerprints on every surface."

"Dad redecorated his office not long ago." Laurel spoke up. "And surely the killer was in there."

"The police went over the office during the initial investigation. I'll talk to them about our new theory of a separate intruder who hid in the building and see what they have." Tony typed something into his laptop.

"Jack Sinclair is still top of my list." RJ looked from Tony to Nikki. "And now apparently he's spreading the word that he plans to use his new shares to make changes in the company. Nikki, didn't you say his car was parked in a nearby lot on the night of the murder?"

"Uh, I'm not sure it was his car. The police are still looking into it."

"You can use your skills to dig into his corporate activities and see if he's been working to damage our company."

"I'm not sure why he'd do that when he's the biggest shareholder."

"Am I sensing reluctance?" RJ frowned at her. Why did she keep finding excuses not to dig up dirt on Jack?

Nikki blinked and tucked a neat lock of black hair behind her ear. "Of course not. I'll look into the situation from all my usual angles. I'll report back as soon as I find anything."

RJ nodded. "And I'll talk to Brooke and see if she remembers anything else about that night." If he knew she was there he'd have asked her earlier. Even the tiniest shred of evidence in the right direction could get his mom out of jail, which was the most important thing right now.

More important than his affair with Brooke. When he was with Brooke, everything else faded into the background. He forgot about his responsibilities and worries. He needed to pull off the rose-tinted glasses and find out exactly what was going on in that sharp mind of hers. How could she have been so thoughtless?

When the others had left his office he pulled out his

phone and saw the call he missed was from Brooke. He pressed the button to return the call, and as soon as she picked up he said, "I'm coming over."

Nine

No amount of sun salutations could calm Brooke down after RJ's brusque phone call. He'd told her he'd be there in twenty minutes, then hung up. She rolled up her yoga mat and put it in the closet, then commenced to wiping down her kitchen countertops—again—like someone with obsessive-compulsive disorder.

She jumped a good few inches when she heard a loud knock on the door.

"Coming." She tried to steady her breathing as she pulled the latch.

RJ's fierce blue gaze hit her like a blast of icy air. He walked into the room, as tall and erect as a statue.

She closed the door. *Hi, RJ. How are you doing? Did you have a good day?* Normal pleasantries stuck in her throat.

"You told the police you saw my mother on the night

of the murder." He spoke quietly, but his voice held an edge of steel.

"Yes, I did." She managed to keep her voice from shaking. "I never suspected her, but I did see her as I was leaving, and when they asked me, I simply told them."

"Your testimony is the reason she's being held without bail. You're the reason they consider her a suspect."

She felt herself shrink under his gaze. "All I said was that she was in the elevator when it stopped on our floor, carrying a large bag."

"With dinner for my dad."

"I didn't know what was in the bag."

"You said she seemed…distressed." His eyes narrowed. She fought the urge to step back, away from the force of his fury.

"She had tears in her eyes, or the beginning of tears. And she looked anxious. I think that's what I said. It's hard to remember, it was weeks ago." She felt tears rise in her own eyes. "I never imagined they'd arrest her."

"You knew the police were investigating a murder and looking for suspects." His gaze bored into her.

"Yes." She swallowed. "All I did was tell them the truth."

"Why didn't you say anything to me? We've all been wondering why they're holding Mom without bail, and it's because of your testimony."

"Why?" She blinked back the tears that still threatened. "I suppose I knew you'd be angry."

His eyes flashed with a mix of anger and confusion. "I'm not angry that you spoke the truth, but for you to keep it secret all this time, while we were together and so intimate." He shook his head. "I don't understand it and it makes me feel like I don't know you, Brooke."

She took a step back, shrinking under the force of his stare. "I'm truly sorry I didn't say anything. I wanted to but the time never seemed right and then it was weird that I hadn't already told you." She hadn't wanted to mess up their budding romance. That seemed to have gone right down the toilet. She'd better hope nothing resulted from their little mistake last night. A thick, heavy sadness descended over her.

"Why didn't you tell me my mom looked upset? Don't you think I'd want to know?"

"I didn't see you until the next day when we all arrived to the news that your dad was dead. I never got a chance to talk to you in private until after the police interviewed me." She shivered slightly, remembering that terrible day. Yellow crime scene tape in Reginald's office, swarms of investigators everywhere, press jamming the doorway to the building.

"So you were one of the last people in the building before the murder."

She nodded. "I wish I could be more help in finding out who did it."

"Maybe you can." He rubbed his temples. "Did you notice anything unusual?"

She hesitated. "Your mother being there was unusual. I don't remember her bringing him dinner too often."

His eyes narrowed. "You do suspect her, don't you?"

"No, I'm just answering your question." She lifted her chin. She'd tried to do the right thing. It didn't occur to her at the time that her few words would lead to an arrest.

"She said she and Dad had an argument the night before, and he left for work in a mood, then called saying he'd be working late, so she decided to soften him up by bringing his favorite roast beef and potatoes." RJ crossed his arms. "Not exactly suspicious."

Brooke kept her mouth closed. She could see why the police were suspicious, especially given all the information about Reginald's infidelity that came to light after his death. She hadn't known about any of that when she spoke to the police.

The corner lamp in her living room threw RJ's strong features into high relief. Why did he have to be so handsome? Her life would be so much easier if her boss was a balding, middle-aged guy with a potbelly. Even now, with tension hardening the lines of his face and darkening his blue eyes, he was stunning. And the way he leaped in to defend his mom only showed what a loyal family man he was.

Her heart ached. "I so wish I'd seen someone else, or noticed anything strange. I've gone over that evening so many times in my head, but it was just a regular day in so many ways, until we discovered what happened."

"My dad was murdered within minutes of you leaving. The killer must have been in the building."

"What does your mom say? Did she see anyone?"

He shook his head. "No one. She said she went to Dad's office and the door was closed, so she knocked. He didn't answer, so she opened the door and he was sitting at his desk. He told her to go away."

"What?" She'd never heard Reginald speak that way to anyone.

"Yup. Nice, huh? She was totally shocked. She told him she brought dinner and he said he didn't want any and for her to go home, now. She said he almost growled it at her."

"That's terrible."

"And that's her last memory of my dad. Now she's in jail for killing him. And you just *forgot* to tell me you shared the elevator with her that night."

She lowered her eyes. "I'm so sorry, RJ."

"We need to take a break from each other. I'd like you to take a paid leave of absence, starting immediately." She glanced up, to see his brows lowered in a frown. "In fact, I'll double your pay if you'll stay home until things clear up around here."

Brooke's knees went weak. Did this mean she was fired? She'd already figured out that her relationship with RJ was over.

"Tasha can take over your duties in the meantime. If there's anything personal at the office, I'll have her send it here."

She felt like she'd been slapped. RJ's pained expression tugged at her heart and she wanted to reach out to him and say she never meant to hurt his mom, but he wanted her to vanish.

"I'll get my laptop. Tasha will need it." Her voice barely rose above a whisper. She tried her best to keep tears out of her voice. She moved to her work bag, which was near the kitchen table, and fished out her laptop. Her hand trembled as she handed it to RJ. Her fingers brushed his thumb as he took it from her and she steeled herself against the jolt of energy that passed between them.

Last night she'd lain in his bed. Tonight she'd sleep here alone.

RJ was already at the door. "Your increased pay will

be wired directly into your account. You will not return to work until further notice." He avoided her gaze. He hesitated with his hand on the door handle. "But if you learn of anything…unexpected…"

Her mind flew to his reaction this morning when he realized they forgot to use a condom.

"I'll call you if anything important happens." Her voice sounded so tiny, like it was coming from far away.

RJ turned one time to look at her, eyes hooded and face set in a hard line, then he tugged open the door, stepped out and closed it firmly behind him.

Brooke collapsed onto the sofa, and the tears flowed like summer rain. This beat all the bad outcomes she'd imagined for their relationship. Obviously she hadn't been creative enough in imagining how things could go wrong. He'd literally ordered her to keep away from him, and was paying her twice her salary to stay out of his sight.

She hugged herself, suddenly cold. If only she'd told him sooner about her encounter with his mother. He might still have been annoyed that she told the police, but he could hardly blame her. Her secrecy, however— born of cowardice—was inexcusable. She knew that. His anger was justified, and seared her like a hot brand.

RJ slammed the door of his Porsche and fired up the engine. His entire body was on fire with rage and hurt. Brooke had been his port in this crazy ongoing tempest, and all the time he'd held her, and lain with her and kissed her, she'd neglected to tell him that she had identified his mom at the scene of his father's murder.

You really couldn't ever know people. His father's

untimely passing and the wake of chaos it left behind should have hammered that home. Everyone had secrets that grew and tangled like briars, snaring them in a web of deception.

He roared through the streets, wishing he could drive fast enough to blow right out of this dimension into another life where none of this was happening.

He wanted to go visit his mom, but he hadn't obtained special permission to see her in person and the thought of talking to her via a video monitor made his chest hurt. It was past visiting hours anyway.

He swung into the underground parking of his building and pulled into his space. For a moment he rested his head and hands on the wheel. How could he face going back to his empty apartment when only last night he and Brooke had shared such a joyful night? At least until he realized how his foolish mistake could have ruined everything. The last thing any of them needed at a time like this was an unexpected pregnancy.

He hauled himself out of the car and took the elevator up to his apartment. As expected the large space seemed chill and empty. He'd barely even been there without Brooke for the last couple of weeks. They'd grown so used to each other's company that it seemed stranger for them to be apart than together.

The answering machine light flashed green, so he walked over and pressed the button. "RJ, it's Lily. Mom's been released! The lobby door being unbolted from the inside late at night was enough to make her eligible for bail. She's on her way home right now. Come over and join us for a celebration."

"Yes!" RJ did a fist pump. "About time." He picked up the phone and dialed Lily. "I'll be right there."

Glad to leave the lonely space of his apartment, he almost ran back to the elevator. It was as quick to walk to the family mansion as to drive, so he set off along Charleston's familiar streets with renewed vigor. Despite everything that had happened with Brooke, his heart soared with relief that his mom was out of that grim place, back in her beloved home.

Her body felt frail and thin when he hugged her in the front hallway of her house. "I'm desperate to style my hair." She patted her dark hair self-consciously. "My gray roots were previously a secret between my hairdresser and myself. I'll have to see if he can squeeze me in first thing tomorrow." Her soft, old-Charleston lilt was music to his ears.

"I can see you have your priorities straight, Mom." Kara squeezed her again. They all crowded around her in the big family room, crackling with excited energy. "You need a lavish dinner after all that jailhouse food."

"I think I'll make my fortune by writing a book called *The Prison Diet.*" She glanced down at her shrunken frame. "I thought I was slender before, but apparently there was plenty of room for improvement if you believe the old saying you can never be too rich or too thin."

"I'm glad your sense of humor survived intact," said RJ. "We Kincaids take some serious lickings."

"Where's Brooke? I heard she came for dinner on Sunday." His mom's sharp green eyes met his.

He hesitated. His mom didn't need to hear any bad news. "She's at home."

"Why don't you invite her to join us?"

RJ glanced at Matt. He knew, as did the others, that Brooke had kept her words with the police secret. Part of him yearned to pick up the phone and invite her back into their lives, but some cooler, more practical instinct told him to maintain distance. "I think it's better if we enjoy your newfound freedom as a family." He didn't comment on the fact that Susannah and Lily and Laurel's fiancés had joined them. He wasn't engaged to Brooke, after all.

"I hope my newfound freedom is permanent. And you all better hope I don't skip out on the two million dollars bail they made you post."

"Cheap at the price, Mom." Matt kissed her slim cheek.

Kara handed Elizabeth a glass of champagne she'd poured. "And if you skip you'd better take us with you. I don't think any of us could stand that kind of separation again."

"Much as I hate everything that's happened to our family in the last few months, there's no denying it's brought us closer than ever." Laurel sat on the sofa next to Eli.

"And now you guys can really start planning your wedding." Kara's eyes lit up. "Mom, Laurel wouldn't even look at invitations until you were released."

"Oh, I think we need some time for things to settle, don't we?" Laurel looked at Eli.

"Sure, yes. A lot going on right now." He patted her hand in a reassuring way. "We have the rest of our lives to plan our wedding."

"Of course you do." Elizabeth Kincaid smiled at the handsome pair. "No sense rushing into marriage. It's a big commitment and sometimes involves a good deal of sacrifice."

RJ could understand Laurel's reluctance to launch into marriage. Especially now they knew their parents' marriage wasn't quite the rosy union they'd grown up imagining.

"Mom." Lily leaned forward. "Did you really know about Dad's second family?"

She hesitated for a moment, then nodded. "Not all the time. Just the last couple of years. I didn't see any reason to burden the rest of you with the news."

"It wasn't right for you to bear it alone." Lily stroked their mom's arm.

"Maybe that's the only way I could bear it." She shrugged her shoulders. "It's a lot harder now the secret's out, and when anyone looks at me I wonder if that's what they're thinking about. Have those two boys been causing any trouble?"

"Jack's stayed out of the picture." RJ frowned at the very thought of Reginald's true oldest son. "So who knows what he's up to. If you ask me he's responsible for the murder. I still can't believe Dad gave him a controlling share of the company." He shook his head and blew out a disgusted breath.

"Alan's been lovely, though," Kara chimed in. "He's really quite sweet. I know he was devastated to hear that you'd been arrested, and he's been very supportive. He seems quite keen to become part of the family, even though he's not related by blood."

"Well, perhaps that's something good to come out of this mess. We Kincaids can always stretch to welcome a new family member." His mom's smile warmed RJ's heart. "And what a relief it is to be back in my own home, surrounded by all of you."

They took champagne glasses from a tray and raised a toast. Still, despite the bubbly and festive mood, a cold sorrow settled in RJ's gut. Brooke should be here. He still resented that she hadn't told him about her talk with the police, but she'd woven herself tightly into the fabric of his life and his arms now felt empty without her in them. He missed her with a painful ache he'd never known before. Was this love? If so it wasn't exactly a happy feeling.

"You okay, RJ?" Laurel nudged him. "You look a bit dazed."

"Overwhelmed, I guess." He took a bracing swig of champagne. "I'll be fine." Already he regretted driving Brooke away in such a cold and cruel manner. Paying her to stay away from him? His shock and anger had gotten the better of him.

And what if she was pregnant? For a single, mad instant, he had a vision of Brooke gazing, with her kind, loving expression, at their baby.

He took another swig. Everything was moving so fast and he didn't know where he'd be from one day to the next. Jack could take over the company and boot him out. The last thing he needed was to establish some kind of permanent relationship. He'd better keep his options open and his feet ready to dodge bullets.

Still, he had to apologize to her.

"Dinner's ready!" Pamela opened the door bearing a steaming dish of food. "Come into the dining room. I set the table already."

The apology would have to wait. He was needed

here for now. RJ followed the others into the elegant dining room, where the silver cloche opened to reveal their mom's favorite roast lamb and potatoes au gratin. Matt poured wine and they settled down to enjoy their first real family dinner since the arrest.

"Okay, let me get this straight." Evie's voice emerged from Brooke's phone, set on speakerphone so she could pace around her living room. "Since I was at your house—oh, two hours ago—and you were telling me you loved RJ, he's now dumped you and fired you."

Brooke inhaled an unsteady breath. She'd already cried once; surely she could keep the tears in for now. "That's pretty much it. I'm not technically fired. I'm on paid leave. In fact he was so keen to get rid of me that he's paying me more to stay home than I'd get to come to the office. He's furious with me."

"All because you neglected to mention that you shopped his mom to the cops."

"Evie! Are you my friend?"

"I'm teasing. You didn't tell him because you thought he'd dump you and fire you. Apparently you were right." She could tell Evie found this slightly funny. "I'm thinking he's not quite so fabulous as you originally told me."

"He's a very passionate, proud family man. He was raised to be head of the Kincaid family, and they come first. I admire that."

"Even when it means you come last?"

Brooke bit her lip hard. "I wish the two weren't mutually exclusive. If I could figure out a way to get his mom out of jail, he might forgive me."

"Elizabeth Kincaid is out of jail!" Evie's voice boomed out of the tiny phone. "I saw it on the news not fifteen minutes ago. She's been granted bail."

"She's out?" RJ hadn't told her. Then again, why would he? He didn't want anything to do with her. Her heart crumpled.

"They showed a video of her leaving the jail. She's one of those people who manages to look like a society matron even in that situation, polite smile at the cameras, and all that."

"That is good news." She shoved a hand through her hair. "RJ must be thrilled. I wonder if they know who the real killer is." If his mom was truly freed, he might not be so angry with her anymore.

"From what you said, it sounds like you and Elizabeth Kincaid were there right at the time the murder was committed. Did you see or hear anything odd?"

"The building was pretty much empty. But apparently the intruder hid somewhere after the murder and crept out when the guard was in the bathroom."

"So they probably snuck in well before the murder. Were there any unfamiliar people around the office?"

"I didn't notice any but it was a very crazy day. There were at least three big meetings, one of them offsite at the architects. I had a terrible time struggling back with all those blueprints." A thought struck her. She stopped pacing and stood still in the center of the room. An entire, fully formed memory sprang into her head. "My God, the blueprints. I brought them to talk with RJ about the plans for the new retail development on the waterfront. RJ went off to a meeting and I came back to the office with armfuls of blueprints. It was right before closing and pouring rain and I ran from the car park to the front door, trying not to get them wet, but I couldn't get into the revolving door."

Suddenly the whole scene was crystal clear in her mind. The fish smell of the rainstorm, her face and hair wet in the heavy shower, big drops splashing on the crucial blueprints.

And a man in a raincoat, who took half of the blueprints, opened the revolving door for her, and stepped in with her.

They'd emerged on the other side and she'd thanked him profusely as he handed back the rest of the tall cylinders of paper, then they'd walked to the bank of elevators. He didn't get in with her, and that was the last she saw of him.

But he hadn't stopped to sign in at the security desk.

"Brooke, have you been struck dumb?"

"The man, who came through the door with me. He was quite tall, but not quite as tall as RJ." Why did her thoughts spring so readily back to him? "He wore one of those felt hats, you know, the Indiana Jones kind."

"I call those jerk hats, because that's the kind of person who usually wears them. In fact my last boyfriend before—"

"Evie! This is important. His hat was dripping from the rain, and he had little round glasses, the kind with the metal rim, thick lenses, so you could barely see his eyes."

"What about his features. Did you recognize him?"

"No. He had a beard and moustache. Damn, I can't remember the color. Gray, maybe? He was an older guy. And he had a Boston accent, I remember it. You know the kind. *I pahked the cahr in Hahrvad Yahd.*"

Evie laughed aloud. "He sounds very suspicious."

"He didn't stand out much at the time. The coat and hat kind of fit, with the rain. It was so wet, and dark, one of those intense, stormy days. Besides, we get quite a few characters at the office, especially since we've branched into real estate. You wouldn't believe the kind of people who just happened to own a derelict dock in North Jersey."

"Or Massachusetts."

"Exactly. I didn't really think anything of it, but since it was five everyone was leaving, security was in the middle of a shift change and he was with me so he breezed by the security desk without anyone stopping him."

"When he wasn't actually with you."

"No. Not at all."

"He could have been waiting for that opportunity."

"I suppose so." A tingle of anticipation—or was it fear—shot up Brooke's spine. "I think this is important."

"You should call RJ and tell him."

For a moment her fingers itched to hang up on Evie and dial RJ immediately. Then an awful thought occurred to her. "Do you think RJ will be happy to hear I let the killer into the building?" If anything, this made things worse.

"Since he's mad at you already, what's the harm?"

Brooke hugged herself, and stared out the window onto the dark street. "I think I should call and tell the police. I can't believe I never thought of this when I first spoke to them. Then again, maybe this guy had a reason to be there? Perhaps he's not relevant at all."

"Or maybe you've just helped to identify Reginald Kincaid's murderer. RJ will be over the moon that you've cleared his mother of all suspicion, and he'll run right over there and ask you to marry him."

Bright moonlight fell at an angle on the cars parked outside, casting long, sharp daggers of light that fell through her window and across her carpet. "I doubt it."

Ten

"Where's Brooke?" Matt appeared in RJ's office doorway, then cast a glance back at Brooke's empty desk.

RJ shoved a hand through his hair. His chest ached and his head hurt. "On a leave of absence." He said it coolly, hoping Matt would drop the subject.

"Is she sick?" His brother looked worried.

"Nope. I just thought it better if she was home for a while. Things were getting too complicated."

Matt cocked his head. "Don't say I didn't warn you."

RJ stood up from his chair and stretched. Or tried to. Every muscle in his body was tight as a bowstring. He felt Brooke's absence like a missing limb. The office seemed dark and empty without her sunny presence. "I didn't plan it. What a cliché, to have an affair with my assistant. I lost my mind."

And then I lost my heart. He cursed the unwanted

thought that sprang into his brain. Another cliché. Mom read him too much poetry when he was a kid.

Matt moved in and closed the door. "Is she making threats?"

"God, no."

"You're angry she didn't tell you she saw Mom on the night of the murder."

"I was angry. I'm still confused by it. And there's something else." Adrenaline pulsed through him. He picked up a paperweight on his desk and studied it in the light. A tiny model ship trapped in glass, sailing nowhere.

Matt raised a brow. "Care to tell me?"

"I forgot to use a condom."

His brother's eyes widened. "You think she's pregnant?"

"No idea yet, but she could be. Can you see how things were getting complicated?" His heart squeezed. Was Brooke sitting somewhere alone and worried? He cursed the violent urge to take her in his arms and comfort her.

"What a mess. Still, it's not nice to banish her when she's worrying about it, too. She didn't mean to get mom into trouble."

"We needed some space. Things were too intense." At least that's how he tried to explain the strange commotion of feelings that left him unsettled and edgy.

"You miss her, don't you?"

RJ placed the paperweight back on the desk with a thud. "I don't know how I feel. Too much happening all at once."

"I know the feeling." Matt grinned. "It all came

thick and fast between me and Susannah. I think you should go with your gut instincts."

"I'm not sure I have any." His gut was in turmoil right now, maybe because he couldn't face breakfast. Or because he couldn't face a day without Brooke in it. "Besides, we have work to do. To make Jack Sinclair richer." He attempted a wry grin.

Matt crossed his arms. "Don't change the subject."

"Why not? Isn't that what we're doing here? You'd think Jack would be here himself pitching in, since he owns forty-five percent of the company. And what's with Nikki stalling on digging into his books?" Phew. He'd managed to get off the topic of Brooke.

Matt shrugged. "I don't think she suspects him of murder as much as you do."

"Me? What about you?"

"I barely know the guy. Too soon to draw any conclusions. Things aren't always what they seem. Besides, I heard from Tony that the police have new eyewitness testimony about a strange man in the building on the day of the murder."

He sat up. "That's great. Details?"

"An older guy in a trilby, with a Boston accent." Matt shrugged. "I can't think of any clients with Boston accents, can you?"

RJ shook his head. "No, but this is great news. I'm going to call Tony for the full scoop. Hopefully they'll drop all charges against Mom and we can put that ugly chapter behind us."

"Brooke is the new eyewitness. Apparently she called the police last night after remembering the man."

RJ froze. Could Brooke have made this new suspect up? For a moment he cursed himself for the disloyal thought. But he didn't trust Brooke anymore. The realization hit him like a fist to the gut.

"Why the grim expression?" Matt shrugged off his jacket and threw it over his arm.

"Seems very convenient that she suddenly remembers a mysterious intruder, right after everyone's angry with her for surreptitiously fingering Mom."

Matt stepped forward and clapped his hand on RJ's upper arm. "Bro, you're all on edge, but Brooke is not the type to lie. That's why she told the police the truth in the first place. We've both worked with her long enough to know it."

Emotion gripped his chest like a nutcracker. He knew Matt was right. "She never did lie, she just didn't tell me the whole truth." He rubbed his forehead. "Because she was afraid the truth would upset me. If anything, it's my fault she kept silent." He blew out a hard breath. "I owe her an apology." His neurons fired with energy, spurring him forward. "I'm going over to her house."

Matt grinned. "Glad to hear it. I hope she'll forgive you for overreacting."

RJ grabbed his jacket off the back of the chair and pulled it on. "Me, too."

Brooke didn't know what to do. It was midmorning and usually she'd have sorted through a ream of mail and coordinated several schedules and possibly attended a meeting or two. This morning all she'd done was drink a cup of coffee (decaf in case she was pregnant), do some halfhearted yoga poses and dust her bookshelves. She'd be wise to start looking for another job, but she didn't have the heart.

She let out a long sigh and poured the dregs of her coffee into the kitchen sink. She felt like someone had taken a hunting knife to her chest and cut her heart right out of it. All the excitement and happiness of yesterday had crashed and burned so fast she was still too numb to even react properly. She knew pain was coming but right now she was still too shocked and dazed for it to touch her.

How quickly RJ had gone from cherishing her to despising her. He must have never really cared about her in the first place. A sharp pang of disappointment stung her. She still cared about him. She should be angry with him for dismissing her so harshly, but she couldn't blame him. He was under stress and his family came first. She knew both those things before they got involved.

It was her own stupid fault she wasn't brave enough to tell the truth about seeing his mom there that evening and telling the police. Now he'd learn that she let the killer into the building, which was hardly likely to help him forgive her.

She brought her empty coffee cup down on the sideboard with a light thunk. What a mess. Still, time to get dressed. No sense spending the day moping around in her pajamas. If she was pregnant she'd need to be strong for her child, and she might as well start now, just in case.

She'd turned on the shower and started to take off her PJs when the doorbell rang. She frowned. The mail had already been delivered and no one could expect her home at this time. She pulled her T-shirt back down again, turned off the water. Maybe it was the police. She'd spoken to a detective at the station yesterday and they said they might want to speak to her again. She grabbed a robe off the back of the door and slid her arms into it. She couldn't face those flint-eyed officers in her heart-print shorts and top.

As she slid back the chain and undid the lock she couldn't stop a massive, painful flash of hope that it might be RJ on the other side. This in no way diminished her surprise when she opened the door to his tall, imposing presence on her doorstep, dressed in a dark suit.

"May I come in?" His deep voice barely penetrated her shock. She hadn't said a word.

Her pulse now pounded hard and fast. "Yes." She stepped aside and he walked in. Didn't try to kiss her. Didn't shake hands. Still, a rush of energy crashed through her as his body passed within inches of hers.

She closed the door behind him and turned to face him, still no idea what to say. Why was he here?

His bold blue eyes met hers. "I've missed you."

"I've missed you, too." The words fell from her mouth. So much for playing it cool. "Very much." She bit her lip to stop more confessions pouring forth.

"I've come to apologize." His eyes darkened. Brooke held her breath. "Banishing you from the office was out of line. I've been on edge, upset about my mom being in jail. I overreacted to hearing that you were the eyewitness." Morning light shone through the window onto his hard profile.

"I should have told you it was me. I kept trying to pluck up the courage to tell you, but I was so afraid you'd be angry, and I only made it worse."

His expression softened. "My behavior proved you were right. I flew off the handle and it was inappropriate." He hesitated. The air thickened with tension and anticipation until Brooke felt faint. "I'm sorry."

Sorry. Her heart sank. What had she hoped for? He was sorry. For sending her home. For sleeping with her without a condom. For sleeping with her at all. For kissing her. For ever hiring her in the first place…

Her head hurt and she fought to keep herself from shaking, as RJ's tall presence filled her living room.

"Brooke." He stepped forward, and again, pathetic hope rushed through her like a burst water main. He took her hands. Her fingers tingled and heated inside his. "All these years we worked together, sitting in meetings and discussing correspondence and spending all day with each other." She held herself steady. "And all along I never realized I was working side by side with the perfect woman for me."

She blinked. The perfect woman for him? Her tongue seemed stuck in her mouth. Surely she should say something here, but no words rose from her confused and anxious brain.

"I love you, Brooke." His voice deepened as he said the words, and something dark and powerful flashed in his eyes. "I've felt empty and hollow every second I've been without you. All I could think about is coming to see you, to hold you in my arms, and beg you to forgive my cruel behavior. When I thought I might have made you pregnant I panicked about making our lives more complicated than they already are."

He hesitated, frowned slightly, and looked away. Brooke's stomach turned over. Doubts crept back into her mind. Maybe he was just here trying to "do the right thing" in case she was pregnant. Her hands grew cold inside the cocoon of his fingers.

"Brooke, I want to marry you." His eyes met hers again, with a jolt. "I want to have children with you. I want to spend the rest of my life with you." His words, spoken fast and gruff, wrapped around her and swirled through her mind. Did she imagine them? Was this some kind of crazy dream or delusion? It couldn't possibly be happening, right here in her living room, on an ordinary weekday morning.

Could it?

"Brooke, are you okay?"

"I…I don't know." She searched his face. His strong features were taut with emotion. "What did you say?" Her ears must be deceiving her.

One of his dimples appeared. "I said I want to marry you." His eyes twinkled. "You, Brooke Nichols, and me, RJ Kincaid, getting married."

She drew in a ragged breath. He wanted to marry her? Her heart soared, then her excitement screeched to a halt again. Better clear the air. "Is this because I might be pregnant?"

"Not in the least. I want to live the rest of my life with you, for better or for worse. For richer for poorer. All that stuff. How does that sound?"

"It sounds…good." Joy sparkled over her. What an insane roller coaster her life had been lately. Suddenly she'd shot up the ladder to the top of the game board again, and could hear party whistles and see streamers as she approached the final square. Images of her and RJ, walking down a church aisle hand in hand, flooded her mind. "Really good."

Then something hit her like an icy thunderbolt.

RJ didn't know that she had likely let his father's

killer into the building. That she was, in some way, responsible for his dad's death.

Her joy drained away.

"What's the matter? You've turned pale." RJ's dimples disappeared again.

"You don't know, do you?"

"Know what?"

She swallowed. Her hands tightened into cold fists inside his grasp. "I let the killer into the building."

RJ dropped her hands as if they burned. "What are you talking about?"

Pain trickled through her as his expression darkened. She inhaled a shaky breath. "I remembered, when I thought hard, that a strange man came through the revolving doors with me. I didn't think anything of it at the time, since I didn't know him. There's no record of him and no one knows who he is. In all likelihood he went to hide somewhere, and then…" She gulped. "Shot your dad later that night."

She looked down at the floor, not wanting to see RJ's appalled expression.

"Matt told me you'd seen someone and that you spoke to the police again." His voice was strangely hollow. "He didn't say you opened the door for him."

"He was just another person hurrying into the building on a stormy afternoon. It was right at the end of the day. I didn't really even register him at the time." Tears rose inside her. "I'm so, so sorry." She looked up, to find RJ's eyes filled with pain.

But instead of striding away, he stepped toward her and took her in his arms. "I know you'd never do anything to hurt my family, or the company." His warmth enveloped her, and the stirring male scent of him soothed her ragged nerves. "We all know that." He pulled away from her long enough to look her in the eye. "No one blames you for Dad's death. The good part is now we have a real suspect and the police can go after him." She shuddered as he buried his face in her neck and his breath heated her skin. "And I can't even tell you how much I've missed you." His words swirled around her, spoken with gruff passion.

"I've missed you, too." Her voice sounded so small. Her heart filled so fast with all the hope and love she'd locked away in the last day, thinking she'd never need it again. He'd told her he loved her! "I love you, RJ. A part of me has loved you for years, but since we became close…" Words failed her, which didn't matter because RJ's mouth covered hers in a heady kiss.

He pulled her tight against his muscled chest and she sank into his strength. When their lips parted, she felt his chest fill with a mighty breath. "God, Brooke, I couldn't stand my life without you in it. Can you ever forgive me for being such a jerk?"

His wry expression almost made her laugh. "You were under stress. You're still under stress."

"We all are, but that's no excuse for the way I behaved. I'll do anything in my power to make it up to you." His face hovered close to hers, kissing and nuzzling her, stirring sparks of arousal that mingled with her joy to create an electric atmosphere.

"I don't want anything from you." She stroked his hair, and relished the rough feel of his hard cheek against hers. "I just want you."

RJ's ragged breath revealed the depth of his emotion. "And I just want you. Will you, Brooke? Will you marry me?"

"Yes." The tiny voice emerged from somewhere deep inside her. Somewhere hope had survived during all the drama and upset of the last few weeks. "I will."

They held each other tight, half-afraid some fresh drama would fly in through the window to blow them apart again. They stayed silent for some time, then RJ spoke. "It's okay if you're pregnant. In fact, it's more than okay." He pulled back far enough to meet her eyes. "Once again I overreacted and lost sight of the big picture. I'd love to have a child with you, Brooke."

Her chest tightened, or was it her heart that swelled even further? "Me, too." She smiled. "Though there's an excellent chance that I'm not pregnant, so don't get too excited. I wasn't at the right place in my cycle."

"Then we'll just have to try again." Hope sparkled in his eyes. "Because I see us having a big family."

Brooke swallowed. She'd always dreamed of a house filled with children, so unlike her solitary childhood. "I'd love to have a big family, like yours."

"Then we'll need a big house. Maybe a historic one near downtown? Or would you prefer something out in the suburbs?"

"I love downtown. It's nice to be able to walk to the shops, and restaurants. And work." She froze. Work. Would they keep working together after they were married, or would that be too weird?

RJ raised a brow. "Are you thinking what I'm thinking?"

"I'm not quite telepathic enough to know. But I was wondering if I'm still banished from the office."

"Definitely not. But I think you should move into your own office. You've done enough time manning the desk outside mine. I think it's time you're promoted to management."

Brooke blinked. So he had remembered their conversation where she'd shared her career goals? The subject hadn't come up again so she'd tried to forget about it. "I'd love that. I'm happy to work at The Kincaid Group in any capacity, but I'd like to stretch myself and develop new skills that can help the company."

RJ laughed. "Hey, you're not on a job interview. I already know you're an organizational genius. And if things go south with Jack Sinclair running the show, maybe we can start our own company together."

She smiled. "That might be fun."

"I think anything we do together will be fun, as long as we can keep our perspective, and I promise I've learned a lot about myself over the last day or so." He took a deep breath. "From now on I'll put our relationship first and everything else second. Or even third." His dimples appeared. "Or fourth."

A sudden thought clouded Brooke's happiness. "What will your mom think about us?"

"She'll be thrilled." He stroked her cheek. "I couldn't understand why no one, including her, would tell me who the eyewitness was. Later I realized she didn't want me to know it was you. She really likes you. She asked about you several times during dinner last night."

"She doesn't mind that I'm not from local aristocracy?" She couldn't help voicing the worry that had nagged at her from the first time RJ asked her out.

"Not at all. Mom judges people on their own merits, not the arcane rules of the society she was born into.

That's why she married my dad, even though a lot of the local snobs thought him beneath her."

"I don't think I'll ever understand the rules of Charleston society."

"Don't waste time trying, because they don't make any sense." He kissed her on the nose, which brought a smile to her lips. "We'll make our own rules to live by."

Their mouths met in a kiss that melted the tension in her body and replaced it with a flush of pleasure. RJ's arms enclosed her in their protective circle. Everything they'd been through hadn't torn them apart forever, but had pulled them closer together.

"Rule number one," she breathed, when they finally parted lips for a few moments. "No shoving me off on paid leave when I get on your nerves."

RJ winced. "I made a real ass of myself. If you can't ever forgive me for that, I can understand."

"I'll let you off just this one time." She dotted a kiss on the end of his nose. "Since you're devastatingly handsome." The sheepish look in his slate blue eyes made her smile.

"That's quite a compliment coming from the loveliest woman in Charleston."

"Flatterer."

"It's all true. Best figure, too." He squeezed her rear. "And since I seem to have talked my way back from the brink of disaster, I hope I'll be sharing a bed with it tonight." He grew still and his gaze darkened. "You did say you'd marry me, didn't you?"

Brooke chewed her lip and pretended to look confused. "Did I?"

"I think you did but it might have been wishful thinking."

She shrugged her shoulders. Arousal trickled through her like hot liquid. "It's been a confusing time, lately. Maybe we should stop talking and just go to bed right now."

RJ's dimples appeared. "That's the best idea I've heard in a long time."

* * * * *

Turn the page for an exclusive short story

By USA TODAY bestselling author
Day Leclaire.

THE KINCAIDS: JACK AND NIKKI, PART 3
Day Leclaire

Morning came, streaks of blushing red, glittering amber and a deep bruising purple. It gave an incredible punctuation mark to what had been another amazing night and offered a joyous wakeup kiss to what Nikki Thomas hoped would be an equally amazing day.

She stood on the deck of Jack Sinclair's beach house, a place she'd frequently stood since that morning after they'd first made love. Of course, the term "beach house" seemed such a ridiculous description for such an elegant, stylish home. Beach mansion came closer to describing it. She rested her forearms on the salt-treated wooden railing and stared out at the ball of fire heaving itself from greenish-blue water. Breakers curled in long, uniform sets, rolling toward shore, and she drew in a deep breath of fragrant, salt-laden air, filled with the wealth of springtime promise.

Had she ever experienced anything more idyllic? A

pair of strong, masculine arms slid around her, pulling her against a broad, naked chest, as powerful and indomitable as the ocean stretching toward the horizon. She released a sigh and relaxed against Jack. Okay, *this* was more idyllic.

"Is that coffee I smell?" she asked.

"Maybe. How grateful would you be if I brought you a cup?"

"Very grateful." She turned, wrapped her arms around his neck and drew him down for a deep, lingering kiss. Dear Lord, the man could kiss, his lips firm and possessive and slightly crafty, edging a simple caress into something that had her melting against him in desperate longing. "In fact, I might be grateful enough to make us both late for work."

"Tempting. More than tempting." Regret shimmered in his eyes, the early morning sunlight catching in the robin's egg blue intensity of them. "Unfortunately, I have a meeting at The Kincaid Group today."

"With your…your father's family?" As if she didn't know.

"The Legitimates," he confirmed. "The legitimate side of the family tree, forced to deal with the bastard in the family. My father's dirty little secret."

Where before his expression had been open and relaxed, now it hardened, reminding Nikki that the man with whom she'd been having a passionate affair for the past month was considered one of the most ruthless businessmen in all of Charleston, South Carolina. She'd do well to remember that. Not that a single day or night went by without her worrying about his unearthing the secret she continued to keep from him.…

How would he react if he ever discovered she worked for The Kincaid Group? That as their corporate investigator, she'd been assigned to investigate *him*. To dig into his corporate activities in order to determine whether he'd been working on the sly to damage TKG as part of an effort to absorb the company into his own, Carolina Shipping.

Of course, her affair with him had begun weeks before RJ Kincaid assigned her to the investigation. But that didn't change a thing. Eventually the truth would come out about her role at TKG and their affair would end. Badly. Equally as bad, she doubted the Kincaids would take it well if they found out she and Jack were involved in an intimate relationship.

But until that happened, she intended to treasure every single minute. Indulge herself to the fullest. And hope, desperately, that a solution presented itself, one that would take her out of the equation. Not likely to happen, particularly considering she had another secret, one she'd kept from Jack *and* the Kincaids. A secret that kept her squarely between all the various combatants in this little war.

"What about you?" he asked. "Still working on your top secret project for your top secret employer?"

It was the story she'd given him when their involvement blossomed into something more serious than the dinner date with him she'd won through a charity auction. He'd asked about her job when they'd first become involved and because she'd been unwilling to face a fast end to an amazing relationship, she'd told him the information was confidential. Well, it hadn't been a total lie. What she did for TKG was most definitely confidential, even if the identity of her employers wasn't. Fortunately, due to the nature of her work the Kincaids kept her name very low-key, on a need-to-know basis only.

She rested her head against his shoulder so she wouldn't have to look at him, so he wouldn't see the guilt that must be written all over her face. "Yes, still working on that project."

He captured her chin in his hand and tilted it upward. "Just reassure me about one thing," he insisted. "Promise me you aren't in any danger."

Oh, God. How did she answer that? Yes, she was in danger. In terrible danger. In danger of losing her heart to a man she could never have, a man she wanted more than any she'd ever known, but who could never share a future with her.

"I'm in no physical danger," she informed him.

"Swear it."

"I swear it." She risked a quick, teasing smile. "Now do I get coffee?"

"I think I can make that happen."

He drew her up for another kiss, one as hot and potent as the sun at her back, filling her with warmth and a sweet, sharp desire. How was it possible that she'd tumbled so fast? That in just one short month Jack could come to mean so much to her? It was frightening and wonderful and ultimately tragic when their relationship couldn't end any other way than badly. Even with the knowledge ripping through her, she wrapped her arms around his neck and surrendered to a bottomless passion.

With a groan of demand, Jack swept her into his arms and carried her through the French doors leading from the deck to his bedroom. She dropped her head to his shoulder and snuggled into the embrace. "Bringing me to the coffee instead of the coffee to me?" she asked.

"Not quite."

Nikki's breath hitched as she recognized the intent beneath the clipped words. "What about your meeting with the Kincaids?"

"Some things are more important." He lowered her to the bed, followed her down. The fit of angles to curves caused her to shudder from the intensity of her need, from the helplessness of it. "Right now, you're the most important thing in my world."

She closed her eyes. "Please don't say that."

He brushed her hair back from her face, tracing the line of her jaw and cheekbones. Lingering in a scintillating caress. "Why not?"

She looked at him then, saw something in his eyes, something she didn't want to identify. Something she suspected was reflected in her own. "Because it's perfect," she whispered helplessly.

A smile eased the hard, tough curve of his mouth, turning his customary ruthlessness into something that made him approachable. Something and someone she could lose herself in, who put her heart at serious risk. "Maybe there's a reason for that," he replied, his eyes dark and serious.

Not a reason she dared look at. Not now. "Why you?" she demanded. "Why did it have to be you?"

"I don't have a clue."

She pulled him down, inhaled him, drew him in. "Maybe because I'm a lucky, lucky woman."

He smiled with a tenderness that devastated. "You have that backward, sweetheart. I'm the lucky one."

* * *

After escaping Jack's bed, Nikki decided to work from home that morning in order to avoid running into him at TKG. She emailed RJ Kincaid to warn him that she wouldn't be in until after lunch. He shot her back an immediate response asking her to join him at her earliest convenience, no doubt so they could discuss his meeting with Jack.

She arrived at the office to find the three Kincaids most intimately involved in the daily running of The Kincaid Group just concluding a meeting in the main conference room. Matthew Kincaid, tall and sporting a swimmer's physique, lounged back in one of the leather swivel chairs, a look of concern disturbing the even tenor of his expression while he listened to his sister.

"This could turn into a nightmare from a PR standpoint," Laurel Kincaid was saying. As tall as Nikki, the eldest Kincaid daughter was a stunning redhead, the image of her mother. "We can't allow Sinclair to throw any question on the stability of TKG by claiming he's going to run the company once we elect our new CEO at the June meeting."

"And gaining new business between now and then will also be problematic," Matthew added. "Who wants to hire a company who may not have a Kincaid at the helm in another three months?"

RJ nodded wearily. "We've been around this and around it and I don't see an easy solution. We have got to find something to hang Sinclair with. Speaking of which…" He waved Nikki into the room. "We'd appreciate an update. Please tell us you've found something. Anything."

Oh, God. What did she say? Nikki cleared her throat

and wished with every fiber of her being that RJ didn't look so much like Jack. But the two were definitely their father's sons. Tough features, deeply scored by sophistication and experience, they both had a multitude of life's lessons marking the striking blue brilliance of their eyes. Each was also tall and broad, their muscular builds delineated by the superb cut of their suits. Even the deep tenor of their voices was uncannily similar, which had caught her off guard more than once over the past two months.

"So far everything checks out," she said. "I wish for all your sakes, that it didn't. Carolina Shipping is a solid company with a sterling reputation. There have only been two lawsuits against Jack Sinclair. I'd classify them as nuisance suits, both settled in his favor."

"What about on the personal front?" Matthew's green eyes sharpened on her. "You've socialized with him, right?"

RJ looked momentarily startled by the question before making the connection and nodding. "Of course. The bachelor auction. Your dinner date." He edged his hip onto the conference table and folded his arms across his chest. "The family has only associated with him at the lawyer's office and in a business setting. His half brother, Alan, has surprised me by being downright friendly. Seems a decent enough sort. As for Sinclair… I couldn't get a true personal read on the SOB. He's much more self-contained."

Laurel sighed. "Our meetings with Jack couldn't be considered the best circumstances in which to get to know anyone, let alone our—surprise—half brother."

RJ's mouth tightened. "Assuming we wanted to get to know him." At the mention of Jack's name, his eyes took on an expression identical to Jack's whenever the Kincaid name was mentioned. It was downright freaky, not to mention distressing. "Which we don't. Maybe if he was as innocuous as Alan, it might have been a different story. But it's clear he despises us. And equally clear he'd like to destroy TKG."

"He doesn't realize you work for us, does he, Nikki?" Matthew asked in concern.

She shook her head. "No. I've kept that quiet."

"Give us your assessment of him on a personal level," RJ prompted.

Nikki hesitated, choosing her words with care. "He's more relaxed. I guess he would be all things considered. Still hard. Still tough. But if I were to attempt to describe him, I'd say…" Her gaze arrowed toward RJ and she shrugged. "He's a lot like you."

Insult spread across his face, spiked through his body and he straightened. "That's a hell of a thing to say."

She refused to back down from her assessment. "You know I call it like I see it. You're both a lot like your father. You have boundaries and God help anyone who steps across those lines. You're both brilliant businessmen. But when crossed you're…" She forced herself to acknowledge the truth. "Ruthless."

RJ took a moment to absorb her words before nodding. "No doubt Brooke would agree with that description."

Matthew continued to watch Nikki with a sharpness she tried to ignore. He opened his mouth to speak, then much to her relief, reconsidered. "We need more information than you have so far. Insider information. Information that will help us by June."

Now it was Laurel watching her, this time with a woman's gaze and a woman's understanding. "Are we done here, guys?"

The two men nodded. After thanking Nikki, they switched to a shorthand wrap-up on a business matter on the way out the door. Laurel lingered, touching Nikki's arms with unmistakable sympathy. "Would you rather we assign someone else to research Sinclair?" she asked gently. "I can arrange it without raising any flags with my brothers."

The offer tempted Nikki beyond measure. Even so, she shook her head. "I can do my job."

"Is it serious?"

A smile wobbled across her mouth. "It won't be when he finds out I work for TKG." Normally, she wouldn't have been so forthcoming, especially since she was concerned about how her affair with Jack would affect her job. But something about Laurel's calm, understanding gaze had her opening up. "Of course, if he somehow manages to gain control of the company, working for him won't be a problem since I'm sure his first act will be to fire me."

Laurel's laughter held a dry edge. "Right after he fires us." Her green eyes turned defiant. "Not that that's going to happen. Not while we have anything to say about it."

"I wouldn't do anything to betray your family," Nikki stated, aware it needed to be said. "You know that, don't you?"

Laurel nodded without a moment's hesitation. "We all know it. My father once told me you took after your father. That one of the defining qualities you shared was an unswerving sense of honor. It's part of what made him such an outstanding policeman and has made you such a valuable employee."

The observation caused tears to prick Nikki's eyes. "Thank you for telling me that about my father. It means the world to me that others saw him the way I did. As for me…" She closed her eyes. "Somehow I'm not feeling too honorable about the way I've handled all this."

And she didn't. She'd kept a secret from both parties, a secret she'd promised Reginald Kincaid she'd keep. But in order to honor that promise, it compromised what she considered her integrity and duty on another front. And then there was the lie she lived with Jack. She should have been up-front with him about who she worked for right from the beginning. She'd planned to tell him over that first dinner together after she'd placed the winning bid at the bachelor's auction. Instead of alerting him to the connection, she'd slept with him. Granted, the next morning she had intended to confess the truth. Would have if he hadn't said one small thing that had stilled her tongue.…

It was the morning after their bachelor auction dinner date. The morning following the first night they'd made love. Nikki woke to find Jack standing on the deck just off his bedroom, brought him a cup of coffee and a confession. But one look at the brooding starkness on his face made her hesitate a moment too long.

He held a thick envelope in his hands that reeked money and class, and tapped it against the railing as though the contents contained a terrible emotional burden. It was heavily creased and careworn, but still sealed. She caught The Kincaid Group's distinctive logo decorating one corner, the ink blurred from frequent handling. "I'm taking them down, you know," he announced.

Even though she guessed who he meant, she forced herself to ask. "Who are you taking down, Jack?"

"The Kincaids." He turned, accepted the coffee with a hard smile, remained blissfully unaware her confession had slipped away like a forgotten dream. "Ironic, isn't it? By giving me 45 percent interest in TKG, my own father handed me the very weapon I needed to destroy his family. Why do you suppose he'd do that?"

"Maybe he didn't consider it a weapon," she suggested hesitantly. "Maybe he hoped you'd realize they're your family, too."

"They're not my family," he instantly retorted. "They will *never* be my family."

Nikki waited a beat so he'd hear the anger and defensiveness in his own voice before deliberately instilling a hint of calm in her reply. "Then maybe your father considered it an olive branch, an attempt to correct past errors in judgment."

Jack drew a deep breath and gathered himself. "Could be. There's one way I could find out." Steam from the mug caused a curtain to form between them while he sipped, before parting again when he set the mug on top of the envelope, pinning it to the railing. "I can tell that startles you."

"Only because your father's dead, so I'm not sure how you can get any real answers."

He flicked a corner of the envelope. "He left me a personal note. And no doubt a lengthy explanation for why he refused to acknowledge me all these years.

Why he never told the Legitimates that I existed. Why he felt it acceptable to betray his wife and take my mother for his mistress. I wonder if he asks for forgiveness or simply attempts to excuse his behavior."

She glanced again at the seal. "You haven't opened it. Why?"

"Because I'm tempted to burn it."

"Unread?"

He turned to her, genuine amusement brightening the intense blue of his gaze. "You think I'd regret it if I destroyed the damn thing without reading it?"

"I…" She almost said, "I don't know." But she did know. There wasn't a single doubt in her mind. "Yes. Yes, I think you'd regret it. If not now, at some point."

He turned back to the letter, lifted the mug for another swallow of coffee. A bitter-dark ring marred the creamy white of the envelope. A dark smudge that reflected Jack's birthright…or birth wrong. And yet, a ring that connected all the Kincaids within that unfortunate darkness. "I decided to give it more time for just that reason. First impulses aren't always the best choice."

"Bidding for you at the auction was a first impulse. So was sleeping with you."

He leaned in, soothed the worry from her brow with a tender kiss. "The exception that proves the rule."

Confession time. "Listen, Jack, there's something you should know—"

"There are some who suspect—hope—I killed my father."

Damn, damn, damn. "Did you kill Reginald Kincaid?" she asked evenly.

She asked the question deliberately, hoping to jar

Jack out of his odd mood. And that's when she saw it. The stillness. The flash of pain. The weary acceptance. Each expression reflected an emotion she knew—knew without a minute's doubt—he'd experienced countless times in the past, a lifetime's accumulation of slights and insults he'd absorbed, all of which had left scars. How many were due to his birth? How many to the fact that he was Reginald Kincaid's son by blood, but never by name? How many were because his mother was Kincaid's mistress? How many were because he'd lived his entire life in the shadows, unable to claim kith or kin, always living beneath a cloud of shame?

She went to him, took the coffee from his hand and set it aside. She wrapped him up in the warmth of her embrace, waiting for his instinctive resistance to fade. Little by little he surrendered to the comfort she offered. The instant he rested his cheek against the top of her head she knew she'd won him over, eased some tiny part of his burden.

She also knew she couldn't tell him about her ties to the Kincaids, that to do so would cut him adrift once again. She couldn't do that to him. Even more, she couldn't do it to herself. She wasn't ready to lose him. If she toed the line she always had in the past, the line that demanded she follow a certain code of honor, he would end things between them before they fully began. And she wasn't ready for that.

Nikki cupped the back of Jack's head and lifted her face to his, drawing him down and into a slow, lush kiss. Warmth flooded over them, capturing them within the brilliant rays of the sun, adding even more heat to their embrace. He ran his hands over the simple silk shirt she wore—his shirt from the night before.

And then he swept under, tracing the naked curves he found beneath. It made her desperately grateful he owned extensive land around his home and had planted trees that blocked any possibility of being seen, other than from the empty stretch of beach.

He cupped her buttocks, lifting her against the rigid line of his arousal, aligning her more acutely to sheer masculinity. Then upward still further to cup the fullness of her breasts. His thumbs traced the tight peaks of her nipples and he inhaled her groan of pleasure, incorporated it into their kiss.

"I want you." He backed her toward one of the large, cushioned deck loungers and came down on top of her. "I can't seem to stop wanting you."

"Make love to me. Here and now."

"Not my usual venue."

She laughed, filled with a recklessness she'd never experienced before other than with him. Only with him. "I have a confession."

"You're secretly a Kincaid?" he teased. She stiffened, unable to help herself, her shock communicating itself to him. His eyes narrowed in abrupt suspicion. "Tell me you're not somehow related to the Kincaids and are secretly on their side in our little war."

"I'm not secretly related to the Kincaids," she answered without hesitation, the truth of her modified statement reflected in her eyes and voice.

"Swear it."

"I swear it."

"Sorry." He shook his head and released a gruff laugh. "These days I'm seeing Kincaids lurking behind every tree. Maybe because half the time they are."

She ran her hands over his chest, hoping to distract

him, tracing the ridges of power that rippled across the impressive expanse. It worked like a charm. He shuddered beneath the gentle caress. One by one he opened the buttons of her shirt—his shirt—and spread the silk wide. She lay beneath him, utterly exposed, so bared she worried that he could see straight through to her heart and soul and those tiny secrets that hid there. He cupped her breast, lowered his head to nip, to pleasure. She surrendered to him, helpless to do anything less. All he had to do was touch her and she was his for the taking.

He took his time, exploring where the sun dappled. Somehow making them one with the give and take of the sea. The pounding surf that echoed the kick of her heart. The swish of water dragging across sand that matched the movement of his mouth and tongue across her body. The desperate, helpless drive of salt water against shoreline that mirrored the desperate, helpless drive of passion that sent her climbing, climbing, climbing. The relentless rush that couldn't be stopped before the break of wave, the powerful tumble that nature demanded.

Her cry of climax joined with that of the sea, with that of the man whose body mated with hers. And in that moment she realized there was no going back. Not now. Not ever. No matter how this ended. Slowly they subsided, the crash easing to bliss. They held and clung for untracked time.

He turned his head to meet her stunned gaze. "Still think I killed my father?" he asked.

She winced, aware she'd hit a serious hot button earlier. She rolled onto her side and snuggled in. "Considering you just sent me straight to heaven, I may have to rethink my original opinion."

He chuckled, tucking her closer still. "You asked me that question deliberately, didn't you? Not because that's what you believe, but rather to watch my reaction. Did you learn that technique from your father?"

"Guilty," she confessed, her voice muffled against his shoulder.

"Quite effective. I'll have to try it sometime, maybe with the Kincaids."

"Oh, Jack." She tilted her head back and looked up at him. "How will ruining the Kincaids solve anything? It won't make Reginald any more or less your father. It won't change how you were raised."

"Let's just say I'll find it satisfying."

"To ruin The Kincaid Group?"

He lifted a dark eyebrow. "Who said anything about ruining the company? That would be counterproductive, since I now own 45 percent."

She relaxed ever so slightly. Maybe she'd misread the situation. "Oh. Well, okay then."

"No, I want TKG to prosper when I take it over and one by one take each and every last Kincaid down. They've had their reign. They've spent their entire lives at the top. Reginald Kincaid's sons and daughters. The Legitimates." Ruthless intent burned in Jack's eyes, carved a pathway across his features. "Now it's my turn. Now the Kincaid bastard takes over."

And that's when Nikki realized she was in serious trouble, that she'd put herself in an impossible situation, one in which she felt honor-bound to protect both sides in a war no one could possibly win. The only thing she knew with dead certainty...

When this war ended, she would be the ultimate loser.

* * * * *

ON THE VERGE OF I DO
HEIDI BETTS

An avid romance reader since school, national bestselling author **Heidi Betts** knew early on that she wanted to write these wonderful stories of love and adventure. It wasn't until college, however, when she spent the entire night before finals reading a romance novel instead of studying, that she decided to take the road less travelled and follow her dream.

Soon after she joined Romance Writers of America, Heidi's writing began to garner attention, including placing in the esteemed Golden Heart competition three years in a row. The recipient of numerous awards and stellar reviews, Heidi's books combine believable characters with compelling plotlines, and are consistently described as 'delightful,' 'sizzling,' and 'wonderfully witty.'

For news, fun and information about upcoming books, be sure to visit Heidi online at HeidiBetts.com.

Dear Reader,

I can't tell you how much I enjoyed writing *On the Verge of I Do* for the The Kincaids series, and have to take a moment to thank Senior Editor Stacy Boyd and Associate Editor Charles Griemsman (with a shout-out to Assistant Editor Shana Smith) for once again trusting me to take part in such a wonderful continuity.

Kara and Eli's story is right up my alley, and I absolutely loved spending time with them in Charleston, South Carolina, and the surrounding area—albeit vicariously. Any mistakes you may notice concerning this beautiful city are entirely my own, of course, but working on this story certainly gave me a great excuse to watch tons of southern-set television shows and movies in the name of 'research.' (Join me on my blog—HeidiBetts.com/WIP-SandChains—if you'd like to see a list of my personal favourites and share some of your own!)

Until then…

Happy reading, y'all!

Heidi

HeidiBetts.com

With thanks to JoAnn Ross and Geremy Kephart for all the great Charleston and Hilton Head information you provided. I may not have used it all, but you helped me with this story more than you can know and I really, *really* appreciate it!

One

"This is a lot of work. I don't know how you do it on a daily basis."

Kara Kincaid chuckled as she turned another page of the catering catalog spread open on the glossy surface of the low black lacquer coffee table in front of them.

"And I don't know how you keep half a dozen luxury hotels and resorts up and running. I'd rather pore over guest lists and seven-course menus any day than try to keep all of that afloat," she told her older sister's fiancé.

Eli Houghton was tall and handsome and mouth-wateringly well-built. With chocolate-brown eyes and wind-blown, coffee-brown hair, the man could make a woman's heart skip a beat without even trying. When he did try…well, that was enough to stop a woman's heart from beating entirely.

"You're selling yourself short, darlin'," he told her, flashing a smile that made her own internal organs do things she didn't think her personal physician would approve of. "We may have different talents, but we've both managed to build successful businesses for ourselves."

"Except that Houghton Hotels and Resorts is worth millions of dollars, and I run Prestige Events out of my home office."

They were sitting on a black leather sofa in Eli's impressive ninth-floor office, but ordinarily they would be having this meeting in the small ground-floor library-turned-workplace of her meticulously restored circa 1806 French Quarter row house on Queen Street.

She loved the quaint, three-bedroom/three-bath home, which was more than enough space for a single gal like herself. But she did sometimes worry that running her business out of her home gave the wrong impression to potential clients. Not for the first time, she realized that she should probably give some serious consideration to renting an office elsewhere.

Possibly even an entire building where she could host tastings, put up displays and store reusable decorations so she wouldn't have to rent them from vendors. She might hire an assistant—or even *employees,* plural, one day—to help her, since she'd been running things pretty much single-handedly so far.

She didn't regret the hard work. Prestige Events was, after all, her baby. The business she'd started on her own, stepping away from her family's interests in shipping and real estate to do it. But it might be nice, just once, to not have to be responsible for *everything,* for everyone else. Or at the very least, to have a handful of workers on staff that she could turn to when two arms, two legs, two ears and one mouth just didn't seem to be enough to get the job done on time.

"Give it time, sugar," Eli said in a voice as smooth as Kentucky bourbon, drawing her attention back to their conversation. "Keep doing what you're doing, and I'd be willing to bet that in a few years you'll be planning the wedding of one of the Obama girls."

Oh, her sister was a lucky, lucky woman. It was a good thing Kara was sitting down. The man oozed charm, and his softly spoken encouragement had her bones melting like butter on a biscuit.

Clearing her throat, she took a deep breath and straightened her spine. This was not the time to be going all weak-kneed over a man. Not the time *or* the man.

Eli was Laurel's fiancé, for Pete's sake. In less than a month, the two would be married.

Yes, Kara found Eli attractive. She'd be willing to bet she was no different than any other red-blooded woman in South Carolina—or heck, the entire Eastern seaboard—in that regard.

Yes, she'd sort of had a crush on him from the time they were teenagers. Again, that was no great surprise. Every girl in school had had her eye on the football player.

Well, almost every girl, anyway. Kara couldn't remember Laurel ever showing more than a passing interest in him while they were growing up. They'd always been friends—all of them, the entire Kincaid brood and the lone boy who lived with the Youngs on the neighboring estate—but it wasn't until much more recently that the two of them had decided to get engaged.

And Kara was happy for them, truly she was. It just wasn't easy to plan a wedding for her sister and the man for whom she'd spent the past ten years carrying a moderately flickering torch.

But she was doing her best. And her best required putting aside any inner turmoil she might be feeling to pull off what could arguably be considered the Wedding of the Year within Charleston's high society circles. The fact that it was her sister's wedding only raised the stakes, made the event that much more important to Kara, both personally and professionally.

Reaching past the catering brochure, she scooped up her glasses and slid them onto her nose. She didn't really need them, but she always felt more sure-footed with them on, and she could certainly use a little added confidence—not to mention an added barrier between herself and Eli—right now.

"Once you and Laurel decide which proteins you want

for the reception, it will be a lot easier to narrow down your choices. And that will actually be the fun part, since you'll be taste-testing samples before we plan the final menu."

Eli leaned back against the sofa, spreading his arms across the buttery-soft leather and crossing his legs to rest an ankle on the opposite knee. "We should probably leave that up to Laurel. I'd hate for us to have our first fight at the wedding reception just because I told you to order fried chicken instead of crab tarts."

Kara checked her watch. Her sister was already twenty minutes late. They'd purposely agreed to meet at Eli's office so his workday wouldn't be turned upside down, but Laurel's tardiness made it look as though that's exactly what was going to happen.

"She should be here any minute," Kara told him.

With a solemn nod, he said, "I'm sure she will be."

He sounded so certain…and so patient. More patient than Kara suspected she would be, if she were in his shoes.

The truth was, in all her time as an event coordinator, all the times she'd dealt with giddy, nervous, and even monstrously spoiled and demanding brides, she'd never put together a wedding for a woman as distracted and seemingly disinterested as her own sister.

Granted, there was a lot going on with their family at the moment. Bad enough that their father had been brutally murdered late one night in his office by someone who had tried to make it look like a suicide…. Bad enough that they'd discovered only after his death that he'd been leading a double life—and had another adult son with another woman…. But now their own mother, Reginald's rightful widow, had been accused of killing her own husband.

Kara didn't care what secrets her father had been keeping or how hurt her mother might have been when she'd discovered his betrayal. Elizabeth Winthrop Kincaid would never have raised a hand against him. Her mama could barely squish a spider, let alone shoot her husband of nearly forty years in the head.

No, it was an absolute impossibility. And every single one of the Kincaid siblings felt the same; they were one-hundred-percent behind their mother. But tell that to the prosecutors who had accused Elizabeth of murder. Luckily, new information had surfaced about a mysterious man seen entering Reginald's office building the night of the murder, which was enough to get Elizabeth out on bail—for now.

So it was no wonder, really, that Laurel—the oldest Kincaid daughter—had more on her mind than just her upcoming nuptials.

Still, it struck Kara as slightly odd that her sister didn't already have a clear vision of her perfect wedding day. Most women did. Most *girls* did, starting around the age of eight.

Kara had never met a bride who didn't already have wedding colors firmly in mind. Who didn't already have an idea of the type of wedding dress she wanted to wear. (Laurel would be wearing a very traditional 1920s vintage gown in vanilla rather than white lace, but only because Kara had pushed and prodded and dragged her to fittings, essentially demanding her sister make a decision before time ran out.) Who showed up late for each and every scheduled meeting, be it about picking flowers or setting dates for the bachelorette party, rehearsal dinner, and ceremony itself.

She wondered if Eli had noticed his fiancée's peculiar—at least in Kara's opinion—behavior, and if he found it as perplexing as she was beginning to.

From the looks of him, he either hadn't, or Laurel's frequent delays didn't bother him. He seemed totally at ease, even dressed for business, as he was now, in a charcoal suit and pomegranate-red tie.

He also didn't seem the least concerned with how much this wedding was going to cost. Traditionally, the bride's family footed the bill, and the Kincaids could certainly afford to host the celebration. But given the family's current troubling state of affairs and ongoing legal predicament, Eli had told the Kincaids not to worry about it and ordered Kara in no uncertain terms to be sure that all the bills associated with the upcoming nuptials were sent directly to him.

It was a gesture that hadn't surprised Kara. Eli had always been kind and generous and understanding. Growing up in the foster care system, he knew what it was like to have nothing, to go without. But even now that he'd made such a success of himself, he didn't pinch pennies or hoard his millions like a miser.

She only hoped he was still feeling as benevolent once he caught a glimpse of the invoices that were headed his way. The tally was already hovering around the six-figure mark in deposits alone.

As the seconds ticked past, marked by the heavy *tock tock tock* of the antique grandfather clock standing sentinel against the far wall, Kara began to wonder what else she could discuss with Eli that would be wedding-related and not a repeat of previous exchanges. She could probably go back to the beginning of the catering brochure and explain the myriad choices again, in greater detail, but she knew Eli would see that for exactly what it was—a stall tactic.

And then she didn't need to stall, because the office door swung open and Laurel walked in. The epitome of feminine business chic, she was wearing a sage-green skirt and a matching tailored suit jacket the same color as her eyes over a white blouse. On her feet were stylish but practical taupe pumps, and her long, dark auburn hair hung around her shoulders and down her back with just a touch of curl at the ends.

Like their mother, Laurel was a true beauty. She could stop traffic with just a look, and had always had her choice of handsome and attentive beaux. Though until Eli, she'd never seemed willing to settle on any of them.

"Sorry I'm late," she murmured, not making eye contact with either Kara or her fiancé as she slipped a pair of oversize sunglasses into her designer handbag.

Eli, who had gotten up the minute she'd entered, went to her and gave her a quick peck on the cheek. "Don't worry, your sister has been keeping me plenty entertained. Apparently, we have more than three hundred different choices when it comes to entrées, each of which Kara was more than happy to describe in detail."

He turned back to Kara with a smile. "Details I'm sure she'll be regaling you with next."

He didn't seem the least bit put out at the prospect of hearing her catering spiel all over again, which prompted her to return his smile.

The corners of Laurel's mouth lifted in response, but her eyes were flat, her expression tense. Her fingers clutched the strap of her purse so tightly her knuckles were white.

"Can we talk?" she asked Eli in a low voice. Then to Kara, she said, "I'm sorry, but can we do this another time? I really need to speak with Eli."

"Of course," Kara replied, getting quickly to her feet to gather her things.

Folders under her arm and portfolio in hand, she started for the door, but paused before the couple. Eli still looked completely at ease, but tension radiated from Laurel in waves, and Kara tried without words, sister to sister, to convey her concern and ask if everything was all right, if there was anything she could do.

"Call me when you're ready to reschedule," she told them simply, offering Eli a short nod and brushing her hand encouragingly down her sister's arm as she continued on her way.

Closing the door behind her with a soft click, she hoped everything was all right and knew she would be calling her sister to find out what was going on as soon as she got home.

From the look on Laurel's face, and the fact that she'd sent her sister away, Eli knew something was wrong. He just hoped it was nothing too awful. Laurel and the rest of the Kincaid family had had a hell of a year already; he honestly wasn't sure she—or they—could take much more.

Then again, if whatever had his fiancée's Southern belle skin turning even paler was connected to her father's murder and her mother's subsequent arrest for the crime, or anything else related to her family's recent troubles, surely she would have shared the news with her sister rather than asking Kara to leave so they could talk privately. That prospect had his brow puckering and the wheels in his head turning at a rapid pace.

"Here, come sit down," he said, taking her hand and drawing her over to the sofa he and Kara had so recently vacated. Her long, slim, perfectly manicured fingers were chilly against his own, her movements stiff as she sat.

"Is everything all right?" he asked, suspecting it wasn't when she refused to meet his eyes.

"I'm sorry, Eli," she said, her voice wavering slightly. Her dark auburn hair fell around her face and shoulders like a shroud, shifting only when she finally raised her gaze to his. Taking a deep breath, she seemed to steel herself for whatever it was she was about to tell him.

"I'm sorry," she said again, the words rushing together, "but I don't think I can do this. I don't think I can go through with the wedding."

For a second, Eli was certain he'd heard her wrong. Maybe his mind had been on something else, and her words had gotten jumbled with his wayward thoughts.

"Excuse me?"

In a burst of energy unlike any she'd shown since arriving at his office, Laurel jumped up, letting her purse fall to the floor while she skirted the coffee table and began to pace. Back and forth, back and forth, long, agitated strides wearing a path in front of his desk.

"This was a mistake," she said, twisting her hands together at her waist, keeping her gaze straight ahead as she spoke. "We rushed into things. And even though it seemed like a good idea at the time, circumstances have changed."

Stopping on a dime, she turned to him, her arms falling to her sides. "My life is a mess right now, Eli. My father has been murdered, my mother was accused of killing him, I've suddenly got one new half brother and another step-*ish* brother I didn't know existed..."

He'd never heard a woman's voice be both strong and weak at the same time, but hers was. Her words were filled with conviction, even as emotion caused them to tremble.

"You've been amazingly supportive, and I know Mama has been keeping a stiff upper lip. She always wears a smile, tells us everything will be fine, insists we go forward with the wedding because she doesn't want to admit how precarious the future is—for her, as well as the rest of us."

She took a breath, her chest rising as she drew air in, then blew it out again on a sigh. "But I don't think I can do that. Everything isn't okay. My whole world has been turned upside down, and I have no idea what tomorrow might bring. There is just no way I can get married right now, no matter how disappointed people might be. I'm sorry."

Eli sat in silence, watching Laurel's green eyes glisten and the tight line of her mouth quiver while she waited for him to respond.

He wondered if she expected him to be upset. To shoot to his feet and go red in the face as he shouted at her about wasting his time and money. Or maybe to not take no for an answer, insisting that she *would* go through with the wedding, regardless of the nightmare she was currently going through with her family.

He probably should be feeling those things, at least to some degree. He was being dumped, after all. Dumped, jilted, for all intents and purposes, left at the altar. Shouldn't his male pride be rearing on its hind legs, bristling with indignation?

Instead, he found himself not feeling much of anything. He was sitting there, staring at his now *ex*-fiancée, thinking that her eyes weren't quite as vibrant a green as her sister's.

They were pretty, of course. Laurel was, without a doubt,

an extremely lovely woman. Every inch of her, from the crown of her salon-perfect head to the toes of her six-hundred-dollar designer shoes, was the picture of classic, genteel beauty.

But the green of her eyes lent itself more to jade, while Kara's were a deep, glittering green that reminded him of emeralds or South Carolina's own lush salt marshes.

The fact that thoughts like those were even circling in his head at a time like this was probably a fairly good sign that Laurel was absolutely right to call off the wedding. She might be using her family's recent upheaval as an excuse not to go through with it, but he was beginning to think that they simply might not be right for each other.

Their courtship had certainly not been any romantic, whirlwind affair. More precisely, Eli had begun to feel that it was probably time for him to settle down, and Laurel had seemed like a wholly logical choice of wife. They'd grown up together, been friends for years, and when he'd proposed to her—in more of a business proposal than proposal-proposal fashion—she'd accepted with a gentle nod and a kiss to the corner of his mouth.

From there, events had carried along in a very systematic, well-planned manner, just like everything else in both of their very systematic, well-planned lives.

They'd never even slept together. Something that Eli was just now realizing should have been another bright, flashing, fiery red flag. Though at the time, through all the months of their extended engagement, it hadn't seemed unusual at all. Not even for Eli, who considered himself a man with a more-than-healthy sex drive.

Pushing to his feet, he crossed the short distance to Laurel, wrapping his hands around her upper arms, just above her elbows. He stared into her worried eyes for a moment, then leaned in to press a comforting kiss to her cheek.

"I understand," he told her gently, pulling back to offer her an encouraging smile. "Don't worry about a thing. I'll even talk to Kara about cancelling the arrangements. You just take care of yourself, and do whatever you need to in order to be there for your family."

Eli felt, as well as saw, the tension leave Laurel's body. The hard line of her mouth, her stiff spine, and the stillness of her chest while she held her breath all relaxed in a whoosh of relief.

"Thank you," she whispered, letting her head fall against his shoulder. "Thank you so much."

"I want you to be happy, Laurel. I would never want our marriage to feel like a duty or make you *un*happy."

Lifting her head, she smiled up at him, her eyes glittering again, but for a different reason.

"You're a good man, Elijah James Houghton. And one day, you're going to be a wonderful husband to a very lucky woman. I'm only sorry I'm not that woman."

Going up on tiptoe, she bussed the hard line of his jaw before collecting her handbag and letting herself out of the office, leaving him once again alone and woefully unattached.

Two

Eli sat on the far bench seat of his regular booth at Tamblyn's, nursing three fingers of Scotch on the rocks and waiting for his longtime friend, Rakin Abdellah, to arrive.

The two men had met during their days at Harvard Business School, rowing together on the university team and bonding over their mutual lack of immediate family—Eli having been a foster child from a very early age, and Rakin having lost his parents in a light plane accident when he was young. And now they were working together, too, with Rakin's overseas import/export company supplying many of the essential items for Eli's hotels and resorts.

Eli had been at the restaurant for nearly half an hour now, and was on his second glass of Scotch. But Rakin wasn't late—Eli was early.

He'd stayed at the office until his usual quitting time, but couldn't say he'd gotten a hell of a lot done after Laurel dropped her bomb.

He wasn't sorry, exactly, and he certainly didn't blame her.

Even if her personal life hadn't been in upheaval, prompting her to call things off, he wouldn't have wanted her to go through with the wedding unless she felt one-hundred-percent sure it was what she wanted to do. Neither of them deserved to spend the next fifty years in a miserable, loveless marriage.

But he did regret that their engagement had come to an end. There was a certain level of embarrassment involved. The humiliation of having to tell people the wedding they'd expected to attend in only a month's time had been cancelled. Of having to face his friends and business acquaintances and wonder if *they* were wondering what had happened…if he had done the dumping or she had, if he was happy to once again be a free agent or was wallowing in misery….

But more than that, he was disappointed to find himself without a serious relationship prospect.

It wasn't that he was desperate. Lord knew he'd had his fair share of girlfriends, some sticking around longer than others. He'd also had his fair share of one-night stands. Glancing around, he decided he could probably pick up any single woman in this restaurant in about ten minutes flat.

The problem was, he didn't want any of the women in this restaurant. He wasn't sure he'd entirely wanted Laurel—not the way a husband should want a wife. But she'd been a good match for him, and he'd been hopeful that in time, passion would grow.

It wasn't even the idea of being without a woman—a serious girlfriend, an intended, a bride-to-be—that bothered him, it was the extra distance that had been put between him and his desire for a family.

Without a doubt, he loved his foster parents. Warren and Virginia Young had taken him in when he was twelve years old. While most families preferred toddlers or babies, the older couple had been happy to take in a preteen boy and raise him to adulthood. They had even suggested, more than once, that he allow them to adopt him legally.

As much as he appreciated the offer and the deep sentiment

behind it, he'd politely turned them down. They were his parents, and he was their son, in nearly every sense of the word. Absolutely.

But something inside of him would always make him a bit of a lone wolf. He didn't want to take someone else's name, because he wanted to make something of his own. He didn't want anyone to ever look at him and think that he wouldn't have amounted to anything if it hadn't been for the charity of the wealthy, deep-rooted Southern family who had taken him in.

He was sure some folks already thought that, and in all honesty, his prospects probably had improved tenfold when he'd moved in with the Youngs. Without them, he would have been left to languish in the foster care system, and for that, he would always be grateful.

But with the exception of a stable home environment and an Ivy League education, everything he had and everything he'd built, he'd earned and done on his own. Though several million of them had been offered, he hadn't accepted so much as a dime from his parents to start Houghton Hotels and Resorts.

Eli took another sip of the super-smooth Scotch, scanning the front of the restaurant for his still-missing dinner companion. It wasn't yet six o'clock, and Rakin was normally quite prompt, so he was sure his friend would be there soon.

Swirling the remaining liquid at the bottom of his glass, he let his mind drift back to his current situation.

He had solid family roots. He'd created, and was running, a very successful Fortune 500 corporation. Now he found himself yearning for a wife and kids and the whole picket fence American dream—or his adaptation of it, at any rate.

He'd thought marrying Laurel would be the first step toward realizing that dream, but now he'd been forced two steps back.

Ah, well, he had time. He was only thirty-five, after all. And according to statistics, there were plenty of women in the world looking for rich, eligible men. He just had to be careful that when he met one, she was as interested in him as she was in his millions.

"You look deep in thought."

The low male voice caught him by surprise, even though he'd been waiting for Rakin to arrive. Eli lifted his head just as his friend slid into the opposite side of the booth and settled against the soft, russet-colored leather.

Raised for most of his life in Diyafa by his paternal grand-parents after his parents were killed, Rakin possessed the jet-black hair, brown eyes and darkly tanned skin of his Middle Eastern heritage. But he was also half-American, which meant he'd spent holidays, vacations and much of his college years in the United States with his mother's family, making him com-fortable in either country and both cultures.

"Business troubles?" Rakin asked, raising an arm to signal for the waiter.

"Nothing so simple as that," Eli muttered.

Rakin raised one dark brow in question. They'd been friends long enough that words weren't always necessary. Rakin knew that if something was wrong, and if Eli wanted him to know the details, he would share in his own good time.

"Let's order first," Eli told him, "and discuss that shipment of linens for the Seabrook Island location. Then maybe I'll be ready to tell you about my day." After a bite to eat and a few more fingers of Scotch.

When their waiter appeared, they asked for drinks, then pored over the leather-bound menus until they arrived. Eli knew why he was drinking, of course, but was surprised when Rakin ordered the same. He suspected he might not be the only one having a rough day.

Once their orders had been placed, the two men squared off, hands wrapped around their respective glasses. After a few seconds, one corner of Eli's mouth curved in a grin. Rakin's quickly followed suit. They both chuckled.

"You first," Eli said.

"The linens are on their way," Rakin told him. "Everything

is on schedule. I should have them for you late next week. At the moment, they're scheduled to be delivered directly to Ocean Breezes, but there's still time to change that, if you'd prefer they be delivered to your office here in Charleston."

Eli gave an approving nod, but that's not what he'd meant, and they both knew it.

"And…" he prompted. Partly because he was genuinely interested in what was going on in his friend's life, and partly to buy time until he had to reveal the latest turmoil in his own.

Rakin sighed, dropping his attention to the table. "Grandfather is threatening me with disinheritance."

Eli sat back, eyes going wide. "What? Why?"

Lifting his gaze back to Eli's, Rakin said, "He wants me to marry. He's been pressuring me about it for quite some time, but now he's serious. He wants it done sooner rather than later, and doesn't particularly care about my opinion on the matter."

For a second, Eli didn't say anything, just let the words sink in, the irony of the situation wash over him. Then he let out a bark of laughter.

"This is funny to you," Rakin said. It was a question, but it came out more of a statement—a very disgruntled one.

Eli shook his head. "I'm sorry. It isn't funny. But if you knew what happened to me today, you'd be laughing, too."

"All right, I'll bite. What happened today?"

"Laurel called off the wedding." He said it quickly and succinctly, like tearing off a bandage, then downed the last of his second glass of Scotch.

It was Rakin's turn to look shocked. "What? Why?"

Eli's mouth curved in amusement. Weren't those the exact words he'd uttered only moments before when Rakin had told him about his grandfather's command that he marry? Surely his friend could see the humor in that.

"She says things are too erratic right now, her life too chaotic with everything that's going on with her family."

Rakin inclined his head sagely. "I can understand that, I suppose. The Kincaids certainly have had their share of bad luck lately."

Eli nodded in return. "Agreed. Although I think Laurel's reasons for backing out of the marriage have more to do with her feelings for me than anything that's going on with her family. Her feelings…" he muttered into his empty glass, "or lack thereof."

"You don't think she loves you?" his friend asked quietly.

"I think she cares for me," he answered honestly, "the same way I care for her. As friends. I'm just not sure that's enough to build a marriage on."

Rakin cocked another brow. From the expression on his face, Eli could tell he finally recognized the irony of their situations.

"I guess I'll have to let you know, since I have to enter a loveless marriage or risk being disinherited," Rakin told him.

"Something you're *not* willing to risk, right?"

His friend gave him a look—a cross between *What do you think?* and *Would you?*

As CEO of his family's multi-million-dollar import/export company, Rakin had worked too hard and had too much to lose to gamble that his grandfather would change his mind.

"Well, if you're interested," Eli told him, feeling less troubled than he had since walking into the restaurant, "I can introduce you to a very attractive single young lady from a very respectable Southern family. She was engaged, but I have it on good authority that she jilted her fiancé only a month before they were supposed to exchange vows."

"Yes, I imagine you could," Rakin replied dryly just as the waiter returned with their entrées. Once the young man made sure they had everything they needed and left to refill their drinks—this time, both men switched to coffee—he added, "Let me try one more time to change Grandfather's mind. If I can't, I may just take you up on that."

It was nearly 9 p.m. by the time Eli and Rakin finished dinner and parted ways outside the high-priced restaurant.

Despite the fact that Eli had drunk three Scotch on the rocks straight, he'd then downed a very filling meal and just as many cups of coffee during the rest of the evening, so he was far from intoxicated.

He was also far from in the mood to go home and sit alone for the rest of the night. If he did, he knew he'd only end up opening another bottle of Scotch and starting all over again.

He was restless, and quite frankly, didn't want to be alone. Which didn't mean he was lonely, per se, but as nice as his high-rise luxury apartment was, it would still be empty and too quiet for his current state of mind.

Almost before he'd realized it, he was driving toward the French Quarter, headed for Queen Street. It was late, but there was a chance Kara would still be up. And after all, he had promised Laurel he would take care of informing her sister about the cancelled wedding.

Ten minutes later, he was standing on the stoop of her yellow chiffon row house, raising a hand to the brass knocker on the black lacquered door. The building itself was a couple of hundred years old, but showed no signs of wear. It had been kept up well by the prior owners, and Kara had done quite a bit of work herself to see it fully restored.

Even though most of the trim was painted white, the shutters and wrought-iron window dressings were black to match the front door. Fire-engine-red azaleas sat in giant pots on either side of the steps and hung from every windowsill, bringing the house to bright and summery life.

At least during the day. At night, they simply added more contrast to the already shadowed street.

To be safe, Eli glanced up at the front of the house, not letting the knocker fall until he spotted lights on in an upstairs window. Even then, he didn't knock too loudly in case she'd fallen asleep. If she was awake, he wanted to talk to her, but if she wasn't, he didn't want to disturb her.

The seconds ticked by while he waited, debating whether to knock again. Just as he'd decided to turn around and go home to his empty apartment, the outdoor sconces flipped on. Another beat passed, then he heard the scratch and click of locks being turned and unlatched, and the door swung open.

Kara stood less than a foot away, the yellow cast of light from the front stoop and the far-off upstairs hallway at her back causing a halo effect all around her. Her generous curves were encased in a silky, pearl-white robe covered with purple violets, her chestnut hair falling around her shoulders in a veil of loose, natural curls. A few inches below the hem of her robe, her feet were adorably bare, the nails painted a shimmering shade of seashell pink.

Attraction, sharp and immediate, hit him point-blank in the solar plexus. Knocked the air from his lungs. Damn near rocked him back on his heels. When he could draw a breath, he did, hoping his instant and unexpected lust wasn't written all over his face—not to mention other parts of his body.

Maybe he'd had too much to drink, after all. Wasn't that the only logical excuse for such an intense reaction to his ex-fiancée's sister? Especially when that fiancée was only an ex by a handful of hours.

Then again, maybe his response to the sight of Kara ready for bed was purely that of a man who'd gone too long without the pleasures of a woman's body. And Kara's lush body was one to make any man sit up and take notice.

"Eli," Kara greeted him softly, tiny lines crinkling over her nose as she frowned in confusion. "What are you doing here?"

Resting a hand on the jamb and leaning slightly in that direction, he said, "I'm sorry. It's too late to be dropping by, isn't it?"

She studied him for a moment, raking her gaze from the top of what he suspected was his tousled head, over his tired face, down the line of his disheveled shirt, jacket and dress slacks, and back again.

"Please tell me you didn't drive over here after drinking," she chastised, eyes narrowing with disapproval.

He held up the middle three fingers of his free hand. "Three

Scotches. But that was more than three hours ago, and I've had dinner and several cups of coffee since. I'm sober, I swear." This time, he held his hand up as though taking an oath on a Bible in a court of law.

She considered that for a moment before letting out a soft sigh and taking a step back into the foyer. "You'd better get in here before my neighbors get suspicious," she told him, opening the door wider to allow him entry.

Stuffing his hands in his pockets, he moved inside, waiting for her to close and lock the door behind them. When she turned to face him again, he knew without a doubt that she knew. She knew and felt sorry for him.

"I talked to Laurel," she admitted in little more than a whisper, her gaze hovering somewhere around his chin rather than meeting his eyes. "I'm so sorry."

Dammit, he didn't want her pity. He didn't want anyone's pity. And if this was the reaction his own almost-sister-in-law had, he could only imagine how awful it would be to deal with all of his other friends and acquaintances once they found out Laurel had dumped him.

"Christ," he swore in a manner he almost never did, especially in a lady's presence. "I don't need this."

Running a rough hand through his hair, he started to pace the length of her entryway. His steps tapped out a brusque, staccato trail back and forth across the glossy hardwood floor. "I don't need the rumors or the sympathy or the negative attention this is going to draw. I don't care that she called off the wedding," he charged to no one in particular, "but I damn well don't need the fallout it's going to cause."

He was driving his fingers through his hair again, working himself into a good huff, when Kara touched his arm. That one light touch halted him in his tracks and brought his head around until he met her gaze.

"Let's go into the kitchen," she told him in a gentle voice. "I'll make us some tea, or even pour you another glass of

Scotch, as long as you promise to spend the night here instead of trying to drive yourself home."

And just like that, his tension leeched away. He followed her past the stairwell leading to the second floor and down a long, narrow hallway to the kitchen that ran nearly the entire width of the back of the house.

This wasn't his first time wandering around Kara's home, and not because he'd been here so often recently to discuss wedding plans. When she'd first moved in, the entire family and a few friends—Eli included—had come by to help her unpack. Then later, she'd thrown a housewarming party to show off "her baby" and given everyone the grand tour.

It had been a while, though, since he'd been farther inside than the office she used for Prestige Events at the front of the house, and he had to admit he liked what she'd done with the place. Not only was it neat as a pin, but the decor looked like something that should grace the pages of *Better Homes and Gardens* or *Garden & Gun*.

He wondered briefly if she'd decorated it herself, or hired someone. And then that if she'd done it herself, she could make a hell of a fall-back career for herself if she ever gave up event coordination. Or maybe she could consider expanding Prestige Events into Prestige Events and Interior Design. Lord knew he'd paid an arm and two legs to the woman who had styled his apartment, and it was only about one-third the size of Kara's house.

Leading him into the state-of-the-art kitchen, she glanced at him over her shoulder, sending her curls bouncing. "So what's it going to be—tea or Scotch?"

His mouth opened, but she stopped him from getting a word out with an upheld hand. "Before you answer, I should probably warn you that I don't think I even have Scotch. It's never been my drink of choice. I maybe have a bit of vodka or some gin, but aside from that, your hard liquor choices are somewhat limited."

"If you didn't have Scotch," he said slowly, "why did you offer?"

She lifted one slim shoulder in a shrug. "I wanted you to stay, and didn't know if you would otherwise."

Eli smiled, and he was surprised by how easily his lips curved, how much better he felt just being here with her. "Well, then…tea, it is."

With a short nod, she turned to collect a stainless steel teapot, fill it with water, and put it on to boil. Enjoying the gentle sway of her hips and occasional bounce of her breasts as she moved, he made his way to the island in the middle of the room and pulled out one of the oak stools to take a seat.

Next she collected a delicate china tea service—cups and saucers, teapot, creamer, sugar bowl, a plate for lemon wedges—and set it all on the island in front of him.

"You don't have to go to all this bother," he told her.

She shot him a crooked grin. "This is how tea is done in Charleston, no matter the day or the hour. Mama would faint dead away if she found out I was doing it any other way."

"So no convenient, pre-packaged tea bags dipped into mugs of microwaved water, huh?"

"Hush your mouth," she chastised, letting her natural Southern accent go even deeper. Going to a nearby cupboard, she removed a fancy tin full of loose tea leaves, shaking them at him for emphasis.

Ten minutes later, she was perched on the stool next to him, facing him on the same side of the champagne-marble-topped island. She crossed her legs while she poured the tea, causing her robe to slide open and reveal a long expanse of smooth, alabaster skin from knee to thigh. Eli's gaze zeroed in on that strip of sleek flesh, making his groin tighten and his mouth go dry.

"Something tells me you're not much for tea, no matter how it's prepared," she remarked, handing him a steaming cup on a matching saucer before filling her own.

"Guilty," he admitted. "I'm definitely more of a black coffee kind of guy." Even so, he took a sip of the hot, dark brew. "But I've sat through my fair share of afternoon teas with Mom, so I can hold my own when I need to."

Kara smiled, distractedly rearranging the folds of her robe to cover her legs. More's the pity.

Long moments ticked by in companionable silence, the only sound in the room the ticking of the wall clock hanging over the bank of ovens.

"I really am sorry about what Laurel did," she said suddenly, dragging him straight back down to earth with an unpleasant thud.

He was starting to feel like a broken record, having had a similar conversation with Rakin less than an hour before, but he carefully returned his cup to its saucer and told her the truth. "I'm not. Not really."

Her eyes widened slightly, as though his response surprised her…or she didn't quite believe him.

Making sure to hold her gaze so she could see that he was sincere, he said, "I mean it. I don't want Laurel to marry me if she doesn't *want* to be married to me. That's a recipe for disaster, and the fastest way I can think of for us to end up miserable."

Kara lowered her gaze, using one fingertip to trace around the rim of her tea cup. "But the two of you made such a lovely couple," she murmured. "I know things are kind of crazy with our family right now, but that didn't seem to bother you, and if Laurel loved you…if you loved each other…"

She trailed off, her voice growing to little more than a whisper. Then she lifted her chin, her eyes locking with his. "If you love each other, I wouldn't think there was anything that could keep you from getting married."

Three

Kara didn't know why she'd said that. It was none of her business, and the last thing she wanted to consider too closely was Laurel and Eli's romantic relationship.

Bad enough she'd been writhing with guilt for months over her secret attraction to her sister's fiancé. Now she was bouncing like a Ping-Pong ball between feeling genuinely sorry the engagement had come to an end and being almost relieved, because it meant she wouldn't have to spend the rest of her life watching Laurel and Eli living their happily ever after together.

It would be better for her to keep her mouth shut and play the role of the concerned, but not overly invested wedding planner rather than sister to the ex-bride-to-be and friend to the ex-groom-to-be. She should be more focused on the unraveling of all the wheels that had already been set in motion for the coordination of the Big Day itself than in the myriad emotions involved in the dissolution of such an event.

But she wasn't just any wedding planner. She was also a sister. She was also a friend. And it would be selfish of her to pretend otherwise when Eli, and probably her sister, needed her support and understanding.

The very idea, though, had her stomach in knots. How could she commiserate with Eli when Laurel was her sister? Or with her sister when she was secretly glad Laurel had called off the wedding?

Grabbing her cup, she brought it to her lips and swallowed the piping hot tea in one giant gulp, wishing it were laced with a dash or two of that Scotch Eli had mentioned. Since it wasn't, she reached for the teapot and poured herself another serving… for all the good it would do.

"I think that might be the sticking point," Eli said, toying with his tea more than he was drinking it.

She could feel his eyes drilling into her, willing her to return his gaze. Stomach churning, she wiped her damp palms on her robe and forced herself to do just that.

As always when she looked at him straight-on, her heart did a little swan dive behind her rib cage. She imagined herself having to sit across from him every week at the Kincaids' Sunday family dinners while he was married to Laurel, while he started a family with Laurel…and the small prick of guilt that lived inside her grew to a full-blown cottonwood tree.

Because she was *glad* those encounters were no longer a part of her projected future. She was glad that the rare times Eli joined the family for Sunday dinner—he'd had a standing invitation since they were teens, thanks to her mother—it *wouldn't* be as Laurel's husband.

"We were the perfect couple on paper," he continued. "Both successful. Both from good families, Charleston-born-and-bred. Well, you know…" he said, alluding to his foster child status with a self-deprecating grin. "We would have looked wonderful in all the photographs for the paper and *Garden & Gun*. Our children would have been frighteningly beautiful."

Laurel and Eli's children. Oh, yes, Kara had imagined those, as well. And they *would* have been frighteningly beautiful;

anything else was a genetic impossibility, given their parents' striking good looks.

It was enough to make her want to cry.

"But at best, Laurel and I would have had a good partnership. Almost akin to a savvy business partnership."

Kara frowned. "I don't understand," she said, feeling as though she'd missed something.

"Laurel doesn't love me," he told her point-blank. "Not as more than a friend, at any rate."

Now that he said it, Kara could see the truth of the statement. It explained her sister's disinterest in the details of her own wedding. The dress, the flowers, the guest list, the date... Kara had had to press for decisions and lead Laurel by the hand through every step of the process, something she wouldn't have had to do if Laurel's heart had truly been in it.

Which meant her betrothal to Eli had been one-sided, with all of the love and emotion needed to keep a relationship afloat coming from him.

Oh, this night just kept getting better and better.

Licking her lips, she forced herself to whisper the words she was far from feeling. "I'm sorry."

Eli gave a sharp shake of his head. "Don't be. It has nothing to do with you, and I'm better off coming to terms with this now instead of a couple years into the marriage."

A short pause and then, "What did Laurel say when she told you?"

"Just that the wedding was called off," she answered honestly. "By her, because of everything that's going on with Mama, and Daddy's murder investigation, et cetera. She didn't seem inclined to say more, and I didn't press."

She took a sip from her second cup of tea before it grew cold, then offered him a weak smile. "This is new territory for me, and I'm afraid I'm not quite sure how to properly balance the fine line between sister and wedding planner. Or friend and wedding planner, either."

He returned her lopsided grin with one of his own. "Have

you ever had to deal with a situation like this before in your line of work?"

Kara shook her head so hard and so fast she nearly gave herself whiplash. "I've dealt with demanding brides and even more demanding mothers-of-the-bride. Grooms with cold feet. I've had bar mitzvahs canceled or anniversary parties rescheduled at the last minute. But this…this is all very new to me. Until now, all of the weddings I've been involved with have gone off with only the usual number of minor, to-be-expected hitches. Which is maybe why I should have recused myself from planning this one from the beginning."

"Recused yourself?" he repeated, poking fun at her choice of words.

"You know what I mean," she told him. Her tone was light, the same as his, and for the first time all night, she felt her chest loosen, some of the tension in the room ease. "I should have recommended another wedding planner and just stuck with being a bridesmaid."

Eli quirked one coffee-colored brow. "But then I'd be sitting in some other woman's kitchen, and I'll bet she wouldn't know how to pull off a proper Southern tea service."

His tone was low and suggestive, at least to Kara's ears, rolling through her veins like warm honey. Lord have mercy, the man was a danger to female hormones everywhere.

Once she found her tongue and thought she could speak without sounding like she lived deep, *deep* in the bayou, she said, "Well, I'm glad you felt comfortable coming here. Even if we both know you'd prefer Scotch over a cup of hot tea."

She flashed him a tentative grin, and was rewarded by a chuckle of agreement.

"I do have sweet tea," she told him, "if you'd prefer that."

Leaning back an inch or two, he glanced at the bit of china as though it were a tightly coiled snake, then at her. "Am I that transparent?"

"Not at all." She hopped off her stool and rounded the island to retrieve a glass from the cupboard, then ice cubes and a pitcher of chilled sweet tea from the stainless steel refrigerator.

"I've seen lots of things more transparent than you," she added as she set the filled glass and pitcher in front of him. "Windows. Water. Cellophane…"

"Yeah, yeah, I get it. You can read me like a book." He downed half the glass in one long swallow, then released a satisfied sigh before returning it to the countertop with a soft clink. "But I really am glad you're our event coordinator. It will be a lot easier to go through the process of dismantling everything with you than with a near-stranger."

She inclined her head. She'd never had to completely undo all the plans for such a large event, but she would do everything she could to see that it went smoothly, and that it had as little impact on Eli and Laurel as possible.

"So where do we start as far as that's concerned, anyway?" he asked.

She blinked, caught off guard by the question.

"You want to talk about that tonight?" She was surprised he wanted to talk about the end of the engagement at all so soon, let alone the steps that would need to be taken to cancel the wedding.

"Why not?" he replied with a shrug. And then he let his gaze slide down the length of her body and back up again. "Unless you wanted to get to bed. I really shouldn't have dropped in on you so late."

He put one foot on the floor, prepared to stand up and let himself out, but she stopped him with a hand on his wrist.

"Don't go," she told him, feeling her throat close with unexpected emotion. "It's fine. My only plans for tomorrow were to…" She trailed off, not entirely sure how to finish that sentence.

"Work on more of the arrangements for the wedding?" he supplied wryly.

She gave a reluctant nod.

"Well, the good news," he said, sounding cheerier than she

would have expected, "is that you don't have to change your plans. Just alter them a little to start *cancelling* the arrangements instead of setting them up."

"As long as you seem to be in a fairly good mood," she said, "I should warn you that the chances I'll be able to get your deposits back are slim to none. They're non-refundable, and of course I'll do my best to talk the vendors into reconsidering, but—"

"Don't worry about it," he cut her off to say. Then when she didn't respond, he added, "I expected as much. And even though it's no small amount of money, I'd rather let it go than add to your stress level by making you fight to get it back."

"Are you sure?" she asked quietly. It was a very substantial "no small amount" of money; anyone else would be livid at the thought of losing it.

Taking another drink of his sweet tea, he tipped his head in the affirmative. "My relationship with Laurel was an easy one. There's no sense in complicating matters now that it's over."

"I'll take care of everything," Kara promised. "I don't want you or Laurel to have to worry about anything."

"With you at the helm? Never," he offered gently. Then he glanced at his watch. "It's getting late. I'd better go and let you get to bed."

She padded after him in her bare feet when he slid off the stool and headed for the front of the house. He opened the door, then turned to face her, hand still on the brass knob.

"Thanks for keeping me company tonight."

"It was my pleasure," she told him. "And I really am sorry things didn't work out with you and Laurel."

He didn't respond for a second. Instead, his attention seemed to be locked on her lips. She licked them self-consciously, wondering if she had a spot of tea there, or some smeared lipstick from earlier.

"At least I still have you," he murmured in a low voice without lifting his gaze.

Kara didn't know what to make of that. Of the words or his tone.

But she didn't have long to wonder about it, either. One minute he was staring at her, so intently she almost began to fidget. The next, he was moving in, coming closer and closer until his mouth covered hers.

Everything inside of Kara went stock-still as soon as their lips touched. She stopped moving, stopped breathing, stopped thinking.

The kiss was warm and soft and tasted of sweet tea, with a hint of the Scotch he'd consumed earlier. It was everything she'd ever imagined and more. It started out so slow and tentative, just a brush of lips on lips. Then, as though a match had been struck, it was so much more.

Grabbing her by the upper arms, Eli dragged her against him. She could feel the heat of him through the thin silk of her robe, the press of his arousal at her belly.

In all the years she'd dreamed of kissing him, her fantasies had never been like this. Sometimes she'd imagined light, chaste kisses that made her feel like the princess in a fairy tale. Other times, she'd imagined uncontrollable passion that incited him to sweep her into his arms and carry her off to the bedroom à la *Gone with the Wind*.

But this was nothing like either of those scenarios. It was real and raw and made her feel as though her entire being was going up in flames.

She clung to him as the heat radiated through her. His mouth enveloped her, his tongue sweeping inside to claim her in a way she couldn't ever remember experiencing before.

And then it was over. Without warning, he pulled away, took a step back at the same time he set her a step away from him in the opposite direction.

Reality slapped Kara in the face more effectively than a bucket of frigid ice water falling over her head. They were both breathing heavily, chests heaving while they struggled to look anywhere but at each other.

"I should go," he said in little more than a mumble.

The words buzzed in her ears, sounding as though they were coming to her through a very long wind tunnel. Her ears, she realized, were ringing in time with the spinning of her head. The best she could do was nod in agreement as he opened the door and walked out into the night without a backward glance.

Kara stood frozen in place, the events of the past few seconds flashing through her mind. It had been wonderful…it had been terrifying. She wanted it to happen again…she wished it had never happened.

The man of her girlhood dreams—oh, who was she kidding?—her girlhood *and* womanly dreams…had just kissed her half-senseless. And all she could feel was horrendous guilt over the fact that he was her sister's only very recent *ex*-fiancé.

Eli took the long way home. The "long way" being three loops around Kara's block on foot before finally making his way to his car and back to his apartment. The same dark, empty apartment he hadn't wanted to return to earlier.

He didn't particularly want to return there now, but it wasn't as though he had much choice unless he wanted to spend the night in one of his own equally dark and empty hotel rooms.

He'd seriously considered his options during his extended walk, though. Part of him had wanted to lope back up Kara's front steps, pound on the door until she opened it, and burst inside, sweeping her into his arms and upstairs to her bedroom. The other part—the part that ruled his head rather than his libido—wondered how the hell he could kiss his former fiancée's sister like a house afire on the very same day his engagement had been called off.

How he could be lusting after her even now.

Had he ever felt this way after kissing Laurel? He didn't think so. Or at least, he didn't remember so.

All of the kisses with Laurel that he could remember had been fairly chaste…just like the entire rest of their relationship. They had been a lovely, upstanding couple. From the outside, they had probably looked perfectly prim and proper, candidates for gracing the cover of *Garden & Gun*'s "Who's Who of Charleston" edition.

Inside, however, there had been no passion. Respect and friendship, certainly—and that wasn't about to change, regardless of Laurel's decision to call things off.

But until he'd kissed Kara—and he still didn't know what in blue blazes had prompted him to do it—he hadn't realized just how lacking in passion his relationship with Laurel had been. Kissing Kara had been like touching a live wire. It had scorched him from his lips to the top of his head and all the way back down to his toes. He couldn't recall ever having such an intense reaction to kissing a woman…or if he had, she'd blown the memory straight out of his brain.

The question was: what the *hell* was he going to do about it?

The smart thing would be to go home, take a shower, climb into bed, and forget that the kiss had ever happened.

The blood still pounding in his head and through his veins—not to mention lower extremities—with the force of molten lava told him that was clearly going to be an impossibility.

Which put him back at square one with *what the hell was he going to do about this sudden, powerful attraction to Kara Kincaid?*

Four

Kara hadn't slept a wink the night before. How could she after that kiss? It had been as though she had two invisible demons sitting on either shoulder, pulling her in opposite directions like a wishbone.

Those little invisible entities hadn't taken the forms of the typical devil and angel, though. Oh, no. Instead, they'd very clearly sported the faces of Eli and Laurel.

Eli smiling, winking, being his usual charming self, doing his best to smooth-talk her into another soul-shattering kiss with that smooth Southern drawl. (Just because she shared that accent didn't mean she couldn't still be affected by it.)

And then Laurel on the other side, frowning, her eyes filled with hurt, asking, *Why, Kara? How could you do this to me... your very own* sister?

No, she didn't sleep a wink with *that* preying on her conscience.

So here she was, up at the crack of dawn. Which wasn't all that unusual—a lot of her days began before the sun started its slow climb into the sky.

Normally, however, she was functioning with eight solid hours of sleep to keep her upright. Also normally, she would be dressed for work, and either already in her office at the front of the house or on her way to her first appointment.

But today was far from normal. Instead of continuing to plan her sister's wedding, she was supposed to be in the process of dismantling it. Instead of being dressed in a stylish, professional skirt and blouse, she was in her bare feet, wearing one of her favorite light-as-air sundresses covered in giant orange poppies, with a thick, neck-to-knee apron over that. It was hot pink, with white lace along the top and at both of the pockets in the center, and had *Everyone has their price...mine is chocolate* stitched beside a delicious-looking pile of chocolates.

Like a lot of women raised in the South, when the going got tough, the tough got cooking. Or baking, as the case may be.

Even growing up as she had, in a house filled with servants—or household help, as was probably the more politically correct term these days—any time her mother had felt undue stress, she'd ended up in the kitchen, up to her elbows in flour with a rolling pin in her hand. Sometimes she'd baked her weight in biscuits. Other times she'd fried enough chicken to feed the entire Confederate army. And still others, she'd made so many cookies all of the Kincaid children had been sent to school the next day with bags enough to become homeroom heroes.

Elizabeth had also taught each of her girls to cook—and the boys, too, if they were willing to learn. At least enough that they wouldn't starve if they were ever left to their own devices.

Thanks to her mother's talented instruction, Kara made a mean honey-glazed ham and created desserts so yummy that she'd briefly considered opening her own bakery before deciding to go into event planning instead. Mainly because she was only motivated to bake when she was emotional, for some reason—angry, sad, nervous...or in this case, guilty and confused. And what kind of bakery could stay open if the owner baked only when she was in the mood?

As it was, she didn't know what she was going to do with the butter pecan cookies that even now were beginning to cool on her marble countertop. All she knew was that she needed to keep busy. Needed the precision of measurements, the therapeutic act of mixing, and the repetitive movements of dropping dough onto cookie sheets, then sliding them off with a spatula when they were done.

At exactly 8:15 a.m., the phone rang. It startled her. This was her personal line, not the business line in her office, and she rarely got personal calls so early in the morning...unless something was wrong. And considering her family's current troubles, something could indeed be wrong.

Her stomach clenched and her fingers tightened inside her oven mitt as she set another cookie sheet on top of the stove. Lord, what now? Her father had been murdered, her mother had been arrested for his death, her sister had called off her wedding... What more could happen that hadn't already—fires, floods, pestilence?

The minute the thought crossed her mind, she shook herself and wished she could call it back. There was no better way to jinx something than to ask that exact question, and her family sure as all get-out didn't need any more jinxes falling on them.

Shedding the oven mitt and saying a quick prayer that this was *not* going to be more bad news, she picked up the cordless receiver from its cradle and hit the talk button.

"Hello?"

"Kara, hon, it's Penelope from Eli's office."

The familiar voice sang over the line, lifting the cloud of foreboding that had begun to weigh her down. She blew out a breath even as she wondered why Eli's assistant was calling her on her personal line. They'd had plenty of interaction over the past few months, setting up meetings to go over wedding plans, but that had always been on her business line.

"Hello, Penelope. How are you?"

"Just fine, sweetie. How about you?"

"Fine," she replied by rote.

"Mr. Houghton asked me to call you at home and set up an appointment for this afternoon. Are you available?"

Kara's heartbeat sped up and her lungs began to burn until she realized she'd stopped breathing. Inhaling quickly, she told herself to stop being such a ninny and asked, "Do you know why he wants to meet?"

A short pause. "I just assumed it was more to do with the wedding. Why—are you busy today?"

It was a simple enough question, but Kara heard the eager curiosity underlying the words.

"No, no," she answered before Penelope became any more suspicious than she already was.

Eli obviously hadn't said anything about his broken engagement, and Kara wasn't about to be the one to start the Charleston rumor mill churning. Penelope was a dedicated employee, but this was the South—gossip was practically a sporting event.

"I'll be happy to meet with him whenever he likes," she added. He probably just wanted to get together to discuss the cancellations and make sure she covered all the details.

And if he could act as though nothing untoward happened last night, so could she.

The doorbell rang forty minutes later, a full hour earlier than she'd been expecting. With a jolt of panic, Kara dropped the last of her dirty utensils in the dishwasher and took a quick glance around the kitchen to make sure it didn't look like a natural disaster had struck.

The problem with baking, she grumbled silently on her way to the front door, was that once you started, you couldn't stop. Not unless you wanted everything ruined and gone to waste.

So even though she'd told Penelope she was at Eli's disposal and agreed to meet with him at 10 a.m., as soon as she'd hung up the phone, she'd had to go right back to sliding cookies hot from the oven onto cooling racks, spooning fresh batter onto empty sheets, and repeating until she'd run out. She'd done it all as quickly as humanly possible, but the laws of physics only allowed these things to move so fast.

Which left her not much time to clean up, ditch the apron, change her clothes and refresh her hair and makeup. If Eli had shown up as scheduled instead of devilishly early, she might actually have made it. As it was, she was hoping against hope that someone else was at the door. A neighbor asking to borrow sugar—something she was low on, thanks to her early-morning baking binge—or maybe one of her brothers needing a favor... or wanting to grab a handful of cookies, since they seemed capable of smelling the scents of her kitchen from a mile away.

Wiping her hands on her apron, she yanked open the door... and released a sigh of resignation. Of course.

"Good morning, Eli," she said, stepping back to invite him inside. "You're early."

He shot her a dazzling smile. "What can I say? I was eager to see you again."

Caterpillars broke through their cocoons and turned into butterflies inside her stomach. So much for pretending last night hadn't happened.

"Actually, I have meetings all afternoon and wanted things hammered out with you before I get distracted. I hope you don't mind."

She asked, "What things did you have in mind?"

Rather than answering, he tipped his head to the side and sniffed. "Do I smell pie?"

"Cookies, actually," she corrected.

He lifted one brow and gave her a look.

Her lips twitched as she struggled not to grin. "Would you like some?"

"Yes, please," he said with enthusiasm, actually clapping his hands and rubbing them together.

"Come on." Reaching behind her, she loosened the ties of her apron as she led him back to the kitchen. Once they arrived, she slipped it over her head and folded it to set on one of the stools beside the center island.

"You must have gotten up awfully early to do all this," he remarked, taking in the dozens upon dozens of cookies covering every flat surface in the room.

She ignored that, instead busying herself by collecting a small plate and filling it with cookies, then setting it on the counter in front of him. He was sitting in the same spot as last night, looking infinitely comfortable. As though he was used to lounging around in her kitchen. As though he belonged there.

Lifting a cookie halfway to his mouth, he paused to study it.

"Butter pecan," she supplied a scant second before he took a bite and let out a long, appreciative moan.

Eli wasn't new to her baking skills. They'd grown up together, and he'd spent enough time with her family as an adult that he'd been the recipient of plenty of both her and her mother's culinary creations.

But for some reason, having him here with her—just the two of them, in her home, in her oven-heated kitchen—felt more… intimate than any of the other times he'd sat across from her, eating her cookies.

Clearing her throat in an attempt to shake off the uncomfortable tingle building beneath her skin, she asked, "Would you like something to drink with those? I know you're not overly fond of tea, but maybe a cup of coffee or…" She trailed off, running a mental inventory of her refrigerator.

"Got any milk?"

It was her turn to raise a brow. Milk was certainly the perfect choice of drink to go with a plate of fresh-from-the-oven cookies, but for some reason, she hadn't expected such a request from a man like Eli, who just last night had shown up on her doorstep filled with double malt Scotch.

"Of course," she told him, moving first to the cupboard, then the refrigerator.

She poured them each a glass before hopping up on her stool and snatching a cookie for herself. Eli had already chomped through three of the rich, fattening blobs, but Kara rarely did more than sample her own treats. After all, she knew what went into them and how many calories she would be forced to burn off at the gym if she overindulged.

"So," she prompted, after they'd both spent a few minutes chewing and washing the crumbs down with sips of cold milk. "What is it you wanted to discuss? Concerns about the dissolution of the wedding plans?"

She cringed inwardly the moment the words were out of her mouth. How could she be so thoughtless? Why hadn't she kept her stupid mouth shut?

It was too early to be bringing up the called-off marriage vows in such a callous fashion. Eli had to be stinging still from Laurel's rejection. She could have just as easily sat here while they enjoyed their cookies and let him get to his reason for dropping by in his own sweet time.

Eli, however, didn't seem fazed. He finished off the cookie in his hand, washed it down with a gulp of milk, and then wiped his mouth with the napkin she'd provided, before speaking.

"You said you could handle all of that, so unless you need me for something, I'd rather leave everything to you."

"All right," Kara replied carefully. If he didn't need to talk to her about that, then what *did* he need to talk to her about?

Please not the kiss...please not the kiss...please not the kiss...

"I'm not sure I've mentioned before how impressed I was with your work on the wedding plans."

He said it in the same tone of voice he might compliment her cooking. No hint of pain or resentment or happiness.

"You're very efficient and have great taste."

"Thank you," she responded, still choosing her words carefully.

"Which got me to thinking that Houghton Hotels and Resorts might benefit from your expertise."

All right, Kara thought slowly, that was unexpected. But aloud, she said, "How so?"

"We do a lot of high-end events—weddings, anniversaries, birthday parties, bar mitzvahs—especially at the Ocean Breezes location. The one on Seabrook Island," he clarified, as though she wasn't already more than familiar with every one of his half-dozen-and-growing hotels.

"At the moment, we have a resort employee handling that sort of thing, but I think we could do an even better job and become even more of a go-to site for large, upscale special occasions if we had a professional on board who really knew what she was doing, and whose only job was to plan and oversee those events."

Seconds passed while she absorbed his statement and tried to make sense of it. "Are you asking me to give up Prestige Events and work for you instead?"

He shook his head, sneaking another cookie. "Of course not. Prestige is your baby, I understand that. But if you'd be willing to branch out a bit, maybe sub-contract some work, I really think I could use your input."

She let another beat or two go by. "What, exactly, are you asking me to do?"

"Come with me to Ocean Breezes for a few days," he said casually around half a bite of butter pecan. "I know the wedding was the only project on your agenda for the next few weeks, so now that it's been called off, I assume you're free. With the exception of canceling everything, of course, but since we've got telephones and fax machines at the Seabrook Island location, that shouldn't be a problem."

"And what would I do once I got there?" she asked, amazed at how calm she sounded when inside she felt as though a Fourth of July parade was marching up and down her spine. She tingled all over, torn between the excitement of an offer that could lead to some *very* lucrative business for her firm, and the trepidation of being forced to—getting to?—spend more time in Eli's presence.

"Look around. Talk to the woman I've got in charge of special events for the resort at the moment. Review some of our past events to see what we're doing right, and what we might be doing wrong."

"And then...?" she prompted.

Downing the last of his milk, he set the empty glass on the countertop with a clink. "And then we'll talk. You can give me your honest assessment of how we've been handling things. I suspect I'll want to discuss the possibility of contracting Prestige Events for a bit of work in the future, but I'm happy to take things a step at a time."

"So you just want me to visit the resort with you, offer my planning expertise." She made it a statement, but it was really a question.

"Exactly."

He flashed her a dazzling smile, one not dotted with a single crumb, while she would probably look like Cookie Monster if she smiled that wide.

"Look at it this way," he added when she kept her mouth firmly closed. "If it ends up being a waste of time, business-wise, at least you got a nice, all-expenses-paid weekend get-away out of it."

She thought that over for a minute, weighing all of the pros and cons in her head—or at least the ones she could fathom at that particular moment.

Pro: This was Eli, a man she'd known since adolescence and *knew* she could trust. He might be an accomplished business-man and drive a hard bargain when it came to negotiations, but he would never cheat or try to take advantage of her.

Con: This was Eli, the man she'd had half a crush on for three-quarters of her life, and who had kissed her last night like he meant it.

Pro: Being asked to consult for one of Eli's multi-million-dollar hotels—any of them, but the uber-luxurious Seabrook Island location, especially—was a huge opportunity, profes-sionally speaking.

Con: Her sister had just broken up with him the day before. Both the kiss last night and his offer today were likely responses to being jilted by his fiancée only a month before they were scheduled to exchange vows.

Pro: Getting out of town for a few days and keeping his mind on business would probably be one of the best ways for him to avoid a lot of the gossip, and help him heal from the breakup with Laurel. Not that he would ever admit he was suffering or needed time to recover.

Con: Going away with Eli—regardless of the fact that it would be business-only—might not look good to outside observers. *Sister of bride-to-be runs off with groom-to-be the week after wedding is called off...* It was a headline waiting to happen.

And how would Laurel feel about her doing such a thing? Would she understand that Kara was simply exploring a golden business opportunity, or would she see it as a personal betrayal by her very own sister?

It was like being on a seesaw—back and forth, good and bad.

Tipping her head to the side, she studied him, trying not to let his handsome face or cappuccino-brown eyes influence her decision.

"All expenses paid, hmm?" she murmured.

"Yep."

"That's an awfully tempting offer."

"Wait until you get there. You'll think you've died and gone to paradise."

He wiggled his brows, making her chuckle in spite of her determination not to.

"I'd like to say yes," she told him, "but think I should sleep on it at least one night. And...I'm sorry," she said after a slight hesitation, "but I need to talk to Laurel about it first. With everything that's going on right now, I wouldn't feel comfortable taking off unless she and the rest of my family are okay with me being gone."

"Of course," he responded quickly, pushing back from the countertop and climbing to his feet. "Take as long as you need…as long as you don't take too long," he added with a wink.

She followed his lead, trailing him out of the kitchen.

"If you decide you want to go, we can leave as early as Friday morning," he said as they reached the front door. Just like the night before, he turned with his hand on the knob.

At the memory of that, and of what had come next, Kara tensed, her nerve endings going on high alert. She hoped to heaven he didn't try to kiss her again…and at the same time wished he would.

"And if I decide I don't?" she ventured to ask.

He cast her a glance that clearly said he didn't expect to be turned down, no matter how long she took to make up her mind.

"Then I'll hie you away to one of HHR's closer locations instead," he said simply.

A shiver tightened her belly and squeezed her throat. She knew he was talking business, but he made it sound for all the world like an intimate proposition. Like a visit to one of his hotels would be spent in a penthouse suite, burning up the five-thousand-thread-count Egyptian cotton sheets rather than touring the location and offering advice for improving their event-hosting skills.

As though he could read her mind and knew exactly what was making her temperature rise, one corner of his mouth lifted.

"Thanks for the cookies," he murmured. "Call me when you decide what you want to do."

And then he was gone, slipping out the door and leaving her alone in her foyer. *Without* attempting to kiss her again.

Five

Eli was in the middle of reviewing a handful of renewal contracts with some of his hotels' vendors when his receptionist buzzed.

"Kara Kincaid on line three," she said, then clicked off without waiting for a response.

Taking his time, he glanced at his watch.

Four hours. That was fast. He hadn't expected to hear from her until at least tomorrow, given her comment that she needed to "sleep on it."

Of course, he didn't know that she was calling to accept his offer. She could just as easily be calling to give him a short and sweet rejection.

Hoping that wasn't the case, he picked up the receiver and brought it to his ear.

"Hello, darlin'," he greeted her in his—he hoped—friendliest and most cajoling voice.

It must have caught her off guard because the only thing he heard for the count of ten was silence.

"If you're still interested in having me go to Seabrook Island with you," she said slowly, as though she were weighing her words carefully, "then I accept your offer."

"Excellent," he drawled, trying not to let his mouth curve into a Cheshire-cat smile and failing miserably. "I'll pick you up at eight o'clock Friday morning. Will that work?"

"That will be fine," she replied primly.

"Pack for the beach," he told her in a low, just-this-side-of-seductive tone. "See you then."

He hung up before she could reply and while his luck was still running strong.

He pulled up in front of her row house bright and early Friday morning, five minutes before eight. Normally when he visited his resort on Seabrook Island, he drove his BMW Z4 Roadster convertible. It was a sexier, sportier vehicle, and he enjoyed the sting of the open air as he tooled down the expressway, then past burgeoning marshes and canopies of oak and cypress trees as he got closer to the magnificence of the Atlantic Ocean.

But this time, because he wanted to appear harmless and lull Kara into a false sense of security, he was driving the Mercedes-Benz. Safe, comfortable, subtly impressive—it should create the perfect impression for Step One of Operation Win Over Kara Kincaid.

Amazing, he thought, that only two days after being dumped by his fiancée, he was preparing a systematic seduction of her sister. It sounded shameless, even in his own mind, and he was sure there would be plenty of folks within Charleston society who would whisper and shake accusing fingers behind his back.

Not that he gave a tinker's damn. They could say anything they wanted to about him, the same as they had when he was a scraggly foster kid newly moved in with the Youngs—one of the wealthiest families in Charleston, with blood that was very blue and could probably be traced back to the Mayflower.

Boy, he'd had a chip on his shoulder back then. He'd been bitter and angry about the hand life had dealt him, putting on a tough front to keep from being hurt again. He'd been scared, too, never knowing when another shoe might fall or what might be waiting around the next corner.

But having the Youngs take him in, treat him like their own, and not give up on him no matter what, the way so many other foster families had in the past, had taught him self-assurance. They had raised him to be confident in his own thoughts and decisions, regardless of others' opinions.

He wanted Kara Kincaid, and just as he'd gone after building his multi-million-dollar enterprise with his head down, full steam ahead, he intended to go after her.

Until this week, he'd thought he had his life together, both personally and professionally. It was startling to realize how far off-base he'd been in that assessment.

He'd thought he was happy with Laurel—and would be for the next fifty years. Now, the only woman on his mind, the only woman he could fathom spending the rest of his life with, was Kara.

He'd been dating the wrong sister. Planned to marry the wrong sister. Thank God Laurel had put a halt to things when she did, otherwise they both might have made the biggest mistake of their lives.

Cutting the engine, he stepped out of the car and pocketed the keys. At this time of morning, most of the residents on Kara's street had already left for work, but a few people were out walking their dogs or tending their flowers.

Stopping at the curb, he waited for an older woman to pass, offering her a polite smile. She was obviously out for her daily walk, dressed in a hot pink tracksuit with matching head and wristbands.

She was also eyeing him like the captain of the Neighborhood Watch. He wouldn't be surprised if she hit the corner, turned around and came back to see if he was welcome on Kara's doorstep or deserving of a call to the police.

Biting back a chuckle, he crossed the sidewalk and strode to the front of Kara's house, using the antiqued brass knocker to give a couple good raps. Moments later, Kara opened the door.

Her hair was down, falling around her face and shoulders in fat chestnut waves instead of pulled back into a loose bun or intricate twist the way she normally wore it when she worked. Her glasses were also missing, another habit he'd noticed more often than not when she was on personal time and didn't need to look quite as pulled-together and professional.

Her clothes, too, were more casual and beach-worthy, just as he'd advised. She wore a short-sleeve floral blouse made of some sort of flowy, lightweight material, with a lime-green skirt and sexy but comfortable sandals on her feet.

Minimum jewelry—just a small gold cross necklace and gold hoops at her ears. It was understated, but classy and totally Kara. He liked it.

But as beautiful as she looked, she also looked nervous. Her eyes were hooded, her mouth crooked as she nibbled on the inside corner of her lower lip, and he couldn't help but notice the constant, fidgety movements of the hand hanging at her side.

Eli almost felt sorry for her. He'd tried hard not to make her uncomfortable with his invitation to visit his resort. He'd avoided touching her or getting too close, and he'd very pointedly *not* mentioned the kiss they'd shared, even though it was practically the *only* thing he'd been able to think about since.

The smell of her, the taste of her, the feel of her soft body pressed ever so lightly against his own... Just the memory of that short kiss had the power to heat his blood all over again.

He was hoping for an encore very, very soon, but couldn't let Kara know that was his number one priority. If he did, she was likely to get spooked and run all the way back to Charleston.

Not that Eli could blame her. He suspected she was just as interested in him as he was in her, but the circumstances were far from ideal.

A week ago, he'd been on the fast track to becoming her brother-in-law. Now, he had his sights set firmly on her. He could just imagine the checklist she would come up with of all the reasons they should avoid each other like the bubonic plague.

Which meant he had only the weekend to convince her otherwise. To convince her that the attraction humming between them was worth exploring, regardless of the gossip it was likely to create.

Gossip died down…eventually. But he wasn't sure his yearning for her would. Or that, if he let her go, he would ever get another chance at something like this. A chance to be with a woman he thought might be The One.

It was a bold move for him. Deciding to propose to Laurel had taken months of careful consideration. He'd analyzed every aspect of their relationship—past, present and possible future—before concluding that she was a prudent choice to become his wife. And that only after taking even longer to decide he wanted a wife at all.

For the past few years, he'd felt as though something was missing from his life. He had a good, solid family now, and had long ago come to terms with his past and childhood origins. His business was booming, too, so there were no holes there.

The same couldn't be said about his personal life, however. In that respect, he had been sadly lacking.

Which was why, after mulling it over, he'd decided settling down and starting a family was the wisest course of action. It had taken quite a while longer to narrow down his list of possible brides-to-be and land on Laurel Kincaid.

She'd seemed so perfect. On paper, anyway.

Little had he realized how overrated on-paper perfection was.

Laurel was a lovely woman, inside and out. She would be a wonderful wife for some man someday. Of that, Eli had no doubt. But that didn't mean she was the perfect wife for him.

No, he suspected that role might be better suited to Laurel's sister. Which was awkward, to be sure—but not impossible.

He only hoped he could convince Kara to be as open-minded as he was feeling these days. But in order to do that, he had to start slow and do his best not to let her know he had more than simply business in mind for their weekend away.

"Good morning," he greeted her, keeping things casual, upbeat. He was still on the other side of the threshold, one hand resting against the doorjamb. "Ready to go?"

She nibbled the inside of her bottom lip a minute longer, both corners of her mouth drawn down in a worried frown.

"Are you sure this is a good idea?" she asked. "With everything that's going on, maybe I shouldn't be leaving town. Especially with you."

He slapped a hand over his heart, pretending to be wounded. "Why, darlin', I do believe you've hurt my feelings."

She chuckled at that, knowing darn well he was kidding.

"Fine," she told him, reaching for the handle of one of the overnight bags at her feet. There were three in varying sizes and shapes, all part of a matching designer set. She thrust the largest at him before picking up the other two and stepping outside, shutting and locking the door behind her.

"But if anything happens and I can't be here with my family when they need me, I'm blaming you."

"It's just Seabrook Island," he reminded her as they headed for his car and he popped the trunk to load her bags. "A single phone call from your family, and I can have you back to Charleston within the hour. Less, if you want me to put a helicopter on standby."

She shot him a withering glare before ducking into the passenger seat. "That won't be necessary."

He grinned back at her, then slammed the door and walked around to the driver's side. They drove in relative silence until they hit the expressway before broaching a subject he'd been curious about ever since she'd first called to accept his invitation-slash-job offer.

"I take it Laurel was okay with you running off with me for the weekend," he said, keeping his tone light and just this side of flippant.

For a moment, she seemed to hesitate, then she gave a short nod. Readjusting her seatbelt, she turned slightly to face more in his direction.

"She said she didn't mind at all. She even claimed to think that my working with you was a good idea."

He couldn't resist a tiny smirk. "Told you so."

"She sounded distracted, though," Kara added without rising to the bait. "I don't know if it's Daddy's death and Mama being blamed for it, or calling off the wedding to you, or something else altogether, but she hasn't been herself lately."

"You've both got a lot on your minds these days. Anyone in your situation would."

Kara tipped her head to one side, whether in agreement or simply in thought, he wasn't sure.

"Laurel and Mama were supposed to travel next month before the wedding. Mama can't go, of course, now that she's being accused of Daddy's murder, but she doesn't want Laurel to cancel the trip. I think there's a part of Laurel that still wants to go, if only to get away from all the craziness here at home. But there's another part of her that will feel guilty if she goes, because it will be like abandoning Mama or running off when the family needs her most."

"Sort of like you running off with me this weekend."

Eli purposely let his words hint at a double entendre, curious to see what Kara's response might be. Would she immediately deny that they were "running off" or rush to clarify that it wasn't *that* kind of trip? Or would she let it slide, silently acknowledging that it may indeed turn out to be *that* kind of trip?

To his surprise and delight, she let it slide.

"Yes. I told her she should go. It sounds selfish, but I think she could use the time away. She'll come back with a clearer head, feeling more refreshed. And just like you said about me this weekend, if anything comes up that she needs to be here for, she can get home in a matter of hours."

"Exactly," he agreed, reaching over to take her hand. He twined their fingers together, pleased when she didn't try to stop him. "So now that you believe getting out of town for a few days is a good idea for your sister, maybe you'll start to believe it's a good idea for yourself, too."

She chuckled, her fingers tightening around his. Whether it was accidental or deliberate, however, he wasn't sure.

"I guess I have to, otherwise I risk being a hypocrite, don't I?"

"You certainly do," he agreed.

"Hmm," she murmured. "I think I'm beginning to learn what makes you such a successful entrepreneur. You're a tough negotiator."

"Damn straight."

Though she didn't know the half of it. But by the end of the weekend, she very well might. He would beg, borrow or steal to convince her to launch into a steamy, clandestine affair with him.

"Of course, it helps that I'm simply stating the obvious."

"Arrogant, too," she quipped. "How lucky that I get to spend the entire weekend with Mr. Know-it-All."

"You love me, and you know it," he shot back, bringing her hand to his mouth and pressing a quick kiss to her knuckles.

Eli wasn't certain why he was pushing her so far so soon, when he'd been determined to be a perfect gentleman until they were comfortably settled at Ocean Breezes. But after dropping the first hint that there might be more to their relationship than she wanted to admit and not having her deny it, he felt compelled to press again.

Both his words—the *L* word, coupled with the declaration that she had feelings for him—and the intimacy of the kiss to her hand were designed to test her boundaries. Would she pull away? Would she correct him? Would she laugh it off or concede that, yes, she did love him, but only as a friend?

Oh, how that one would hurt. Because they *were* friends, but he wanted them to be more. And everybody knew that once a woman soundly relegated a man to the "friend" column, he had a better chance of sprouting wings and flying to the moon than ever making it even close to the "potential lover" category.

He didn't expect her to jump across the console and molest him while he was driving, but when she untangled their fingers and slowly pulled her hand away to rest in her lap, he caught his breath. Anticipating the worst and wishing he'd kept his damn mouth shut.

"I do love you," she said quietly.

So quietly, he barely heard her. When he chanced a quick glance in her direction, he found her no longer leaning toward him, but sitting up straight, staring ahead out the windshield.

"You're one of my dearest friends."

Bum-bum-BUM. The impending doom score from every movie he'd ever seen reverberated through his head.

Well, there it was. The kiss of death. A minute ago, he'd been pulsing with anticipation of the weekend to come. Now, he was almost sick with dread and wondering how the hell he was going to get through the next three days.

"I don't think I've ever thanked you for all your support when Daddy first died. Being there for me, day or night."

He'd been one of the first callers to show up at the Kincaid Mansion as soon as he heard about Reginald's untimely death. It had been a suspected suicide then, which had left the family reeling. But then, finding out later that it was murder hadn't been much better.

He liked to think he'd been there to support all of the Kincaids, doing whatever he could to help them in their time of need. But after the reading of the will, when each of Reginald's children had gone home with a letter written specifically to them by their father, Kara had been the one to call him, sobbing.

There hadn't been anything particularly pertinent in her letter. Kara wasn't greatly involved in the family businesses, so there were no instructions on how to run the Kincaid Group or last requests for something Reginald wanted to see done. It was simply a father reaching out to his daughter one final time, telling her how much he loved her.

Eli had stayed on the phone with her well into the night, saying what he could to comfort her, listening to her voice her grief and share special memories of her father that no one else—not even her brothers and sisters, in many cases—possessed. And he'd been happy to do it, grateful that there was *something* he could do for her at a time when he felt pretty damn helpless otherwise.

"Any time," he said now. "You know that."

"I do," she said in barely a whisper. "I do know that."

They were the last words spoken between them all the way to Seabrook Island.

Six

This was a mistake.

At a time when she should be taking in the view, enjoying a leisurely drive to a gorgeous ocean resort, Kara was a bundle of nerves, and all she could think was that agreeing to take off with Eli, even for business purposes, had been a terrible mistake.

How in the name of heaven was she supposed to get through the weekend with him, feeling as she did right now?

From the moment he'd dropped that bomb—*you love me and you know it*—her heart had kicked up like an electric power generator and had been chugging along at full speed.

She did love him, just as she'd admitted. But while she'd focused on their friendship, deep down she was afraid she wanted more than that. Not in some ethereal, childhood fantasy, dream lover way, but in a very solid, realistic, forever kind of way.

It couldn't happen, of course. Despite the kiss they'd shared—which was likely the combined result of stress from a broken engagement, exhaustion from the late hour and too many scotches with dinner—Kara knew he didn't really have *those kinds* of feelings for her.

He liked her well enough, felt warmly toward her because of their shared childhood and appreciated her support after Laurel had dumped him. But he didn't *want her*-want her. Didn't want to toss her on the bed, tear her clothes off and have his wicked way with her.

She shivered at the very thought, because that's exactly what she'd like him to do.

Then she thought of her sister and felt her face flush with the sting of shame.

How could she even be *considering* such things about her sister's former fiancé? How would Laurel feel if she knew Kara was lusting after Eli, and had since she was a teenager?

The most likely answer—that even if Laurel wasn't ready to marry him herself didn't mean she was willing to hand him over to her own baby sister on a silver platter—was the biggest reason this weekend *was a huge mistake*.

They were on Seabrook Island now, drawing closer and closer to his resort, and Kara didn't have a clue what she was going to do once they arrived. Would she be able to tamp down her emotions and act as though nothing was wrong? As though they were nothing more than friends doing a bit of mutually beneficial business? Or would she spend the weekend walking on pins and needles, teetering on the ragged edge of a panic attack?

Crushed shells crunched beneath the Mercedes's tires as they traversed the curving drive leading to the front of the seaside resort. She'd been to Ocean Breezes once before, for the grand opening and ribbon-cutting ceremony. She'd been so proud of Eli that day—as proud as he'd been of his new "baby." Ocean Breezes wasn't just a hotel, after all, which all of his other ventures had been up to that point, but a full-blown resort with everything a guest could possibly want in an island getaway.

A private beach, private golf course, on-site spa and in-room spa treatments. Exclusive shops and a high-end salon right on the premises. Restaurants to die for. And, of course, all the amenities for those once-in-a-lifetime special events she would be consulting on: weddings, anniversaries, bridal and engagement parties, even the occasional sweet sixteen celebration.

She couldn't wait to experience the true luxury she knew stood beyond the front doors.

Eli pulled beneath the wide portico shading the main entrance, and a second later a valet was rounding the hood of the car to open her door for her. The young man was dressed in black slacks, white button-down shirt and a maroon vest with the Ocean Breezes logo emblazoned on the breast pocket. He greeted her with a wide smile, waiting for her to step out before moving again to Eli's side of the car.

"Welcome back, Mr. Houghton. It's a pleasure to see you again."

"Thank you, Robert," Eli returned, passing the boy his keys, along with a folded bill of what looked to be a high denomination as a tip.

At the same time, another Breezes employee removed their luggage from the trunk, placing it on a wheeled, brass-plated cart. When that was done, Eli tipped him, too.

"They all go to my private suites," he told the other young man in a low voice. "And see that strawberries and a bottle of champagne are delivered there, as well. Thank you, Julio."

Kara was more than impressed that he knew his staff by name. She wondered if that was true of all of his hotel and resort locations, considering how many he owned now and how many individuals he must retain at each.

As the car rolled away in one direction and their luggage in another, Eli came to her side, taking her arm and tucking it securely within his own. He began leading her through the glass doors and into the lobby, their heels clicking on the glistening marble floor.

"Strawberries and champagne?" she murmured, repeating

what she'd overheard, but making it a question rather than a statement.

"To celebrate," he said simply.

"Celebrate what?"

"The start of what I expect to be a very lucrative and successful partnership."

"A thank-you note would have sufficed," she told him flatly.

He chuckled, leaning over to press a quick kiss to her temple. "Don't be silly, darlin'. A woman like you would never be impressed by something so mundane."

"Are you trying to impress me?" she asked.

"Of course," he replied without hesitation. "I always try to impress lovely ladies when I want something from them."

Kara's pulse leapt, her breath catching in her lungs for a brief second. They passed the reception area, Eli nodding to the two doe-eyed young women behind the registration desk, who were practically giggling behind their hands at their rich, attractive boss's very presence, before leading her to the bank of elevators off to one side. He pressed the up arrow and the gleaming silver doors slid open.

She waited until they were inside the car, alone, and he'd used a special key card to unlock the button for his private level before clearing her throat and forcing herself to ask, "What do you want from me?"

The doors slid open once again. "For you to join me for strawberries and champagne," he responded matter-of-factly, stepping out into the entry area of his private quarters.

Kara exited the elevator, but then stood nailed in place, taking in her opulent surroundings. She'd grown up with money, so she was no stranger to luxury. She'd also toured several of the guest rooms, suites and private bungalows on the premises during the grand opening.

But while those spaces were impressive even by luxury resort standards, Eli's was a cut above that. It also didn't look like a typical Ocean Breezes suite; it looked like a personal residence.

Hardwood floors instead of plush carpeting...sheer white curtains billowing with the breeze blowing in from the ocean instead of heavy, light-blocking drapes...a full, nearly gourmet kitchen instead of a kitchenette...and unique, personally chosen furniture instead of cookie-cutter pieces.

From what she could tell from a glimpse through the French doors on the opposite side of the large sitting area, he also had one of the most magnificent views in the entire resort. Possibly the entire island.

"Don't be afraid," he said from halfway across the room. "You can come in. I won't bite."

She moved away from the elevator, taking slow, deliberate steps as she continued to study the intricacies of the suite. Through a set of double doors off to one side of the living and dining area, she spotted an immaculately made-up king-size bed.

Their bags were stacked at its foot, which meant the bellhop must have really hustled to get in and out of the suite before they arrived. Pausing only a few feet from Eli, she kept her eyes locked on that luggage and the wide, wide mattress beyond.

"I never agreed to stay here with you," she told him, still without peeking in his direction. "I thought I would have my own room."

From the corner of her eye, she saw him shrug a single broad, tailored shoulder. "This will be better. Besides, you're not just another resort guest, you're *my* guest, and we'll be working quite a bit this weekend. It will benefit us to be in close proximity."

Being in *close proximity* to Eli was the problem. She was having trouble enough beating her runaway hormones into submission just standing three feet away in an otherwise spacious room.

How was she supposed to stop the images flitting through her brain and turning her insides to mush if they shared a living space for three days and two nights? It didn't sound like much, but considering the fantasies she'd been entertaining ever since he'd murmured "I won't bite," three *minutes* and two *seconds* had become too long an amount of time to be alone with him.

"I'm not sure I'm comfortable with that," she told him truthfully. Of course, she didn't reveal the *why* of it.

He started toward her, and she finally turned to face him. As always when she saw him, a jolt of electricity skittered through her veins, sending shock waves to every extremity.

He was just so darned handsome. She was certain he knew it—the man did own a mirror, after all, and tended to have random women fawning over him day and night—but he never acted as though his model-perfect features and physique made any difference to him.

He didn't act cocky or entitled. He didn't use them to sway people to his advantage. He didn't even—to her knowledge, at any rate—use them to seduce women into one-night stands.

Oh, she was sure he had affairs, and possibly even girlfriends, though she couldn't remember him ever mentioning a serious relationship other than the one he'd had with Laurel. But while just about every red-blooded woman would be willing to throw herself at him before she even knew his name, Kara had never known him to take them up on their offers just for the sake of quick, sweaty sex.

When was the last time *she'd* had quick, sweaty sex? she suddenly wondered. Or any sex at all.

It had been a while, to say the least.

Let's see… She'd dated Bradley pretty seriously back in college, and they'd experimented with each other in ways that could still make her blush. At the time, she'd believed they would get married and live happily ever after. Too bad Bradley had had other ideas—along with every cheerleader on the pep squad.

It had taken her a while to get over Bradley's betrayal, so for a few years, celibacy had been the name of the game. Then she'd met Christian.

She'd had no delusions that Christian was the man of her dreams, but he'd been funny, good-looking and knew how to show her a good time. The sex had been decent, and she'd enjoyed it, knowing everything about Christian was temporary with a capital *T*.

And that was it—her two claims to sexual adventure. The last of which had ended some time ago.

Meanwhile, Eli's last relationship had ended only a handful of *days* ago.

With her sister. Her sister, her sister, her sister. She really needed to remember that.

"I only see one bed," she pointed out, holding his coffee-brown gaze even as she wanted to look away and take a cautionary step backward. "Where, exactly, am I supposed to sleep?"

Lifting a hand, he brushed his fingers over her cheek and into her hair, tucking a loose strand behind one ear. "You worry too much, darlin'. Now stop frettin' so we can enjoy our weekend and get a little work done."

Oh, it was so simple for him. Obviously, he didn't have an entire race of tiny alien creatures tap-dancing on his nerve endings the way she did.

She opened her mouth to argue, but a chime sounded near the elevator. Dropping his hand, Eli moved around her and went to deal with it.

After he pressed a button on the panel beside the elevator, the doors whooshed open to reveal the same bellhop who'd taken their luggage standing behind a cloth-draped room service cart.

"Mr. Houghton," he greeted Eli with a respectful nod.

Eli inclined his head in return, waving an arm to welcome the young man into the suite. He pushed the cart to the center of the sitting room, smiling at Kara as he passed.

"Would you like me to open the champagne for you, sir?"

"No, thank you, Julio. I can handle it."

With that, the young man moved back to the elevator. "Is there anything else I can do for you?" he asked.

"Not right now, thank you."

"Enjoy your stay, sir," Julio said before stepping into the elevator and disappearing from sight.

Eli lifted the champagne bottle from the ice bucket and wrapped it in a pristine white cloth napkin.

The cork fell from the champagne bottle with a small pop, and he picked up one of the crystal flutes and began to pour.

With both flutes now filled with the bubbly, he held one of them out to her. Kara stayed rooted in place for a moment, feeling as torn as Eve must have been when tempted by the serpent.

Oh, she could spot a neatly baited trap when she saw one. *Come closer, my dear. I won't bite.*

She'd heard that before, hadn't she? And from Eli's very own soft, seductive lips. Never mind the wolf's razor-sharp teeth glittering in full view.

And yet she found herself moving forward, feet dragging even as she reached for the champagne he was offering. She lifted the glass only to have him stop her before she could take a drink.

"Ah-ah-ah. Don't forget the best part."

Taking a strawberry from the bowl sitting on the room service cart, he brought the ripe, red fruit to her lips. She hesitated for a second, desire battling her better judgment…until desire won out.

Opening her mouth, she allowed him to slip the tip of the strawberry inside, then bit down, letting the tart juices coat her tongue and drip down her throat. She was having trouble chewing, though, and when Eli put the same berry to his own lips, taking an even larger, more succulent bite…well, swallowing became all but impossible.

Of course, he didn't seem to be having nearly the same difficulties. He chewed his strawberry with gusto and just before swallowing, took a drink of the champagne, never taking his eyes from her face.

Because she wasn't sure how long she could keep the bite of berry between her teeth without choking to death—especially considering how tight her lungs were growing—she, too, began to chew.

"Now take a sip," he murmured, putting two fingers to the base of her glass and tipping it toward her mouth.

She did as he encouraged, just barely managing to get it down. Not because there was anything wrong with it; on the contrary, both the berry and the bubbly were exquisite.

But being this close to Eli, almost intimately close, in his own personal suite of rooms had her dangerously on edge. Her whole body was tense, vibrating with expectation. Though in expectation of what, she wasn't certain.

As soon as she'd swallowed, Eli was there again, holding another ripe, luscious strawberry up to her mouth, tempting her to give up. To give in.

And, oh, how tempting it was.

But she couldn't let her heart run away with her good sense. Pursing her lips, she shook her head, refusing to let him ply her with any more intoxicating food or wine until she knew exactly where she stood with him.

"What is this, Eli?" she blurted out the minute he lowered his hand, strawberry and all. "You asked me here on business, but this feels like something else. It feels," she said in a much softer voice, "like a seduction."

He lifted one broad shoulder. "Maybe it is," he said in a casual tone. "But then, who says we can't mix a little pleasure with our business?"

Seven

Eli hadn't intended to admit the more wily part of his plan so soon…or at all, frankly…but when Kara asked him point-blank what he was up to, he couldn't bring himself to lie to her.

In retrospect, perhaps the champagne and strawberries hadn't been the best way to open the weekend. They were a bit obvious.

Then again, he was relieved to have the truth of the matter out in the open. He would have felt like a heel if he managed to lure her into bed, only to be forced later to admit that had been his goal all along.

So there it was. His cards were on the table, and now she knew that he had something more in mind for the weekend than simply talking event planning.

How she would react to that admission, however, was yet to be seen. And he knew there were some tall hurdles to jump when it came to making Kara feel comfortable about engaging in an illicit affair with him so soon after his engagement to her sister had ended.

Because she looked like a deer caught in the crosshairs of a hunting rifle, Eli made a quick adjustment to his plans. Returning his champagne and the uneaten strawberry to the room service cart, he took her glass and did the same, then grabbed her hand and tugged her toward the elevator.

"Where are we going?" she asked after he'd pressed the button.

"You'll see."

A moment later, the doors slid open, and he pulled her inside, pressing the button for the lobby. He continued to steer her as they stepped out and crossed the wide-open space. The same two young ladies who had been behind the reception desk when they arrived were still there, and he offered them a polite, if distracted, tip of his head.

Moving across the lobby and down a long, carpeted hallway, he led Kara to the main ballroom where the majority of their large-scale events were held. It was empty at the moment, literally empty of everything but thick carpeting, a centrally located faux wooden dance floor, and an immovable dais along the far wall.

A row of French doors ran the entire length of the room, opening onto a wide verandah that overlooked the ocean. Several yards away, at the end of a grassy, peninsula-shaped bit of land surrounded by a rocky ledge sat a large white gazebo where many a wedding ceremony had taken place.

"So this is our largest, most booked, and *most coveted* area for events," he told her, letting her enter ahead of him. "People enjoy the view and the breeze coming in off the ocean, and both the gazebo and verandah as a backdrop for pictures."

"This is lovely," she said, beginning to wander around, taking in the details from all different angles.

She no longer seemed distracted by the incident in his suite. "It's perfect for weddings."

"We get a lot of those," he agreed. As well as bookings for the honeymoons that came after.

She moved to the French doors, standing in place for several long minutes. And while Kara studied the landscape, Eli studied her.

She was stunningly beautiful, even turned away from him. Her auburn hair fell around her shoulders in soft, gently curling waves. The lightweight blouse and skirt she was wearing accentuated her feminine curves, from shoulders kept finishing-school-straight to the indent of her waist and back over the flare of her hips. She had great legs, too, whether she was wearing heels or flat sandals like now.

Why did things have to be so damn complicated? he wondered with a silent curse.

He wanted to sidle up to her, stroke the hair away from her neck and kiss the long line of her throat. Spin her around and kiss her senseless. Toss her over his shoulder and carry her back up to his suite, heedless of who might see them.

From there, he wanted to do all manner of wicked, delicious things that would make her forget he'd been engaged to her sister...forget that their being together could be qualified as forbidden...forget everything but the feel of his lips on hers, his naked length pressed to hers, his body moving inside of hers.

The very thought turned him semi-hard and had him shifting uncomfortably from one foot to the other.

But then, he'd always been of the mind that anything worth having was worth working for. If being with Kara were easy, he might not be as interested in her as he was.

Sighing under his breath, he started forward, prepared to open one of the sets of French doors and escort her outside, show her around a portion of the grounds before leading her back to some of the smaller rooms used for lesser events. Only steps from reaching her, he was stopped in his tracks by his name being cried from the opposite doorway.

"Eli!"

He and Kara both turned to see Diane Montgomery swishing her hips as she rushed toward him. Standing on tiptoe, she hugged him a bit too tight, kissed his cheek a bit too close to his mouth.

Long ago, when the plans for Ocean Breezes were first being set in motion, he and Diane had been involved in a short-lived affair. Considering their history, hiring her as the resort's on-site event coordinator probably hadn't been the wisest idea, even if her résumé showed her to be more than qualified for the position.

At the time, she'd been unemployed and somewhat desperate, and she'd done a decent job up to now, even if she did get a little possessive with him and behaved with too much familiarity on occasion.

Bringing Kara in for her professional input on making Ocean Breezes a premiere event location was sure to cause a few bad feelings and a slightly bruised ego for Diane. He only hoped she wouldn't make a scene or do anything to scare off an already skittish Kara.

"The girls at the front desk told me you were here, but I didn't believe them. If you'd let me know you were coming, I could have made sure things were ready for you."

"Everything is fine," he said without intonation, returning her greeting with much less enthusiasm.

Pulling Kara up beside him and keeping her close, Eli introduced the two women. "Kara, this is Diane Montgomery. She's been in charge of events here at the resort since shortly after we opened. Diane, this is Kara Kincaid."

He chose his words carefully, not yet wanting Diane to suspect that Kara might be her replacement, or to imply that she wasn't doing an acceptable job. He also didn't want Kara to know he'd been involved with Diane, even if the relationship was very much past tense.

Kara held her hand out. "Pleased to meet you."

Diane took her hand and gave it a quick shake, but whether Kara noticed it or not, Eli saw the other woman giving her a thorough up-and-down examination. He could almost see the wheels in her head turning, wondering who, exactly, Kara was, what she was doing there and what she meant to Eli.

He certainly wasn't going to enlighten her. Not here, not now…maybe not ever, since who he chose to spend time with was none of her business.

"I was just giving Kara the grand tour," he said. "But I will need to speak to you while I'm here."

Apparently picking up on his all-business tone of voice, Diane glanced at him, then Kara, and back again. The corners of her mouth turned down in a slight frown as she took a step away from them.

"Fine. I'll talk to you later, then."

She turned on her heel and stalked from the ballroom.

"Does she know I'm here to consult on her position?" Kara asked as soon as the other woman was out of sight.

"No," Eli answered simply. Taking her elbow, he led her through one of the unlocked French doors onto the wide verandah.

"I'll tell her when the time comes, if need be. But until you've given me your opinion of the operation here, and how we can improve, I don't see the point in borrowing trouble."

"Fair enough."

"Thank you," he said with a grin, slipping his hand down her arm to link their fingers.

He expected her to pull away, to show the same uneasiness she had back in his suite when he first brought up the idea of turning business into pleasure. Instead, she not only let him twine his hand with hers, but gave him a gentle squeeze in return.

It surprised him how much that small gesture warmed him. Gave him hope that he would be successful in his plan of seduction, after all.

He took her out to the gazebo, which was designed with giant American Beauty roses climbing in a deep blush pink all around the railing and up the posts toward the circular, sloped roof. They didn't go inside, but stood closer to the rocky ledge that overlooked the ocean. A hundred yards below, waves crashed against the shore, sending a salt-tinged breeze up to stir Kara's hair and plaster their clothes to their bodies.

Though the view was breathtaking, Eli didn't normally spend a lot of time on this side of the resort. He didn't like the strong, sometimes violent wind whipping at him, blowing in his face and hair and making it difficult to keep his eyes open.

But experiencing it with Kara suddenly made him see it from a different perspective. Despite the number of weddings they hosted, he'd never considered Ocean Breezes particularly romantic before.

Maybe because he hadn't been paying close enough attention. Or hadn't been standing in the right place, looking out over the churning sea with the right person.

Kara *made* him feel romantic. She made him *want* to order strawberries and champagne, not just because he thought it was a wisely calculated move on his path of seduction, but because she deserved strawberries and champagne, and he wanted to spoil her.

He wanted to take long walks on the beach with her, when the idea of sand in his shoes had never appealed before. He wanted to gaze at her across a candlelit dinner table while they spent three hours paying more attention to one another than their meals.

At that very moment, though, more than anything else, he wanted to reach out and brush the hair away from her face, tip her head back and kiss her.

So he did.

Giving in to temptation, he speared the fingers of his free hand into the hair at her temple, smoothing it back behind her ear, then away from the side of her throat. Leaning down, he pressed his lips to the pulse pounding there. Quickly, erratically. At the same rate his own pulse was pounding in his ears…and lower.

When she didn't pull away, he moved his mouth farther down, to her collar bone, letting his tongue dart out to skim the sharp jut of that sexy protrusion. Then back up, continuing to push her hair out of the way ahead of him so that he could kiss around to her nape, along her shoulder, down toward her shoulder blade.

"Eli."

Her voice came to him in a whisper, one he barely heard over the crashing of the waves below and his own arousal thrumming in his ears.

"Eli," she said again with a reluctant moan.

"Hmm?" he replied without pausing in his exploration of skin that tasted of flowers and honey.

"What are you doing?" she asked on a hush of exhaled breath.

"Kissing you," he murmured against her skin, "what do you think?"

"Why?"

That nearly made him chuckle. It did make him grin.

"Because ever since the kiss we shared in your foyer, I haven't been able to think of a damn thing other than kissing you again," he told her, trailing his mouth over every speck of skin he could reach.

"Because I couldn't resist a minute longer." He nipped the lobe of her ear and traced the line of her jaw.

"Because kissing you is the only thing I can get away with out here without scandalizing guests and starting the rumor mill running at full throttle."

Grasping her chin, he turned her face the last inch to meet his and finally kissed her the way he truly wanted to. His mouth covered hers, grazing her lips, teasing with his tongue until she opened beneath him.

His fingers tunneled into her hair to hold her in place while the kiss deepened. At the same time, he took half a step closer, pressing them together from chest to knee.

A moan rumbled up his throat at the feel of her breasts flattened against him, her legs brushing his, her belly and the apex of her thighs molding to his growing erection through the double layers of her skirt and his trousers. Slipping one hand from the knot of her hair to the small of her back, he tugged her tighter, letting her feel just how much he wanted her. Right here and now, if she would agree…and if they weren't bound to have an audience within a matter of minutes.

Realizing just how true that could be and that they might very well be attracting an audience already, he forced himself to lighten his grip, lighten the pressure of his lips on hers and begin to pull away.

He was breathing hard when they separated. So was she, he was satisfied to notice.

Her lips were swollen a rosy pink from his kisses, her eyes dazed and unfocused. And whether it was the wind blowing in off the Atlantic or the aftereffects of their kiss, she seemed to sway on her feet.

It was the perfect opportunity to sweep her away. Back to his suite and straight into his bed. She was stunned, pliant, and most likely confused about both his actions toward her and her feelings for him.

But as much as he wanted to jump at that excuse, he couldn't. He couldn't take advantage of her. At least not this way. Not yet.

Lifting a hand to her mouth, he used the side of his thumb to wipe away a smudge of lip gloss. He liked it; the smear and bee-stung look made him feel possessive.

Taking a deep breath of salty ocean air to fortify himself, he dropped his arm and clasped one of the limp hands at her side. "Come on," he said, turning on his heel and tugging her with him.

Hurrying to keep up with his long strides, she asked, "Where are we going?"

He slowed his steps and let her catch up, walk beside him rather than running behind. Just because he was frustrated on a massive scale—sexually and otherwise—didn't mean he should take those frustrations out on her.

Pulling her beside him, he wrapped an arm around her

shoulders, pressing a soft kiss to the crown of her head. He held her close, but not too close. Familiarly enough that she would get the point, but not so much that they would garner curious looks from other guests. Or worse yet, his employees.

"I promised you a tour," he told her. "I'm going to give you one before we get distracted and move on to more pleasurable things."

Eight

This was not the weekend Kara had envisioned on the drive down to the island. Even knowing it would be difficult for her to spend so much time in such close contact with Eli, she'd never expected *this.*

How could he suddenly be so interested in her when he hadn't been before? It wasn't just that until a few days ago, he'd been engaged to Laurel. He'd *never* shown an interest in her.

Had he?

She tried to think back on their history together, from middle school on. To all of the times they'd spent together and their countless interactions.

He'd always been kind to her, friendly. But then, he'd been kind and friendly to everyone.

He'd always been there for her, it seemed, through thick and thin. When she'd broken up with her high school boyfriend… when she'd been torn over which college to attend…when her father had died. And in the good times, too—he'd attended her graduations and birthday parties, celebrated with her after the opening of Prestige Events.

But surely he was like that with all his close friends. She imagined he'd been run nearly ragged ever since her father's death. As close as Eli was with the entire Kincaid clan, she was sure each and every one of them had called him at some point since the murder. She was equally sure that he'd spent hours listening to each and every one of them, offering his sympathies and support the same as he had with her.

So that didn't make her particularly special, did it?

Yet when she was with him, she *felt* special.

Of course, her feelings for him had never been in question. She'd always been enamored of him, always had this dreamy, schoolgirl sort of crush on him.

It was *his* feelings for *her* that she wasn't quite as certain of.

Was he toying with her?

At that thought, her heart squeezed almost painfully. If that was the case, she honestly thought she might hurt him. She had carried a torch for him much too long to be seduced and then discarded.

But somehow, she didn't think that could be true. She'd never known Eli to be less than one-hundred-percent honest about anything, and couldn't believe he would ever be so cruel as to make sport of her affections.

But if he wasn't tormenting her, then what was he doing?

It was almost too much to hope that he might truly be interested in her, especially so soon after being engaged to her sister. And yet, here they were.

Kara swallowed hard, doing her best to act as though she was paying attention, while in reality, her mind and pulse were racing.

Eli had shown her the portions of the grounds that were often used for events. He'd taken her through more ballrooms of varying sizes and given her a tour of the kitchens used to cater on-site celebrations.

Now they were headed back to his suite. At least, that's

where she assumed they were going, since there wasn't much more for her to see at the resort that was related to event planning.

He'd promised to schedule an appointment with Diane during their visit so they could sit down and go over dates and figures and paperwork. Kara would need to review how things were currently being run in order to know where there was room for improvement, but she suspected Eli was as reluctant to meet with the other woman as Kara was.

After all, Kara was here to check her work, point out the flaws in her business acumen, and possibly even take over her position as event coordinator for Ocean Breezes. Frankly, Kara wasn't much looking forward to that face-to-face.

At the moment, however, Kara had bigger problems, bigger dilemmas. They were on their way back to Eli's suite of rooms, and she had no idea what she was going to do once they arrived.

Worse, she had no idea what *he* was going to do. Or try to do. Or expect.

She was torn between feeling as though she was walking around in a fairy tale, whisked away for a romantic weekend by a handsome, charming prince…and being swamped by insecurities and guilt.

It was wrong. Giving in to her weakness for Eli was only going to complicate matters. She might be able to get away with it here on Seabrook Island, with no close family to take note of her actions and few prying eyes to watch her every move.

Well, there were prying eyes. The majority of Eli's staff seemed unable to tear their gazes from them any time they passed by. Of course, the fact that Eli had set them up to both stay in his private quarters didn't help matters.

As they reached the bank of elevators, Eli punched the button to call the car.

The elevator doors slid open and they stepped inside. Eli swiped his pass key and punched the button for his private suites.

The doors slid closed, shutting them in together, alone. One minute she was staring at their blurry reflection in the polished silver of the double elevator doors. The next, she was spinning like a top, coming to rest between the hard wall of Eli's broad chest at her front and the cool steel of the doors at her back.

"I can't wait one more minute to do this," he growled.

She opened her mouth to ask *Do what?* but didn't get to voice the first syllable before his mouth crushed down on hers. It took her by surprise, cutting off her oxygen and making her muscles go limp as noodles.

Against her better judgment, when his tongue licked the seam of her lips and he attempted to nudge his way inside, she let him. It was just a kiss, after all. Just one…tiny…kiss.

Somewhere over their heads, a bell dinged. The sound didn't have time to register in her fog-laden brain before the doors behind her slid open and she fell backward.

Eli stumbled after her, catching them both before they ended up in an undignified pile on the foyer floor. Keeping them on their feet, he continued backing her across the entryway until she was once again stopped by a wall. He pinned her there with his body, touching her from collarbones to knee bones.

He kissed her again, not nearly as gently as he had in the elevator. If the kiss in the elevator could be called gentle, which it couldn't. But he didn't wait for her compliance, didn't give her time to adjust or a chance to open her mouth in invitation. He simply took what he wanted.

For long, languid moments, they stood there, tasting, touching. His hands clutched her waist. His erection pressed into her belly. In return, she pawed at his shoulders, her nails kneading him through the material of his suit jacket.

When he released her mouth, she gasped. Then, while she was sucking air into her scalded, much-abused lungs, he caught her off guard by scooping her into his arms.

She let out a startled yip to find herself suddenly horizontal, literally swept off her feet.

"What are you doing?"

"What do you think?" he retorted, not the least bit out of breath, even though she was still struggling not to pant.

Now that he wasn't muddling her mind with steamy kisses and subtle strokes of his hands up and down her sides, she could almost think straight, and she knew this wasn't right. Knew they couldn't do what he was carrying her off to do.

Pressing a palm to his rock-solid shoulder and wiggling slightly in his embrace, she said, "Eli, no. We can't do this."

"Yes," he told her in no uncertain terms. "We can."

Reaching the bedroom doorway, he elbowed open the pocket doors and headed straight for the massive king-size mattress at its center. The entire room was decorated in shades of the ocean—sand, turquoise, salmon—and the bed was made up with a thick golden comforter with enough pillows against the woven bamboo headboard to build a fort.

That's all she had time to notice, though, as he carried her to the side and set her on her feet so he could begin tossing those pillows onto the floor and tearing back the covers. Snowy white sheets in what she was sure was the finest Egyptian cotton lay beneath, just begging to be dirtied and rumpled.

Uh-oh. She took a step back in self-preservation.

Eli noticed her retreat immediately.

"Oh, no, you don't," he mumbled, grabbing her wrist and tugging her toward him.

Her hands went up to stop her from bumping into his chest, but he apparently wanted her to do just that, because he kept tugging until she made contact.

"We can't do this, Eli," she said again, trying to make him see sense.

"Yes," he returned with even more resolve than before, "we can."

He was all hard edges and single-minded determination, but when he looked at her, something in him softened. His eyes turned from coffee-black to melted milk-chocolate-brown and his lips parted ever so slightly. Offering her a small, cajoling smile, he brushed the side of his thumb back and forth across her cheek.

"Don't say no," he told her, barely above a whisper. "I know you want me. As much as I want you."

The words, spoken in such a heartfelt tone, made Kara's throat clog with emotion. Oh, how she wanted to believe them—wanted to believe him.

But she knew better. She knew this was just a momentary whim for him, a rebound fling to help him get over Laurel. And what better way to roll getting over and getting back at his ex-fiancée into one neat little package than by having a quick, tawdry, *meaningless* affair with her younger sister?

"What about Laurel? What about—"

He shushed her in that age-old fashion of placing a finger against her mouth. "She's not here, Kara. She never was. I've never brought her here, and she isn't a factor, not in this."

He continued to stare into her eyes, his hands moving to her hair and doing wicked things to her scalp. Things that made her want to moan. Things that turned her brain to mush.

Then he stopped trying to smooth-talk her. He stopped talking altogether. Tilting her head back, he slanted his mouth across hers.

She brought her arms up, linking them around his neck even as every other bone in her body turned to butter. It was useless. She was powerless against his charm, his blatant sexuality, against his very personality, every aspect of which she'd known and admired since childhood.

She might hate herself—and him—in the morning, but at the moment, she didn't care. Inside her head, she heard the immortal words of that famous albeit fictional Charlestonian, Rhett Butler: *Frankly, my dear, I don't give a damn.*

And she didn't. Not when Eli was kissing her like a starving man at his own personal oasis. Not when his arms were wrapped around her and her breasts were pressed to his chest. Not when the very thing she'd been wanting for half her life was finally within her grasp.

To hell with *should*s and *shouldn't*s, *maybe*s and *what-if*s.
To hell with reputations, and propriety, and all the confessions
and atonements she'd have to make once she got home.

Right here, right now, she was going to be selfish. Not just
give in to Eli's successful persuasion, but do what *she* wanted.
Take what she wanted.

And she wanted Eli. More than ever before. More than she'd
thought possible, even after so many years of wishing, dreaming, fantasizing. Lusting from afar.

His hands were at her abdomen, fumbling with the minis-
cule buttons running down the front of her blouse. That small
display of susceptibility on his part actually worked to make
Kara feel more in control, more sure of herself.

Leaning back, she let him work. Not only because this was
part of her fantasy, but she suspected it was also part of his.

His fantasy. A shiver raced down her spine at the realization that—at this moment, at least—Elijah James Houghton
wanted her as much as she'd always wanted him. It tightened
her throat, made it hard for her to breathe.

Then her blouse floated open and Eli's hands slid inside to
cup her breasts, teasing the nipples through the lace of her bra
with the pads of his thumbs, and she was not only breathing,
but gasping with delight.

His mouth quickly followed the direction of his hands.
Bending her back over one arm, he suckled the material, damp-
ening both it and the skin beneath.

Kara could have sworn her head was spinning. Literally
whirling around on her neck, taking the room with it.

From head to toe, she flushed with heat, her body slowly
beginning to incinerate from the inside out. And they'd barely
gotten started.

With his free hand, he found the tab of the zipper at the back
of her skirt and dragged it down, the *snick-snick-snick* of the
teeth echoing through the room like the boom of a cannon. He
shifted just enough to let the garment fall past her hips to the
floor.

Giving the back of her blouse a tug, he pulled it off her shoulders and down her arms until it followed the direction of the skirt, landing in a puddle at her feet. Without those two pieces of clothing, she was left in only her bra, panties and strappy sandals.

It was too late to turn back, and no matter how much she was wearing, Eli would have had her out of it in a blink.

Catching her off guard, he released her breast and pulled her upright, then in practically the same motion, scooped her up and tossed her to the center of the bed. She bounced there before using her elbows in an attempt to sit up.

"Ah, ah, ah." He gave her a dark look, pinning her in place with his expression alone. "Don't move. Not one muscle."

Still standing beside the bed, gazing down at her without ever breaking eye contact, he started to flick open the buttons of his starched white dress shirt. One at a time, methodically, with only one hand. The other was at his belt, slowly loosening the thin strip of leather.

"I might have to tie you to the headboard," he said, arching a brow as he tugged the tails of his shirt from the waist of his slacks. He shrugged out of what was probably a five-hundred-dollar suit jacket and the shirt beneath both at once, kicking off his shoes in the same motion.

"You've been so jumpy and so reluctant to be with me," he continued, slipping into a deep Southern drawl. "I don't want you hopping up and trying to escape at an inopportune moment."

The sight of his bare chest had her drooling. It was broad and sleek, with just a smattering of crisp, dark hair forming a T-shaped pattern across his pectorals and down to his abdomen. The muscles there rippled, attesting to the time he put in at the gym and calling to her like a half-off shoe sale at Saks.

Every inch of him was golden and lovely.

She licked her lips, watching as he lowered his fly and let the pants drop to the floor with a *whoosh*. Her heart stopped thudding in her chest, moving up to lodge firmly in her throat.

She tried to swallow, but failed the minute she glanced at him again—from head to toe and back up, getting stuck somewhere in between.

Looking at him, she had no problem with his threat to restrain her. The very thought of being tied down, at his mercy, made her go hot and turned her insides to molten lava. Never mind that the shape of the headboard didn't allow for anyone to tie so much as a shoestring to it; she would happily help him scout out other locations.

Even though she sounded like a pack-a-day smoker, she smacked her lips and swallowed until she could speak. "I'm not going anywhere," she told him in a graveled voice. "Not this time."

Nine

A jolt of lust tore through Eli at her words. He was pretty sure that if she'd tried to bolt, he'd have gone after her. Naked as a jaybird, if need be.

Never mind that his reputation as a hard-nosed business tycoon would be tarnished beyond redemption if his employees and the resort's affluent guests saw him racing across the shore after a half-naked woman. If it meant catching and keeping Kara Kincaid, it would be well worth the embarrassment and a short stint in the local mental ward.

But hearing her say she had no intention of running, no intention of changing her mind or trying to get away from him again relieved him of those worries. It also set his blood ablaze and made him want to get *her* naked as quickly as possible.

Climbing onto the bed, he advanced on her. She shimmied back a few short inches, but didn't get far before he caged her in with his body. His hands flat to the mattress on either side of her head, his knees against her thighs.

"Now you can't get away, even if you want to," he rumbled, staring down into those flashing green eyes.

"I don't want to," she said.

His entire body twitched. His skin began to tingle. And for the first time since adolescence, finishing almost before he'd gotten started was a very real possibility.

Careful not to touch her with any other part of his body, he dropped his mouth and kissed her. Slowly at first, savoring the taste and texture of her lips. Smooth and soft like rose petals or spun silk. Sweet and tangy like the strawberries they'd eaten earlier, with a hint of honey from the gloss she was fond of wearing. He nibbled, suckled, teased her as well as himself.

Beneath him, she writhed provocatively, making tiny mewling sounds deep in her throat. Sweat broke out along his brow and his pulse kicked up another thirty beats per minute.

Deepening the kiss, letting his tongue dance along the seam of her lips before pressing inside, he carefully lowered himself until he was stretched atop her entire length, pressing her into the downy mattress.

The lace of her bra scratched against his chest, but in a very good way. The feel of her matching panties cushioning his rigid arousal was even better. Rubbing slowly back and forth, he created a gentle friction between their bodies to match that of their tangled tongues.

Slipping a hand behind her back, he found the hook of her bra and released it, tugging the straps clear of her shoulders. But when he tried to remove the slinky material completely, Kara's hands came up, holding the cups in place.

As loath as he was to do so, Eli lightened the kiss, slowly pulling away until he could lift his head to look down at her.

"Don't," he whispered, holding her gaze. "Don't turn shy now. And don't hide from me. Ever."

She didn't say anything, but he felt her relax beneath him. Her hold on the bra went slack and she dropped her arms back to her sides.

He grinned—he couldn't seem to help himself. But not because she'd followed his orders. Because her acquiescence proved that she trusted him in one of the most intimate ways a woman could trust a man—with her body.

And because her breasts were magnificent.

Kara was far from fat, but she wasn't model-thin, either. She had curves—full thighs, lush hips and bountiful breasts—in all the right places. Curves that could make a man sit up and pant. Invited him to invent some first-rate fantasies or stick around awhile and explore to his heart's content.

Eli counted himself among the lucky few who were going to be allowed to linger. But he didn't have the patience or the fortitude to linger very long this time around.

Nevertheless, he relished the view. Her flushed skin, slightly parted lips, the rise and fall of her chest as she lay beneath him. She was at his mercy…but whether she realized it or not, he was also at hers.

He snagged her lips for a quick, hard kiss before trailing his mouth down her chin, her throat, the center of her chest. She arched her back, bringing her breasts even closer to exactly where he wanted them.

He caressed them with his fingers and thumbs, tweaking the nipples before lowering his mouth for his very first taste. She moaned, putting voice to the sensations swamping them both. He rolled one puckering bud beneath his tongue for several long seconds before moving to the other. He could have gone on forever, back and forth between those two soft, amazing mounds.

Could have, except for the fact that Kara raised her legs and wrapped them around his hips. Raised her arms and wrapped them around his neck. Her nails raked languidly up and down his spine; her thighs cradled him, rubbing maddeningly against his arousal.

Growling with mounting frustration, he abandoned her breasts and slithered down her body. She tightened her grip to keep him from moving, but she was no match against his size or determination.

She clung to him while he kissed his way down her torso, swirled his tongue around her navel, then dipped inside. Hooking his fingers into the waistband of her panties—which were little more than a scrap of white lace to begin with, held in place by an even smaller strip of elastic—he worked them down, slowly revealing the V of her femininity inch by tantalizing inch.

She squirmed against him, murmured his name in such a needy, breathless tone that he nearly gave in. But he knew what he wanted, and what she needed to push her as close to the edge as he was already.

Ridding her of the panties altogether, he tossed them somewhere off to the side, not particularly caring where they landed. Then he spread her legs, tucking them up and over his shoulders.

Kara gasped when she realized what he was about to do, but he wouldn't let her wiggle away. He pinned her in place, absorbing her heat, breathing in her essence.

Kissing her like this was just as pleasurable as kissing her mouth, but in a million other, very different ways. He used his lips and tongue and fingers to explore her folds until her mewls of protest turned to moans of delight.

She writhed beneath him, her hands tangling in his hair—whether to urge him on or still attempting to budge him, he wasn't sure. And it didn't matter. He had no intention of stopping until he'd wrung from her every ounce of pleasure she was capable of giving.

He could feel her body tensing, every muscle and tendon tightening like a bow as her nails dug into his scalp. Redoubling his efforts, he licked and stroked, driving her up and up until she cried out and went over.

He stayed with her until she calmed, floating back down to earth in a heap of boneless limbs she didn't even have the strength to keep wrapped around him any longer. The corners of his mouth twitched as he tried to hold back a self-satisfied grin.

Tried, but failed. He smiled his way back up the line of her body, trailing kisses all along the way. When he reached her mouth, he kissed her there, too, long and deep and hard.

Her hands, shaking with the aftershocks of her orgasm, came up to frame his face, caressing the slight stubble on his jaw. Eli groaned at the gentle touch, feeling his own skin ripple, the muscles beneath constricting in anticipation of what would come next.

Trailing his fingers over her hip and between her legs, he found her opening, slick with a mix of moisture from his mouth and her own feminine juices. Centering himself, he pushed inside. Slowly.

An inch.

He gave a silent but heartfelt moan.

Then another.

His nostrils flared as he tried to school his breathing. In, out. In, out.

And another.

Maybe if he concentrated on something else. He thought about his company. Of pending business, upcoming meetings and contracts that were sitting on his desk yet to be reviewed.

It didn't work. Heat and pressure built in his groin, radiating outward.

Drawing her legs up, he wrapped them around his waist. She crossed her ankles to hold them in place, arching up to meet him, which only worked to drive him deeper.

They gasped together, breaths mingling. And then he was fully embedded, buried to the hilt.

As taut as he was, every fiber of his being pulled tight with building tension and expectancy, he didn't rush toward the big finish. Instead, he held perfectly still, soaking up the sensations of being this closely linked to Kara.

He'd dated a lot of women. Been involved with them on varying levels, from meaningless one-night stands to lengthier, more significant relationships. Never before had he been anywhere near thinking the *L* word.

With Kara, though, it was easy. Just thinking about her made him go soft inside. Being with her, seeing her smile, hearing her voice and her smooth-as-Southern-Comfort laugh, warmed him from head to toe. And thinking about being with her *like this*…on top of her, under her, inside of her…made him go hard.

He'd certainly never reacted that way to Laurel. Not in the entire time they'd been engaged.

That had to mean something, didn't it?

Not that he was going to spend much longer contemplating the matter. He was busy with something more important.

Canting his hips, he began to rock gently back and forth, in and out. Kara's heels dug into his thighs and buttocks, and he returned the favor, clutching her bottom to bring her up on each of his downward thrusts.

They moved together like synchronized swimmers, every move in perfect harmony. But it was also *hot.* She cushioned him, squeezed him, struck a match somewhere deep inside that flickered, sparked, then burned him nearly to ashes.

Holding her tight, he rolled them across the wide bed, coming to a stop on his back so that she was on top. Once she caught her breath, she sat up, both hands flat on his chest as she straddled his hips.

She shook her head, sending her dark curls swirling around her face and shoulders. Her hair was rumpled and sexy as hell. Maybe because he'd been the one to muss it up.

Her cheeks were flushed, her lips rosy and swollen, and he'd done that, too.

A surge of possessiveness poured through him, making him feel strong and powerful. *Me Tarzan, you Jane* manly.

Reaching up, he tangled his fingers in her hair, mussing it even more as he tugged her down by those big, soft curls. He took her mouth in a hard, soul-stealing kiss, wanting to mark her as his own, ruin her for other men forever.

Lower, she started to move, shifting just enough to begin the exquisite friction of body against body, skin against skin, hard against soft. He released her mouth and she straightened again, curling back like Lady Godiva on her trusty steed. And in this instance, Eli had no problem whatsoever being her ride.

She placed her hands flat on his chest, the half-circles of her nails digging into his pecs. Her breasts hovered just inches from his face, pushed together by her arms. Those raspberry nipples, drawn tight and dimpled, called to him. He wanted to feel them, taste them, test their sensitivity.

He covered both breasts with his hands, weighing them, kneading them, using his thumbs to tweak their tips. Then he leaned up and took one rigid nipple into his mouth.

Kara moaned, sucking her bottom lip between her teeth. Eli grasped her hips, guiding her motions while he continued to play with her breasts as long as he could.

But eventually, instinct took over. Sensation swamped him. Bone-deep need drove him, and he knew it was driving her, too.

Falling back to the mattress, he sucked in gulps of air, a steel vise closing around his rib cage tighter and tighter while she gyrated on top of him. She looked like a goddess, but was doing things to him that only a temptress could manage.

His fingers dug into the flesh of her bottom as she rose and fell on him faster, harder, sharper. Her own breath came in pants, her eyes fluttered closed and he could feel her clenching around him.

She cried out, stiffening above him. Her whole body rippled with climax, sending shimmers through his own until he couldn't hold back and followed her blindly over the edge.

Ten

Kara was lying on her side, watching the sun slip beyond the horizon. It was a bright ball of orange, the sky glorious streaks of pink, yellow, purple, all sliding into the wide expanse of the gently rolling blue of the ocean.

Without a doubt, Eli had the best view of the entire resort. It paid to be the owner and CEO of such an amazing enterprise, she supposed.

It was one of the most beautiful sunsets she'd ever seen, and she'd never felt so happy, so comfortable, so satisfied and content. Or she would have, if guilt weren't swamping her in steady waves.

She'd just slept with her sister's fiancé. *Ex*-fiancé, but the *ex* part was so fresh and new, it might as well not even be there.

So instead of basking in the warm relaxation of afterglow, she was lying there worrying.

Worrying about Eli's arm circling her waist and what emotions or intentions it might symbolize.

Worrying about what she would say to Laurel when she got

home…or how she would ever again be able to look her sister in the eye if she *didn't* confess this weekend's sins.

Worrying about what to say to Eli, a man she'd known most of her life and yearned for almost every one of those years.

Being with him had brought to life a million fantasies, made a million of her dreams come true. But they couldn't last. And worse yet, she was afraid she might only be a temporary distraction for him. A rebound relationship designed to help him get over his breakup.

Which only added to her misery, because if there was one role she'd never played in her fantasies of being with Eli, it was a substitute for the woman he truly craved.

"This was a mistake," she murmured, still staring into the distance.

She should be leaping away from his touch, grabbing her clothes and fleeing his room, racing back to Charleston. Not that she had any idea what she'd do once she got there. Lock herself inside her own bedroom, maybe, and refuse to come out, refuse to speak to anyone until her guilt and humiliation wore off. If it ever did.

"No, it wasn't," Eli responded without missing a beat.

His nose nuzzled her hair, his lips grazing her earlobe. The arm around her waist tightened, pulling her even closer to his bare—and obviously masculine—length. He wasn't fully aroused, but he wasn't soft, and he made no secret of the fact.

"What are we going to tell Laurel?" she asked, her voice crackling with the sinking of her heart.

"Nothing. She has nothing to do with this. With us. We're consenting adults. We don't owe her, or anyone else, an explanation."

If only it were that simple.

"We didn't use protection." The flip-flop of her stomach at that knowledge—realized too late to do anything but panic—joined her rapidly descending heart until everything in her felt heavy and weighted down.

"I know," Eli admitted. "You got me so worked up, I completely forgot. I'm sorry."

He pressed a kiss to her temple, sliding his arm higher until it just brushed the undersides of her breasts. "I don't want you to worry, though. If anything happens, you know I'll do the right thing."

Wonderful. So if she wound up unexpectedly pregnant to her sister's ex-fiancé, he would "do the right thing" and marry her, giving even more grist to the overactive Charleston gossip mill. That had never been part of her fantasies, either.

She felt, as well as heard, Eli's long sigh. With a tug at her shoulder, he rolled her onto her back. She held the sheet to her chest, but otherwise just lay there, passive and pliant.

Propping himself up on one arm, he hovered over her, gazing down into her eyes.

"You need to stop worrying so much," he told her. "About other people, and about what they think. You're not responsible for the entire world, you know. Or even your family."

She raised a brow, knowing she should be offended, but lacking the energy to get worked up. "That's a terrible thing to say. I love my family."

"Of course, you do. *I* love your family. But you spend so much time taking care of everyone else that you never stop to consider what you need or want." He splayed his fingers and ran them through the hair at her temple. "You have a right to your own life, Kara. A right to be happy."

"I am happy," she protested.

"Happy enough," he agreed. "You're not sitting in a bathtub with a straight razor, that's for certain."

She wrinkled her nose at the image that created. She preferred to sit in a bathtub full of bubbles, with maybe some candles, rose petals, soft music, a glass of wine... And the only razor she took in with her was of the leg-shaving variety.

"But your first thought is always for others. What you can do for them, what they need, how you can help them. Even your job is about fulfilling everyone else's wants and needs over your own."

Okay, she was beginning to get some of her strength back. Annoyance was building.

"Since when is not being a selfish jerk such a crime?" she charged.

He shook his head. "It's not a crime. You are an amazing, caring, *selfless* human being. I just want you to admit that we're enjoying ourselves, and that there's *nothing* to be guilty about."

"When a person does something that hurts, or has the potential to hurt, another person, they *should* feel remorseful."

Eli cocked his head, still hanging over her, still stroking her hair. "Who are we hurting?"

She opened her mouth, a name popping immediately to her mind, but he covered her lips, stopping her before she could speak.

"Don't say Laurel." He sighed, a shadow passing over his coffee-brown eyes. "Dammit, Kara, you're not her keeper. She's the eldest sister, so if anything, she should be yours. But even that doesn't matter, because she is not a part of this. Laurel is a grown woman, she can take care of herself and make up her own mind, and that's exactly what she's done. She called off the wedding because she doesn't want to be married to me."

Licking his lips, he held her gaze. *Glared* down at her might be a better description. But despite the harsh lines of his face and the darkness of his glower, she could see the sincerity in his expression and had no choice but to believe him, no matter how strongly her gut told her to deny his words.

"And I'm fine with that. After giving it a bit of thought, I don't think I really wanted to be married to her, either. But I *do* want to be here with you now. And I want *you* to want to be here with me."

A sob worked its way up from her diaphragm and she swallowed hard to hold it back. She knew he meant what he said, *believed* he meant it.

She wasn't sure it was enough to override all of the issues

still clamoring between them, but for the moment, it was enough to make her forget.

Her hands came up to stroke his shoulders, his biceps, back up to cup his square jaw. "I do want to be here with you," she told him barely above a whisper.

It was easier to admit than she would have expected. Maybe because it was so very true.

A wide smile spread across his face, lifting the shadows.

"That's something, anyway," he murmured.

Then he kissed her, mashing his lips against hers, snaking his tongue inside to duel and suck and claim her as thoroughly as his body had during their lovemaking less than an hour before.

For long minutes, they were twined together. Her arms and legs tangled with his while he rested in the cradle of her thighs. His mouth devoured her, overwhelmed her, but in the best way possible.

When he lifted his head, his ragged breaths dusted her face with warmth. His smile was still there, making him look happy and youthful and carefree. The emotions were contagious, and she couldn't help but smile back.

"Now that we've got that out of the way, I have a proposition for you."

She raised a brow. "Another one?" Hadn't she been compromised enough for one day, one weekend, one lifetime?

The corner of his mouth hitched higher. "Yeah. Another one, I guess."

She waited, her stomach taking only minor dips at the thought of what foolhardy endeavor he might suggest next, but it took him just a beat or two to fill in the blanks.

"Stay the week with me."

Kara's eyes widened in surprise, and Eli was glad he was currently lying on top of her, holding her in place. Otherwise, she might have already exited stage left. As it was, she went statue-still beneath him, and he found himself holding his breath, waiting for her eventual, full-blown response.

The tip of her tongue darted out to wet her lips, and a stab of heat hit him center mass. They were in the middle of a conversation that needed to be finished, but there was no way she could miss his growing arousal. And if she was even a tenth of a percent willing to do something about it, he knew every coherent thought he possessed would be driven from his head in the blink of an eye, possibly never to be heard from again.

So he needed to hold his ground, grit his teeth and bear it until she answered him—preferably with the response he was looking for.

"I don't understand," she said. "I'm already staying with you through the weekend. More than I ever intended."

"I know, and I appreciate it," he responded, nudging her slightly beneath the sheets and waggling his eyebrows. Thankfully, she giggled, which let him know she wasn't on the verge of screaming bloody murder and hitting him over the head with the bedside lamp just to get away.

"I'm talking about staying the whole week, though. So you can do what you came here to do, and we can still have time to be together without a clock hanging over our heads."

"But what about Prestige? What about my family?"

He didn't gloat, even though he wanted to. The fact that she was questioning him, posing dilemmas he'd already mapped out solutions for, meant she was considering his invitation.

"You are Prestige," he pointed out, schooling his features and warning himself not to go too far too fast. "And the only event you're working on at the moment is unraveling my no-longer-upcoming wedding. No one would expect you to be in the office or pick up new events until after that would have taken place."

He purposely avoided mentioning Laurel—her name had been spoken too many times in this bed for his peace of mind, as it was. The fewer reminders of Kara's sister while he was trying to convince her to spend a decadent, illicit week with him, the better.

"As for your family...you know how I feel about that. We

don't owe them any explanations. But if you're set on sharing the most intimate details of your life and coming clean about something you shouldn't feel guilty over in the first place, well then, I would think you'd welcome an extra week's reprieve before that particular confrontation."

He shrugged, shifting so that his forearms aligned on either side of her upper body and his hands could frame the heart shape of her beautiful face.

"We're already here, in a spot a lot of people would say comes close to Paradise. We're obviously enjoying ourselves… or at the very least, I am," he teased, rubbing against her again in case she'd somehow forgotten that she had a heavily aroused man lying on top of her. "Let's stay here, continue to enjoy ourselves. Reality will intrude soon enough, believe me."

Rather than tense beneath him and try to push him away, or launching into a second round of arguments, her features softened, and he felt her release a sigh.

"Have you ever heard the term 'silver-tongued devil'?" she asked.

A question that didn't require an answer, but one side of his mouth hitched upward all the same. Her lips twitched in return.

"I think I've just met him," she confessed. "You're a very smooth talker, even for a Southerner."

"Only when I'm properly motivated," he told her, slipping into an even deeper Carolina drawl. "And you, darlin', are very proper motivation."

Lowering his head, he covered her mouth, going for a drawn-out kiss meant to persuade. The downside being that attempting to turn her soft and pliant had the exact opposite effect on him. He went hard and ready, and it was all he could do not to slide into her right that minute, bringing them both to an almost immediate climax.

But he'd been careless once, and owed her better than that next time around.

Pulling away—reluctantly—he leaned across her, careful not to crush her, and dipped into the top bureau drawer. He came out with the box of condoms he kept there just in case, though he'd never before had reason to use them.

"I promise to be more careful from now on, but we only have twelve of these, so I may have to run down to the gift shop and buy more."

"That's rather brash of you," she replied.

"We'll be together for a week. A case of condoms may not be enough."

She chuckled. "Now I know how you managed to build your very own hotel empire in only a matter of years—all that cocky self-confidence drove you."

"Of course. You don't think I got where I am on my good looks alone, do you?"

"Oh, and modest, too!"

Her humor and lightheartedness were contagious, and soon they were both laughing.

Had he ever laughed in bed before? With a woman and while he was sporting an impressive erection, that was, rather than simply sitting alone, catching up on paperwork and watching something funny on television.

If he had, he couldn't recall it. In his world, sex and hilarity didn't mix. But now that he was experiencing it firsthand, he found that he liked it. He could see himself laughing in bed with Kara again and again. Even doing things purposely to amuse her so that they could.

He would pour champagne into her belly button and noisily slurp it out...dot her nipples with whipped cream and chocolate sauce, and see how many tries it took to get the cherries to stick... With a bit of thought, he could probably even come up with a couple ideas that didn't involve food, too.

Of course, there was no time like the present, and he realized suddenly that he was famished—for more than just Kara, though she was definitely on the menu. But with the exception of a few nibbles of strawberry when they'd first arrived, neither of them had eaten since breakfast, so it was high time to remedy that.

Rolling away from her, he reached for the telephone and dialed room service.

Eli ordered appetizers, entrees and all of the ingredients for the hot fudge sundae he was suddenly craving—provided he could eat it off of Kara's ripe, voluptuous body. Then he asked them not to deliver it for another hour. That should give him enough time to ravish her at least once without any awkward interruptions.

"Expecting company?" Kara asked as he turned back around.

"No, why?"

"You ordered enough food to feed the U.S. Olympic team."

Shrugging that off, he said, "I'm hungry. But we have time before everything arrives to put at least one of these to good use." He shook the box of protection as he returned to her, gathering her into his arms.

She gave a long, exaggerated sigh. "Fine. But do me a favor—if you do have to go down to the gift shop for more of those, put on a disguise first. Bad enough everyone who works here knows I'm staying in your suite with you, I don't need them knowing we're having sex, too."

He quirked a brow. Surely she couldn't be that naive. "Hate to break it to you, sugar, but chances are they're already thinking that's exactly what we're up here doing."

Her mouth folded into a proper moue and she lowered her lashes in the best imitation of Scarlett O'Hara he'd ever seen.

"Presuming and knowing are two different things," she told him primly.

Eli started to chuckle, then bit back the sound, doubting she would appreciate him being amused by her modesty. He might think it unnecessary, but it was obviously important to her. And if it was important to her…

"All right. But you may have to help me go incognito. I left my Groucho Marx glasses in my other overnight bag."

"That's okay," she said, taking the box from him, opening it, and removing a single foil square. She waggled it in front of him between two slim fingers. "I'll lend you one of my sundresses and a pair of heels. No one will suspect a thing."

Snatching the foil packet away from her, he set it and the box of others aside. "I am *not* dressing up as a woman. Not even to protect your modesty," he told her in no uncertain terms.

She shrugged, feigning nonchalance when he could clearly tell she was biting back a grin.

"Suit yourself. You're the one who wants to extend our visit to a full week so we can stay in your suite and have hot, sweaty monkey sex. I was just trying to help."

For the count of twenty, he simply stared at her in astonishment. Where had *this* Kara come from? he wondered.

Slapping his arm out, he grabbed the loose condom and the box of extras right along with it, dragging the entire bunch back beside them.

"To hell with it," he growled, ripping the corner of the first packet open with his teeth. "I'll wear the dress."

Eleven

Kara never did make Eli wear one of her dresses—not that he would have fit into it, if he'd tried. But she wouldn't let him shop for fresh protection in his own resort's gift shop, either. Her face flamed at the very thought of the clerk knowing exactly who he was using those condoms with, and then running off to spread the news with every other employee.

At least this way she could still walk through the lobby with her head held high. Speak to the room-service waiters, registration receptionists and current event coordinator, Diane, with only a small spot of self-conscious color reddening her cheeks.

Then again, she'd compromised her family loyalties, her entire belief system and a good chunk of her self-respect to spend the week with him. It was the most clandestine, illicit and guilt-ridden affair she'd ever participated in or even heard about, so as far as she was concerned, he owed her one. Or twenty.

She owed him one, too, though. She'd come to Seabrook Island to investigate and revamp his event planning system… or at least that's the request he'd made in order to get her down here so he could sex her up, down and sideways, the lying bastard…and she intended to do that before they headed back to Charleston. If she didn't, she would forever know that she'd run off with her sister's ex-fiancé for a week of sex on the beach—or darn close to it—without even the guise of doing actual work.

Thankfully, Eli was of the same mind. Oh, he took advantage of every opportunity to sneak up behind her and kiss the sensitive spot beneath her ear…or pull her into his arms for a hot, demanding kiss…or tug at the knot of her towel just after she'd stepped from the shower, getting her dirty all over again (in the very best way) before she could dry off and dress.

But he'd also admitted that there was some business he could attend to as long as they were at the resort. Work that, if he took care of it during their current visit, would save him another trip at the end of the month.

So while he was off picking up protection for whatever erotic trouble he planned to start after they finished a private dinner…and taking care of *his* work, she'd decided to bite the bullet and sit down with Diane.

It wasn't that Kara was nervous, exactly, but from the moment she'd first met the woman, she'd gotten the feeling Diane Montgomery didn't care for her. Maybe because Eli was an eligible bachelor of the rich and handsome variety and she had her eye on him for herself. Kara could certainly understand the other woman's jealousy, if that was the case.

Of course, if Diane had confronted her about that at their first meeting, Kara would have laughed and shrugged it off. Her own secret, long-term feelings for Eli notwithstanding, she *hadn't* thought she was here to sleep with him. She probably would have handed him over on a silver platter, much as she had when she'd first noticed Eli and Laurel getting involved. Instead of jumping up and declaring her own longtime feelings for him, she'd kept her mouth shut and suffered in agonizing silence.

The other reason Diane might have for disliking Kara on sight was that she suspected Eli had brought her here to…

evaluate her work, dissect her past efforts and possibly even take over her position at the resort. Eli had never said as much, at least not within Kara's hearing, but that didn't mean word hadn't gotten around that that might be his purpose.

Which meant Kara had to be very careful about how she handled things. She needed to do right by Eli and figure out how well his on-site event planner was doing her job, but without making the woman feel as though she was undergoing an IRS audit. Something Kara should be able to handle quite easily…as long as Diane's discomfort around her was professional rather than personal.

As professional as Kara needed to be, she also had to keep things casual, otherwise Diane would be put off from the very start. To that end, she was wearing a simple sundress perfect for the cool spring weather, with flat, strappy sandals and no pantyhose. She'd also kept her jewelry to a minimum to avoid looking too flashy. Small, gold hoop earrings, a braided gold necklace and matching bracelet, and one filigree ring on the middle finger of her right hand.

Crossing the wide-open lobby, she made her way down a series of tiled hallways toward a rear section of the resort where the offices were kept. She found Diane's quickly, thanks to the clearly marked doors and Eli's detailed directions.

He'd offered to take her, actually, and sit in on her first meeting with Diane. To her mind, having him there could only make things worse. It would put Diane even more on edge, and make Kara feel self-conscious, as well. So she'd said thank-you, but turned him down, sending him off to do his own thing while she did hers.

Tapping gently on the office door, she waited for the other woman to respond before pasting a wide, friendly smile on her face and walking into the lioness's den.

For the second time that day, Eli caught himself whistling. Actually whistling. When he was far from a whistling kind of guy.

But apparently, being with Kara put him in a whistling kind of mood.

Talking her into coming down here with him had been inspired. Never mind that he'd had to bribe her with a work project and a possible future contract with his billion-dollar resort to do it...the point was, she'd come.

And just as he'd hoped, once they were settled in, he'd been able to lure her into bed with him. It hadn't taken long, either, a fact that caused him to preen a bit, sure, but that he was also just damn thankful for.

With only one short weekend—now extended to one short week—to convince her that *she* was the Kincaid sister he wanted to be with, he didn't have time for the usual amount of wining, dining and patient romantic wooing. Instead, he was taking more of a shock-and-awe approach.

If he could shake her up by getting her away from Charleston, distancing her from her business and family, then he might have a chance of getting through to her. If he could bring her here, sweep her off her feet, and show her a side of himself she'd never seen before, then she might believe him when he suggested they make things permanent.

He had to be careful, though, not to move too fast and spook her. Or smother her with his desire to keep her close, to be with her nearly twenty-four-seven.

How pathetic was that? He thought as he walked with purpose from his office on the first floor of the resort's main building across the lobby to the elevator. A thirty-five-year-old man who didn't want his lover of seventy-two hours out of his sight.

Some might call him whipped. And in a way, he supposed he was. Kara had certainly woven a mesmerizing spell around him in a very short amount of time, but it was a spell he'd walked into willingly.

Of course, it was no hardship to be in her company practically around the clock. In bed with her...in the shower with her...up against the bureau with her... But also sitting across the table from her, watching her eat and enjoying sparkling conversation.

She was witty and smart; opinionated, but not obnoxiously so. He could introduce almost any topic, and she would discuss it with him passionately and at length. Just the other night, they'd spent nearly an hour debating a handful of political issues, but rather than getting heated, he'd found her views astute and invigorating.

The elevator dinged as it reached his floor, and he stepped off, automatically scanning the suite for Kara. He didn't see her or hear movement from any of the rooms, but that didn't mean she wasn't here. In the bathroom or out on the balcony, maybe.

"Kara?" he called. No answer.

After checking the rest of the rooms and finding them empty, he moved to the bedroom and tossed the paper sack he was carrying on the bed. At Kara's urging, he'd spent the afternoon taking care of resort business. There wasn't much for him to do; he employed an excellent staff who handled most of the day-to-day running of the place for him. But he *was* the boss, and as the saying went, the buck stopped with him. Even if he hadn't devised a creative pretext to bring Kara to Ocean Breezes with him, he'd have made the trip down in the next few weeks, anyway, for one of his routine inspections and overviews.

It was good to have a lot of that finished and out of the way. Now he would be able to set aside business matters altogether and focus on what he was really interested in—seducing Kara. Again, and hopefully again.

He was still wearing the shorts and summer shirt he'd put on at Kara's urging to make his cloak-and-dagger excursion outside the resort property to the nearest gas station-slash-convenience store that carried condoms. He hadn't had to go far, thank goodness, and he was pretty sure no one had recognized him. Especially since he'd also been wearing sunglasses and a baseball cap.

Checking his watch, he picked up the nearest phone and called down to the kitchen to check on the progress of his earlier order. They were assuring him that everything would be ready at the appointed time when he heard the elevator bell ding again and the doors slide open.

That would be Kara. He'd given her a key card that would allow her entrance to the private suite of rooms whether he was with her or not. The only other people with pass cards were staff members, and none of them would come unless he requested it or gave them permission.

He met her in the sitting room, taking a moment to bask in her unmitigated beauty while her nose was still buried in an oversize book resting on top of a stack of other books and folders.

How was it possible for a woman to look mouthwateringly sexy and cute as a damn bug at the same time? The two descriptions were contradictory, to be sure, and yet they both suited her to a T. He was torn between wanting to grab her and tuck her against his chest in a tight, protective embrace…and drag her off to the bedroom to do some very adult, very non-protective deeds with her.

Dragging her off to bed was close to winning out, but he'd made plans, dammit. It had taken him half the night to come up with the idea, and half the morning to put everything in motion.

By dropping the ball now, he would not only risk portions of his staff thinking he was losing his edge, but risk losing ground with Kara. That was more important than anything else, even satisfying his raging libido.

Tamping down on his desire, he cleared his throat to keep from startling her before stepping closer. Her head came up and she blinked like an owl. He'd been right about her not realizing he was there.

"That must be fascinating reading, to keep you so engrossed."

She made a noncommittal sound deep in her throat, then

closed the cover of the book and set the entire pile on the nearby credenza.

"What is all that?" he asked.

"Work. More than I expected," she murmured. Then she shook her head and met his gaze. "Sorry. I mean, scrapbooks, as well as paperwork for past events held here."

Eli cocked his head. "You've already formed an opinion of how things are running, though. I can tell."

Rather than respond, she started to nibble at her bottom lip, which was answer enough for him.

"Great," he mumbled, more to himself than to her. Rubbing a spot at the center of his forehead, he wished he'd waited to begin this conversation.

"All right, we'll talk about all of that. Later. For now, I have a surprise for you."

He'd been hoping for a spark of surprise, maybe the hint of a smile. Most women would be squealing and jumping up and down at his pronouncement, eager to find out exactly what the surprise was. But then, Kara was definitely not *most women,* a fact he'd known and appreciated from the beginning.

Instead, she looked wary.

He couldn't decide whether to be annoyed or amused by her reaction, but opted for amused. She was still a little gun-shy. Nervous about what they were doing, confused about her feelings for him and even more unsure about the ramifications of both.

So he would cut her some slack. Besides, if this evening went as well as he hoped, he would be one step closer to allaying all of her fears and convincing her that they could—*should*—be together in spite of the odd circumstances.

"Stop with the frown," he ordered with mock severity. "You're going to like this, I promise."

His assurances were met with continued silence and a doubtful expression. He just managed to hold back a sigh of frustration.

"Fine. I'll show you, then you'll believe me. Now, before we leave, do you need to use the restroom or change your clothes or anything?"

She raised a brow. "Where are we going?"

"I told you, it's a surprise. But we'll be a short distance from the resort, so I want to be sure you're comfortable and won't need to come back for any...emergencies before we're through."

She seemed to think about that for a moment, then gave a sharp nod. "Give me just a minute."

He did, watching her retreat into the bedroom. Several minutes later, she returned. Her hair had been brushed and tied back in a loose ponytail, and she was carrying a small clutch purse. Typical, he supposed, since she didn't know where they were going, and women rarely went anywhere without at least the bare minimum of a wallet, comb, lipstick, make-up case, the kitchen sink...

When she got close enough, he punched the elevator button, taking her hand while they waited. She didn't pull away, which he found encouraging. Hadn't, actually, any of the times he'd touched her or reached for her since the first time they'd made love. To him, that meant progress, and he would take what he could get.

Twelve

From the moment Eli took her past the reception desk to pick up a giant fabric tote with the resort's name and emblem stamped on the side, and then through the kitchen to collect an oversize picnic basket, Kara had a pretty good idea of what his surprise was going to be. She didn't let on that she knew, though, because she didn't want to ruin it for him.

She was also having trouble breathing, feeling almost overwhelmed by the emotions the situation evoked. He was being so sweet and thoughtful and romantic. And it had been a really long time since anyone—especially a man—had been any of those things to her.

Oh, she was sure Eli was on his best behavior this week. He'd set out to seduce her—a fact she still had trouble wrapping her mind around—and was apparently pulling out all the stops.

But since she was already sleeping with him, since he'd gotten exactly what he wanted from their impromptu trip to Seabrook Island, there was no reason for him to go above and beyond any longer. He could have just as easily ordered room service, then kept her upstairs, in bed, for the rest of the night. Something she wouldn't have minded in the least.

Instead, he led her out of the resort's main building through a side exit and down a narrow stone path toward the beach. Her fingers were clasped in his left hand, tangled up with the straps of the bag. In his right, he carried the woven wicker picnic basket that bounced against his thigh with every other step.

As they hit the sand, he stopped. "You might want to kick off your shoes," he told her, doing just that with his own.

She shed her sandals. Then, because his hands were already full, she leaned down and collected both pairs, letting them dangle from her fingertips. From there, she followed him instead of walking beside him.

Sand slid between her toes as her feet sank deep, slowing her steps. The wind blowing in off the ocean ruffled her hair, pulling thin strands out of the ponytail holder and whipping them around her face. The salty tang of the sea air stung her nostrils and lungs. Three sensations she absolutely loved.

Living in Charleston, she was very close to the water, but never seemed to find the time to truly enjoy it. She'd forgotten how refreshing the ocean breeze could be. How easily the sights and sounds and smells could bring almost instant serenity.

The farther they moved along the shore, the less "touristy" it became, giving over to rougher, rockier terrain. Then she began to notice the signs.

Private beach—no guests permitted beyond this point.

A few yards later: *No trespassing. Violators will be fined.*

And finally: *DANGER: Shark-infested waters. Enter at your own risk.* With a rudimentary drawing of a bloodthirsty shark devouring a hapless swimmer.

Granted, there could be sharks in pretty much any stretch of the Atlantic Ocean…or pretty much any large body of salt water, she supposed. It *was* their terrain, after all. But she'd never known the waters off Seabrook Island to be "infested" and didn't remember hearing any reports of recent attacks.

"Please tell me you haven't brought me here to feed me to the sharks," she said, raising her voice to be heard over the crash of the waves.

Eli glanced back over his shoulder and shot her a devilish grin. Pausing for a second, he waited for her to catch up so they could once again walk side by side, and she knew that if his arms hadn't already been full, he would have reached for her hand.

"Like that?" he asked. "I thought it was rather inspired myself."

With a chuckle, he added, "I asked one of my employees to section off part of the beach so we could be alone. He found that sign at the back of a storage closet, and we both agreed that if the others didn't deter visitors from poking around, the last certainly would."

"I should hope so."

A short distance past the last warning sign, they rounded a curve of beach and entered an area that was almost an island unto itself. Set back slightly from the rest of the shoreline, it was dotted with small trees and bits of grass, and a bed of sand that was flat and dry, with only a few feet at the front being hit by the surf.

Eli dropped the items he was carrying and began digging around in the bag. He removed a giant blanket and spread it out on the ground, taking extra time to straighten the corners. Then came plates and flatware, glasses and a bottle of wine.

"Sit," he said, waving a hand at the blanket while he moved to the picnic basket.

Setting their shoes aside, she folded her legs beneath her, careful to keep the skirt of her dress down around her legs. The steady breeze blowing in off the water wasn't helping.

As she watched, he laid out a platter of crab cakes pan-seared a golden brown, a bowl of chunky, savory southern slaw, and sautéed green beans with slices of onion and bits of crispy bacon stirred in. For dessert, there was a tray of tiny little berry tartlets topped with a dollop of what she was certain was fresh-made, not-from-a-tub, hand-whipped cream that he set aside just to tempt her. It was pretty much a GRITS's—Girl Raised in the South's—idea of a perfect meal, and the very sight of it had Kara's mouth watering.

Eli filled a plate and handed it to her before making one for himself. Then he opened the bottle of wine—a deep, dark claret—and poured them each a glass.

"This is delicious," she said after they spent a few minutes eating in silence.

"Our chef is one of the best," he said.

She cringed. "Actually, that's something I need to talk to you about."

"What—you're eating these amazing crab cakes that Jean-Philippe whipped up from scratch, and you have the nerve to imply he *isn't* one of the best chefs in all of South Carolina?"

He raised a brow as though he knew *that* was impossible.

"No, of course not. Jean-Philippe is clearly a genius," she assured him.

After all, she'd been the one to recommend him in the first place, back when Eli was just building and beginning to staff the resort. Eli had wanted the food at Ocean Breezes to be five-star…ten, if he could have managed it…and had asked for her opinion about hiring a head chef, since a big part of event planning revolved around catering.

"But I met with Diane today, and have been going over the files and scrapbooks for a lot of the past events that have been held at the resort."

"And…?" His voice was flat, unemotional. A businessman waiting to hear the bottom line before any decisions were made.

Feeling uncomfortable at having to point out the flaws in how his resort's events were run, and especially in the event coordinator herself, Kara's gaze skittered off to the side and she toyed with the fluted edges of her dessert tart. Finally, she took a deep breath, lifted her head and looked him in the eye.

"Diane has been offering guests primarily package deals. If someone comes to her wanting to hold their wedding here, she offers them standard, pre-arranged choices. Menus are already designed…the same bands and DJs are used over and over… decorations reused and stored between events."

She shrugged a shoulder and took a small sip of wine.

"There's nothing wrong with that at a certain level. I have sample menus for clients who don't know what they want. I have the names and numbers of several bands and DJs on hand, depending on a client's needs and the type of event I'm planning. And I have entirely too many decorations in storage myself that I pull out when necessary."

"But…" he prompted, ever a step ahead of her. It almost made her smile.

"But this is *Ocean Breezes.*" She stressed the name, because in most of the high-class social circles Ocean Breezes catered to, the name really did say it all. It was one of those *Lifestyles of the Rich and Famous* destinations—the wealthy spent their weekends and vacations there, and the less-than-wealthy aspired to someday at least drive by and see how the other half lived.

"A luxury resort. A dream getaway for half of the United States. Anyone holding their wedding ceremony or fiftieth anniversary celebration here doesn't want the Surf and Turf Menu from Column B of the Seafarer Party Package. They want flowers and ribbons and other assorted frippery chosen just for them…a menu designed just for them…every detail to be exactly as they've imagined in their wildest fantasies, and unique only to them."

Leaning back, Kara blew out a breath, grateful to have that little speech out of the way. Now she just needed to wait and see how he would react.

"In other words," he murmured after several long, tense seconds had ticked by, "we're tantamount to the Plaza delivering motel-quality arrangements."

Her mouth twisted. "Something like that."

"What would you suggest we do to fix things?"

"I think that depends on how far you're willing to go."

He gave a low chuckle, turning the situation from awkward to once again comfortable and relaxed in a split second.

Reaching for his wine, he took a long, leisurely swallow. "I think you know me well enough to know I go all the way," he replied with a sexy wink, the double entendre in his words clear.

"I want my hotels to be the best, and Ocean Breezes is the crown jewel of Houghton Hotels and Resorts," he added plainly. "Whatever changes need to be made, whatever the cost, I want it done. So…what are your recommendations?"

Lowering her gaze to her plate, she continued to pick at her food while she told him the truth. "I think you need to find out what your clients want and give it to them. Don't just give them options to choose from, but be willing to fulfill their every desire."

"I kind of thought that's what we were doing," Eli mumbled. Then, "Give it to me straight, darlin'—does Diane have what it takes to do this job, or doesn't she?"

With a sigh, Kara dropped the fork she'd just used to stab a series of green beans and met his eyes. "I don't want to answer that. It's not my place to evaluate your employees. I mean, I know you brought me here to do just that, but…" She shook her head. "I'm a guest. I spoke with her for all of two hours. I haven't even finished going through all the files."

"But your instincts are already telling you something, aren't they? You've already made up your mind, even without proof." He gave an approving nod. "I follow my gut, too, when it comes to business, and I want to know what yours is telling you."

"Fine," she said, even though her chest felt tight and she really, *really* hated what she was about to do.

"Diane is a nice enough woman. She's probably very good with people."

"I've always thought so."

"But she doesn't seem to *care* about the events she's organizing. She seems to be…phoning it in, for lack of a better description. She likes the packages she's concocted because it makes her job easy. She never has to race around off-island searching for a supplier of pink calla lilies when they're out of season. Or spend two days on the phone trying to find a kettle drum band."

"And that's the sort of thing you do for your clients," he said, making it a statement, not a question.

She laughed, popping the beans into her mouth. "You have no idea. I once flew a magician in from Seattle for a birthday party and picked him up at the airport. On the drive, he made me hold three of his rabbits on my lap. They weren't in a carrier. And they *weren't* potty-trained."

"Oh, no."

His eyes danced with amusement and he was trying not to laugh, she could tell.

"Oh, yes. For the record, you don't try to launder a skirt that three rabbits have pooped and peed on. You throw it away, take a long, hot shower, and buy a new one the next day. Having the car detailed isn't a bad idea, either."

This time, he did laugh. A low rumble of sound that rolled up from his chest. "I hope you billed the client for all of that."

"I did," she assured him, silently remembering how relieved she'd been that the father of the birthday boy had very deep pockets and hadn't batted an eye at the exorbitant bill she'd handed him after the event. He'd simply written her a check and then sent several new clients her way in the months that followed.

"I can't envision Diane holding a rabbit on her lap, never mind letting it pee on her."

"And poop," she reminded him with a small shudder. "There was also poop."

He chuckled again, and she reached across the blanket to smack him on the arm.

"I'm sorry," he said, not sounding the least bit sorry, since he was still shaking with mirth. "But I've got a picture in my head now, and it's really funny."

"I'm sure it is. Did I mention that the magician was in costume the entire time? But not your typical magician's outfit. He was wearing a sparkly purple jumpsuit, complete with full-length cape. Imagine walking through the airport with someone dressed like *that*. Getting him through security on his way out of town was a nightmare."

He was imagining it, and rolling with laughter. He wasn't even trying to control himself, but was flat on the ground, holding his stomach and guffawing. And the terrible thing was that *she* was laughing right along with him.

"All right," she admitted after he'd settled down and she'd caught her own breath. "I suppose it was somewhat funny— *after* the fact. But my point, if you'd allow me to finish making it before you find any more amusement at my expense," she added with mock severity, "is that you have to be willing to go above and beyond to give your clients the best day, the most memorable event, of their lives. I don't think they're getting that from Ocean Breezes right now, and I think if they were, you'd get more bookings and word-of-mouth endorsements."

Back to serious business mode, Eli said, "I guess I'll have to let Diane go, then. Would you be willing to take over for her?"

Kara sat back slightly, eyes going wide. "You're offering me a job? *Her* job?"

"If you're interested."

"I— You— But—" Brushing her hands over her face, she took a minute to collect her thoughts, then tried again. "I'll be happy to help you out, you know that. But I can't give up Prestige and leave Charleston to come down here and work for you. I'm sorry."

"Of course not. I would never ask you to give up your business. You've worked too hard to get it off the ground and make it a success. I was thinking more along the lines of you splitting your time between Charleston and the island—at least to start. Then maybe hiring a few very capable employees to help you at Prestige so that one of them can come down here to work for the resort full-time."

She must have taken too long to respond, because he prompted her. "You have been wanting to hire extra staff for Prestige Events, haven't you? Someone to help you out so you don't have to run things single-handedly."

"I have," she said, with no little bit of awe leaking into her tone. "I just didn't know you knew that."

He flashed her a grin.

"I know more than you think. Of course, it helps that I'm wildly intelligent, pay close attention when I need to, and am invited to Sunday dinner with your family every week."

She smiled back. "There is that."

"This would be the perfect opportunity to finally do it. You would oversee everything, but one of your employees could be here five days a week—or even three, if that's all that's warranted—to run things to your standards."

It was tempting, very tempting. Gnawing her lower lip, she considered it from every angle. And then she realized that she couldn't possibly make a decision like that right here, right now. She needed more time to really think about it and reach a smart, informed conclusion.

"I'm not saying no," she told him after a moment, "but I can't say yes, either. Not yet. May I make a suggestion?"

He quirked a brow. "I thought that was the whole point of this conversation."

"Let Diane stay on. Let me work with her to plan a big summer to-do. A barbecue on the beach, maybe, or a lobster bake. Something substantial and seasonal and open to everyone. Use it to promote the resort, and show the world what kind of events can be held here, as well as the quality of care you offer when guests book special occasions with Ocean Breezes."

"All right, I like that idea. Then what?"

"We'll see if Diane rediscovers her enthusiasm for the job. It may simply be that she's gotten into a rut, and having something new and unique to work on will put her back on track. If not, you can consider terminating her, and I'll reconsider your offer to hire on extra help and station someone here on a semi-permanent basis. It will cost you, though," she warned him.

He grinned. "I'd expect nothing less. But you get what you pay for in life, and I'm willing to pay for the very best."

"You," she said, waggling a finger at him, "are trying to

butter me up with all this talk of taking over your event planning for the resort, hiring on employees for Prestige and having an unlimited expense account."

"I don't remember saying anything about an unlimited expense account."

"Oh," she said, glancing down at her nails as though examining her manicure and feigning innocence. "I could have sworn you did."

"Nice try," he tossed back, lips curled in a smile.

She lifted a shoulder. Chances were, if she did end up working for him on an extended basis, she wouldn't even need an expense account; he would readily pay whatever she charged without argument. That's just the kind of man he was. Especially since he knew how honest she was and that she would never cheat him out of so much as a dime.

"So what am I buttering you up for, do you think?"

"Sex."

That caught him off guard, and she had the pleasure of watching his face go slack at her forthrightness. She didn't imagine it was a feeling he experienced very often and nearly grinned that she'd managed to surprise him.

"You just want me for my body," she added, curious to see what his reaction would be to that slightly loaded observation.

"You're wrong about the 'just' part," he told her in a low voice, staring into the liquid depths of her emerald-green eyes, "but I definitely want your body."

"Sex on the beach?" she teased, running her fingers through his hair, along the curve of his scalp, down to his nape and up again. "I thought that was a mixed drink."

He waggled his brows, sliding his hand from her waist to the underside of her breast. "How do you think it got its name?"

At that, he began to nuzzle her neck, running his tongue in featherlight strokes along her soft skin. She let her head fall back and gave a low purr.

"I've never had sex on the beach," she murmured, her words

beginning to slur as desire thickened her blood. "The act or the drink."

With a chuckle against the silken flesh of her collarbone, he said, "We'll rectify that, I promise. Sex first, room service later."

"What if I want the room service now? I am feeling a bit parched."

Eli knew darn well she was teasing him, but he happened to be in a good mood. Having a beautiful, willing, soon-to-be-naked woman in his arms had a way of doing that to a man.

"If you're really thirsty," he said, as he continued to dot her body with kisses, "I'll call now. You'll have a drink in your hand in ten minutes. Only problem is, by the time the waiter gets here, you'll be naked and under me. Do you really want to risk that?"

She tensed a fraction, and he heard her swallow. "No," she responded primly, "I don't think I do. So sex first, drinks later."

He nodded. "Smart decision."

"I'm a smart woman."

"Yes, you are. A damn sexy one, too," he added, running his palm up her calf, the inside of her thigh, and past the hem of her skirt.

Her lips curved in a wide grin. "I'm glad you think so. I think you're pretty damn sexy yourself."

"Together, we made a damn sexy couple," he quipped. His fingers toyed with the elastic edging of one leg opening of her panties, threatening over and over again to delve beneath. "Who are about to have damn sexy sex on a very private beach."

"Mmmmm." She rolled the sound around in her mouth, letting her head fall back as his mouth trailed the valley between her breasts. "I'm becoming less and less interested in the drink by the minute."

"Good. Now let's see if I can get you more and more interested in the act."

Thirteen

Early the next morning, Kara was reconsidering her decision to turn down Eli's offer of a full-time position at Ocean Breezes. The resort was gorgeous. The island was gorgeous. The people were friendly and accommodating.

Could anything be better than waking up in the morning to the sound of the ocean lapping against the shore? Or the smell of the tangy salt air? Or the sight of the sun rising on the far side of the water, slowly turning it from onyx black to sapphire blue?

It was paradise, pure and simple. Heaven on earth.

Or maybe that was the happiness talking. As often as she'd cautioned herself not to get caught up in the romanticism of this weeklong getaway with the man of her dreams, it seemed she'd fallen and fallen hard.

A picnic on the beach. Gulls floating overhead. A gorgeous man sitting across from her. Delicious food, amazing surroundings, better company.

He'd flattered her, romanced her, listened to her, laughed

with her. And then he'd closed the distance between them and kissed her, caressed her, made love to her.

Right there on the beach, where anyone could have seen. Except no one did because he'd cordoned off the area ahead of time with warning signs and threats of shark attacks.

And he'd delivered on his promise of letting her try a Sex on the Beach—the cocktail this time—soon after they'd enjoyed the real thing.

How could any woman resist?

She certainly couldn't. And she was getting tired of trying.

After returning to their room from the picnic dinner and sandy-but-worth-it seduction, they'd both needed showers. She hadn't voiced a word of protest when he'd started the water running, stripped her of her clothes and then his own, and climbed in with her.

Less than a week ago, she would have screeched, slapped at his hands and fought him every step of the way. Not because she didn't want it, but because she didn't think she *should* want it. Or had the right to another woman's man—her sister's man.

Somewhere along the way, however, her guilt over her possible betrayal of her sister had started to fade away until all she was left with was want and need and love for Eli Houghton. She'd also started to believe that he might have true feelings for her. Not just a need for hot and dirty rebound sex, not just a desire for revenge against Laurel, but actual romantic and serious emotions for *her*. It warmed her, made her feel fuzzy and cozy like a comfortable old sweater.

She laughed to herself, glad no one else was around to hear her as she wandered through the hallways at the rear of the resort's main building. Comparing her newfound adoration for Eli to an old piece of clothing might not sound very poetic, but it was apt. There were some items in her closet that she absolutely loved and wore on days when she was feeling sad or nostalgic. She would never get rid of them, and if anything ever happened to them, she knew she would probably cry.

And just as she suddenly had an urge to go home and climb

into her favorite cable-knit sweater—which would have been perfect for the beach; she really should have brought it with her—she had a sudden urge to see Eli. See him, touch him, talk to him. Just to be close to him and ask how his day was going so far.

Never mind that they'd been together less than an hour ago. She'd awakened wrapped in his arms, pressed like cellophane to his hard, hot body exactly as they'd fallen asleep after a final, incredible bout of lovemaking that had nearly sent her eyeballs rolling back in her head.

And then they'd made love again. She'd never realized how much she enjoyed morning sex, but with Eli, she was practically a nymphomaniac. Morning, noon or night…bed, floor, sofa, sandy beach or the backseat of the car… Anywhere he wanted her, she was more than willing. And if he didn't approach her first, she was more than happy to initiate.

But as much as she might want to track him down and jump his bones, she wouldn't. She would maintain her composure, act like the lady her mother had raised her to be and wait until they were alone again, likely much later that night. *Sigh.*

She would fill the hours until then doing what she'd set out to do when they'd parted ways the first time—tour the resort buildings and grounds, and familiarize herself with both the layout and the leisure interests it had to offer. She knew most of the details already, but if she was going to be working at Ocean Breezes with Diane Montgomery to arrange a Fall event—she and Eli were contemplating August or September for the barbecue, a month when most people's summer vacations would be over, but the weather would still be nice and warm—then she wanted to be sure of her options.

So far, she was contemplating a number of activities for the event—tennis lessons, spa treatments, sailing and jet or water skiing, beach volleyball, possibly even horse-drawn carriage tours of the resort grounds and island. She just had to be sure that everything was both adult- and child-friendly.

Legal pad in hand, she headed for the same ballroom Eli

had shown her when they'd first arrived, trying to get a feel for the sizes of the different indoor areas at her disposal and then wanting to get a closer look at that gazebo again.

"Ms. Kincaid!"

With her hand on the door, ready to push it open, she turned at the sound of her name being called from down the hall.

"Diane," she said when she spotted the woman hurrying toward her. "I was going to drop by your office in a bit to discuss a late summer event Eli is interested in hosting."

"Sure, fine, whatever Eli wants," Diane replied with a distracted nod. "That's actually why I was looking for you—I want to talk to you about why you're here. I realize you might be feeling special right now, thinking Eli brought you here to take over my job."

Kara cringed inwardly. She'd been hoping to avoid just this sort of confrontation and thought she had by convincing Eli to give Diane a second chance. She opened her mouth to respond—though what she planned to say, she wasn't certain—but Diane barreled ahead.

"I can assure you, that isn't the case." The woman's nose went up a good three centimeters. "I'm here because Eli loves me. We've been involved for years. Why do you think he created my position in the first place? It's so that I would be here whenever he came down for a visit, without anyone knowing about our affair."

She shook her blond hair, surgically altered breasts popping forward as her shoulders went back. "It was important to keep our relationship a secret so that he could go ahead and romance your sister. I can't say I was happy about their engagement, but I certainly understood—Eli has always wanted to marry into a wealthy, influential Southern family to solidify his own growing fortune and reputation. Your sister was going to be a trophy wife. I'm the one Eli truly wants to be with."

"Excuse me?" Kara choked out, feeling as though she'd been hit over the head with a two-by-four. She heard the words, understood them in a Webster's Dictionary sort of way, yet couldn't seem to put them in order or make logical sense of them.

"I have to admit, I was relieved when your sister called off the wedding. It meant we could carry on as planned. But then you came along, and I guess he decided to move forward with marrying into the prestigious Kincaid family, after all."

Swallowing hard, Kara struggled to maintain her composure. No matter how much she might want to burst into tears or kick Diane in the shin with the toe of her pointy-pointy shoe, she wouldn't give this woman the satisfaction.

"Why are you telling me this?" she asked instead, hoping her face was as blank and emotionless as she was trying to make it.

Diane shrugged again. "I just want you to know that—no matter what Eli might have told you to get you down here—there's no way he'll ever actually get rid of me and put you in my place. Even if the two of you marry and he gets the high society bride he's always wanted, we'll still be involved. But don't worry…"

She fluttered her lashes and gave Kara a cold, calculating smile. "I'll continue to take excellent care of him, in bed and out."

With that, she turned on her heel and sauntered away. Kara watched her hips sway from side to side, her waist-length hair bob as her long legs in their four-inch heels ate up the carpeted hallway.

For long minutes, Kara stood frozen in place, feeling dazed, confused. It was almost as though she was having an out-of-body experience, her consciousness floating far above her form while she watched and heard everything like a third-party observer.

When her head began to spin, she realized she was holding her breath and made herself inhale. Exhale. Inhale. Exhale.

The sea air she'd so enjoyed earlier that morning now smelled stale and rancid, making her sick to her stomach, and despite the April temperatures that kept the entire island cool, she was fever-hot and starting to sweat.

Pushing away from the ballroom door, she forced her feet to move. Right, then left. One step, then another. She walked all the way back to Eli's rooms without looking at or seeing anyone, without even remembering how she got there.

The suite was empty when she got there, thank goodness. She honestly didn't think she could handle facing Eli right now.

She'd loved him and thought he might truly love her. She'd fallen for his charms, begun to believe all his honeyed words and romantic gestures.

But all the while, he'd been playing her. Just as she'd feared, he'd come to her only after Laurel had broken things off. If he couldn't tether himself to one Kincaid daughter by marriage, he'd take another; apparently, he wasn't particular.

Guilt and humiliation swamped her. She'd gone away with him, fallen into bed with him, betraying her family, and for what? To feel like a first-class fool.

Retrieving her suitcase, she began to pack, her movements stiff and methodical. Tears clouded her vision, but she refused to let them fall.

Eli might have used and lied to her, but she'd been the one idiot enough to let him. She couldn't fix it. She couldn't go back and undo anything she'd done this week, and she certainly couldn't un-feel any of the feelings she'd ever felt for him.

But she could stop them in their tracks.

She could stop being so gullible and easily swayed.

She could leave Seabrook Island and never look back, hoping that her family would forgive her for her sins and her stupidity—if she even had the courage to tell them what she'd done, how quickly she'd gone from being her sister's maid of honor to sleeping with her sister's ex-fiancé.

Pulling her luggage behind her, she traveled back downstairs, all the way to the car rental office. Half an hour later, she was speeding away from Ocean Breezes and home to Charleston, leaving the resort, the island, Eli and nothing but tainted memories behind her.

Fourteen

Such a small, inconsequential noise shouldn't have the ability to strike fear in a person's heart, but when the brass knocker sounded on Kara's front door, that's exactly what happened. In the middle of steeping a cup of hot tea, she jumped, sending the spoon clinking against the mug and water splashing everywhere. With a curse, she reached for a nearby hand towel to sop up the mess but didn't make a beeline for the door. Mostly because she didn't want to answer it. She didn't want to know who was on the other side.

It had been a week since she'd driven back to Charleston, angry and alone and well over the speed limit. She hadn't told anyone she was back in town, not even her family.

Never mind that she'd originally felt guilty about leaving for even one short weekend…and then a whole week…given everything going on with the investigation of her father's murder and her mother being suspected of the crime. When it came to running home with her heart broken and her tail tucked between her legs, she'd been too distracted and miserable to think of anything—or anybody—but herself.

She was wallowing and acting pathetic, and she knew it. She'd been chastising herself for days, annoyed that she'd let a man reduce her to such a state.

And she was just about to shake off her melancholy...really, she was.

But if it was Eli knocking, seeing him again was sure to set her back and cause her to remain housebound for another month, at least. She'd already avoided a dozen of his calls and refused to play back any of the messages he might have left.

The knocking persisted, but didn't turn to full-out pounding, which made her think maybe it wasn't Eli. And then she heard the faint sound of a woman's voice she thought might be her sister's.

Abandoning her tea and the towel on the kitchen island, she made her way less than enthusiastically toward the front of the house. Family was better than Eli at this point, but not by much. She honestly didn't know if she could face them after what she'd done...what had been done to her...and the secrets she was harboring.

At the door, she peeked through the peephole and nearly groaned, letting her head fall against the cool wooden panel. Of all the family members who might have dropped by when she was still feeling like algae at the bottom of an abandoned swimming pool, it had to be Laurel. It just *had* to be Laurel.

"Kara," she heard her sister call out from the other side of the door. "I know you're in there. Open up—*please*. We're really starting to get concerned about you."

Kara's heart squeezed and she sniffed back a wave of emotion. Family—her family, at any rate—was always there for her. Always worrying about her, watching out for her, ready to leap to her aid or defense, if necessary. The least she could do was let them know she was all right.

Taking a deep breath, she straightened her spine and unlocked the door, opening it to a wall of bright sunshine and one very agitated older sister.

"Thank God," Laurel huffed, pushing past her into the house. "I was about to call the police or ask one of your burly neighbors to break down the door."

"I don't have any burly neighbors," Kara murmured.

Laurel was dressed for work in a taupe suit with chocolate-brown edging and a brown clutch purse that matched her heels. Even as upset as she obviously was, she looked completely poised and pulled together.

A sharp contrast to Kara's current state of dress, that was for sure. She'd been in pajamas or ballet pants and tank tops since returning from Seabrook Island, and since it was early yet—hey, it wasn't quite noon—she was still wearing the cotton shorts and camisole she'd slept in the night before.

Laying her purse on the hallway credenza, Laurel sighed and asked, "Are you okay?"

It took some doing, but Kara managed to hold back a ragged sob, nodding silently instead.

"Eli has been calling. Everybody. He said something happened at the resort and he's worried about you." She paused, giving Kara a chance to fill in the blanks. When she didn't, Laurel said, "Do you want to talk about it?"

"I really don't," Kara told her, not surprised when her voice cracked slightly. Swallowing hard, she cleared her throat and added, "Not right now."

Another beat passed, and then, like the wonderful sister she was, Laurel let it drop. With a cheery smile Kara knew was solely for her benefit, her sister put her hands on her hips and cocked her head to one side.

"Okay," she said, "you can fill me in later. Right now, you need to go upstairs and get changed. We're going out to lunch."

"We are?"

"Yes, ma'am. You've been holed up in here long enough. I don't know what's going on, and you don't have to tell me until you're ready, but there have been some new developments with Daddy's case that I thought you might like to hear about."

Kara's shoulders went back and she suddenly stood a couple inches taller. "What developments?"

Laurel grinned. "If you want to find out, you'll have to stop moping, get dressed and come with me."

"I haven't been moping," Kara protested, sounding petulant, even to her own ears. "I've been working. Quietly and alone." Often in the dark. But she *had* gotten some work done since getting back, in between bouts of feeling sorry for herself.

Laurel raised a disbelieving brow, and Kara sighed in defeat.

"Fine. Give me twenty minutes," she told her, heading for the stairs. "There's a cup of hot tea in the kitchen. Help yourself, if you want it."

They ended up seated at one of the outdoor tables of a local bakery-slash-coffee shop within walking distance of Kara's house, rather than driving to a sit-down restaurant. Partly because Kara was too eager to hear the latest about the investigation, and partly because she'd been doing almost nothing *but* eating since her return from Seabrook Island.

While Laurel picked at a giant cranberry-orange-nut muffin, Kara kept her hands wrapped around the oversize ceramic cup of her low-fat cinnamon dolce latte that she hadn't yet bothered to taste. For the first time all week, she wasn't interested in food, only information.

"All right, all right—stop with the torture. Tell me what's going on."

Wiping her hands on her napkin, Laurel finished chewing and swallowed quickly.

"You know Cutter Reynolds, right?" she began.

"Of course." Cutter was an old friend of the family. Kara couldn't remember a time when she hadn't known him, and he'd been acquainted with her parents even longer.

Laurel leaned in conspiratorially, even though no other patrons were sitting close enough to overhear or even care what they were talking about. "He and Mama have been having an affair."

Kara's mouth fell open, and she jerked back in shock.

"Mmm-hmm. Apparently, it's been going on for a while."

"Oh, my stars."

"And garters. I *know*."

"I can't believe it," Kara said, still feeling as though she'd been run over by a giant paddlewheel boat.

Although she didn't know why she was so surprised. If she'd learned anything in the past few months, it was that not everything was as it seemed...and that her family—her parents, especially—were exceptionally adept at keeping secrets. Big ones.

Her father spending years living a double life and carrying on with a second family.

A half brother, and what amounted to a step-brother, she'd known nothing about.

And now her mother's extramarital affair with a man Kara had always thought of as an uncle of sorts.

"None of us could," Laurel said. "Although, considering how Daddy was carrying on for so long, I don't suppose we should hold it against her. It sounds like she really loves him, and she swears they never got involved until *after* she discovered Daddy had another family."

Kara nodded. She wasn't surprised. Her mother was a true Southern lady, in every sense of the word. She might have strayed, but not until after she learned her husband had been unfaithful. Otherwise, Elizabeth Kincaid would have gone down with the ship, remaining true through thick and thin.

"Mama told everybody she was taking Daddy dinner that night. Later, though, she had to admit that the real reason she was at Daddy's office the day he died—" a fact that had moved Elizabeth to the top of the police's list of suspects "—was to tell him she wanted a divorce so she could marry Cutter. But at the time Daddy was actually...you know..."

Laurel trailed off, caught up suddenly in the emotion and

remembrance of having a loved one murdered. Emotions and memories Kara shared. Regardless of their ages, they had lost their father—in a violent and gruesome manner—which made them all feel like small, frightened children inside.

As though it had been choreographed, they swallowed past the lumps in their throats.

"I know," Kara whispered, reaching out to take Laurel's hand. They squeezed each other's fingers.

"When it happened, Mama was with Cutter," Laurel told her in a low voice.

"So Cutter is Mama's alibi."

Laurel nodded enthusiastically. "And that's not all. Nikki Thomas—you know, the investigator we hired to find out whether Jack Sinclair is doing anything to undermine the company—heard from some of her police contacts that surveillance cameras from a parking lot near Daddy's office picked up Jack's Aston Martin. It was parked there when Daddy was shot."

Kara's eyes went wide. "I thought he had an alibi."

"He does…or did, anyway. Several of his employees swear he was at his office all evening the night Daddy was killed. But this…well, video doesn't lie. This definitely casts doubt on that and points *away* from Mama as the murderer."

"That's incredible." Kara released her sister's hand and slumped back in her chair. "I can't believe I leave town for a couple of days and the whole world goes topsy-turvy. But at least it went topsy-turvy in a good way for a change," she added.

"You were gone more than just a couple of days," Laurel pointed out, raising a curious brow. "And then you locked yourself inside the house for a week after you got back, refusing to answer the phone or talk to anyone."

Kara winced. It was true, and as they said, the truth hurt. "I know, I'm sorry. I just…needed to be alone for a while."

Laurel took another small bite of her muffin and washed

it down with a sip of espresso. "Are you ready to talk about it yet? Because I'm ready to listen."

Her sister's soft tone, filled with concern and support, brought tears to Kara's eyes. Blinking them back, she said, "Can I ask you a question?"

Laurel chuckled. "That is a question," she teased. "But of course you can. You can ask me anything, you know that."

Taking a deep breath, Kara steeled herself, then met her sister's warm, moss-green gaze, so much like her own.

"Are you still in love with Eli? I mean, I know you called off the wedding, but do you regret that decision? Do you still have feelings for him?"

Laurel studied her for long, tension-filled moments.

"I never loved him enough," her sister said finally. "That's why I called things off. I care about him, as a friend. Despite everything, I hope we'll still be close. That we can still laugh together at Sunday dinners and run into each other at functions without any awkward, uncomfortable moments. But no, the way you mean…I don't still love him."

Kara held her sister's gaze—and her breath—for several more seconds. Then she looked away, unsure whether to be relieved or more confused.

"You do, though, don't you?"

Kara's head snapped up at Laurel's soft question. Her sister was watching her much the way their mother used to when she knew one of them had done something wrong, but was giving them the chance to confess before she doled out a punishment for both the crime *and* the lie.

"It's all right, you know. If you have feelings for Eli, I'll give you my blessing. Happily. You don't have to worry that you'll be stepping on my recently engaged-to-be-wed-to-him toes."

Kara had been doing so well. So far, she'd managed to keep all of her breakdowns private, bursting into tears only when she was alone and sure no one else would see.

But her sister's words, so heartfelt and sincere, put another crack in the dam of her emotions. And apparently, all it needed was one more crack to crumble completely, flooding her with every drop of guilt, anger, sadness and fear she'd been working so hard to hold back.

With a ragged sob, she broke down, covering her face with her hands as tears streamed down her face.

"Oh, sweetie."

Laurel's chair scraped the ground as she stood up and dragged it to Kara's side. Wrapping her arms around Kara, she hugged her close, stroking her hair and whispering for her to hush.

"It's okay, sweetie. Whatever it is, it can't be that bad."

Of course, that just made Kara cry harder, because it *was* that bad. Kara was a terrible, horrible person, sneaking around behind her sister's back to have an affair with her sister's ex-fiancé.

Meanwhile, Laurel was practically a saint. Handling her broken engagement like a trouper, giving her *blessing* to her sister who'd lied and tried to steal her old beau out from under her.

And now Saint Laurel was comforting her, absolving her of guilt and trying to make her feel better. It was enough to make a low-down dirty snake like herself want to slither out onto a dry, hot highway and let traffic run over her until she was flat and dead. It was no less than she deserved.

After Kara had soaked the front of Laurel's beautiful suit jacket for about ten minutes, and given herself a nasty case of bloodshot eyes, swollen nose and raw throat, her sister patted her back one last time before grasping her shoulders and pushing her upright. Tucking loose strands of hair behind her ears and away from her face, Laurel wiped her cheeks with a napkin, then sat back and fixed her with a stern, determined glare.

"There. Now that you've gotten that out of your system, tell me everything."

So Kara did. She went all the way back to the beginning, admitting to the crush she'd had on Eli since girlhood.

To which Laurel said, "Oh, honey."

Kara expressed how hard it had been to watch the relationship between Laurel and Eli develop.

"Oh, honey."

That she'd pushed her own feelings aside, struggling to be truly happy for them and doing everything she could in her capacity as an event coordinator to give them the best wedding possible. But that after Laurel had called things off and Eli had come to her for help—both with his own business and the dissolution of the wedding plans—she'd let herself get swept up, carried away…let herself pretend and believe and almost… almost…

Fresh tears spilled down her cheeks, and Laurel pulled her close a second time.

"Oh, *honey*," she murmured again, stroking her hair like a mother comforting a distressed child. "You poor thing. Why didn't you say something—*years ago?* I never would have started seeing Eli if I'd known you had feelings for him."

Kara shook her head, which was still buried in her sister's neck. "He never showed any interest in me, and I didn't want to ruin it for you, if you were in love with him."

Instead of giving her another encouraging *tsk* or comforting pat on the back, Laurel laughed. Startled, Kara sat up, holding her breath and blinking her wet lashes.

"You know I love you," Laurel said, "and I would never want to do or say anything to cause you pain, but sweetie…you've got to stop worrying about everyone else and worry about yourself for a change."

With a sigh, Laurel reached for another napkin and started dabbing at Kara's newly damp cheeks. "You are a wonderful sister. A dedicated daughter. Nobody could ever, *ever* accuse you of being selfish or not being there for your family when they needed you. But you don't have to be a martyr for us. You don't have to give up your own happiness for someone else's, or spend your life being miserable because you don't want to rock the boat."

"I'm not miserable," Kara said in a tiny, quiet voice that certainly sounded miserable. At least, she hadn't thought she was. She might not have been deliriously happy, twirling around on a mountaintop like Julie Andrews in *The Sound of Music,* but *miserable* was a bit of a stretch.

"You're sitting here, crying into your latte," Laurel pointed out. "Your hair is a mess, your makeup looks as though it was applied by Picasso and when I arrived at your house this morning, you were still in your pajamas. If I'm not mistaken, the same ones you'd been wearing for a couple of days."

Laurel raised a brow. "This, to me, does not scream personal contentment."

Oh, my god, it was true. She was a mess. She *was* miserable.

Hadn't Eli said nearly the same thing to her back on Seabrook Island? Not the miserable part, but the part about always putting others first, not spending enough time looking out for herself.

That made two people who knew her pretty darn well telling her the exact same thing.

So maybe she should listen.

"Does Eli feel the same about you?" Laurel asked.

Her eyes stung and her throat began to close at the mere mention of him, at the flood of memories from their time together. But she *wouldn't* start crying again. She needed to buck up and face this head-on, even if it meant reassessing her life and the way she dealt with others—especially her family.

Taking a deep breath, she was completely honest. "I don't know. He said he did, but then the things Diane said… What if they're true? What if he was only seducing me because he failed with you, and he really is after the Kincaid name and fortune?"

Laurel frowned, mouth turned down and brows forming a sharp V over her wrinkled nose. "I don't believe that, and neither do you. We've known Eli for years. He's one of the best men I've ever met," she said with conviction. "Not only is he a millionaire in his own right, he's noble and honorable. He doesn't need our money, and probably wouldn't take it if we offered it to him on a silver serving tray. He's proud of who he is and what he's accomplished."

She paused only long enough to pick up her cup and take a quick swallow of her now tepid espresso. "As for wanting to ride our coattails or marry into the Kincaid family to better himself…" She gave an unladylike snort. "If anything, I'd expect him to avoid the very possibility like the plague, knowing how vicious the rumor mill can be with that kind of fodder. The fact that he'd date either one of us is clearly a sign of the opposite—that he *doesn't* care about our name or social prominence, and is perfectly comfortable and confident with who he is."

Kara hoped she wasn't grasping at straws, but what Laurel was saying made sense to her. Parts of it, anyway.

"What about him jumping from you to me so quickly?" she wondered. Half-aloud, maybe, but really wanting—*needing*—an answer. "He couldn't have been ready to marry you, then suddenly develop feelings for me in the space of a single week. Could he?"

"No, I don't think he could," Laurel said, her features softening. "I think maybe you're the one he's been interested in all along—even if he didn't realize it. He was only marrying me because he thought it was time to settle down and start a family, and we'd always been close. Good friends who could maybe grow to be something more."

Reaching out, Laurel took her hand. "But, honey, we weren't sleeping together. That's one of the things that helped me realize we probably shouldn't be married. We'd kissed, of course, but even that was…bland. There was no spark between us, no need to be together or inability to keep our hands off each other. We were *just friends*, and I was afraid that's all we'd ever really be."

The air got trapped in Kara's lungs and she suddenly

couldn't breathe. No sex. No spark. Just friends. Three things that definitely couldn't be said about *her* time with Eli.

With them, there had been enough sparks to light up the entire North American sky on the Fourth of July. The sex had been spectacular. They'd done it round-the-clock…and tried to find time to squeeze in even more.

And the *just friends* part… They were friends, but didn't think they could ever again be defined as "just friends." Maybe they hadn't ever been; maybe there had always been more between them but lying dormant. Lurking beneath the surface, waiting to be let loose.

She lifted her head to find Laurel grinning at her. "The sex was good, huh?"

"Phenomenal," Kara admitted, barely able to hold back a starry-eyed sigh.

"I told you," Laurel said, looking entirely too smug and self-satisfied. "He's always been closer to you than the rest of us."

It was Kara's turn to frown. "What do you mean?"

"Kara," her sister said gently, "haven't you ever noticed how solicitous he is of you? At Sunday dinner, he always finds a way to sit next to you. Even while we were engaged, he somehow managed to finagle himself so that you were on his one side and I was on the other."

She hadn't noticed, though thinking back, she realized he *did* end up next to her during most of her family's gatherings.

"He calls you 'sugar' and 'darlin'," Laurel continued. "He never used endearments with me. I was always simply 'Laurel'."

That was true. He called her those things all the time, she just hadn't realized he didn't also use them with her sister or other women.

"And whenever we all get together, he seems to gravitate to you. Sitting on the arm of your chair…hanging out in the backyard while you help Mama with her flowers…offering you a hand while you're in the kitchen putting together a plate of cookies or making a pitcher of sweet tea."

True.

True.

True.

"He never did those things with you?" she asked.

"No," Laurel replied. "He was a gentleman, don't get me wrong. He pulled out chairs, brought me drinks, walked me to the door after we'd been out to dinner. But he didn't look at me the way he looks at you. His voice didn't go whiskey-soft when he spoke to me the way it does when he talks to you. And he never took me away for the weekend so he could ravish me within an inch of my life."

Kara flushed at her sister's pinpoint accuracy—and the knowing grin on her face.

"I don't know what the deal is with this Diane woman," Laurel volunteered, "but I'd be careful about taking her at her word too easily. Talk to Eli. Ask him flat-out whether or not he's having an affair with her behind your back." Her lips twisted in distaste. "While you're at it, ask if he was seeing her behind *my* back, just because I'm curious. If he was—and is— then he's just about the biggest jerk on the face of the earth, and I think we should hire a mercenary to take him into the jungle, stake him spread-eagle to the ground, and leave him as fresh meat for big cats and flesh-eating ants."

The image made Kara chuckle, even though she would never actually want to see Eli subjected to such an act. Then again, if he was a cheating, two-timing S.O.B., he deserved much worse.

"But, really, ask him," Laurel suggested again. "Give him a chance to defend himself—or come clean, if need be. I'd hate to see you miss out on something *phenomenal*—" she winked, tossing Kara's own descriptive term back in her face "—over little more than a misunderstanding…or a third-party trouble-maker up to no good."

Propping her elbow on the table, Kara blew out a breath and rested her chin in the cradle of her hand. "When did you get so dang smart?" she asked her sister, slightly annoyed that she suddenly felt like she deserved to sit in the corner with a dunce cap on her head.

Laurel chuckled, reaching for the final bite of her muffin and popping it into her mouth. "I've always been this smart. You just never noticed before because you didn't want to admit your older sister might actually be able to teach you something about life."

They both knew that wasn't entirely true, but if Laurel wanted to gloat, Kara was more than happy to let her. This time, at least.

"Well, you've taught me something today," Kara told her. "Thank you."

"You're welcome. Though I'd appreciate it more if you were thanking me for keeping you from making the biggest mistake of your life…and for helping you find true love."

With a wide smile—the first she'd let slip out since she'd returned from Ocean Breezes—Kara leaned over and hugged her sister tight.

"Give me a little more time," she said just above her sister's ear. "Maybe I still will."

Fifteen

Once Laurel was certain Kara had no intention of climbing back into her pajamas and under the covers with a pint of fudge ripple to wallow in self-pity for another week, she agreed to leave her to her own devices. Seeing her home, she gave her a hug and a peck on each cheek, then headed back to work.

Her sister had nothing to worry about, though. Kara felt excited, energized, hopeful.

As soon as she shut the front door behind her sister, Kara tossed her purse at the hall credenza and raced upstairs, kicking off her shoes and beginning to undress along the way. To go out with her sister, she'd thrown on a simple pair of white shorts and turquoise camisole top embellished with sequins and beading along the neckline. But that wasn't remarkable enough for what she planned to do next.

Because her makeup was, indeed, a mess from her crying jag, she washed her face a second time, then left her skin to dry a bit while she rooted through her closet for just the right dress…just the right shoes. She didn't want to overdo it, though.

Look good? Yes.

Show Eli what he'd be missing if he gave the wrong answers or turned out to be a jerk of the first order, after all? Yes.

Look as though she belonged down by the docks, selling her wares to every sailor and fisherman who stumbled off a boat at the end of the night? No.

Look desperate or needy or gullible? Definitely not.

So she bypassed the "evening wear" and "beauty pageant" sections of her wardrobe. The "summer casual" and "work formal" collections were out, too. That left her everyday, nine-to-five clothes—which were actually very nice—and things she wore to luncheons or the country club.

Perfect.

She opted for a satiny slip dress in butter yellow with blue piping at the arms and throat, and tall blue bachelor's buttons at the bottom as though they were growing up from the hem. Next came a pair of retro wedge sling-back espadrilles, and then she was off to the bathroom to fix her hair and re-apply her makeup.

Half an hour later, she retrieved her purse from the floor beside the credenza and darted out the door. It took what felt like forever to get through midday traffic to the business district where Eli's office was located and make it up to his floor. She was positively vibrating the entire elevator ride.

With a quick finger-wave to the main receptionist, she headed down the hall to Eli's office. She'd been here so many times, she didn't bother to stop out front anymore, but went straight to Penelope, Eli's personal assistant.

The older woman was sitting behind her desk, fingers flying across the keyboard as she worked. She must have seen Kara in her peripheral vision, though, because her head came up the second Kara stepped through the doorway.

"Well, hey there, Miz Kincaid. How are you today?"

"Fine, Penelope, thank you. How are you?"

"Just dandy, thanks."

"Is Eli here?" Kara asked. "I really need to speak with him."

"I'm so sorry, hon, but he's not in. He took the whole day off, actually."

"Oh." Kara's face fell, taking her heart with it. She hadn't expected that and didn't have a back-up plan.

Penelope cocked her head to the side, giving Kara a sympathetic glance. "I'm not supposed to do this, but I don't think he'd mind me telling you. He's at the park."

"The park?" Kara asked in surprise. That didn't sound like Eli. Except for their time on Seabrook Island, he tended to be a bit of a workaholic. He'd rather be closed up in his office poring over paperwork than out taking a leisurely stroll.

"Yeah. Wannamaker Park. He'll be there for a few hours, at least."

"Thank you," Kara said, spinning on her heel and rushing out of the office.

"Good luck!" Penelope called after her.

Kara couldn't imagine what Eli was doing at the park. On a beautiful spring day like today, the place was packed. Children everywhere—running, playing, laughing. Parents watching, chasing, wiping runny noses and blowing on scraped knees. It didn't seem even remotely Eli's style.

Still, she was here, and Eli supposedly was, so she wasn't leaving until she'd either found him or scoured every inch of the park to be certain he wasn't here. Which was easier said than done.

She checked the playground and the picnic areas. Dodged skateboarders and bike riders.

Just when she was about to give up, she heard loud singing, and turned to see a crowd dotted by balloons and party hats. The group was mostly children, but children of varying ages with a few adults thrown in.

Moving closer, she found herself humming along with the off-key rendition of "Happy Birthday" as she glanced over everyone's heads, thinking perhaps Eli was standing on the other side of the birthday gathering, watching the festivities.

The song drew to a close, followed by a group outcry for

the birthday boy or girl to "Blow out the candles! Blow out the candles!" But when it came to that, six or eight of the children gathered most closely around the table leaned in to do the deed.

Odd, Kara thought, but though she was distracted by her search for Eli, Kara couldn't help smiling at the sheer joy emanating from the partygoers. Warm memories of her own childhood birthday parties, and those of her brothers' and sisters', played through her head.

And then, at the very center of the crowd, a man who must have been crouched down beside the picnic table stood. He was holding a large plastic knife in anticipation of cutting the cake, wearing a yellow, pointy-tipped, glitter-covered paperboard hat and smiling the widest smile she'd ever seen.

Eli laughed at something a young black boy said, and began doling out evenly sliced squares of the giant sheet cake to the two or three dozen other children dancing around, awaiting their sugar high.

Rooted to the spot, Kara watched him. He was dressed very casually in jeans and a blue chambray shirt, sleeves rolled up to reveal his muscled forearms, and looked more handsome than she could ever remember seeing him. Then again, they'd been apart for a whole week, so maybe she was simply starved for the sight of him.

She couldn't quite make sense of what Eli was doing in the middle of a child's birthday bash, but she didn't care. Her head buzzed and her pulse raced while she waited none too patiently for him to finish passing out cake. A woman beside him was adding scoops of ice cream to each plate, which slowed down the process and added to Kara's growing anticipation.

Finally, all the kids and most of the adults had their servings and were digging in, and she couldn't stand it a moment longer.

"Eli," she called out, hoping he would hear her over the voices of the boisterous children. "Eli!"

He turned, his eyes going wide when he spotted her at the edge of the party-hatted crowd. Passing the knife to the woman in charge of ice cream, he started toward her, weaving between children until they stood only inches apart.

"Kara."

He breathed her name, making it sound like a wish, a prayer, an endearment, and her knees went weak. Her heart pounded so hard, she was sure he could see it through her dress.

"I called," he said, shoving his hands into the front pockets of his jeans.

"I know. I'm sorry, I just…"

She trailed off. Now that she was here with him, close enough to reach out and touch him—which she wanted to do so badly her palms were tingling—she didn't know where to start.

"I was upset," she told him honestly. "I needed time."

Eli rocked back on his heels, fighting the urge to drag her against his chest and kiss her senseless. His gaze raked over her again and again, taking in the glorious fall of her auburn hair, her sparkling green eyes, those rose petal lips, and her womanly curves beneath a dress that was pretty enough…but would look even better in a pile on the floor beside his bed.

He couldn't ravish her just yet. They had some things to discuss first. Important things.

She licked her lips, and her gaze skittered over his shoulder. "What is this?" she asked.

He didn't bother looking. The noise level alone told him all was well and everybody was having a good time.

"Never mind that." He shrugged off the question, more interested in getting an answer to his own.

"Why did you leave the island, Kara? I thought we were fine."

Better than fine, actually. He'd thought they were well on their way to damn near perfect. Realizing they weren't, remembering the moment of panic he'd felt when he'd realized she wasn't just late getting back to the suite, but gone— and not coming back—caused his mouth to turn down.

"Then you disappeared without a word."

He watched her chest hitch as she inhaled deeply.

"Because I was hurt. And angry. And felt like a fool."

His brows knit. "Why?" he asked, even though he already knew the answer. He knew more, in fact, than she did at this point, but wanted to hear the situation from her perspective.

Rather than answering his question, she asked one of her own. Tipping her head to the side, she said, "Are you sleeping with Diane Montgomery? And don't you lie to me, Elijah James Houghton," she added in a tone that reminded him entirely too much of his mother, complete with a finger waggled under his nose.

He bit back a grin at her flushed cheeks and riled disposition. If she suspected he found this conversation entertaining in any way, he would be knee-deep in swamp water. She'd likely kick him in the shin or smack him with her purse in front of the entire park full of people. But it was almost impossible not to be amused and even energized by her barely suppressed outrage.

What wasn't amusing was the fact that she'd run away from him in the first place instead of coming to him with her suspicions and concerns…even her fury. If she'd stuck around to confront him while they were still at Ocean Breezes, they could have hashed this all out in a matter of hours and spent the rest of the week enjoying themselves. And each other.

But they were here now, and though he'd have picked a different venue for this discussion, he wasn't going to pass up the opportunity to work this out once and for all.

"No. I am not sleeping with Diane," he told her in no uncertain terms. "We were involved once, a few years ago, but not now."

Kara worried the inside of her bottom lip. "That's why I left," she said softly. "Diane told me you were having an affair. She said you had some sordid plan to marry a Kincaid just to get into the family and increase both your bank account and your social standing, but were going to continue seeing her behind Laurel's—and then my—back. Using Ocean Breezes as your own personal love nest," she added with a disgusted twist of her lips.

Eli scowled. "And you believed her."

She had the decency to flush. "Yes. Or maybe I was just afraid *not* to believe her."

Her gaze dropped to her feet, where she was dragging the toe of one shoe back and forth along the grass. Then her shoulders drooped and she gave a loud sigh before heading away from the party toward an empty picnic table. He followed, knowing they weren't finished with their discussion.

She perched on the end of one of the bench seats, setting her purse on the table and straightening the skirt of her dress to keep from flashing too much leg. He liked her legs; he wouldn't have minded seeing her flash a bit more of them.

Taking a deep breath and finding courage, she turned to face him again. "I let myself get comfortable with you, feel... maybe too much for you."

A stab of optimism shot through him. Her eyes were the dark green of summer moss, brimming with emotion as she spoke. He wanted to haul her into his arms right then, or at least reach across the table and take her hand, but he needed to hear this. He needed to know what she was thinking and how she felt about him now...before he told her the way it was going to be.

"I was really enjoying our time at the resort, but in the back of my mind, I don't think I ever truly believed any of it—anything between us—was real."

His scowl deepened, and he had to bite his tongue to keep from snapping right then and there. But if he stopped her now, he knew he'd never get the rest out of her, and he needed to hear it.

Holding his gaze, she said, "I couldn't believe you wanted me or cared for me as more than a friend, because you'd never shown the least bit of interest in me that way before. And it was *too easy* to believe that you were on the rebound from your breakup with Laurel. Not just a breakup, but practically being left at the altar. It wasn't much of a stretch to think you might be using me to get back at her."

Eli clenched his jaw so forcefully, he could hear his molars grinding to dust. "You'd better get to the point damn quick," he bit out, "because I've got something to say and I'm running low on patience."

Her lashes fluttered at that. She looked just about ready to bolt...which would be a huge mistake on her part. Birthday party or not, park full of witnesses or not, if she made one move to get away from him, he was going to tackle her to the ground like the Carolina Panthers offensive line and ruin that cute little dress of hers.

She swallowed, her chest rising and falling with her shallow breaths. And then, in a tone so soft he could barely hear it over the revelry at his back, she said, "I've been in love with you forever, Eli. Since the first time we met...all through high school, college, our adult lives... It broke my heart when you started dating Laurel. When the two of you started talking about marriage and asked me to plan the wedding."

Her voice cracked and her eyes glistened with moisture. Any anger or frustration he'd been feeling only seconds before washed away, replaced by keen remorse and the sudden understanding that he was a jackass. A complete and utter fool.

Giving in to temptation, he took her hand, linking their arms across the top of the plastic picnic table.

"Kara," he whispered softly.

She shook her head, blinking to keep the tears at bay. "So you can see why I didn't think I could trust your sudden profession that you had feelings for me. Or trust myself to trust you, for fear it was just my long-buried crush spinning out of control."

"Kara," he said again.

She licked her lips before they curved into a crooked, slightly insecure smile. "But I had coffee with Laurel this morning," she told him. "And she had this really smart idea.

She suggested I simply *ask you* about what Diane said, and give you a chance to respond. So here I am. Asking."

Her shoulders went back as she straightened her spine, her chest rising as she inhaled confidence along with fresh oxygen. "Are you in love with Diane?"

Eli sat up straighter, too. If they were going to do this, then they were going to do it head-on. No beating around the bush. It was no-holds-barred, all-on-the-line, do-or-die truth-telling time.

He met her gaze, looked directly into her soul, and invited her to look into his.

"No," he answered firmly.

"Are you sleeping with her—now?"

"Absolutely not."

"Are you still in love with Laurel?"

"I don't think I was ever in love with Laurel," he responded honestly.

"Do you still have feelings for her at all? Other than friendship."

"No."

Kara paused, her toe tapping wildly beneath the table while nerves coursed through her bloodstream. She knew what she wanted to ask next, but once she did, that was it. Game over. His answer would determine the entire future of their relationship—good, bad or indifferent.

But she had to know.

"Are you in love with me?"

Sixteen

Kara's heart lurched against her rib cage over and over again like a Mexican jumping bean while their gazes remained linked. Eli's eyes, dark and glittering with intensity, made her want to squirm, but she refused to look away until she had an answer.

The heavy, razor-sharp silence was killing her. Fear that he might say no or, worse yet, that his face would fill with pity at her awkward confession and pathetic desire for him, turned her insides cold.

But she held her ground, waited, and told herself that if he was going to break her heart into a million pieces, then it was better to be done with it here and now.

She could go home and lick her wounds later. Lord knew she still had the ratty pajamas, unmade bed and freezer full of ice cream ready.

To her surprise, Eli pushed to his feet, coming to her side of the picnic table and pulling her up to stand in front of him. Framing her face in both of his big, strong hands, he smiled, sending a shiver of warmth through her system.

"Yes," he said, his voice rough and graveled and sincere. "Yes, I'm in love with you. I think I have been for years, too. I just didn't realize it until recently."

Running the pad of his thumb back and forth across her bottom lip, he said, "I fired Diane."

He gave a small chuckle when Kara's eyes went wide as saucers.

"When I couldn't find you that last day you were at the resort, I went searching and ran into her instead. She admitted what she'd told you—sounded proud of it, no less. I think she actually believed what she said to you. In her mind, she thought we had a real relationship, while I considered our time together nothing more than a one-, maybe two-night stand. I never would have hired her if I'd known she had an agenda."

"So you fired her?" Kara didn't know whether to be shocked or flattered.

"On the spot. Ordered Security to stay with her while she gathered her belongings and see her off the resort property so there would be absolutely no mistakes and no confusion about my feelings—or lack thereof. I called you right after. And called, and called, but you didn't answer."

"I'm sorry, I—"

He covered her mouth with his finger. "I would have been back in Charleston that very night, on your doorstep with candy and flowers and my heart on my sleeve, but as luck would have it...disaster struck."

His mouth twisted with irony. "I don't know if she did it in an act of payback for bringing you in, or if she was just a lousy event planner, but Diane booked two large golfing events for the exact same time. Guests started flooding in, we didn't have enough rooms for all of them, the courses were double-booked... It was a nightmare. One I couldn't leave the staff to handle alone, so I stuck around to help get everything ironed out."

She nodded. She understood completely. And he'd said

he loved her, which pretty much made everything else in her life—everything else in the world—a non-issue.

"I only got back into town last night. Called you again," he added, "but you still wouldn't answer."

She winced with guilt, nose wrinkling, and he chuckled.

"I was going to come over, but wanted the timing to be right, and I was tired, cranky… I thought it would be better to let us both get a good night's sleep. Then this morning when I got to the office, Penelope reminded me about the party, and I had to be here."

He cast a quick glance over his shoulder, where kids with frosting smeared all around their mouths, and on their hands and clothes, had started chasing each other, playing hide-and-seek and breaking out the party favors.

"I was in charge of picking up the cake."

Something thick and warm unfurled at the base of her stomach at his admission. He sounded so proud.

"What is this?" she asked, just as she had earlier. Maybe this time, he would answer her.

"April's birthday party." At her questioning expression, he explained. "You know I was a foster child, and I lived in a group home as often as a foster one, until Mom and Dad took me in. Well, special occasions and reasons to celebrate are hard to come by in group homes—as are the funds to party properly."

She shook her head. "I didn't realize."

"Most people don't, but I've never forgotten how it feels to lie in bed at night and know no one remembered your birthday—if they even knew it to begin with. So when I started making good money, I made a point of going back. I visit every few weeks, arrange outings to museums or the zoo, and I throw big bashes like this for any of the kids who have a birthday that month."

Kara's chest tightened and tears stung the backs of her eyes. And this time, it had nothing to do with fear that her feelings for Eli might not be reciprocated. Instead, it had everything to

do with feeling like a worthless, self-centered human being…
and realizing that the man before her was not only wonderful,
thoughtful and self*less,* but that she'd gotten very close to letting him slip through her fingers.

Clearing her throat, she said, "You did all this?"

Color bloomed on his cheekbones. "Well, I had some help.
Penelope orders the cakes and decorations, reserves the locations, if necessary. But she lets me take the credit."

"I'm glad." Kara smiled, sparing another glance for the
young partygoers before returning her attention to Eli.

"Will you let me be involved next time?" she asked. "I'd
love to bring some presents or help come up with new ideas
for party themes."

Eli beamed at her, his grin wider and brighter than she'd
ever seen it. He gave her elbows a squeeze and leaned in to
press a quick kiss to her lips. "They would love that. *I* would
love it. We supply gifts, but they're more of the boy/girl variety, not child-specific. If you could help us personalize things
a bit, that would be great."

"Consider it done," she told him. And she meant it. His
kindness and compassion were contagious, and she could tell
these kids were a cause near and dear to his heart. Which meant
that—if things between them played out the way she hoped
they would—they were about to become important to her, as
well.

His hands brushed up her arms, stopping at her shoulders
while he continued to study her. Finally, he said, "I need you
to know something. I was never in love with your sister."

His voice was low and genuine, and an invisible weight she
hadn't known was pushing down on her, lifted.

"I decided I was ready to settle down and start a family, and
I thought we would make a good match. Laurel is classy and
sophisticated, she comes from a good family…" He shot her a
lopsided grin. "All the things you are, of course, but there was
no spark there. Nothing that kept me up at night or made me
crazy with wanting. *You* make me crazy with wanting, Kara.

And you definitely keep me up at night—in more ways than one."

With a giggle, an honest-to-goodness giggle, she buried her face in his chest.

"It wasn't until Laurel called off the wedding and it didn't bother me in the least that I realized I was marrying her for the wrong reasons. Then I went over to your place, and it was as though I was seeing you for the first time. Clearly, through new eyes. It was startling and invigorating and humbling...and I knew, without a shadow of a doubt, that I wanted you. Not just for a night or a weekend or even a year, but forever."

Heart stuttering in her chest, Kara lifted her head and met his gaze. "Say that again," she told him.

The corners of his mouth lifted. "Which part?"

"All of it," she said on a sigh. "Or maybe just the highlights."

Running his fingers through her hair, then lingering to toy with the ends of the curls, he said, "Here are the important bullet points: I love you. I want you. I need you."

He punctuated each declaration with a soft but firm kiss to her lips. Kisses that melted her bones and turned her knees to jelly.

"Now answer one of my questions," he murmured. "Do *you* love *me?*"

Her lashes fluttered and the air skittered from her lungs. "More than anything," she told him.

"And you don't think I'm after your money or your family name? Especially considering that I've amassed a rather large financial portfolio in my own right, and my parents' roots— the only parents who matter, at any rate—go back at least as far as the Kincaids'."

His face hardened, his eyes going dark, but she knew he wasn't really angry. Annoyed that anyone could ever believe that, maybe, but not mad. Still, she couldn't resist teasing him.

"I don't know," she said with an exaggerated sigh. "We are *really* rich. And there are *a lot* of men out there who want me. I'm irresistible."

The corner of his mouth twitched, and she knew she had him.

"You are that," he agreed, obvious humor slipping into his tone. "But I'm afraid I have to have you—money, well-respected Southern name, and all. So what can I do to convince you? Give up my vast fortune? Shout it from the highest rooftop? Eat a bug?"

She just barely managed to hold back a chuckle. "You *could* eat a bug."

He scowled at her, letting her know that wasn't going to happen.

"All right, then, I have an idea," she said.

Standing on tiptoe, she looped her arms around his neck, getting as close as possible. To her delight, he did the same at the small of her back.

"I haven't gotten around to canceling everything for your and Laurel's nuptials." She'd taken care of some of the items on the list, but then got sidetracked by his work-weekend-turned-sexual-rendezvous and the emotional upheaval that went along with it.

"So…if you love me as much as you claim, and truly want to be with me for the rest of your life…" Her entire body hummed with that knowledge and the soul-deep contentment it brought. "You could keep your original wedding date, but marry me instead."

His eyes widened, then began to twinkle. "Marry you? Next month?"

"Two weeks from now, actually."

"Hmm. I don't know, that's awfully soon," he said with mock indecision.

"It is. But think of it this way—once you tie me to you legally, I'll be forced to take your name…and half of your money. It's the perfect solution to all of our problems."

He laughed. "You may be right about that. And something tells me you're going to enjoy spending my money."

"Mmm-hmm. Almost as much as I enjoy spending my own."

"I'll bet." Then he tipped his head, seeming to consider something. "You know, maybe I should go back to Laurel, after all. She may not be as hot as you are, but she might end up costing me less in the long run."

Eyes wide, Kara pulled back and punched him hard in the chest. "Hey! Be careful, bub, or I'll rescind my offer. Then you'll not only be without the hot Kincaid sister, but I'll stick you with all the cancellation fees for the rest of the wedding arrangements."

"We can't have that," he said, shaking his head slowly back and forth. "I guess I have no choice—I'll have to marry you. But only if you promise to remain as sweet, smart, funny, beautiful, wonderful and amazing as you are at this very moment."

She tipped her head, rolled her eyes skyward and gave her best drawn-out Southern belle sigh. "I suppose I could do that. But *you* have to promise to always be as kind, smart, wonderful, patient, sexy and amazing as *you* are at this moment."

With the cocky, self-assured grin she'd fallen in love with so many years ago, he said, "Oh, I think I can handle that, darlin'."

And then he leaned down to kiss her, stealing her breath and taking her heart, her soul, her very being right along with it. When he broke off minutes later, they were gasping for breath.

Eli touched his brow to hers. "I want to take you home and make love to you. Make you mine, once and for all. My place or yours, I don't care which."

She wanted that, too. So much, she was trembling.

"I'm already yours," she told him, and meant every word. "But what about the party? Your guests might notice if their host suddenly disappears."

He groaned, turning his head slightly to check on the birthday celebration. The children were still playing, eating, having fun…but several adult eyes were on them, curiosity running rampant.

"I think you're right," he said. "Our absence would definitely be noted. And commented upon."

Resting the tips of her fingers on one side of his strong, smooth face, she pressed a light kiss to the other. "Tell you what," she said. "Introduce me to the children so I can get a feel for their personalities and what kind of gifts they might like in the future. After a bit, we'll make our apologies, and you can take me home—your place or mine—and have your way with me for the rest of the night."

One dark brow shot halfway to his hairline. "Now that's a plan I can get behind," he told her. "I can see why you're so good at your job, Miss Kincaid."

She met his raised brow with one of her own. "That's Soon-to-be Mrs. Houghton to you, sir."

He flashed her a wide grin, lifting her left hand to his mouth and kissing the spot on her finger where his ring would soon reside. A diamond temporarily, followed by a solid gold band for the rest of their lives.

"Yes, ma'am," he said softly. "It certainly is."

Seventeen

Kara stood outside the front door of her mother's home—also known as the Kincaid Mansion—on Montagu Street, fidgeting like a mouse in a room full of traps ready to spring. The heat from Eli's strong, broad body was close at her back, adding to that of her growing anxiety and the warm April afternoon.

"If you don't calm down," he whispered just above her right ear, his hands resting lightly at her hips, "they're going to know something is up the minute you walk through the door."

"I know." But that didn't keep her nerves from jangling or her pulse from jumping in her throat. Her fingers tightened on the container of homemade apple fritters she was carrying, for fear she might drop them.

"And that's if they don't notice the ring right off."

The lump in her throat plummeted to her stomach. Oh, lord. She hadn't needed to hear that.

After the birthday party at the park, Eli had indeed taken her home—to his apartment, as it turned out—and made love to her *all...night...long...*. Over and over, until she was weak in the knees…and the spine…and the brain stem…and everywhere in between.

The very next morning, he'd woken her with kisses that quickly led to another round of slow, languid sex, followed by breakfast in bed and the pronouncement that they were going ring shopping. As soon as he managed to stop touching her long enough to let her get dressed, they'd strolled hand in hand to the nearest jeweler's he'd approved of, where he'd only let her look at the trays of rings that they kept under lock and key. Nothing from the average, everyday display case for *his* bride-to-be, he'd declared.

She'd walked out with the biggest, most beautiful engagement ring she'd ever seen. A three-carat, princess-cut diamond in a one-of-a-kind yellow gold and platinum floral setting with even more smaller diamonds dotting the band, it was nearly blinding in its brilliance. Showier than she would normally wear, as well, but she absolutely loved it, Eli had insisted, and for once she wasn't going to worry about what anyone else might think. She was blissfully in love, happier than she'd ever been before in her life, and wanted to soak up every minute, every detail, every exquisite sensation.

Which was easier said than done, since she hadn't yet told her family about the latest developments in her personal life, and wasn't entirely sure how they would take it. On top of that, her mother had *just* been cleared on Thursday of all charges connected to her father's murder.

This was the first Sunday dinner they would be attending since the news had broken, and the Kincaid family was sure to be in a celebratory mood. That was good; she hoped they would be equally willing to celebrate when she announced that Eli had asked her to marry him—well, she'd asked him, but he'd readily agreed, thank goodness—she'd said yes, and they intended to follow through with most of Laurel's original wedding plans so that they could hold the ceremony next week.

Her mother was sure to think there was a reason for the rush down the aisle—especially since Lily was four months along with Daniel's child—but Kara simply wanted to be married. To Eli. She'd spent most of her life longing for him; she didn't want to waste a single minute more *not* being legally bound to him and beginning their life together as man and wife. She also had to admit that—because Laurel had seemed so disinterested throughout the planning stages—the wedding Kara arranged for her sister was very close to her own idea of a dream wedding.

She would be picking out her own gown, of course, and adjusting the color scheme and guest list somewhat. But otherwise, everything that was already in place was darn near perfect.

If only her father could have been there to give her away, it would be.

"Do you want me to go in first?" Eli asked, as though they were tromping off to the gallows and he was offering to get in line ahead of her. "Or would you rather we skip out altogether? We could call and tell them we're stuck in traffic…or out of town on business…or were mauled by bears."

She turned on him, eyes wide. "How in the world would we ever be mauled by bears?"

He shrugged. "I'm just trying to help, sugar. If you don't want to tell them about our engagement, I'll understand. We can even push back the wedding."

"No!" Spinning around, she faced him, separated only by the dessert container that she was clutching like a life preserver. "We're getting married next week if we have to fly to Vegas and elope. I'm just nervous about how they'll react, considering that—until earlier this month—you were engaged to Laurel. Some of the details are going to be a little hard for folks to swallow."

"And to explain."

Her mouth twisted with frustration. "You see my dilemma."

He smiled gently, lifting a hand to brush a stray curl away from her face and behind her ear. The gesture was becoming something of a habit for him…but a habit she liked. A lot.

"Our dilemma," he said. "We're a package deal now, darlin'. But I don't think we have anything to worry about. Your family loves me. And your sister is the one who dumped me, not the other way around, so I've got that whole 'innocent party,' 'sympathy card' thing going for me."

She chuckled. "You're right. They're going to feel sorry for you. If we can play on that, we may have a shot at catching them off guard with our news."

"Here's another idea," he suggested. "We could tell them we're engaged, tell them we're hijacking Laurel's wedding plans, tell them they're invited…and then tell them we love each other, whether they approve of the circumstances of our relationship or not."

Grasping her upper arms and tugging her slightly toward him, until the apple fritters nudged at them both, he added, "I've waited too long to find you, Kara. I'm not going to let anyone—not even your family—make me feel guilty or ashamed of how we got together."

He looked positively ferocious. Brows drawn together, mouth pulled taut. She suspected he could take on those imaginary bears, if they showed up now and tried to maul them, and come out of the skirmish without a scratch.

But instead of being intimidated by his dark scowl, it calmed her. Warmed her from her very center outward, and seemed to wash away every last one of her frazzled nerves.

Smiling from ear to ear, she reached up to trace the line of his jaw. "Have I told you lately how much I love you?"

His features softened and he winked. "I recall you saying something along those lines this morning while you were on top of me, riding me like—"

Slapping a hand over his mouth, she shushed him, struggling not to flush with embarrassment even as a sudden wave of erotic memory and equally erotic need crashed over her.

"Now cut that out or we'll never make it inside," she told him sternly, doing her best to ignore the wicked sparkle in his brown eyes. "And for the record, I *do* love you, and I don't feel the least bit guilty about or ashamed of how we got together, either. I only wish we'd been smart enough to do it a decade ago."

Plucking the fritter container out of her hands, he held it aside and dragged her against his chest. He kissed her on the lips, long and slow, licking off all of the color she'd just applied in the car, she was sure.

"Don't worry," he murmured into her mouth, "we'll spend the next decade making up for lost time, I promise."

Then he turned her around and gave her a little shove toward the front door. "Now let's go inside before you get cold feet again."

Following his instructions—not quite as reluctantly this time—she opened the door and entered the wide foyer. Eli had just closed the door behind them, when Laurel appeared in front of them, almost as though she'd been waiting just around the corner, ready to pounce the second they arrived.

With a sigh and rolling eyes, she threw up her hands. "There you are. I was about to send out a search party."

"We aren't that late," Kara insisted.

"No, but Matt and Susannah are in Georgia with Flynn. You *know* how Mama likes everyone to attend Sunday dinner when they can, so she's been frantic you weren't going to show."

"I told her I'd be here." She took the dessert container back from Eli and held it up for Laurel to see. "I even brought apple fritters."

Laurel's gaze darted from Kara to Eli and back again. Then a smug smile started to spread across her face.

"Hello, Eli. It's nice to see you."

"You, too, Laurel."

"So...I take it everything worked out okay between the two of you," she said without a hint of subtlety.

"Everything is fine," Kara told her, and left it at that.

Apple fritters in hand, she started toward the dining room. As she passed her sister, she mouthed, "I'll tell you later."

In the dining room, the long mahogany table was already

set with steaming plates and platters and bowls of amazing-looking food. Which was nothing surprising; Kara had grown up with meals like this, especially on Sunday afternoons. Chicken-fried steak, okra gumbo, red rice, potato salad, grits topped with real butter, pumpkin biscuits…and later, the apple-pecan fritters Kara had made from scratch while trying to fend off advances from Eli—to both her body and her baking.

"Kara!" her mother cried from her seat at the head of the table. She pushed back her chair and came around to give her a hug. "I'm so glad you made it. And Eli…"

Elizabeth beamed up at him, not settling for a polite handshake, but wrapping her arms around him, as well.

"You're just in time. We were about to sit down and say grace, but I didn't want to start without you."

"We wouldn't miss it," Kara assured her.

Her brother RJ and Brooke, his fiancée of less than a month, as well as the youngest Kincaid sister, Lily, and her new husband, Daniel Addison, were already seated. But as Eli and the other women neared the table, both RJ and Daniel rose.

RJ greeted Kara with a kiss to the cheek, then moved to hold Elizabeth's chair for her while Daniel helped Laurel and Eli helped Kara. True Southern gentlemen down to the bone.

Once they were all settled and had said grace, food was passed around until everyone's plate was full. While they ate, they discussed a number of events that had impacted the Kincaid family over the past few months. The charges against Elizabeth being dropped…Lily and Daniel learning they were expecting a girl……RJ and Brooke's recent engagement and talk of either an engagement party or shifting straight to wedding plans—they couldn't decide which.

The general consensus, of course, was that Kara would be the one to help each of them plan whatever type of event they decided to throw. From party to wedding to wedding reception, and everything in between, she was the Kincaids' go-to gal for that sort of thing. And she was happy to help.

But as the conversation turned to upcoming nuptials, she

couldn't remain silent any longer. Eli might say he didn't mind putting off the announcement of their engagement or even their wedding, but *she* did, and the first step toward getting the deed done was sharing the news with her family.

She was lucky they hadn't already noticed the ring sitting on her left hand like a live canary. But then, she'd spent most of the meal hiding it on her lap beneath the table.

Swallowing a last bite of potato salad, she washed it down with a sip of sweet tea, then cleared her throat to get her family's attention.

"Actually," she told them, reaching for Eli's hand beneath, "Eli and I have a bit of news to share, as well."

The entire table grew silent, all eyes on her…with the occasional roll to Eli and then back.

"Eli has asked me to marry him, and I've accepted. Not only that," she rushed to get in before the collective gasp that filled the room could turn into a free-for-all of questions and comments and demands for details, "but we've decided to go ahead and follow through with Laurel's original wedding plans. So I hope none of you have made alternate plans for next weekend."

As soon as she finished, chaos erupted. The women squealed—especially when they saw her ring—and started talking at the speed of light. The men stood and came around to shake Eli's hand and slap him on the back.

In only a matter of minutes, Kara started to wonder why she'd ever been anxious about telling her family to begin with. They were wonderful and supportive and genuinely happy for her, just as they'd been all her life.

The fact that Eli had been engaged to marry Laurel less than a month ago, or that he was suddenly set to marry Kara when they'd known each other forever, but never so much as flirted before didn't even come up, though she was sure there would be questions—*lots* of questions—later. Her mother and brother and sisters simply accepted that she was an adult, and knew her own mind and heart well enough to know what— and who—she wanted.

While the men formed a small circle in one corner of the room for "manly talk," Elizabeth insisted they needed to celebrate, dragging Lily and Brooke with her to the kitchen. Kara didn't know if they would return with wine flutes and a bottle of champagne (and something equally festive, but non-alcoholic for Lily) or simply coffee and her apple-pecan fritters arranged on a fancy silver tray.

Rather than follow along, though, Kara grabbed Laurel's elbow and held her back. The one thing that continued to plague her mind was that her older sister might still be harboring feelings for Eli, despite her continued assertion to the contrary.

She believed her sister, and yet…how could anyone *not* be head over heels in love with Eli? How could any woman—even Laurel—be ready to marry him, only to turn around and be content to see him spend his life with someone else?

Kara would certainly never be able to sit back and watch while something like that happened. Not now that she'd been with him, given him her heart and soul.

"Are you sure you're all right with this?" she asked in a low voice so nobody else would hear.

Laurel gave a light, carefree chuckle. "Of course. Oh, Kara, I'm so happy for you!" She grabbed Kara up for another quick hug. "Eli and I were never meant to be together, but you…you two are positively glowing. You're like separate electrical currents coming together to light up an entire city block."

Kara's throat tightened and she blinked to hold back tears. "I love him so much, Laurel. I never wanted to steal him from you, but seeing him with you was killing me."

"I can imagine," Laurel said with an even heartier laugh. "But you didn't steal him from me. I gave him to you—freely and without hesitation. Or maybe Eli simply wised up and realized who it was he truly wanted."

"Thank you."

"I do have a question for you, though." Laurel tipped her

head. "Since you're recycling most of my wedding plans—which is a fabulous idea, don't even *think* about feeling guilty for that!—can I be your maid of honor? I mean, you were going to be mine, so it's only fair."

"Yes!" It was Kara's turn to squeal. "Oh, yes, I'd love that! And Mama can be there, too, now that the charges against her have been dropped, thank goodness."

"It's all going to be absolutely perfect," Laurel agreed. "In fact, you've inspired me. I'm tired of being so cautious and always playing it safe. You jumped into love with Eli feet-first, and look how things turned out. Meanwhile, I nearly married him because it was comfortable and easy. I need to be more spontaneous, take more risks. Live life instead of letting it just roll by day after day."

Nibbling at the inside of her lip, Kara said, "Taking a chance did pay off for me, but…just be careful, okay? I'm all for spontaneity, but don't go crazy or do anything dangerous."

"No danger," Laurel assured her. "I want to add a little spice to my life, not jump out of a plane head-first."

A moment later, the other women burst back into the room with champagne *and* coffee to go with Kara's fritters. Elizabeth also brought the phone with her so she could call Matthew and tell him the good news.

Soon after she'd spoken with her brother, Kara felt strong arms come around her waist from behind, and she was tugged back against the solid wall of Eli's chest. She smiled, leaning into him with a sigh.

"Since I know my chances of ever being right again once we're married are slim to none," he teased, "I'd like it noted that I *was* right about this. You had nothing to be nervous about with your family."

"You were right," she admitted. "I'll endeavor to listen to you and trust in your impeccable wisdom from now on."

He chuckled just above her ear. "We'll see how long that lasts. I'm guessing not much past the honeymoon."

She gave a little *hmph* beneath her breath, only to feel him press a kiss to her temple.

"Speaking of honeymoons," he murmured, "have you given any thought to where you'd like to go for ours?"

"Oh, lord," she moaned, leaning against him even more. "Everything's been happening so fast, I forgot all about that. Maybe we could go back to Seabrook Island and hide out in your suite again."

Turning her in his arms, he tipped her head up and stared down into her eyes while tracing the outline of her bottom lip with his thumb.

"Ocean Breezes may be one of *the* premiere oceanside re-sorts in the continental United States," he said proudly, "but it doesn't hold the greatest of track records for us, and I don't want to take any chances. Not with our honeymoon."

He made a good point, although she had a lot of wonderful, spine-tingling, swoon-inducing memories of her time there with him, too.

He must have been thinking the same thing, because a wicked glint filled his eyes. "Give some thought to something truly decadent. The French Riviera. The Greek Isles. The coast of Spain."

Her heart leapt higher at each of his suggestions. She could picture them touring any one—or all—of those, and the images were hugely romantic.

"Yes, yes and yes," she told him, puckering her lips to kiss the pad of his thumb as it neared the center of her mouth. "I'm not sure we should travel so far away right now, though. Not with Mama newly freed from suspicion and Daddy's murderer still on the loose."

Taking her hands, he threaded his fingers with hers, hold-ing them down at their sides. "Then we'll put it off until we can do it right. But keep those locations in mind. I'll take you anywhere you like, for as long as you like. Provided we sched-ule plenty of time for me to get you alone. And naked. Several times a day."

"Thank you," she said, rising up to kiss him, wondering how she'd ever gotten so lucky as to end up with a man like this. Then again, she'd always known Eli Houghton was special. It was part of the reason she'd lusted after him for so long.

Pulling away, she fluttered her lashes and gave him her best come-hither look. "I'm not the least bit interested in fritters anymore, but if you split one with me and we gulp down a glass of champagne each, it will make Mama happy. Then I can come up with an excuse to get out of here, so you can take me home and get me naked. How does that sound, Mr. Houghton?"

His gaze smoldered, his brown eyes hot enough to singe the clothes from her body right in the middle of her mother's formal dining room.

"Better than a honeymoon, Soon-to-be Mrs. Houghton," he replied. The use of those names—Mr. and Soon-to-be Mrs.— had become a bit of an inside joke with them. The wedding was only a week away, and yet they couldn't seem to wait to be tied to each other in every way possible.

Lifting his arm, he studied the face of his expensive watch. "One hour. I'm counting down. If you haven't said goodbye to your family by then, I'm tossing you over my shoulder and carrying you off caveman-style."

A shiver stole through her at the thought of that. It might be worth shocking her mother and brother and sisters—not to mention their significant others—just to see if he really would do as he threatened…and then reap the benefits of those Neanderthal-ish tendencies of his.

Leaning up on tiptoe, she put her mouth to his ear and whispered, "If you keep looking at me like that, I might just let you."

Her reward was a deep growl and his hands coming up to squeeze her bottom possessively. She chuckled, pressing a quick kiss to his rugged cheek and breaking away to get in as much family time as he would allow before following through on his warning.

Oh, Eli was definitely the man for her. It might have taken

her half her life to admit it and then work up the courage to claim him as her own, but now that she had him…

She was never, ever letting go.

* * * * *

Turn the page for an exclusive short story

by USA TODAY bestselling author
Day Leclaire.

THE KINCAIDS: JACK AND NIKKI
PART IV

"**Y**ou've been so quiet."

Jack Sinclair joined Nikki Thomas on the deck off his beach house bedroom. Coming up behind her, he encircled her with his arms. The long, lovely sweep of her back fit perfectly against his chest and the sweet curve of her backside shifted against him, arousing him in a way no other woman had. Ever. Why her, and no one else?

"I guess I have a lot on my mind," she admitted.

"Work?"

A tiny sigh escaped her, sounding almost painful in its intensity. "Always."

Together they watched the rising moon sit on the line of rolling breakers, huge and squat, as though attempting to keep the restless sea under control. Of course, that was no more possible than controlling the desperation that exploded between them whenever they came together. The violent need and endless yearning had governed their two-month-long affair. And while Jack suspected they'd both anticipated it would fade over time, it only grew stronger with each passing week.

Nikki was his. Had been his since she first appeared beneath the balcony of the Read and Write literacy auction where she'd bid a thousand dollars for a single dinner date with him—as well as a wish of her choice. Of course, that one date had led to two months of dates, her wish not yet made or fulfilled. She'd continued to be his over that time, their headlong tumble one neither had anticipated.

The moon crept higher into the night sky, silvering a slice of the dark ocean and playing across the foam capping the surging waves. Nikki turned to Jack, wrapped him up in bewitching feminine warmth, then gently, tenderly fit her mouth to his. He felt the heat of passion beneath the softness, knew it would take no more than a simple nudge to move it up a notch. But for some reason, he simply wanted to enjoy the slow, easy slide that spoke of more than sex. That acknowledged the build of a relationship that fired on levels he never thought possible.

He filled his lungs with her sigh of pleasure and teased inward between her parted lips. Sank into her. Relished the sweetness and generosity. Her openness. She initiated a lazy dance, one he followed just as lazily. They drifted across the deck toward the French doors leading to his bedroom. The moon followed them, lighting a silvery pathway. It frosted her skin, giving it a pearlescent gleam and slipped through her thin silk nightgown to outline glorious womanly curves that tempted him beyond reason.

"I'm sorry if I've been a little out of it." She slanted him an amused look, her sapphire-blue eyes glinting in the moonlight. "If it makes you feel any better I'm all here now."

"Well… I was going to suggest you lay back and think of England, but I'm not quite sure what that has to do with my future plans for you."

She chuckled. "I believe that was a suggestion given to British women during the Victorian Era when it came to fulfilling their marital obligations." Her arms tightened around his neck and she caught his lower lip between his teeth, giving it a light tug. "The only thing I plan to think about is you and just what I'm going to do to you."

His voice deepened. Roughened. "And what's that?"

Nikki lifted on tiptoe and put her mouth close to Jack's ear, the warmth of her breath threatening the last of his control. Then her whispered suggestions totally shredded it. A growl rumbled through his chest and he snatched her into his arms and dumped her onto the bed. He ripped her nightgown from her body, made short work of his own sweats and was over and in her welcoming body with a speed that left them both gasping. His name clung to her damp, swollen lips, her want for him burning in her gaze, her unstinting response to his possession driving him to new heights.

He couldn't get enough of this woman. Didn't think he'd ever get enough. As though she could read his thoughts, she moaned in pleasure. "More. No matter how much or how often, I'm always ready for more." She cupped his face, took everything he offered and gave all she had in return. "Only with you. Always with you."

And somehow Jack suspected it would be that way for the rest of their lives.

"Nikki, are you paying attention?"

She jumped, her gaze flashing to RJ Kincaid's, guilt sweeping through her. Oh, damn. What had he asked? She did a quick rewind, relieved to discover that her brain had been recording the conversation, despite her distraction. Police update. He wanted a police update on the investigation into his father's murder.

"I've spoken to Detective McDonough about the camera surveillance discovered showing Jack Sinclair's vintage Aston Martin parked at a lot near The Kincaid Group at the time of your father's death."

"Why isn't Sinclair in custody?" RJ demanded, the fierce expression in his eyes identical to Jack's—as well as to their father's. They were half brothers, "the Legitimates," as Jack referred to them, Reginald Kincaid's legal offspring, while Jack was the product of a decades-long affair with Angela Sinclair, Reginald's mistress. "The police were quick enough to arrest my mother on far less evidence."

Nikki couldn't help it. She flinched at the idea of Jack being dragged off to jail in handcuffs. He wasn't guilty. There wasn't a single doubt in her mind. You couldn't share such an intimate relationship with a man and not know who he was at his core. And while he might be one of the most ruthless men she'd ever met, clearly bent on revenge against his half siblings, that revenge would take a legal form. Like taking over the family business thanks to the forty-five percent interest he'd inherited in TKG upon his father's death. Of course, if he managed to win control of the business, his first act would be to fire RJ, Matthew and Laurel Kincaid.

Nikki sighed. "I've been in touch with Charles—Detective McDonough." He and her late father had been partners for years, before her father had gone down in the line of duty. "Jack claims he was at work at the time of your father's murder and has a number of employees who back him up."

RJ paced the length of the conference room, moving with all the grace and frustration of a caged panther, strengthening his resemblance to his half brother. How many times had she seen Jack pace like that while snapping instructions into his cell phone in regard to his own business, Carolina Shipping, a direct competitor to The Kincaid Group?

"Sinclair's guilty. We all know it. It has to be him. He must have found out about the forty-five percent share of TKG he stood to inherit. God knows, he's been after revenge for years because my father refused to publicly recognize Sinclair as his son. And when he wasn't good enough to beat us by pitting his business against ours, head-to-head, he killed Dad in order to take revenge the only way left to him."

More than anything, Nikki longed to argue with him. But she didn't dare. She was The Kincaid Group's corporate investigator and it was her job to research Jack on their behalf. She'd been given the assignment after the two of them had met at the literacy bachelor auction for Read and Write, and for the past two months she'd walked a tightrope between her feelings for Jack versus her obligations to her employer.

Even worse, Reginald Kincaid had hired her after she'd been unjustly fired by her previous employer. Reginald had believed in her when no one else had. She owed him then and still felt an unshakable loyalty and obligation to the family and business he left behind.

She took her time responding to RJ, allowing her gaze to drift over the three Kincaid siblings currently gathered in the conference room. "While I understand your feelings, the police need evidence. You want your father's killer found. That's only natural. But if you insist they focus their attention in any one direction you run the risk of having them miss something that would lead them to the person responsible. Is it Jack?" She lifted her shoulder in as casual a shrug as she could pull off. "It's possible, though current evidence is to the contrary."

"It's Jack," RJ snapped.

Matt gave a slow nod. She caught a hint of sympathy in his gaze and knew why. He was aware she'd gone out with Jack, as was Laurel. In fact, Laurel knew just how deeply their involvement went. Only RJ remained oblivious. Oh, he was aware they'd dated because of the Read and Write auction. Matt had even asked her to use the time she spent with him to form an opinion of the man and obtain any and all possible information. But she doubted any of them realized just how far the relationship had progressed.

And once they knew?

She released her breath in a silent sigh. She'd be out of a job again. Worse, the instant Jack found out she was a Kincaid employee, what had become an incandescent affair would fizzle like a wet firecracker. And where would she end up? Without Jack and without a job. Probably served her right for not coming clean with both parties.

But how could she? More than anything she hoped to prove

to the Kincaids that Jack didn't deserve their enmity. Just as she hoped to coax Jack into giving his half brothers and sisters a chance. To see if he couldn't form—if not a familial relationship with them—then at least a cordial relationship, one that would prompt him to drop his plan of revenge…which at the current moment was to utterly destroy the Kincaids.

She gave RJ a calm, direct look. "You know I am totally committed to finding out who murdered your father. Totally committed," she repeated. "And I will continue to do everything Detective McDonough will allow in order to help the police with their investigation, as well as research every possible avenue available to me independently."

Some of the tension eased from RJ's body. "Well, I can't ask for more than that, can I?"

Laurel cleared her throat. She was a gorgeous woman who had inherited her striking bone structure, vivid green eyes and deep, auburn hair from her mother, Elizabeth. She spared Nikki a brief, sympathetic glance before addressing her brothers. "We're all frustrated. We expected this to be resolved long ago. We have a board meeting coming up in less than two months that will decide the fate of The Kincaid Group, which has us all on edge." This time she addressed Nikki. "I appreciate everything you've done. When you're personally involved in the situation, it's very difficult to maintain an emotional distance."

Nikki winced. Okay, she could read between those lines. "Is there anything else?" she asked quietly.

RJ released a long sigh. "No, there's nothing else." He offered a swift, charming smile. "Sorry if I came down too hard on you. You're doing a great job."

But she wasn't. How could she when she remained so conflicted? She'd just do the best she could for everyone involved and hope that Charles McDonough found the real murderer. Laurel paused long enough to give her a brief hug.

"Hang in there. This will all work out," she whispered before exiting. "Sometimes you just have to decide to follow your heart instead of doing what everyone expects of you."

Nikki closed her eyes, tears pressing hard. If only she could believe that. How she longed to believe that. But somehow she suspected the situation would get far worse before it ever got better.

If it ever got better.

"I've already told you, Detective," Jack stated evenly. "I was here at the time my father was murdered."

Charles McDonough nodded. He was a strong, well-dressed black man with a gleaming shaved head, and calm, serious dark eyes that reflected his intelligence and determination. "Unfortunately for you, Mr. Sinclair, no one was actually in the room with you."

Jack fought back a flash of impatience. "Granted, my employees weren't in my office every minute of that time, but I couldn't have left the building without being seen or been gone as long as it must have taken without someone noticing my absence."

Charles gave another slow nod and made a notation in his neat, tidy handwriting. "You do have a private exit," he observed.

Jack fought back a flash of temper, well aware it wouldn't help his case. "True. But I never used it that night, certainly not to murder my own father."

"And yet your Aston Martin was in a lot near The Kincaid Group headquarters at the time of the murder." The detective's gaze locked with Jack's, piercing straight through him, warning of a dogged and unrelenting nature. "Did you loan your car to someone?"

"No."

"Have you ever loaned that car to someone else?"

"Never."

Charles smiled, for the first time revealing the man beneath the cop. "Don't blame you," he said. "Don't think I'd let anyone so much as breathe on it."

Jack relaxed enough to return the smile. "Men can be foolish about their toys."

"Yes." And suddenly the cop was back. "So explain how one of your toys—a toy you don't allow anyone else to touch—turned up where it shouldn't have been? If you didn't drive it elsewhere that night, then someone else had possession of your keys or ignition fob. That someone was able to enter your company parking lot and remove your car with no one stopping or questioning him. And then he returned both the car and the keys, with you none the wiser. I find that...odd. Don't you?"

"The lot isn't gated."

"And the keys?"

Jack shook his head. "Detective, I can't explain it, as I'm sure you're aware. I can only repeat that I was here, working on a special project. I've given you the name of the employees who were with me at that time helping with the Berner project. Most were in and out of this office at various times during the evening. It was common knowledge that I planned to work late that night. In fact, I was working late most nights due to a large, complicated project. My car was in its usual place when I finished for the night and left the building. I can't explain how it was spotted in a parking lot near The Kincaid Group at that particular time unless it was someone else's Aston Martin. I assume you've considered that possibility and already ruled it out."

McDonough didn't confirm or deny the assumption. He simply nodded, flipped his notebook closed and stood. "Please remain available, Mr. Sinclair. I'm sure I'll have more questions in the near future."

The Southern version of "don't leave town." "Of course," Jack agreed and stood as well. The two men shook hands before the detective departed.

The second McDonough departed, Jack's assistant entered

the office and dropped a file on his desk. "Hang in there, boss. This will all work out," she said with a sympathetic look.

He spared her a brief smile. "Thanks, Gail."

He wanted to believe that. Really wanted to believe it. But somehow he suspected the situation would get far worse before it ever got better.

If it ever got better.

Nikki exited The Kincaid Group office building, just as Elizabeth Kincaid and two of her daughters, Lily and Kara, approached. All were chatting and laughing. As the women drew level, Elizabeth paused and introduced her daughters, though Nikki had already met Lily at the bachelor auction back in January. Elizabeth appeared relaxed and energized, a far cry from the anguished, drawn woman of the past four months. No doubt it was due to her being released from police custody for the murder of her late husband, Reginald.

"Kara is an events planner," Elizabeth explained. "She owns Prestige Events."

Nikki smiled warmly. "I've heard wonderful things about your company."

"And she's engaged," Lily added. Her blue eyes gleamed with mischief. "To Eli Houghton. They marry this next weekend."

"But, I thought—" Nikki blinked. Last she'd heard Eli's engagement to Laurel had ended less than a month before. Since then he and Kara had apparently fallen in love—because it was crystal clear that the bubbly middle daughter was ecstatically happy. Since everyone else appeared equally happy, Nikki could only assume it had been an amicable transfer of bridegrooms. "Best wishes, Kara," she said and meant it.

"Thanks. We're about to go drag Laurel away from her desk and finalize wedding plans over food and drinks. She's offered to be my maid of honor."

With a cheerful wave, the women continued on their way.

She felt genuinely happy for the Kincaids. They'd been

through a terrible ordeal. But now that Elizabeth had been released on bail, Nikki worried that Jack would become the center of the investigative whirlwind. There simply weren't that many people who benefitted from Reginald's demise. Clearly, Jack was the forerunner in that regard and she knew, both from what Charles McDonough had said—as well as what he hadn't said—that the police were looking long and hard at Reginald's eldest son.

More than anything she wanted to find Jack. As though in response to her silent wish her cell phone rang with the ring tone she used exclusively for him. "Where are you?" he asked abruptly.

"Not far from home. Problem?"

"I could use you, a drink and food, in that order."

She smiled. "I think I can help you with that. Do you want to eat in or out?"

"In. Definitely in."

By the time she arrived home a fine mist clung to the city and the wind carried a chilly edge. They didn't often spend the evening at her place, despite its convenient location, perhaps because the row house didn't offer as much room as Jack's beach house. Or maybe it was because the furnishings were antique and somewhat delicate for a man. Or possibly it was a territorial problem, Jack unable to make his mark in the distinctly feminine environment. Tonight he made one of his rare exceptions.

They entered the small foyer and to her amusement both of their gazes flashed to a section of the wall where they'd collided during their second kiss—a chaste embrace that had exploded into an unexpected wildfire of desire. It had been that way when they first kissed on the night of the charity auction, flamed higher during that crazy second kiss and had continued to build ever since.

"Would you prefer to order out?" Nikki asked. "Or would you like me to throw something together? I probably have enough in the fridge for omelets." Maybe.

"Right now I just want you."

All he had to do was touch her to send her up in flames. His kiss tasted of desperation and need, his hands relentless in expressing that need and driving her own to the breaking point. Their clothing created a trail of passion leading upstairs to her bedroom. While the bed cupped them in silk and softness, the deepening night encased them in a protective dusk. Want perfuming the air, their husky cries lending music to their passionate dance. And when the moment was spent and the fires banked, they clung, two hearts beating in synchronicity, male and female locked together in perfect accord.

"You make it so much easier," he whispered. "I don't know how or why. But I don't think I could get through this without you."

"Get through what, Jack? What's happened?"

He rolled onto his back and rested his head on his folded arms. A pale wedge of light from the hallway sliced across the upper portion of his face, silvering his robin's-egg-blue eyes. Hardness glittered there, as it so often did. But she knew him well enough to see the pain that lurked beneath. The intense grief. The Kincaids weren't the only ones to lose their father. Jack had lost his, too.

"McDonough came to see me today."

"And?"

She caught a glimpse of a smile, though it contained little humor. "I've been told not to leave town."

"Oh, Jack," she whispered, reaching for him, telling him with a single touch that she was there for him. "Why? What do they have on you?"

He rolled onto his side to face her, feathering his hand through the silken length of her dark hair, then tracing the curve of her cheek. In the two months they'd been together she'd noticed that he had a need to touch, to stroke, to maintain a physical connection between them even during sleep. It was one of the qualities she loved about him. "Someone helped themselves to my car the night of Dad's murder and parked it near The Kincaid Group office building."

She stilled and tiptoed into what promised to become a minefield, praying he didn't pick up on her tension. "Who could have taken it?"

"That's the million dollar question, one I'd love to have answered." He'd finished tracing the angles of her face and crept lower, following the line of her neck to the sensitive joining of her shoulder. He smiled at the helpless shiver that rippled through her. "So would the police."

"They think it's you." She didn't bother to phrase it as a question.

His hand stilled briefly. "I suspect McDonough does, yes."

"How do they know your car was parked near The Kincaid Group?"

"They have a photo from a security camera I guess. Maybe video." A frown etched across his brow and his hand shifted, continued to stroke. "What I don't get is… If they have a photo or video, why don't they also have evidence of who was driving the car? That's all it would take to clear me."

"Good question." A very good question. One she'd be certain to ask Charles. "Who do you think killed your father?"

He closed his eyes, his expression turning grim. "I wish I knew. I can't imagine who'd do such a thing." He looked at her then, allowing his grief to leak through. "I could almost understand it when the police thought his wife had shot him. If she'd found out about my mother and they'd argued…"

"This wasn't a crime of passion," Nikki objected. "At least, it wasn't executed in a passionate manner."

"No, I came to that realization as well, which is why I have trouble suspecting any of the Kincaids. Someone had it in for Dad. As much as I despise the Legitimates, I can't see any of them pulling the trigger." He grimaced. "Not even RJ, though I don't suppose he feels the same way about me."

She almost answered, catching back the words in the nick of time. "Have you talked to him about it?"

"Of course not. All of our dealings have been strictly business-related. I requested and received a report on The Kincaid Group's assets, expenses, projected growth, as well as a comprehensive customer list back in January. Since then all we've done is have a number of terse, bitter conversations about how to handle the running of the business. It's clear we both hope to take control at the June board meeting." He traced his finger between the swell of her breasts and the edge of the sheet, then dipped beneath, causing her to inhale sharply. "I guess it all comes down to that missing ten percent."

The breath stuttered in her lungs. "What missing ten percent?" she asked.

"The Kincaids between them own forty-five percent of TKG stock. I now own the other forty-five percent. That leaves ten percent missing." He rolled on top of her, bracing himself so his forearms took most of his weight. "Though, not for long."

"No?"

His expression turned teasing and everything within her melted. "Nope. I'm going to hire someone to find the owner of those missing shares."

He lowered himself to her, inch by delicious inch, driving her insane with need. She opened to welcome him. "You are?" she asked weakly.

"Yes, I am. Someone I happen to know is a brilliant investigator and is well motivated to find the information I need."

She stiffened. Oh, no. Oh, please, no. "Who? Who is that?"

He joined their bodies, driving every coherent thought from her head...right up until he said, "Why, you, of course."

* * * * *

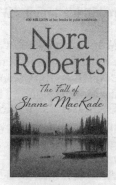